Piano man PROJECT

Kat French lives in the midlands with her husband and two young sons. She is a romance junkie – she loves watching it, reading it, and most of all, writing it.

Kat is also a *USA Today* bestselling author of erotic romance under the name Kitty French.

Please visit www.katfrench.co.uk for all Kat's latest news and to sign up for her newsletter about upcoming books.

Other books by Kat French:

Undertaking Love

THE Piano man PROJECT

KAT FRENCH

AVON

AVON

A division of HarperCollins*Publishers*
1 London Bridge Street,
London SE1 9GF

www.harpercollins.co.uk

A Paperback Original 2015

First published in Great Britain by
HarperCollins*Publishers* 2015

Copyright © Kat French 2015

Kat French asserts the moral right to
be identified as the author of this work

A catalogue record for this book is
available from the British Library

ISBN-13: 978-0-00-757760-6

Set in Sabon LT Std by Palimpsest Book Production Limited,
Falkirk, Stirlingshire

Printed and bound in Great Britain by
Clays Ltd, St Ives plc

MIX
Paper from
responsible sources
FSC® C007454
FSC
www.fsc.org

FSC™ is a non-profit international organisation established to promote
the responsible management of the world's forests. Products carrying the
FSC label are independently certified to assure consumers that they come
from forests that are managed to meet the social, economic and
ecological needs of present and future generations,
and other controlled sources.

Find out more about HarperCollins and the environment at
www.harpercollins.co.uk/green

Acknowledgements

Huge thanks to everyone at Avon, you're all brilliant and I feel very lucky to be part of the Avon family. Extra huge thanks to my superstar editor Katy Loftus for being endlessly patient, supportive and encouraging through all of my various health woes whilst I wrote this book, and for loving Hal as much as I do. We got there in the end!

Thank you also to Sabah Khan at LightBrigade for helping to spread news of Piano Man far and wide.

Lots of love to all of the bloggers and peeps on twitter and FB, you're all amazing – chatting with you guys brightens my working day no end and your help with my many random questions is always appreciated.

I also couldn't get through my working days without my writing besties, the all-round gorgeous minxes of romance.

Last but never least, thanks of course to my own fabulous lot, my friends and family.

For James, with love. Grouchy is the new sexy, right? You just need to get that cooking thing down . . . x

CHAPTER ONE

'Don't you think there's something sad about buying your-self a new vibrator for Valentine's Day?' Honey picked up a lurid pink model and eyed it with distaste.

'Why?' Tash laughed. 'My last one was the best boyfriend I've ever had. When it gave out I buried it in the back garden and planted a phallic cactus over it as a tribute.'

'How the hell did you break it, anyway?' Honey frowned at the hunk of neon plastic in her hand. It looked pretty indestructible.

'Overuse, probably,' Nell chimed in on her other side. With her big brown doe eyes and smooth chignon, she was a study of tidy perfection.

'We can't all lead cookie-cutter lives, Nellie,' Tash chided.

Nell sniffed. 'I don't hear you complaining when those cookies end up in your kitchen cupboard.'

'True,' Tash laughed. 'Just don't go looking for your next cutter in here. Although actually, maybe you should. I'd pay good money to see your mother-in-law dunking cock-shaped shortbread in her tea.'

Nell shot her a sarcastic smile, privately needled by Tash's good-natured teasing. *Had her life become too cookie cutter?* Looking at the alien things on the shelves around her, there was every chance it had. A frown of concentration crumpled her forehead. She'd read enough magazines and books to know that a stale marriage was a step away from disaster.

In both looks and life, Nell and Tash were polar opposites, and Honey knew that her place in the world was somewhere between them. If they were traffic lights, Tash would be green; all flashing emerald eyes and come-hither grins that had men falling at her feet. Nell would be red: stop; don't cross; clear and direct. For Honey, the amber light. Warm, never quite sure, approach with caution. Or perhaps it was closer to 'don't approach at all', if the lack of decent men in her life was anything to go by.

'It went rusty.' Tash scanned the shelves with an expert eye, her riotous red waves swishing around her shoulders. 'Don't ask. Oh thank God, a waterproof one.' She grabbed a gleaming turquoise vibrator and kissed the box. 'Hey there, handsome. I need you in my life.' She dropped it in her basket with a grin.

'How 'bout you, Honeysuckle? Something for the weekend?' Tash waved towards the army of vibrators lined up on the shelf like a platoon of soldiers ready to spring into action.

'Not for me.' Honey slid the pink vibrator back into place on the display.

'There's no need to be so sniffy,' Tash said. 'I mean, it's been quite a while since your last, er . . .'

'Not that long, thank you,' Honey snapped. It had been more than twelve months ago since she'd split from her last boyfriend – not that Mark had ever really qualified for the title. She seemed to have a knack of attracting the wrong kind of men, men who were more interested in football and beer than romance or flowers. Or orgasms for that matter, besides their own.

Her only long-term boyfriend of note had been Sean at uni, a biology student who'd treated her body like an extension of his textbooks, something to study for cause and effect. It was little wonder that her body had refused to perform under such intense scrutiny. She'd eventually given him the push when he'd pulled a magnifying glass out of his bedside drawer before unbuttoning her jeans.

'Honey?' Nell said, and she realised that both she and Tash were looking at her and waiting for an answer.

'I don't know. A year or so, maybe?' She shrugged and looked away from her friend's raised eyebrows.

'Fuck! A whole year without sex?' Tash threw a second vibrator into her basket. 'I'm buying you this. It's a gift. You need it more than I do.'

'Ha-ha.' Honey took it back out of the basket. 'Thanks, but don't waste your money. They don't work for me.'

'They work for everybody, Honey.'

'Not me.'

'Have you ever tried?' Tash asked.

'I don't need to, okay?' Honey turned away, uncomfortable with the turn the conversation had taken. 'I just don't . . . well, you know.'

Tash and Nell grasped an elbow each and turned her back around to face them.

'You don't what?' A frown rumpled Nell's smooth brow. 'Orgasm?' She whispered the question.

'Don't stare at me like I'm a criminal,' Honey muttered. A sex shop was so not the place to discuss this. She felt like an atheist in St Paul's cathedral.

'I'm no prude, I like sex. I just never have an orgasm. It's no big deal.'

Tash stared at Honey as if she'd grown an extra head. 'No big deal? It's friggin' huge! I'd die if I didn't come at least once a day.'

'Even when you're between men?' Nell asked. Her diamond wedding band glinted as she fiddled with the buttons on her polka dot silk blouse, which came straight from the 'glamorous teacher all the dads fancy' pages of the Boden catalogue.

Tash tapped the package in her basket. 'Meet my new boyfriend.'

Honey glanced away. Glittery red hearts dangled throughout the store like a love grotto, although the dummies clad in crotchless knickers and peephole bras made it more 'sex den' than 'romantic arbour'.

'What is all this stuff?' Nell murmured, wide eyed as they passed through a heavy velvet curtain. She picked up a dark string of beads and wrapped them around her wrist. 'I didn't know they did jewellery.' She twisted her arm to admire them. 'These would be perfect with my new purple dress.'

Tash laughed. 'Yes. How thoughtful of them to make their bum beads multi-purpose.'

Nell yanked them off, her cheeks a good match with the violet beads as she tossed them down. 'That's revolting.'

4

'Don't knock it till you've tried it, girlfriend.' Tash raised a knowing brow.

Nell sat down and crossed her ankles, the image of a prim school marm. 'I think I'll wait for you here.'

''Kay. But just so you know, you're sitting on a sex couch,' Tash winked.

'Christ!' Jumping up, Nell smoothed her hands down her navy pencil skirt. 'Is nothing normal in this place?'

'This *is* normal, Nell. Simon would probably love to see you in crotchless knickers.'

'He most certainly would not. He'd tell me to return them because there was a bit missing.'

Tash shook her head and huffed. 'You know, I think he probably would.'

Honey slid the handcuffs she'd been examining off her wrists and grinned. Simon and Nell were the perfect couple. Childhood sweethearts. Mr & Mrs Vanilla. He'd probably have a heart attack if Nell wore anything more risqué than M&S white cotton. 'Come on, Nell, let's get you out of here. Tash, we'll meet you next door in five.'

'So, Honey. About the orgasm thing,' Tash said as she slid into the booth in the crowded bar ten minutes later. Honey sighed.

'Jesus, Tash. Don't start. I really don't need to talk about this.'

'Okay, okay, you're right,' Nell soothed. 'But . . . when you said you don't, you didn't mean you never have . . . did you?'

Honey reached for her wine in resignation. 'It really doesn't bother me.'

'Well, it should. It's bad for your health, if nothing else.'

'No, Tash. It would be bad for *your* health. I don't miss what I've never had.'

'Are you one hundred per cent bona fide certain that you never have?' Nell asked.

'Jesus, Nell. If she had one and missed it then there really is something wrong with her.'

Honey cleared her throat.

'Err, I'm still here, remember?'

'I just don't get how you can't once you're in the heat of the moment, to be honest,' Tash said, looking genuinely perplexed. 'You must have been sleeping with the wrong men, Honey.'

'It's no one's fault,' Honey shrugged.

'Do you think you're getting too wound up about it and then that makes it impossible to relax enough for it to happen?' Nell frowned.

Honey shook her head. 'Please . . . just stop? I'm not wound up, and I'm perfectly relaxed. I don't expect it to happen, and it doesn't happen, so let's just move on, okay?'

'I can't believe we've been friends for ten years and you've never mentioned this.'

'That's because it's honestly no big deal.'

Nell and Tash reached for their own glasses with something dangerously close to pity on their faces.

Tash narrowed her eyes. 'When did you last flirt with a man?'

Honey twisted her bangles around, a jumble of gold and bright-coloured metals. Men worth flirting with were thin on the ground in her day-to-day life. She briefly entertained the idea of flirting with Eric the Lech who occasionally came in to the charity shop she managed, but the idea turned her stomach. He already tried to squeeze her bum most days as it was. One flicker of encouragement from her and he'd have her round to view his ancient Y-fronts over an episode of *Antiques Roadshow* in his sheltered accommodation. No.

'You can't remember, can you?'

Honey shook her head and sighed. 'I just don't meet men I could flirt with. I spend all day serving old dears, and on the rare occasion I meet anyone fanciable they always turn out to be dickheads.'

'You've just been with the wrong men,' Nell soothed.

Honey couldn't argue. The few men she'd slept with wouldn't win any awards for technique, but deep down she knew it was more than that. She'd simply been born without the orgasm gene. Fact.

'Let us pick someone for you,' Tash said.

'No way!' Honey could just imagine the men her friends would come up with; jet-set playboys with perma-tans on one side, trainee teachers in jesus creepers on the other.

'You know what you need?' Tash swayed her glass in Honey's direction. 'A specific. Something to sort out the men from the boys.'

'I'm not with you.'

'Well, take me. My specific is money. No money, no Tash.'

'You are so shallow.' Nell laughed.

Tash shrugged. 'I prefer to say realistic.'

'Well, I'm not fussed for rich.'

'No, but there has to be something,' Tash said.

'Good father. That was my specific.' A faraway smile

kissed Nell's lips, doubtless thinking of Simon and their year-old baby daughter. She'd never known her own father, so Simon was her lover, friend and hero all rolled into one.

Michael Bublé crooned something sentimental from the speaker behind Honey's ear. 'Reckon you can fix me up with Michael Bublé?'

'Tall order, chick.' Tash sat up straight in her chair. 'But . . . that has just given me a great idea for your specific.' She paused, sparkle eyed. 'You need a pianist.'

Nell laughed. 'Where the heck is she supposed to find a pianist around here?'

'Hey, if you can rustle me up the Bublé or Robert Downey Jr, I'm all for it,' Honey said.

'Think about it. All those hours of practising scales would make a man talented with his hands.' Tash warmed to her theme. 'And only clever, sensitive men would bother to learn the piano.' She sounded too certain for anyone to question her logic.

'Tash's right, Hon,' Nell chimed in. 'You need a pianist.'

'Well I don't know any.'

'Not yet . . .' Tash winked. 'But you will.'

'Er . . . how?' Honey reached for the wine bottle.

'No idea.' Tash pushed her glass towards Honey.

Nell grinned. 'We need to check out dating sites.'

'No way!' Honey sloshed wine onto the table in panic. 'There's no way I'm signing up for online dating.'

Tash and Nell eyed each other. 'Of course not,' Nell said. Tash coughed.

Honey narrowed her eyes. 'Have you got your fingers crossed behind your back?'

Nell shook her head and uncrossed her fingers.

'I can't even think of any other famous pianists, let alone regular joes.' Honey frowned.

'Elton John?' Tash suggested.

'He's gay. And married. I don't want married. Or gay.'

'Liberace?'

'Great. *Dead* and gay.'

'Right,' Nell intervened. 'So we're looking for straight, breathing pianists with a thing for boho blondes.'

'And gorgeous,' Honey said. 'He has to be gorgeous.'

'Well, I think it's genius,' Tash said. 'In one easy swipe you've managed to eliminate ninety-nine per cent of the male population, leaving only a small pool to fish in for the catch of the day.'

Honey laughed and shook her head to dislodge the image of herself in waders reeling in an unwilling Michael Bublé. 'A fishy pianist. Every girl's dream.'

Hal heard female laughter and doors slamming well after midnight in the shared hallway outside his flat and yanked the hard, unfamiliar pillow over his head.

Great. His new neighbour had a laugh like an alley cat as well as no respect for anyone else in the house. Had he been in a charitable mood, he might have acknowledged that she actually had no clue he'd moved in that afternoon, but her laughter annoyed him too much to be reasonable. Laughter annoyed him right now. As did people. Laughing people were a particular bugbear. He'd been here for less than a day, but he hated this house already.

CHAPTER TWO

Honey squinted like a gremlin against the glare of the morning sun. Or was it afternoon? After a morning spent lounging on the sofa, her hangover had been replaced with the dire need for a bacon sandwich and a bucket of coffee. Pan on and bacon in, she started to feel a little less deathly and ran to grab the ringing phone before it clicked to the machine.

'Hello?'

'You sound as rough as I feel,' Tash grumbled. 'What did we drink last night? Meths?'

'The tequila was your idea.' Honey grimaced. 'Did you get home okay?'

'Course. The taxi driver made me hang my head out of the bloody window in case I threw up, but yeah.'

Honey laughed at the image of Tash like a family dog on a road trip.

'I wonder how Nell is?'

'Fine, no doubt. She'll have drunk two pints of water

10

before bed, and have Simon on hand with Alka-Seltzer and a bowl of hand-mixed muesli. Lucky cow.'

Honey knew Tash well enough to detect fondness behind the grouch.

'It's our own fault,' Honey laughed. 'Nell didn't have tequila. It's the mixing that kills.'

'Does she always have to be so friggin' sensible?'

'Yeah, but who would you rather be this morning?'

'Er, waking up next to Simon, the dullest man on earth?' Tash said. 'I'll stick to the tequila and the headaches, ta very much.'

Honey yelped as a screechy wail assaulted her ears.

'What the fuck is that noise?' Tash yelled.

'Crap! The smoke alarm! Gotta go, Tash. Love you.'

Honey belted into the kitchen. Smoke and burnt bacon. Double crap. At least there were no flames yet. She hurled the pan in the sink, wincing as the high-pitched alarm battered her already thumping head. She scrabbled onto a chair and pressed reset, weak with relief as the noise stopped. Then she tilted her head. It hadn't completely stopped. Triple crap. Wow, she'd done a thorough job. When she opened her front door the alarm out in the hallway was going full throttle, and the damn thing was too high for her to reach.

She clamped her hands over her ears, then jumped out of her skin when the door to the empty flat opposite hers flung wide open.

'Is the fucking house on fire?'

Whoa. Where did he come from?

'No, sorry. I burnt my bacon. Just give me a minute . . .'

Honey tried to hide her surprise at finding a dishevelled Johnny Depp type yelling at her in her own hallway. Well, strictly speaking it was a shared hallway, but as the flat opposite had been vacant for months she'd become kind of territorial.

She squinted at him. Dark glasses at lunchtime hinted at a fellow hangover sufferer. Maybe he was some famous rock star hiding out. She could dream. Whoever he was, the faded black t-shirt clung to his body in a way that suggested fit, and the tattoos inked down his arms suggested sexy. It was a shame then that his personality rendered him thoroughly repellent.

'Just shut that fucking racket up, will you? I'm trying to sleep.'

'Umm . . .' Honey stared at the alarm in panic. Her head was thumping, and out here the noise was even louder than in her kitchen. 'I would, but I can't reach it. Could you possibly . . .?'

He was well over six foot; with a stretch he'd make it, no problem.

'No I fucking cannot. What sort of grown woman can't cook bacon? Sort your own mess out.' He curled his lip and slammed his door.

Honey reeled. Her life was full of people who, on the whole, were decent human beings. To come up against someone so outright obnoxious came as a shock.

'Fine!' she shouted. 'Fine. I'll do it myself.' She made a half-hearted attempt at jumping to smack the alarm box. Futile. At five foot five and not very athletic, it had always been a long shot.

Plan B was required. Honey took her slipper off and hurled it upwards, but still she missed the alarm by a good foot. Then she spotted her tall, red polka dot umbrella propped in the corner of the hallway. Bingo! Could she reach the reset button with the metal end spike? She tried, but the damn thing wobbled too much for accuracy and the close proximity to the noise threatened to burst her eardrums.

Gah. The next time she wanted bacon she'd go to the café on the corner.

Honey sighed and opted for the only source of action left. She swung the umbrella above her head and whacked the alarm clean off the wall. It bounced hard against her new neighbour's door, then landed with a squawk, before dying. She closed her eyes in relief.

Johnny Depp wrenched his door open again.

'What?' he growled.

'*What* what?'

'You knocked my door.'

'Oh.' Honey bent to pick up the mangled alarm. He recoiled as she straightened, as if her nearness offended him.

'I didn't knock. The alarm hit your door on the way down.'

'You smashed it.'

No shit, Sherlock.

'I suggest you don't attempt to cook again. You might burn the fucking house down.'

The stony look on his face told her that he wasn't amused. As did the door slammed in her face. Again.

Prick.

'I can cook perfectly well, thank you,' she yelled, annoyed by his assumption. This was her home. He was on her turf. If he thought he could roll up and chuck his weight around, he could think again.

13

In a valiant last stand the alarm case pinged open, and the battery plopped out pathetically onto Honey's foot. A bubble of laughter filtered up. She'd murdered it.

She threw a glance at the door opposite.

Hello new neighbour. It's good to meet you too.

One thing was for sure. This guy was no Simon. There wasn't a meek or mild bone in his body. Tash would love him – as long as he was loaded. Their wine-fuelled conversation from last night floated back. Her specific. She knocked on his door.

'Umm, you don't happen to play the piano, do you?' she shouted, knowing how funny Nell and Tash would find it when she told them.

He didn't need to open his door for her to hear him howl *fuck off*.

On the other side of the door, Hal inched along the hallway. Ten paces to the kitchen work surface, where he'd left the half-empty whisky bottle last night. The cool glass against his sweaty palms soothed his rattled nerves. The wail of that alarm had kicked him straight into DEFCON 1 mode.

Stupid airhead woman. 'Could you possibly reach it?' Her question still taunted him. He tipped the bottle to his lips, and the harsh burn of the whisky took the raw edge off his anger.

She'd smelled of strawberry shampoo and bacon smoke when she'd stepped close, and the ever-present laughter behind her voice had told him she didn't take life seriously.

Well, she should.

14

He fumbled his way to the bedroom and walked until his shins hit the edge of the mattress. The unmade sheets scratched his skin when he sprawled out, whisky in one hand, the other balled into a tight fist of frustration. He hated this house, and now he hated Strawberry Girl too.

CHAPTER THREE

Honey emptied out the latest bin liners on Monday morning and picked through the worn polyester blouses and elasticated skirts without enthusiasm. When she'd first started work at the charity shop, this had been one of her favourite bits of the day – tipping out the innocuous black bags in the hope of unearthing vintage treasure, or that some It-girl might have cleared out her summer wardrobe of all last season's Prada to make room for her winter collection.

It hadn't taken long for the shine to wear off. Honey had soon come to realise that the average age of people who gave to charity was around eighty. Either that or it was families clearing the decks of a deceased relative's possessions. Cheap chain store separates. Moth-eaten dresses or suits that had been held on to for sentimental reasons that had died with their owners. Thrift shop jewellery with broken catches. Chipped teacups long since separated from their saucers. Stiff leatherette handbags with brass clasps and screwed-up bingo tickets in the bottom, or a yellowed letter that relatives hadn't cared enough to hold on to. Honey could never bring herself to throw treasured mementoes away, so she slipped them into a drawer in the old bureau that doubled up as her desk in the small back room of the shop.

'Tea.' Lucille popped out of the kitchenette, a vision in tan support tights and an egg yolk-yellow sundress cinched in at the waist by a rhinestone belt. Lucille and her sister Mimi were the lifeblood of the charity shop, full-time volunteers who asked for nothing in return for their services apart from company and the occasional bright string of beads. They were magpies for colour and sparkle; or rather a pair of colourful canaries, singing wartime hits as they fluttered from customer to customer and batted their eyelashes against their heavily rouged cheeks to encourage a sale. Honey adored them both; fabulous aunts she'd chosen rather than had foisted upon her by the inconvenience of bloodline.

'Thanks, Lucille.' Honey took the dainty teacup and saucer. 'No Mimi yet this morning?'

Lucille bent to pull a sequinned dress from the pile at Honey's feet and shook it out at arm's length in front of her. 'She was entertaining last night.' Her perfectly lipsticked mouth puckered into a tight, sour little raspberry as she turned the dress inside out to squint at the label.

'Was she really?' Honey whistled. 'Not with Billy Bobbysocks again?'

Lucille sniffed. Her sister was far too smitten with Billy for her liking. Exactly what Mimi saw in him, with his ridiculous quiff and purple drainpipe trousers that were indecently tight for a man well into his eighties, was anyone's guess.

Honey glanced down to hide her smile. Both Lucille and

Mimi lived in fear of the other leaving, when history really ought to have taught them better. Men had come and gone in each of their lives, but their sibling bond had remained undiminished by romantic entanglements. It was a bond Honey well understood, having spent her formative years in the comfortable sweet spot between her elder sister Bluebell and their equally fantastically named youngest sister, Tigerlily. Their mother Jane, a failed actress forever saddled with the moniker 'Plain Jane Jones', had made certain that her daughters would never suffer the same indignity of anonymity.

Honey sorted the last of the clothes into washing and ironing piles and moved on to unpick the sticky tape from around a dog-eared cardboard box. The musty smell of long-discarded possessions assailed her nostrils as she peeled back the lid, and just as she was about to reach inside to remove the top layer of yellowed newsprint the telephone trilled in the office.

'It's probably Mimi ringing to say that she's still indisposed,' Lucille said with a scandalised arch of her eyebrows.

Honey grinned at the idea of being too swept away by the tides of passion to go into work at the ripe old age of eighty-three. 'I sincerely hope so.'

But when she picked up the receiver, she found herself doubly disappointed. One, it wasn't a love-swept Mimi and secondly, it was Christopher, the manager of the shop and the attached old people's residential home. A man of much influence and no charisma, which he masked with borderline rude officiousness.

'Staff meeting. Seventeen hundred hours. Don't be late or I'll start without you.'

'But we don't close until five p.m.'

'So close early. You're not exactly Tesco's, are you? And don't bring those old women, either. Paid staff only. Got that?'

'Loud and clear, Christopher. Loud and clear.'

Honey sighed as the dial tone clicked in her ear. 'Yeah. Goodbye to you too,' she muttered into the empty ether. Would it kill the man to feign politeness? Lord knows how he got people to entrust their frail relatives into his care; Honey wouldn't trust him with so much as a hamster. It was a great shame, then, that her financial security rested in his sweaty little hands.

Several long and eventful hours later, Honey dropped her plastic shopping carriers down on her front step and groaned with relief as she flexed her bag-sore fingers. Baked beans and tinned tomatoes were heavy but essential items on the non-cooking cook's shopping list.

Her heart lurched at the crunch of broken glass as she shouldered the door open. Shit. Had she been broken into? Honey flicked her eyes over the undamaged panes in the stained glass door, confused, until she noticed the pink tulips strewn across the parquet hallway floor. The very same pink tulips she'd placed in her favourite glass jug in the hallway a couple of days ago to welcome herself home. Or at least it had been her favourite, until now. There was no mending it – whoever had broken it had made a very thorough job.

By the looks of the still dewy flowers and the huge wet patch on the floor, whatever had happened had happened fairly recently, and as everything else in the shared hallway looked ship-shape, that left only one possible culprit. Only one person who would come through here and smash her jug without bothering to clear up the mess or leave an apology note.

Thanks a million, Johnny Depp.

Honey slammed the hallway door shut and leaned against it. It had turned into one hell of a day. Christopher's words at the earlier staff meeting scrolled around inside her head like ticker-tape on the twenty-four-hour rolling news channels. 'Funding being pulled. Threat of closure. Six months. Period of consultation.'

The shop was under the cosh, and unless they secured new funding soon they'd be closed down within a few months. And it wasn't just the charity shop, either; the whole home was under the hammer, leaving thirty residents facing eviction. What do you do when you find yourself unexpectedly homeless at ninety-seven? Honey had no clue, and Christopher had offered precious little in the way of answers. The day had gone from bad to worse as she'd struggled home with heavy shopping on the packed bus, standing next to a drunk teenager who had touched her bum at least twice. He'd been lucky not to have a can of beans wrapped around his head, but Honey was all out of fight. Until now.

The sight of her pretty jug and dying flowers strewn across the floor turned out to be the straw that broke the proverbial camel's back.

'Hey, rock star!' Honey yelled at her new neighbour's door as she picked her way over the shattered glass. 'Thanks for nothing!' She dropped her shopping bags by her front door and leaned against it. 'That was my favourite jug. Just so you know.'

She paused. Stubborn silence reigned, even though she was sure she'd heard movement beyond his door.

'Fine. I'll just send you the bill then, shall I?'

It had actually only cost 50p from work, but it had been pretty and his silence riled her. He was in there, she was sure of it. Although, thinking back, Honey couldn't recall seeing his lights on when she'd passed his windows. Another day, another hangover. Too bad.

'You're not the only one who had a bad day, you know. I almost lost my job today.' She screwed up her face as soon as the words left her mouth. Why was she telling a complete stranger her woes? Or worse yet, yelling them at someone who was clearly too much of an arrogant cock to care less?

Hal lay on the sofa, dark glasses over his closed eyes even though he was wide awake, pained by the effort of holding himself still rather than storming out there to tear a strip off Strawberry Girl. Flowers. Stupid, fucking, stupid flowers.

Storm out there. Who was he kidding? It had taken him almost ten minutes to make his way out into the hallway earlier that afternoon. All he'd wanted to do was answer his own goddamn front door. To stop the door-to-door salesman from banging on it, from banging on the inside of his head.

Who the hell put fresh flowers in a communal hallway anyway? How was he supposed to know they were there? The first rule of living with a blind person – don't place unexpected hazards in their way. But then, Strawberry Girl hadn't realised he was blind yet, had she? Thank fucking God, because when she did, she'd no doubt switch straight

21

into that same mode most other people did around him these days, a vomit-inducing mix of sympathy and desperation to make things easier for him. He didn't want to hear that falter in her voice when she first realised he couldn't see, so he lay on the sofa and listened to her berate him instead. Not that he could have gone out there even if he'd wanted to. Not with a soaked crotch and hands still sticky with warm blood where he'd cut his hands to ribbons trying to gather the glass up.

He knew exactly what she'd think. He reeked of whisky, and no doubt looked like he'd tried to slash his own wrists. And on top of that he must look like he'd pissed himself.

A new low, even in Hal's new world.

And she thought she'd had a bad day. She didn't know the meaning of the words.

Honey dumped her bags on the kitchen work surface and headed back into the hallway with the brush and pan. She'd briefly entertained the idea that her mini rant might have piqued his guilt enough to make him clear up, but no such luck. His door remained resolutely closed, and her flowers were still scattered across the floor. She rescued them one by one, and then set to work sweeping the glass shards together. The water still on the floor made the job extra awkward, and tell-tale streaks of red caught her eye as it mingled with the glass and water. She frowned and stilled for a second. If that was blood, then maybe he had attempted to clear up after all. Or, oh God, maybe he'd injured himself and knocked over her flowers by accident, or maybe he'd had some sort of fit, or nicked an artery with the glass and was at this moment lying dead in his flat and it would be all her tulips' fault. The way Honey's day was shaping up, accidentally murdering her neighbour wasn't beyond the realms of possibility. The floor cleared, she took a few steps towards his door and turned her ear towards it to listen. Nothing. She raised her hand to knock, but then stopped just before her knuckles made contact. What was she going to say if he answered? If you're dead or injured then I'm sorry, but if you're not then I'm not really sorry at all?

'Hello,' she called out tentatively. A stony silence filled her ears, and Honey felt the very edges of panic start to unfurl. 'Hello.' She tried again, a little louder, a little firmer.

Still nothing. She bunched her hand and banged on his door. 'Are you alright in there?'

This time she put her ear right against the door and listened hard. Was that a shuffle?

Hal swore under his breath and hauled himself upright on the sofa. Strawberry Girl was fast becoming his nemesis. Why was she thumping on his door? Did she seriously want the money for her stupid bloody jug?

'Look, I know you're in there. I just heard you move.'

Hal shook his head. It was like living next door to Miss Marple's over-zealous granddaughter. She must have her ear right against his door.

'Just answer me, will you? Are you alright in there?'

Fuck. She was already checking up on him, and she didn't even know he was blind yet. He made a mental note to keep it that way for as long as possible. He winced with pain as he rolled his shoulders and flexed his lacerated palms.

She must have heard him, because she thumped on his door even harder.

'Do you need help?' she called out as he made his way along the hallway, for all the world as if she were checking on an elderly neighbour who might have tumbled over their zimmer frame. Sour resentment settled over him.

'What would it take to make you go away?' he grouched through the closed door, and heard her puff out loudly as if she'd been holding her breath. Drama queen.

'Are you always this rude?' Her tone changed abruptly from concerned to snarky.

'Only to people who piss me off.' Her answering gasp made him smile for the first time since he'd moved in.

'I piss you off? Is that why you smashed my jug and left the flowers all over the floor? Because I piss you off?' The fact that she was shouting at him brought Hal perverse pleasure. No one shouted at him anymore.

'That's about the size of it, yeah.'

This time it was her foot that hit the door rather than her hand, and it was in anger rather than concern.

'Pig. What have I done to you? Besides have the audacity to set off the smoke alarm and disturb your sodding hangover?' Her unnaturally fast breathing gave away how riled she was. 'Well, you picked the wrong day to mess with me, pal.'

Hal almost laughed. Miss Marple Jr had just morphed into Rambo. He crossed his arms and leaned against the door as he waited for her to carry on.

'Unlike you, my life isn't just one big round of parties and hangovers. I have responsibilities. I have a job. People who depend on me.'

The sudden rush of anger her words provoked had Hal groping for the door catch. He wrenched it open.

'One big party? Is that what you think this is?' He spat his words out and flung an arm back towards his hallway.

'No,' she shot back. 'I'd say this is your lair. Somewhere to lie low and recover from your hangovers.' Hal could hear the disdain drip from her voice, and he knew she must be taking in the details of his dishevelled appearance. 'Look at you. You stink of booze, and God knows what else. You need a shave and a change of clothes . . .' her voice trailed off, and he knew that she would be drawing all the wrong conclusions.

It pissed him off royally. He wasn't a man given to hysterics before the accident, but keeping his temper seemed much more difficult these days. Strawberry Girl's accusations felt as if someone had hurled a grenade into his brain and pulled out the pin.

'My lair?' he roared. 'My fucking *lair*?' A laugh started way down in the base of his gut, except it felt more like something dark and ugly trying to fight its way out of him. It rattled through his entire body, and he heard it leave him, a harsh, alien sound somewhere between a laugh and a scream of anger.

'This isn't my lair,' he ground out, when he could speak again. 'It's my goddamn prison.'

Strawberry Girl didn't speak, but her shallow breathing told him she was still there, still staring at him.

'What?' she said, eventually. The heat of anger had left her voice, edged out by bewilderment and something else that might have been fear. Hal heard it and knew he had her on the ropes. It would be so simple to go for the kill now, to reveal his blindness and have her fall over herself in her hurry to apologise. In his previous life he'd thrived on being the one in control, and the urge to take control of her now pressed hard against his skull. His aggressive streak had aided his meteoric rise as one of the country's brightest stars in the restaurant industry. And he'd loved it all. The money. The cars. The celebrity patrons. The girls. One girl in particular. And he'd lost it all in a split second of showman distraction.

Life was different now. It was made up of the four walls of this flat, daytime TV he was almost glad he couldn't see and wished he couldn't hear, and microwave dinners that tasted of the boxes they came in.

He screwed his face up and sighed hard. Everything had gone to hell, but none of that was Strawberry Girl's fault. Everything else in his life may have changed, but frightening women had never been his style and he wasn't about to start now.

'No,' he said. 'You're right. You don't understand, and I hope for your sake that you never need to. Can I go now that you've been a good girl guide and checked on your needy neighbour?'

Hal heard her draw breath to answer, but closed the door so he didn't have to listen.

CHAPTER FOUR

'It was so weird, Nell. He had blood all over his hands, and looked like death warmed up.'

Honey perched on a high stool at Nell's breakfast bar, a sleeping Ava nestled in the crook of her arm.

'Maybe he's a vampire.' Nell closed the dishwasher and spun around with a startled look in her eyes. 'God, you don't think he'd been trying to . . .'

Honey shook her head. 'There were no cuts on his wrists, if that's what you mean. I checked. It was his actual hands, but both of them. That's weird, isn't it? I think he'd tried to clear up my glass jug, but then why would he have been so clumsy? And then not finished the job!'

'Prison's such an odd thing to call your home,' Nell said.

Honey glanced around the warm, welcoming kitchen. Nell's tidy, gorgeous home embraced everyone who entered through the door in a big warm hug. Just being there was balm for her tattered nerves.

'He was angry, Nell. Proper angry.'

Nell frowned. 'I don't like the thought of you living alone next to him, Honey.'

'That's another odd thing.' Honey reached for her coffee mug. 'I'm not scared of him, not in that way. If anything, I felt sorry for him.'

Nell leaned back against the kitchen surface with her steaming mug cupped in her hands. 'I'm not sure I do. He's been nothing but rude to you from the day he moved in.'

'Well, I won't be nominating him for neighbour of the year, that's for sure.' Honey stroked the sleeping baby's fragile fingers, struck by how vulnerable and innocent she was. She couldn't imagine the man she now shared a house with ever being like this. She had no clue who he was, but something had happened to him. Something awful, and it had made him just about the most angry, jaded person she'd ever met.

'Tash texted me this morning from Dubai,' Nell said, changing the subject.

Honey glanced out at the rain through the window, her train of thought broken.

'Lucky cow. She moans about that job, but at least she gets to see the sun every now and then.'

'She's found you a pianist.'

Honey looked up sharply. 'Jeez, Nell. It was a joke. She isn't serious?'

Nell shrugged with a half-suppressed smile. 'I think she is. She's going to call you when she gets home tomorrow.'

'Nell. I'm about to lose my job and Freddy Krueger has just moved in next door to me. Do you think I need any more hassle in my life right now?'

Ava stirred, her sleep disturbed by Honey's agitation.

'Probably not,' Nell conceded. 'But then what if he looks like Michael Bublé?'

Honey grinned. 'Then I'd let him buy me dinner.'

Nell eased the half-awake baby out of Honey's arms and into her own, where Ava slipped straight back into contented sleep.

'Just wait and see then, okay?' Nell winked as she headed upstairs to lay the baby down. Honey sighed. The relentless gloom outside was a fitting reflection of her mood, and the idea of having to endure a blind date with some random stranger to satisfy Tash and Nell's ridiculous quest wasn't a welcome addition to her burden.

Honey walked past the chemist on the way home, and then backtracked and went inside. A few minutes later, she emerged with a carrier. When she let herself into the house she approached her neighbour's door rather than her own.

'Umm, hello?' she called out without knocking, as he must have heard her come in. She could make out the strains of music, something heavy metal by the sounds of it. Maybe he hadn't heard her after all. She rapped on the door, loud enough to be heard, but hopefully not loud enough to be annoying. She waited, and then knocked again when he didn't answer.

'I have something for you,' she called out. In answer, he turned the music up full blast, loud enough to drown out any further attempt at conversation. Honey shook her head and growled with frustration. He really was a nightmare neighbour. She bent and left the carrier leaning against his door, and after a few uncertain seconds she turned away and left him to stew in his misery.

*   *   *

29

Hal sat in the hard, unforgiving armchair with his forearms clamped against the sides of his head to drown out the noise of MTV and Strawberry Girl's knocking. Only when he was sure he couldn't take it any longer without putting his foot through the TV did he turn it off. The sudden silence was almost as deafening as the music. Was she still out there, waiting for him? He sat stock still and listened for a while until he was sure she'd gone, then sat there some more with his head in his sore hands, for some considerable time. He wanted a drink. He needed whisky, but the empty bottle was on his bedside table after he'd tipped the last of it into his mouth last night. He ran through his options in his head. Go without. Not an option. He could call someone, but who?

His close friends would no doubt feel duty bound to let his worried family know where he was, and anyone who didn't care very much about him would value the gossip above his friendship. Poor old Hal, living in a grotty flat with just a whisky bottle to talk to. Such a shame.

No, calling someone he knew was out of the question. Maybe he could just go out in the street and hope that some kindly passer-by took pity on him enough to take his twenty-pound note and fetch his whisky? He thumped the arm of the chair in temper. How low did he have to go with this fucking thing? It scared him that as low as he was, there were still further depths to which he could plummet. There was only one option available to him; he'd known it even as his mind had cast around for alternatives. Strawberry Girl. He scrubbed his hands over his face and pulled his dark glasses over his eyes, then heaved himself out of the chair and along the hallway which had fast become familiar territory.

Hal paused as his fingers found the catch on the door. He hadn't stepped foot outside since he'd knocked her flowers over. Apprehension encroached on his psyche, but he shoved it aside. He wasn't going to become that man.

He swung the door open and stepped out, then lost his footing over something and slammed hard onto the floor.

Honey heard the almighty crash as she wandered out of the steamed-up bathroom in her dressing gown with a towel wrapped around her hair, still hot from the shower. She dashed for the front door without thinking, and opened it to find her neighbour sprawled face down across the floor, surrounded by the antiseptic cream and bandages she'd left for him.

'Go back inside and shut your fucking door right now!' he roared at her without looking up as his hands scrabbled around on the floor for something.

'What? No, let me help . . .' Honey's hands flew to her cheeks in panic. It went against her every instinct to leave him there, but she was under no illusion – he meant exactly what he'd said. She stepped forward, and her toes touched against something unexpected. When she looked down, she found his dark glasses about to disappear beneath her foot. She bent and picked them up, relieved to find they were still intact.

'Here.' She held them out to him, and at the sound of her voice he went from groping around on the floor to absolutely bone still.

'My glasses?'

Honey nodded, then after a beat she let out the softest

of gasps at the significance of him needing to ask the question. 'Oh.'

He reached out towards her without looking up. 'Give them to me.'

She stepped out of her doorway and placed them in his fingers. He grabbed them and shoved them onto his face, then rolled over and scooted back against the wall, his elbows on his knees, his head in his hands.

Honey moved quietly around him, collecting up the chemist supplies back into the bag and putting them on the hall table. Shit. Why couldn't she have just left them there in the first place?

'I brought you bandages. And antiseptic. It was for your hands,' she murmured, knowing it was insignificant. 'I'm sorry.'

He made a guttural sound and scruffed up his hair with his fingers.

'I was wrong when I called you a girl guide. You're way beyond that. You're a regular Mother fucking Teresa.'

Honey hesitated, unsure whether to stay or go. 'What do you want me to do?'

'Not setting up any more obstacle courses in the bloody hallway would be a good start.'

'Deal.' Honey realised in that tiny moment of thaw that she didn't even know his name. 'I'm Honey, by the way.'

'Well, that's ridiculous. What's your real name?'

'Honey *is* my real name. Well, it's Honeysuckle, actually.'

'Fuck me. That's even more ridiculous.'

Honey was well used to her name being cause for comment, yet still his blatant derision riled her. 'Just another thing about me to annoy you then, rock star.'

'"Rock star"?'

'Yeah. That's your name in my head. Mostly because you're an arrogant twat who swears all the time and drinks whisky for breakfast.'

'I'll take that,' he said. 'Or Hal. Just in case you ever feel the need to revise your opinion.'

'Where were you going?'

'To knock on your door.'

'To apologise about the flowers?'

'Not fucking likely. Do you have any whisky?'

Honey contemplated her answer. She didn't. She did, however, have an almost-full bottle of tequila in the back of the cupboard, but enabling a drunk felt wrong. Was he a drunk? He certainly seemed to drink enough to qualify for the title. 'Not whisky, no.'

'But you do have something?'

Honey sighed. He might not be able to see her expression, but her voice had obviously given her away and lying wasn't her strong point. 'I have tequila.'

'Thank fuck. Can I have it?'

'Mother Teresa wouldn't give it to you.'

'Will you give it to me if I apologise?'

'For smashing my jug, or for calling me Mother Teresa?'

'Either. Both. Hell, I'll even apologise for the fact that your mother named you Honeysuckle if you give me tequila.'

'Do you have lemon and salt?'

He lifted his head towards Honey slowly, and even though his eyes were hidden behind his glasses she could clearly read the incredulous look on his face. For a second she thought he was going to yell again, and then he started to laugh. And not just a snicker. A great, huge, belly laugh that shook his shoulders first, then his entire body, and it went on and on uncontrollably until tears poured down his face.

Honey didn't laugh with him, because it was pretty obvious that despite his current appearance, her mysterious neighbour was far from amused.

She slipped into her flat to dig the tequila out of the cupboard. When she returned to the hallway Hal had pulled himself up to standing and almost pulled himself together, although tear streaks still dredged across his face.

'Tequila,' Honey said, and stepped close enough to touch his arm. He took the bottle she placed into his hand with muttered thanks. 'Is there anything else I can do for you?' she asked. 'You know, any help with . . . stuff?'

Hal huffed. 'Don't start the Mother Teresa thing again just because you know I'm blind.'

'I won't. I still think you're an arrogant twat who drinks too much.'

The smallest twitch of humour tugged at the corner of Hal's mouth. 'And I still think you're a frustrated girl guide with a stupid name.'

'Good. Then we understand each other.'

'Don't bang on my door again.'

Honey watched him turn and walk away, staying close to the wall until he reached his own doorway. 'Fine. But shout if you need anything.'

'I won't need anything you could possibly give me, Honeysuckle,' he said, his voice low and gravelly. He clicked the door closed, leaving Honey alone in the hall – a little enlightened, a little troubled, and, strangely, a little in lust.

34

CHAPTER FIVE

Lucille and Mimi stared at Honey with slack mouths and trembling hands.

'So I'm afraid that unless someone steps in and buys the place, the shop will be closed down. The home too,' Honey finished. She'd waited until the end of the day to tell the ladies, knowing they'd need some quiet time to digest the news.

'They can't do this to us!' Lucille cried, her face anguished.

Honey smiled sadly. 'There's still six months yet, Lucille. Let's hope for a miracle.'

'Over my dead body are they closing our shop.' Mimi squared her fragile shoulders, which were swathed today in the palest lime green cashmere twinset. As was often the case, Lucille had coordinated her outfit with her sister's and had arrived this morning sporting an identical twinset in a complementary shade of lemon. Lemon Meringue and Key Lime Pie. Both ladies had knotted long strings of beads around their necks and large rings sparkled on their fragile

35

fingers. Their outfits sang of sunshine, summer days and sweet spun sugar, but their faces told a far more melancholy story. Lucille's big blue eyes shimmered with unshed tears, and Mimi had a look of fierce defiance that would have caused Emmeline Pankhurst's heart to swell with pride.

Lucille turned to her sister with a flicker of hope. 'Do you think we should fight it?'

'Why ever would we not?' Mimi said, looking from Lucille to Honey.

Honey frowned. Much as she hated the idea of closing the shop down, the idea of actively protesting hadn't crossed her mind until now. Was there any point? For all his official talk of periods of consultation, Christopher had made it sound like a cut and dried decision last night. He'd probably been offered a sweetener to keep him onside, a golden handshake to make sure he didn't allow anyone to rock the boat. He certainly hadn't seemed overly concerned by the plight of the residents. 'Dispersed' was the word he'd used, and one Honey had carefully avoided when she'd tried to explain to Mimi and Lucille how the residents would be rehomed at other places.

'Rehomed. We sound like a bunch of unwanted dogs,' Lucille said, wringing her slender hands in her lap. 'No one wants old animals so they get put down. Is that what's going to happen to us, Honey?'

The wretched expression on Lucille's face tore at Honey's heartstrings. She wished she could offer her friend some genuine hope, but at that moment there wasn't much to offer beyond a hug and a cup of hot, sweet tea.

'What if they can't place us together, Mimi?' Lucille said, and Honey took the violently trembling cup and saucer gently from the older woman's grasp for fear of it spilling on the ivory sunray pleats of her skirt. The sisters had shared connecting rooms in the home with their own bathroom for the last seven years, building a life of sorts amongst the residents and voluntary work in the shop. The idea that they might be placed apart from each other was awful, like adopted siblings being split up to maximise their appeal.

'I'm sure it won't come to that,' Honey soothed, hoping with all of her heart that it wouldn't.

'It won't,' Mimi said, 'because I won't let it, Lucie. I promise.' Ever the protective big sister, even at eighty-three, Mimi sat beside Lucille and put an arm around her shoulders. 'And Honey will help us organise ourselves, won't you, duck? People will listen to you more than us.'

Two pairs of eyes turned up towards Honey, one pair cornflower blue and brimming with tears, the other brown and bright with rebellion. Something in Honey stirred, a resolve to stand up and fight for her friends.

'Of course I will.' She sat on Lucille's other side and put her hand over the older woman's clasped ones, trying not to notice their frailty. 'Of course I will. We have six months. It's plenty of time to work something out.'

'Our angel,' Lucille smiled. 'Where would we be without you?'

'You don't need to think about that,' Honey said. 'I'm not going anywhere, and neither are you without an almighty fight.'

Honey let herself into the house an hour or so later, still mulling over the conversation with Lucille and Mimi. She hadn't considered the idea of trying to campaign to save the home, and she certainly hadn't anticipated the idea of being the poster girl for it – yet it seemed that she might have to, because everyone else involved was at least eighty and looking to her for help. The responsibility weighed as heavy as the shopping bags in her hands as she awkwardly bumped the front door closed with her backside and flicked her eyes around the hall for any new signs of Hal's presence. She glanced towards her neighbour's door, half expecting him to throw it open and yell at her about something, but it remained resolutely closed and quiet. She huffed softly and opened her own door, hauling her heavy shopping up onto the kitchen work surface in the tiny kitchenette. The woefully small kitchen hadn't concerned Honey in the slightest when she'd viewed the flat, mainly because her cooking repertoire didn't extend much beyond cheese on toast or microwaved tomato soup. Rooting through the bags, she pulled out the only item she'd really headed into the store for in the first place. Whisky. As someone who never touched the stuff, the wall of whisky choices she'd found herself faced with had been bewildering. Did Hal have a preferred brand? Was he a single malt man? Given the amount of it that he seemed to drink and the hefty price tag on the decent stuff, Honey settled for the supermarket's own blend. Hal probably wouldn't taste it anyway when he knocked it back without it touching the sides. He seemed to use it more for anaesthetic than pleasure. Picking up the bottle and screwing up her courage, Honey opened her front door, crossed the hallway and knocked tentatively on Hal's door. Nothing. It didn't surprise her.

'Hal?' she called his name lightly. Neighbourly. 'Hal, it's me. Honey.'

He didn't reply, and there were no sounds of life behind the stubbornly closed door, but he was in there, she was sure of it. It was pretty obvious from the way he'd practically begged for her tequila yesterday that he wasn't planning on leaving the house anytime soon. Unease crept through Honey. Couldn't the man just grunt or something, make some acknowledgment that he was alive at least? What if he'd drunk all the tequila and passed out cold? God, what if he'd hit his head?

'Hal.' She threw more power behind her voice, aiming for friendly, but immediately knew she'd failed and come over all officious and girl guide again. Glancing back towards her own open door, she sighed with resignation and leaned against the wall.

'I'm not going away until you answer me, so you may as well make this easy on both of us, rock star.'

Silence reigned, and Honey slid her weary bones down the wall to sit outside his door, the bottle of whisky beside her. 'I'll just sit out here then,' she said, her elbows on her knees, chin cupped in her hands. 'I guess I'll just drink this whisky myself then,' she said after a few minutes, not enjoying the manipulative nature of her comment but glad to be well and truly out of girl guide territory. And besides, it worked. Honey let out a long, slow breath of relief as the sound of movement on the other side of the door told her that he was at least alive.

He was close to the door now, she could hear him breathing.

'What will it take to make you give me that whisky?' he grumbled.

Honey raised her eyebrows, nodding philosophically into her hands. That was how it was going to be then.

'Ah you know. Nothing much. A bit of neighbourly chat, maybe?'

More movement from behind the door, and then his whisky and cigarettes voice again, only lower this time. Closer. As if he were sitting on the other side of the door.

'I don't chat.'

'No?' Honey said casually, not even sure why she was trying to engage him in conversation. She felt like someone trying to entice a kitten into their home with a saucer of milk. 'Maybe you could just listen then, because I've had a pig of a day and I could do with offloading.'

'So what, you thought you'd bribe your blind neighbour with whisky to make him listen? Don't you have any friends?'

Honey half smiled. Was it masochistic that she enjoyed his grouchiness? Glancing at her watch, she tapped the face with her fingertip. 'Something like that. Ten minutes of your time and you get the whisky.'

His exaggerated sigh was unmissable. 'I'm not opening the door.'

'Whatever. Just don't go and do something else while I'm speaking.'

His harsh laugh told her that her comment had struck a chord. 'You mean I can't go back to screwing the horny blonde in my bedroom? I could keep it quiet.'

'In your dreams, rock star.' Honey wrapped her arms around her knees. 'So . . . I just had to tell two old ladies that they might be homeless soon.'

A pause. 'It's not just my life you're intent on screwing up then,' Hal said.

'It's not my fault.' Honey knew he didn't care, but felt

the need to make him understand anyway. 'I manage the charity shop attached to the home they live in. They volunteer in the shop most days. They're my friends, and I feel like shit.'

'Did you tell me already why you're making them homeless?'

'I'm not the one making them homeless. The home is under threat of closure within six months because of lack of funds, the shop too. I'll lose my job, and all of the residents will lose their homes. None of them are a day under eighty.'

'Look on the bright side. They're old. They might not make it through the next six months.'

Honey sucked in a sharp breath, taken aback by his harshness. 'You weren't kidding when you said you don't do chat, were you?'

'If you were looking for Oprah you knocked the wrong door, sweetheart.'

The term of endearment landed soft and hard at the same time. Hal had managed to deliver it with a heavy side order of sarcasm that stripped out any potential kindness. But something made Honey wonder how it would feel to hear him say it under different circumstances, in a different tone of voice.

'Is it too soon to ask for that whisky?' he asked into the lengthening silence following his last remark.

Honey glanced at her watch. Three minutes. Seven to go. 'Yup. Want to tell me about your day instead?'

'Fuck off, Honeysuckle,' he shot back, just as she'd expected that he would. Had she needled him on purpose? Potentially, and if she had it had backfired, because the way

41

he'd said her name made it sound like . . . She let the pause extend this time.

'Come on then, Mother Teresa. Tell me some more about this job you're about to lose.'

'It's not so much my job I'm worried about. Well I am, obviously, but it's Lucille and Mimi mostly, and all of the other residents.' She paused and bit the inside of her lip. 'They want me to spearhead a big campaign to fight the closure.'

She thought she heard him half laugh. 'I hope you're photogenic for the newspapers. Will you wear your girl guide uniform?'

'Do you have to be such a cock all the time? This is the most serious thing that's ever happened to me.'

She heard him sigh, deep and melancholy, and then the soft thud of something against the door, most probably his forehead as he leaned against it.

'You don't know how fucking lucky you are if this is the worst that life's thrown at you, Honeysuckle.'

His voice was close to her ear, and she let the side of her head tip against the door. Against his voice. If the door were to magically disappear, they'd have found themselves sitting shoulder to shoulder, his mouth against her hair.

'Sorry. Didn't mean to be insensitive,' she whispered, feeling a fool and checking her watch and finding that they still had five minutes to fill.

'You weren't insensitive. I was being a cock. It's kind of been my way since the accident.'

It was the most genuine thing he'd said to her since she'd met him. 'Want this whisky now?'

'Does that mean our therapy session's up?'

The ghost of a smile tipped her lips. 'I'll let you have this one on the house, rock star.'

'Does that mean you've written me off as a hopeless case, Honeysuckle?'

Unexpected prickles of awareness stroked over the back of Honey's neck. He'd practically whispered in her ear, sexy and velvet soft words softened with the hint of a smile. If the guy was ever inclined he could have a killer career on the radio, his voice had the capacity to stop a woman in her tracks. Even a woman who didn't especially like him.

She found herself smiling too. 'The jury's out, Hal. Maybe I'll come by again tomorrow to fill you in some more on my soap opera life.'

'It'll beat the shit out of *Coronation Street*. Do people really watch that bollocks?'

Honey laughed lightly. 'You mean you don't?' As soon as the words left her lips, she wanted to suck them straight back in again. 'Shit Hal, I'm sorry,' she mumbled. 'Twice in five minutes is pretty rubbish, isn't it?'

'Just give me the whisky and I'll forgive you.'

Honey could still hear the trace of humour and breathed out in relief. He was a hard man to read; angry when it seemed unreasonable to be so, yet cool about things that might well have flared the temper of someone else in his position. She could hear him moving behind the door and drew herself up onto her feet, the whisky in her hand. She wouldn't make the mistake of leaving obstacles in his path a second time.

As he opened his door and leaned against the frame, she found herself reassessing his appearance. He was as dishevelled as yesterday, maybe more so. A washed-out, rumpled grey t-shirt hung over his chest, in places not quite meeting the waist of his slouchy dark jeans. His dark stubble told her that today was another day when he hadn't had a hot date with his shaver, and his slightly too-long hair looked as if he'd pushed his hands through it all day, or else spent the day in bed with that horny blonde he'd alluded to.

'Hey, rock star.'

Hal didn't speak for a second, silent and inscrutable until she started to feel disconcerted, as if he were staring at her behind those glasses, which of course she knew he wasn't. What was going through his head? Did she need to do something?

'You smell of strawberries again.'

Of all of the things she'd expected him to say, that wasn't it.

'It must be my shampoo,' she murmured, bewildered, touching her hair by reflex with her empty hand. 'It's strawberry scented.'

He nodded slightly, as if he'd sussed that much already.

'What colour is it?'

'My shampoo?' she said, thrown. 'It's kind of pink, I think . . .?'

He sighed, and if he could have rolled his eyes, she felt sure he would've.

'Your hair, Honey,' he said. 'What colour is it?'

'Oh . . . blonde. It's blonde.' For information that would be readily available to a sighted person, it felt absurdly intimate.

He nodded again with a half smirk. 'Figures.'

44

'Cheap shot, rock star.'

He shrugged. 'You made it too easy.'

'I'm considering taking my whisky home with me.'

'I know where you live.'

The idea of him leaving his flat and coming into hers made her itch with panic, and she held the whisky out uncertainly until the glass touched his hand.

'Here.'

His fingers curled around the bottle, brushing hers, silencing them both.

'Thanks,' he muttered ungraciously, drawing it into his body as if she might take it away from him.

'I'll . . . I'll go then,' she said, waving towards her flat even though he couldn't see the gesture.

He nodded, in that silent, brooding way that was fast becoming his trademark.

Stepping backwards, wavering in the no-man's-land between their two front doors, Honey watched his stillness and wondered again what he was thinking of.

As she reached her doorway, she lifted her hand, an automatic gesture of goodbye even though he wouldn't be aware of it.

'See you tomorrow,' she said softly, and for the third time that evening she wished she'd been more considerate with her words. Being around this guy was turning out to be a minefield.

He raised the bottle and inclined his head in quiet acknowledgment of her words, and Honey clicked her door closed.

Hal stood for a few moments longer in the hallway, glad of the fresh supply of whisky. The scent of her lingered in the hallway, and he inhaled until his lungs were as full as they could be. She was chaotic, and she was blonde, and she was the first person to not walk on eggshells around him since the accident eight months ago. He pushed his door to and unscrewed the cap on the whisky.

CHAPTER SIX

'I've found you a pianist!'

Honey looked at Tash over the glass-topped counter in the charity shop. She'd burst through the door about two seconds previously, her wild red curls snatched back and merry eyed with news. Dressed in off-duty sweat pants and vest, she was a world away from the air-hostess glam of her professional life. She grinned as she leaned both elbows on the glass and cupped her chin.

Honey shot a nervous glance towards Tash and inclined her head imperceptibly towards Mimi, who was sorting through a bag of brooches nearby. Too late.

'Why do you need a pianist, Honey?' Mimi said, glancing up and smiling at Tash with her pearly white dentures.

'I don't, especially,' Honey said, aiming for off-hand and counting on Tash to change the subject. She'd expected the whole pianist idea to die a silent death once they were all sober, and the last thing she wanted was for Mimi and Lucille to know about her less-than-scintillating sex life too.

'Only my Billy is a dab-hand at tinkling the ivories,' Mimi said, polishing a glittering flower brooch and then holding it up to the light for inspection. 'I'm sure he'd help you out if you're in a fix, dear.'

Tash snort-choked on the coffee Lucille had just placed in front of her, and Honey screwed up her eyes tight against the vision of Mimi's octogenarian boyfriend tinkling her ivories.

'He's got magic fingers, he makes all the women in the home swoon,' Lucille chimed in as she pulled up a stool on Honey's other side. Honey passed her hand over her lips in case she threw up in her mouth a little at the idea of Billy and his magic fingers. She wanted to kill Tash for mentioning the subject at all in front of Mimi and Lucille.

'I don't think Billy would be suitable for this particular gig,' Tash laughed.

'Don't dismiss him because of his age,' Mimi sniffed. 'He's quite modern for an older man. He knows some up-to-date things too.'

'How can I put this, girls . . .?' Tash sighed and placed her cup down delicately. 'This is a very, umm, intimate gig. As in an audience of like, one.'

Mimi and Lucille frowned in tandem. 'You mean you're looking for a pianist to play just for Honey?' Lucille said.

'Er, hello, I am actually here,' Honey grumbled. 'Now can we change the subject, please?'

'Not to play for Honey,' Tash said, completely ignoring her friend. 'To play *with* Honey.'

'You play the piano, dear?' Mimi said, turning her big brown eyes to Honey. 'How did I not know that? Billy will be thrilled. You can duet.'

'Look, I don't play the flippin' piano, okay?' Honey said, picking her cup up and draining it, then gathering up the empty cups and taking them into the kitchen in order to end the conversation. She realised her tactical error a few minutes later when the trio lapsed into suspicious silence on her return; the conversation had clearly carried on perfectly well without her. Surely Tash hadn't gone into detail about the piano man mission to Lucille and Mimi?

Lucille patted Honey's hand. 'We think it's marvellous that you're doing something about your little problem,' she whispered the last few words conspiratorially, and Mimi covered her other hand with her own liver-spotted one. 'Pianists are definitely good with their hands. Take it from someone who knows. Even at our age, my Billy can . . .' she tailed off and shrugged her slight shoulders, thankfully drawing a veil over the finer details before she and Lucille drifted away to help customers.

Honey shot Tash a murderous look, which she ignored with a cheeky grin.

'So, as I was saying. I've found you a pianist.'

'Tash, I don't want one. Not really. It was a joke.'

Tash frowned and shook her head. 'Uh-uh. It wasn't, and it isn't. Anyway, you can't back out now, because I've set you up on a date with him.'

'What? No.' Honey didn't like the way this conversation was headed. 'Who is he, anyway?'

'Deano. You're gonna love him,' Tash said. 'He's one of the girls I work with's brother's flat mate. Or was it her brother's friend's flat mate?'

'You've never even met him, have you?'

Tash looked shifty. 'Well, not exactly myself, but she showed me a picture and he's hot.'

'So you've set me up with some randomer you've never met called Deano. He doesn't even sound like a pianist to me.'

'Oh, he is. For deffo. Well . . . a synthesiser, but that's practically the same thing, isn't it?' Tash held up her hand to silence the protest on Honey's lips. 'And here's the best bit. He's in a band.'

Honey stared at her friend. 'So. To clarify. You've set me up on a blind date with a bloke you've never met who's in a band and isn't even a pianist.'

Tash nodded. 'Friday night, half past eight at The Cock.'

The Cock Inn was the less desirable of the two pubs in the small market town of Greyacres. Honey shook her head.

'No way, Tash. I'm not doing it. You'll have to go yourself.'

'No can do. I'm seeing Yusef on Friday, a property developer I met on a flight to Dubai last week. He's hot and loaded and he wants me bad ways. Besides, Deano's into blondes.'

'For Christ's sake, Tash, who does he think he is? Rod bloody Stewart? Does he think I'm some sort of groupie? Is he expecting to buy me a pint and a bag of scratchings and then shag me in the alleyway behind The Cock?' She shook her head. 'This was hardly the idea, was it? You promised me Michael Bublé.'

'I'm trying, okay?' Tash said, all big green eyes and pouty lips. 'Just meet him for one drink, yes? Gina said he's a laugh and he's lonely.'

'Lonely?' More alarm bells rang in Honey's head.

Tash cleared her throat and ran her fingers through the strings of beads hanging on a stand on the counter.

'Mmm. He broke up with his girlfriend or something. Details, Honey, details. All you need to know is he's hot and available.' Tash picked up her car keys. 'Don't let me down, Honeysuckle. Live a little. Be in The Cock Friday night at half past eight, okay?'

Honey pushed open the door of the house at just after six that evening, weighed down once more with shopping for both herself and her grouchy neighbour. She'd decided against more whisky. A bottle a day seemed a dangerous amount to encourage Hal to drink, or to enable him with at least. She was pretty sure he wasn't leaving the building himself any time soon and he didn't have a second supplier, so she was pretty much his whisky tap. That knowledge came as something of a relief because he couldn't drink more than she gave him, but on the flip side it was a responsibility she didn't especially want. How much was too much? A bottle a week? Every three days? She was pretty certain Hal's answer would be every day if she asked him, which she wasn't about to do. So she'd brought him different things today. Orange juice. Milk. Cereal. Bread. Cheese slices. Ham. Cans of cola. Crisps. Chocolate bars. Her shopping for him resembled a cross between stuff for a kids' tea party and a welcome pack at a holiday cottage. She'd wandered the aisles looking for things that came in easy portions, hampered by the fact that she didn't have a clue either what Hal liked or how someone visually impaired dealt with food preparation. On impulse she'd picked up a couple of bags of chips from the local chippy too, and after nipping into her own flat to deposit her junk and her jacket, she schlepped across the hallway to Hal's door.

'Hey, rock star,' she called out, tapping her knuckles lightly on the wood. Silence, and after a little while, more of the same. No great shock there then. 'Come on Hal, I know you're in there. I bought you stuff.' She turned her head so that her ear was close to the door. Still nothing. She counted to sixty and then tried again. 'Please? I've got takeaway, and it's burning my fingers, so if you could just . . .' She stopped speaking at the sound of movement in the hallway behind the door.

'What is it today? Meals on fucking wheels?'

Honey raised her eyebrows at his closed door. 'Hello to you too, neighbour. Open the door?' She felt him deliberating in the lengthening silence. 'Please? It's only a bag of chips, but they're good.'

The door inched open just enough for Hal to put his hand out.

'That's not exactly polite, is it?' she said, holding on to his food. He gestured with his middle finger in a way that left her in no way confused about his irritation, and then opened his palm for a second time. Honey flicked her eyes at the ceiling and then gave up, placing the wrapped packet in his hand.

'I have some too,' she said through the gap. 'Want to invite me in and we can eat together?'

'Not unless you bought more whisky.'

Honey sighed and slid down the wall beside his door. 'I guess I'll just sit out here and eat them then.' She ripped a hole in the top of her paper parcel to eat them the old-fashioned way, as if she were sitting down on the seafront watching the waves instead of on the Minton-tiled floor of her own hallway. As hallways went, it was quite pretty, square and airy with a big sash window and original flooring, but as views went it wasn't spectacular. On the other side of the door Honey heard Hal settling on the floor too, and through the inch or so gap heard the tear of paper.

'Mind out. They're hot,' she said, blowing on her singed fingertips.

'I'm blind, not stupid,' he muttered. She almost apologised and then thought better of it.

'No need to be snarky, I was only trying to help.'

The chips were at that perfect stage, piping hot in their paper and Honey had asked the girl behind the counter to be heavy handed with salt and vinegar. Hal lapsed into silence beside her, and the regular sound of crinkling paper told her that despite his grouching he was eating his food.

'Saved the world yet today then?' he said eventually. Honey chalked it up as progress in their relationship that he'd initiated conversation and chose to let his sarcasm slide.

'Not today. Sold two pairs of shoes and a cardigan with a hole in the pocket though, so all's not lost.'

'Wow, your life is one long thrill ride. How the fuck do you cope?'

Honey rooted around in the crinkled corners of her chip packet. 'I get by. How's your dinner?'

'Gourmet. I'm just glad you didn't attempt to cook again.'

'You don't know how right you are,' Honey confessed. 'I'm crap in the kitchen.'

'Tell me something I don't know.'

'You first.'

'Me first what?'

'You tell me something I don't know, and I'll tell you something you don't know.'

Hal grunted. 'You want to play drinking games, lady, you have to supply more whisky.'

Honey shrugged. 'I'll go first then.' She cast around for something interesting. 'Er . . . I'm wearing red cowboy boots?'

'Dull. Something more interesting please.'

'Well, that was rude.' She frowned and considered alternative facts. If he'd found her boots dull, it was a sure fire bet he'd find the rest of her outfit even duller, with the possible exception of the colour of her knickers. Well, she did want to shock him out of his superior sarcasm mode . . .

'My knickers are bright red and say Sunday even though it's Tuesday, and I've got a hot date on Friday night.'

She was rewarded with something that sounded like a half laugh on the other side of the door.

'May I suggest you go for more alluring underwear for the occasion? Or accuracy, at least?'

'Oh, he won't be seeing my knickers. I haven't even met him yet. It's a blind date.' Honey sucked in her breath. 'Fuck! Hal, I'm sorry. I didn't think.'

Surprisingly, he opened the door a fraction more. 'Don't say sorry. The fact that you keep putting your foot in it is the best thing about you.'

Honey smiled at the strange, small compliment and cracked open a can of cola from the shopping bags. 'Drink?'

'It's not whisky, is it?' he said mournfully, knowing full well that it wasn't.

Honey pushed the can into his hand when it appeared around the door. 'Nope.'

She heard him take a drink, and when she closed her eyes she could see him sitting behind the door, feet spread, knees bent and his elbows propped on them, his Adam's apple moving as he tipped his head back and swallowed. Hmm.

'So who's your date?'

His question brought her out of her Diet Coke moment with a bang. 'Some guy called Deano. He's in a band and likes blondes.'

'Wow.' Hal whistled. 'I underestimated you. You're a groupie with bad taste in knickers.'

'I'm not a groupie,' Honey bristled. 'I didn't arrange the date, my friends did. They're on this weird crusade to set me up with a pianist, because . . .' The words dried up in Honey's mouth. This talking through the door thing was a dangerous game. The physical barrier had the bizarre effect of removing the usual conversational barriers.

'Finally she tells me something interesting. Carry on.'

Honey stared at the ceiling. 'I don't want to.'

'All the more reason why you're going to.'

Honey screwed up her nose. 'Honestly, it's stupid.'

'Why doesn't that surprise me?' he said. 'Tell me, Honeysuckle. Why are you dating pianists?'

'Tell me Hal, why do I suddenly feel like Clarice Starling in *Silence of the Lambs*?'

'I'll let you live as long as you answer the question.'

Honey puffed out hard. 'I'm dating pianists because . . . because my friends think my sex life needs spicing up, okay?'

Hal laughed. Actually laughed. And then he stopped, and said, 'But why a pianist? Aren't they all dull as fuck?'

Honey scrubbed her hand over her forehead. Why was she telling him this stuff? It felt akin to being on a therapist's couch.

'I don't know any pianists yet to tell you whether they're dull as fuck or not. I'll let you know after Friday night.' She paused. 'Although strictly speaking, Deano plays the synthesiser, not the piano.'

'I'm going to ask you again, Honey, real slow,' Hal said. 'Why pianists in particular?'

'Jeez, Hal! Do we have to do this?'

'Stop avoiding the question. I'm your poor blind neighbour and you're my only contact with the outside world. Have a heart.'

Honey gasped at his blatant manipulation. 'That's not fair and you know it.'

'Life's not fair. Take it from someone who knows. Why pianists?'

'Christ, Hal!' she burst out. 'Because they're bound to be good with their hands, okay? My friends have this crazy-ass idea that a pianist will make the perfect lover for me because they'll be all skilled and clever and sensitive.'

Hal replied to her outburst with deafening silence. And then, 'How old are you, Honey?'

She sighed. 'Twenty-seven.'

He was quiet again, and then, 'No fucking way. You're twenty-seven years old and you're still a virgin?'

'No! No . . . I'm not a virgin. That's not it at all. I've had my share of men, thank you very much.' She spoke without thinking, and then half wished she hadn't because now she'd backed herself into an even more excruciating corner. She shook her head, rolled her eyes, and decided to just get it out of the way fast.

'Look. I happened to tell them that I don't orgasm during sex and they went all batshit crazy on me. I tried telling them it's no big deal, it's just the way my body is, but they don't believe me, and now they're trying to set me up with men they think will prove me wrong and make me scream louder than Meg Ryan in *When Harry Met Sally*.' She paused to breathe. 'There. Happy now? My name is Honeysuckle Jones and I don't orgasm. Is that interesting enough for you, or would you like more?'

She slumped against the wall, hot cheeked and suddenly exhausted.

After a few seconds, Hal spoke, and he sounded incredulous. 'You mean you don't come during sex, or you don't come at all?'

This was turning into a carbon copy of her conversation with Tash and Nell. 'At all. At. All. Can we talk about something else now, please? It's your turn to tell me something I don't know about you.'

She could almost hear Hal shaking his head. 'Surely you can make yourself come though? On your own?'

Great. They were going to discuss masturbation and they barely even knew each other. 'Hal. Let me spell this out.' Honey crossed her arms over her chest. 'My body doesn't orgasm, not for me or for anyone else. It's a basic, physical fact, one to which I have become well adjusted and believe it or not, am totally fine with. It doesn't make me frigid; I still enjoy sex perfectly well. I'm pretty damn good at it, if you must know.' Her chin jutted defiantly in the air.

He was laughing again, she could hear him. It made her glad and mad at the same time.

'I'm sure you are, given that you've had more than your fair share of men and all.'

Terrific. Now she sounded like a slapper. 'I didn't say more than my fair share and you well know it.' She could hear Hal screwing up his chip wrapper. 'Pass me your rubbish. I'll stick it in the bin outside, save it stinking out your flat.'

Would he open the door? She could hear him moving, and she balled up her chip paper and pulled herself up too. After a few moments of hesitation, the door slowly opened and Hal stood there, louche as always in his uniform of old jeans and t-shirt, his dark hair rumpled in a rock star sexy kind of way.

'Thanks for dinner, Strawberry Girl,' he said softly, holding out his wrapper. She took it and pushed it into hers, digesting the nickname with a half smile and pinpricks of pleasure down the back of her neck. She was almost relieved that he didn't know that her cheeks were as pink as her shampoo.

'I picked up some things for you from the supermarket,' she said, bending down to the carrier on the floor. 'Bread.' She held out the loaf until the cellophane touched his fingers and he took it from her wordlessly, laying it carefully on the table in his hallway.

'Ham.' She passed the packet to him, his fingers touching hers before he placed it on the table alongside the bread.

'Orange juice,' she murmured, the warm brush of his fingertips stark against the cold carton.

'You realise you're taking the element of surprise out of

this by telling me what they are, don't you?' he said as he accepted the cheese from her. His hand stilled over hers for a second. Did his thumb slide over the pulse point of her wrist?

'Yeah, well. I don't want you drinking Domestos and blaming me,' she murmured, passing him the other items one by one, watching his hands. He had good, strong hands.

'That's the last of it,' she said as he placed the milk down on the table. 'If there's anything special you want me to get, let me know.'

'Whisky?' he said, hopefully.

'Sometimes, Hal,' she said, gently.

He nodded and breathed in, a sigh somewhere between acceptance and resignation.

'You better go in,' she said. '*Coronation Street* starts in five minutes. I know you'd hate to miss it.'

Hal's mouth quirked at the edges. 'You know it.'

Dark stubble covered his jaw, and on impulse, Honey reached out and touched it. 'You need a shave, rock star.'

Hal stilled at the contact, and Honey felt his jawbone stiffen beneath the softness of the few days' beard growth. They stood there for a few long seconds, his face warm against her palm, neither of them letting go of their breath. To a casual onlooker they'd have looked like lovers saying goodnight.

'Maybe you could put a razor on that list of yours then,' he said eventually, and Honey let her hand slide away.

'Noted,' she whispered.

'Night, then,' he said, then stepped backwards and clicked his door shut. Honey stared at the pale wood, then at her still-tingling palm, and then moved across the hallway into the safety and solitude of her own flat.

Hal leaned his back against his closed door, the scent of her on his fingers when he scrubbed them over his jaw. What the fuck was it about Strawberry Girl? In his world, women smelt of expensive perfume, died a million deaths at the idea of chips, and their polished sexual routines included a perfectly executed orgasm on cue. Or women in his old world, at least. His world of fast cars and glamorous women, and a job he loved with a passion bordering on obsession. He'd only ever wanted to be a chef, and he'd worked bloody hard for more than a decade to build his reputation to the point of being able to open his own restaurant almost three years previously. Hal wasn't ashamed to admit that he'd enjoyed the trappings of his success – the celebrity clientele, the awards, the sparkling reviews from notoriously hard-to-please food critics. His life had been big, and full, and busy, and thrilling.

And now he was here, alone in this godforsaken place, and the only remotely interesting thing about his door was the girl living on the other side of it. A girl who he now knew wore knickers with the day of the week on, and who said the first thing that came into her blonde head without thinking, and who'd lived her entire life without experiencing the mind-numbing bliss of great sex. He briefly wondered whether Deano the synthesiser player would be the man to show her different, and then just as briefly hoped not. No one should have their first orgasm with a man called Deano.

CHAPTER SEVEN

'I thought I might chain myself to the railings around the home,' Mimi said. 'It wouldn't be the first time, I was at Greenham Common you know.'

Lucille nodded. 'She was. She used her bra as a rope.'

Billy Bobbysocks grinned and skimmed a hand over his artful grey quiff. A loyal lifetime customer of Brylcreem, he still had an impressive head of hair for a man well into his eighties. 'I rather like the idea of you chained up, my darling. May I be the keeper of the keys?'

Mimi's dark eyes sparkled at her beau as Honey cleared her throat. It was a few days after the news about the possible closure, and Honey had called a campaign meeting now that the shop had shut for the day. They were gathered around the rickety Formica table in the staffroom. So far Honey had noted down Lucille's suggestion to contact the local paper, and Nell's idea to involve the residents' families and organise a protest walk. Tash and Nell had turned up together about ten minutes previously. They'd both been eager to help as soon as they'd heard about the closure threat hanging over the home and the shop. As committees went, it was a decidedly rocky start – three women in their late twenties and three octogenarians; they sounded rather like a joke awaiting its punch line. Billy withdrew a silver hip-flask from his jacket and took a nip.

'Anyone for brandy?' he said, waving the bottle around the table at them, shrugging when they all declined and pushing the flask back inside his jacket. Honey's thoughts automatically strayed to Hal, and the fact that he would have had that flask off Billy in a flash.

'What do you reckon, Honey?' Tash said, digging an elbow in her ribs beside her. 'Honey?'

Honey glanced up at her friend, realising she had no clue what had been said since her mind had wandered into Hal territory.

'Sorry, what?'

'Are you even listening? You were miles away.'

Honey chewed the end of her pencil. 'Mmm. What did I miss?'

'Lucille just suggested trying to raise the funds to buy the home from the current owners. It's a long shot, but put it down as an idea anyway.'

A long shot was something of an understatement. 'Anyone know any lottery winners?' Honey said as she scribbled on the list. Unsurprisingly, five heads shook around the table.

'Thought not.'

'I think Old Don's son works for the local rag though,' Billy piped up. 'He'd be a good one to start with.' Old Don was one of the home's most senior residents and his son, in his sixties himself, was a regular visitor. Honey nodded.

'Will you speak to him, Billy? Maybe ask him to swing by the shop for a chat when he's here next?'

Billy nodded. 'Consider it done, my angel.'

'Anything else, anyone? Any other business?' Honey said, mostly because it was the thing people seemed to say to conclude meetings on the television. Tash raised her hand.

'Yes, me please, Miss Jones. What are you wearing for your date with Deano tomorrow night?'

Honey frowned. 'Tash!'

Nell clapped her hands gleefully. 'Ooh, Tash told me about this. Your first pianist. I wonder what he'll be like.'

'I can play the piano,' Billy chimed in helpfully, and Honey felt Nell start to laugh under her breath beside her. Lucille and Mimi cast a knowing glance at each other, and then laid a hand each on Billy's arm.

'Not this tune you can't, darling,' Mimi murmured theatrically as Honey cringed into her chair. If anyone attempted to explain the whole piano man thing to Billy, she was going to die on the spot. How had it happened that almost everyone she knew had become aware of her sexual issue? Hell, it wasn't even an issue to her anymore, not half as much as it was to everyone else, anyway. Even Hal had seemed incredulous. Hal. What in God's name had possessed her to tell him about it all? He seemed to transmit tell-me-the-truth vibes through his solid front door like some kind of weird telepathist.

Honey pushed her chair back, signalling the end of the conversation before anyone could say anything more about the issue. Billy helped Lucille and Mimi to their feet, and then offered them each an elbow to escort them out of the back door and across the lawn to the home. The ladies blew kisses at Honey, Tash and Nell as they moved into the doorway and watched them go.

'Christ, I hope we're like them when we get to that age,' Tash said.

Honey laughed fondly. 'Let's grow old together disgracefully, girls.'

'Deffo,' Tash said, pulling a bottle of red wine from her bag with a grin. 'Time for a quick one?'

Honey reached for the glass cupboard, but Nell picked up her bag instead.

'I can't tonight, ladies, sorry. I need to get home.'

'You sure Simon can't hold the fort for just a little longer?' Honey's fingers lingered hopefully on the third glass.

'Umm. It's not that . . . we've kind of made plans for the evening.'

Both Honey and Tash turned to look at Nell; there had been a strange inflection to her words.

'It's not your anniversary, is it?' Honey was sure it was too early in the year for that.

'And it's not your birthday . . .' Tash added, raising her eyebrows at Nell. 'What's going on, Nellie?'

Pink spots appeared in Nell's cheeks and she shrugged lightly. 'Nothing really,' she murmured. 'We just fancied a bit of an early night.' She glanced down at her shiny shoes and then back up again with wide, almost innocent eyes.

'An early night?' Tash said slowly. 'As in you and Simon have already made plans to get down and dirty tonight? Simon's just gone up in my estimation.'

Honey sloshed wine into a glass and thrust it into Nell's hands, sensing from Nell's coyness that there was something juicier to this story. 'A very quick one,' she muttered, pouring wine into the other glasses and handing one to Nell.

'What gives, Nell?' Tash wheedled as they all perched around the table with their glasses in their hands. Nell sat tight-lipped and looked slowly from Honey to Tash and then back again, and after a moment she reached for her big leather satchel and flipped it open. Honey strongly suspected that they were about to see a positive pregnancy test. Nell had gone all glowy and excitable. She was very, very wrong. Nell didn't pull a pregnancy test from her bag. She pulled out a metallic vibrator instead. Both Tash and Honey gasped out loud at the unexpectedness of the item in Nell's perfectly french-manicured hand.

'He gave me this before he went to work this morning!' Nell squeaked, breathless and bright eyed. 'Straight after his organic muesli!'

Honey started to laugh and put her hand over her mouth.

'I told him a couple of days ago about that store we went into the other day, you know, the sex shop? Well, we'd had a couple of drinks, and I might have given him the idea that . . . anyway.' She waved the vibrator around. 'This. This is the reason I have to get home.' She looked like someone about to throw themselves off a bungee platform, terrified and elated all at once. She placed the vibrator down and took a huge swig of wine in the style of a parched person.

'Go Simon,' Tash murmured. 'You do know what to do with this thing, right?'

Nell shot Tash a look. 'I think we can work it out.'

'I wonder what else he bought from the store? Brace yourself, Nell,' Honey grinned.

Nell's eyes opened wide. 'I hadn't thought of that.'

'Maybe you should have bought those pretty purple beads after all,' Tash laughed at Nell's screwed-up nose.

Nell shook her head and then reached into her huge bag again, this time pulling out a fancy paper bag. 'I nipped into town at lunchtime and got these. Thought I might, you know, be a bit more daring, seeing as how Simon has too.'

She reached into the bag and withdrew a boned demi-cup bra, ethereal wisps of black French lace stitched around the edge with pale pink ribbon. Matching briefs, barely there and black, followed the bra from the bag, along with a suspender belt and seamed stockings.

'Are they crotchless?' Tash asked, gesturing towards the briefs with her wine glass and earning herself a frown from Nell.

'No they are not!'

Honey touched the expensive lace, knowing that despite the presence of a crotch, the underwear was still quite a departure for Nell. 'They're gorgeous,' she said. 'Simon is going to think all of his birthdays have come at once when he sees you in this lot.'

'You think so?' Nell said, exposing the vulnerability beneath her excitement.

'Er, hello?' Tash said. 'He'll be like a schoolboy who found his dad's dirty mag!'

'I very much doubt Simon's dad ever bought a dirty mag,' Nell said.

'Having met his parents at your wedding, I think you're probably right there,' Tash laughed. 'It's a miracle they ever had a child at all. I can imagine it now. "Sylvia! On your

66

back in the bedroom at nineteen hundred hours precisely for intercourse!"'

Tash threw a wink and a sharp military salute at Nell, who shook her head in gentle rebuke.

'They're an established army family, Tash, they can't help being straight-laced. They're really very nice when you get to know them.'

Given his upbringing, Simon could hardly be blamed for his *safety first* default setting, and the idea of him wandering around the store looking at vibrators had made Nell brave enough to buy underwear she'd never usually contemplate.

'I really should go,' she said, tucking the lace back into its bag along with the vibrator.

'You really should,' Honey smiled.

'The on switch is on the base,' Tash said, tapping the side of her nose. 'Just so you know.'

Nell rolled her eyes and got to her feet. 'Jealousy is a terrible thing, Tash,' she laughed, leaning down to kiss both of her friends on the cheek. 'Adios, amigos.'

'You know you have to give us a progress report next time you see us, yes?' Tash said.

'Not a chance,' Nell grinned, swinging her bag over her shoulder and skipping out of the door.

Honey left her flat just before eight o'clock on Friday evening, lingering for a second outside her door to look at Hal's closed one. Each day she'd picked up something for him, food or the occasional bottle of whisky, each thing a legitimate reason to tap on his door. He hadn't progressed beyond opening the door for a couple of minutes at the end of their conversation to take in whatever she had for him. He'd grouched at her yesterday about treating him like her pet project, all because she'd refused to bring any more alcohol so soon. She'd shot back that he really ought to think about being more polite seeing as she was only being neighbourly, and that if he'd rather she butt out then she wouldn't bother again. He'd muttered sweary things and closed the door in her face, leaving her standing in the hallway still holding the shopping she'd bought him in her hand. 'I'll eat these my bloody self then!' she'd yelled at him, and he'd yelled, 'I just hope they don't need cooking!' back as she'd stomped across the hallway.

Hal really was an angry man a lot of the time, but it was the every now and then that he wasn't angry that kept her coming back to his door. She was willing to bet he hadn't left the house at all since his arrival a week or so back, and she was almost as certain that no one had been to visit him. Why was that? How had he wound up here, arriving out of nowhere looking like he was hiding away from the world? There was something about Hal that didn't quite add up, and Honey was intrigued enough to want to know more. Intrigued, and drawn to him in a way that had nothing to do with a desire to help out a neighbour in need and everything to do with the way clothes clung to his body, the rich, easy depth of his voice and the warmth of his fingers when they brushed over hers. He was borderline rude ninety per cent of the time, but the other ten per cent was worth waiting for.

The carpet in The Cock Inn felt decidedly sticky underfoot as Honey stood at the bar twenty minutes later. She was a little early, and so far anyone resembling a synthesiser player called Deano had yet to materialise. Alone and trying to look nonchalant in the way only someone desperately hoping their date turns up can, Honey ordered a large glass of wine and perched herself on a stool, barfly-style. She was halfway down the slightly-too-warm chardonnay when the door opened and a guy came in on his own, his eyes slowly scanning the place and coming to rest on Honey. If she were to be picky then his shirt was slightly too Hawaiian and his hair far too blond for Honey's usual taste, but hey ho . . . she smiled and raised her glass gamely in his direction as he sauntered over.

'You must be Deano,' she said, realising that he was incredibly tall as she slid off her high stool and eyeballed his palm tree-covered chest. Tipping her neck back, she looked up as he looked down and found herself suddenly nose to nose with him.

'And you must be Honeysuckle, my favourite flower.'

'Is it really?'

He looked disconcerted. 'I've been practising that line for the last ten minutes.'

'Sorry,' she said, and she meant it. She'd become accustomed to verbal rallying with Hal, and it wasn't fair to Deano to expect him to fall into the same mould. 'Shall we grab a table?' The pub was filling up with Friday night drinkers and pre-clubbers as she headed over to a small table in the corner. Deano joined her a couple of minutes later with drinks in his hand.

'I guessed at white wine?' he said, placing a glass down next to her almost-empty one.

'Good guess,' she smiled. He was actually quite attractive

in a Germanic way, all strong boned and blond. She needed to relax and try to enjoy his company.

'So, Honeysuckle. What brings a nice girl like you to a place like this?'

'A blind date with an organist called Deano?' she supplied with a smile, hoping he'd relax and drop the one-liners soon.

'Synthesiser, actually,' he said, looking affronted.

'What sort of songs do you synthesise?' she said, knowing even as she said it that it was a ridiculous question.

He frowned. 'Are you taking the piss?'

Shit. This wasn't going well so far. 'Look, I'm really sorry. That was a stupid question. Truth is, this is my first blind date, and I'm kind of nervous. Can we start again?'

His Hawaiian-shirted shoulders slumped. 'I'm nervous too. You're my first date since Selina.'

'Selina?' she said, already guessing that she must be the ex Tash had referred to.

'My fiancée. Or ex-fiancée if you want to be picky, which if you were her you no doubt would, seeing as she broke it off.'

Honey cleared her throat as he picked up his beer and necked half of it. She watched him and couldn't help but notice that he had quite stubby fingers for such a tall synthesiser player. She also couldn't help but notice the hurt in his grey eyes, and she knew without a doubt that Deano was too hung up on Selina to be the man who would make her body and soul sing louder than Aretha Franklin in the bathtub.

'I think it's probably best if we agree not to talk about our exes on a first date,' she smiled, swallowing a mouthful of wine.

Deano nodded. 'Too true. Women. Who needs 'em?'

Honey opened her eyes wide. As things not to say on a first date, that was pretty much up there at the top.

'Present company excepted, and all that,' he laughed, recovering himself not quite in time.

'So what do you do, Deano, besides synthesise?' Honey asked, helping him out of the hole he'd dug for himself.

'I work in accounts,' he said, with a casual shrug. 'Bit dull, but a good crowd.' His face dropped. 'Except Selina works there so I'll probably have to, I don't know, resign or something.'

Selina again. He didn't even seem to realise he'd said it.

'As long as it pays the bills,' Honey said, unsure how to develop a conversation around anything as deathly as accounting. 'You must be good with numbers then?' she ventured.

'Thirty-six, twenty-four, thirty-six are my favourites,' Deano grinned and outlined an hourglass in the air with his hands, then dropped them slowly as if he'd belatedly realised that his best accountant joke was inappropriate for the occasion. 'Er, sorry.'

Honey pulled her glass towards her, sneaking a glance at her watch at the same time. She wasn't certain how much longer she could sit and make lad-chat about Deano's no doubt perfectly curved ex without throwing the wine down the front of his ridiculous Hawaiian shirt.

It was just after eleven when Honey turned the front door key and let herself into the lobby. She hadn't stayed at The Cock for last orders, because the more Deano drank the more morose he'd become about Selina, she of the apparently willowy skier's legs and perfect rack. Honey had left him searching the jukebox for anything by Take That – he'd told her at least four times that they were Selina's favourite and that she had a crush on Gary Barlow, who Deano would quite like to punch.

She tried to close the front door quietly out of consideration for Hal, although given their last encounter it was anyone's guess why he deserved her consideration. As she tiptoed across the lobby, his door swung open.

'Jesus, were you waiting up for me? You're worse than my dad used to be,' she said, letting him have both her annoyance in general at an evening wasted and her annoyance at him in particular for being so rude yesterday.

'I heard you come in. Most people would've, given the racket you were making trying to get your key in the door. Are you pissed?'

'Phhfft. Pissed off, more like. I was quiet and you know it. You were waiting for me.'

He leaned his shoulder against the wall, and the movement hitched the bottom of his t-shirt away from the waistband of his battered jeans. Honey noted the smooth line of skin exposed by the move, and the fine central line of hair that dipped into the denim. How was it that this man had her more aware of his body in two minutes than Deano had managed in two hours?

'So, how was your date?' he said, crossing his arms across his chest.

Honey slung her purse and keys into the glow of the lamp on the hall table, then kicked off her high heels as she moved towards him. Her mind was too relaxed with wine to stay angry.

'Umm . . . it was . . . okayish?' she said, and then corrected herself, standing close to him. 'Actually, it was pretty shit. He wanted to talk about his ex-girlfriend's perfect rack all night.'

Hal scrubbed a hand over the side of his face. 'Sheesh. That's pretty bad. She must have been an impressive girl.'

'Yup.' Honey pulled the artfully arranged pins from her hair and mussed it loose with her fingers, shoving the hair pins into the pocket of her denim skirt.

'So what did you get wrong, Honeysuckle? Are you dressed like a nun or something?'

'Piss off. I made an effort. I wore matching undies and everything, even though he was never going to find out.'

'You mean your knickers actually say Friday?'

'Ha bloody ha, Hal. No. I mean I tried to look nice for him and he didn't even notice.'

She leaned against the wall, suddenly weary with the whole thing.

'You smell good,' Hal said quietly. 'And I'm willing to bet you look good, too.'

Honey swallowed hard. Here he went with his ten per cent of brilliance, and here she went going jelly-kneed on him again.

'I tried pretty hard,' she said. 'This skirt's a twelve, and in a perfect world I'm a thirteen.'

She swayed a little on her feet, and for no reason other than her wine-emboldened hands insisted, she reached out and for the second time in her life, touched his jaw.

He let her, and then stepped closer and let her lift his hand and lay it against her cheek too.

If Deano had stripped her naked and screwed her on the

73

sticky carpet of The Cock Inn he couldn't have possibly fired off more sparks of sexual awareness than the simple touch of Hal's palm against her face. Honey felt it right down to her bones.

'A thirteen, huh? I didn't know they did that size,' he murmured, and she could feel his smile in her hand. It was a rarity, and all the more special for it.

'They don't, but I wish they did,' she said, laying her other hand flat over the steady thud of his heart. She had no clue what she was doing. Instinct and chardonnay-lowered inhibitions were in charge of the situation, and she was close enough to Hal to know that whisky was involved in the equation too. He wasn't drunk, but he certainly matched her on the scale right now.

She turned her back against the hallway wall and Hal moved with her, his body so close she could feel the heat of him.

'Did Deano walk you home at least?' he said. His hand was still on her jaw, and he let his thumb graze along her bottom lip, and then back again more slowly. Honey knew he must have been able to feel her holding her breath.

'No,' she whispered with the tiniest shake of her head, bunching the cotton of his t-shirt in her fingers to tug him nearer.

'Not much of a gentleman, is he, our Deano. Did he kiss you goodnight?' Honey could almost taste the late-night whisky on his breath, and wondered if he could smell the wine on hers.

'No,' she said again. 'Deano didn't kiss me, Hal.'

'What a prick. All good first dates should end in a good-night kiss,' he said, and Honey closed her eyes as he lowered his head to hers and covered her lips with his own. Her arms slipped around his neck as his hand slid into her hair, cupping the side of her head as his mouth started to move, slow and warm, the hint of his tongue delicious against hers. She heard a low moan and wasn't certain if it was hers or his, and moved her hands in his dark hair to hold him to her. Not that Hal seemed to be considering escape; his fingers moved restlessly beneath the edge of her top, scorching the skin of her back until she wanted to rip her own clothes off and feel his hands everywhere.

She was suddenly so glad that Deano wasn't over his ex; so glad he hadn't kissed her tonight, because then she'd have missed out on Hal kissing her breathlessly in their hallway, missed the sexiest couple of minutes of her life. He opened her lips with his own and explored her with his tongue, the hard warmth of his body pressing her into the wall as his fingertips massaged the hollow at the base of her spine. He tasted of scotch, and he felt like heaven under her hands. She learned things about him that only kisses can tell you. She learned that he'd be a skilled, considerate lover, and that he could kiss her in a way that made every inch of her body yearn to be naked against his. The man had skills that should be illegal. And then he took the kiss to a deeper level, open mouthed and so laden with pure lust when he licked inside her mouth that all she wanted was his mouth on hers all night. She pulled his t-shirt up and stroked his back, loving the way it made him groan against her lips. His skin was as smooth as silk sheets and as warm as fresh toast beneath her palms, firm and defined and utterly, utterly beautiful to touch. She wanted to touch him all over.

'Let's go inside,' she whispered against his lips. 'Take me to bed, Hal. Your bed. My bed. I don't care which.'

His hand stilled in her hair, and his heart banging against hers told her that he was as turned on as she was. His mouth slowed to a barely there trace, lingering, tasting her lips as if they held the last drops of precious champagne.

And then he broke the kiss, still holding her, shaking his head a little as if trying to clear it, or worse, as if he were ashamed.

'I don't play the piano, Honey,' he said, his lips moving against her ear. 'I'm not the man.'

'I don't care, Hal. I don't even want a pianist,' she said, clinging to him, hating that she could sense his withdrawal from her. 'I think it should be you. You're the man I need. No one's ever kissed me like that.'

'Then you've been kissing the wrong men,' he said gently, his hands finding her shoulders as he stepped back. 'Go inside, Strawberry Girl. Go to bed. I shouldn't have kissed you. I won't do it again.'

She didn't need to be able to see his eyes to know that he was lying. He'd wanted that kiss every bit as much as she had.

'There,' he murmured, propelling her gently across the tiles. 'You've been walked home and kissed goodnight. Consider your date officially rescued.'

She watched him disappear through his door, knowing with certainty that she'd spent ninety-five per cent of the night with the wrong man.

Hal closed his door and reached out for the whisky bottle he'd left on his hall table when he'd heard Honey come in.

Every encounter with Strawberry Girl taught him new things about her. How she smelled. How she laughed. The colour of her hair, and now the dress size of her clothes. This encounter had taught him more intimate things, hints of how she tasted, of the peach-like softness of her skin, of the dips and hollows of her spine. He'd held her curves in his hands and wanted things he hadn't wanted in months.

He tipped the bottle to his lips, welcoming the harsh spirit as mouthwash to clear away the sweetness of Honey. He'd fucked up majorly out there. It would be easy and convenient to blame it on the whisky, and no doubt that's what he'd do when he talked to her again. Now that she'd gone, their kiss served only as a reminder of all the things that were no longer a part of his life, of the woman who'd said she wanted forever until forever suddenly meant life beside a man who couldn't see her.

He'd loved, and thanks to the accident, he'd lost. He'd lost, and he'd lost, until there was nothing more to lose. His restaurant? Sold. His cars? Auctioned. His fiancée? She'd tried to adjust, but in truth she'd fallen for Hal's life as much as for him and it had been too big an ask. And now he was here in this house, and his plan to adjust to life alone had already hit rocky waters because of his madcap neighbour's search for her goddamn elusive orgasm. He shouldn't have kissed her. He had nothing to give. In the many, many long dark days and sleepless nights since the accident, there was one thing he'd come to realise with perfect clarity. From here on in, his life wasn't going to include romance. He wouldn't let another woman close enough to set him aside when she decided being with him was too difficult, and equally he wouldn't let another woman contemplate a half life at his side. He didn't need a nursemaid and he didn't need a guide. It was finally time to learn how to deal with this fucking nightmare on his own.

Hal made his way to bed, wishing he could turn the clock back and resist the urge to open his front door when he'd heard Honey come in that evening.

CHAPTER EIGHT

'He didn't even kiss you goodnight?' Tash said, looking disgusted as she stirred sugar into her coffee in Honey's tiny kitchen. Honey shook her head. 'I don't think he even noticed when I left,' she said, remembering Hal's kiss instead. Tash had arrived five minutes earlier, a flying visit on her way to work and a long haul stint to Dubai for an update on piano man numero uno, as she'd laughingly referred to Deano when she walked through the door.

'Piano man numero uno was el crappo, if you must know,' Honey had said gloomily as she slid a mug towards Tash across the work surface. 'I think it'd be best all round if we just abandon the whole stupid piano man thing altogether.'

'No way, Honeysuckle,' Tash grinned. 'We're only just warming up. Nell has someone else in mind for you already.'

Honey groaned, wondering why she stayed friends with either of them. 'Who is it?'

'A music teacher who goes into the school she works at,

I think.' Tash blew on her coffee. 'Fancy Nell and Simon getting all kinky! I bet Simon's the type who likes to be spanked. Or, oh my God, what if he buys one of those adult nappies and asks to be treated like a big baby?' Tash looked at Honey's grimace with raised eyebrows. 'It's more common than you'd think. I saw a TV show about it.'

Honey rolled her eyes, not wanting to go there even in her imagination. 'I'm sure they'll stay on the right side of tasteful,' she said. 'Anyway, good on them for keeping the magic alive.'

Tash shrugged philosophically. 'They made a baby, so I suppose he must be doing something right.'

'Exactly.'

'And he makes her orgasm,' Tash added. 'I looked up whether it's possible to be born without the orgasm gene. It isn't. If you've got a clitoris, you've got the ability to orgasm. You do have a clitoris, right?'

'Jeez, Tash! I haven't even had my breakfast yet.'

Tash shot Honey a sage look. 'If Simon can talk about vibrators over his organic muesli, you can discuss basic female anatomy over your morning coffee.'

'Fine,' Honey sighed. 'Yes, last time I looked, I had a clitoris. Not that I actually looked, but you know what I mean.'

'Well, there you go then. Hopefully piano man numero deux will be the one who can make it work.'

'So now I have a broken clitoris?'

Tash drained her coffee cup. 'Just on the blink. You need to get a man in to fix it.'

For the second time since Tash's arrival, Honey's thoughts strayed to the man living across the hall, and for the second time since Tash's arrival she decided to keep her own counsel. If Tash got wind of the fact that the hot man over the hallway had snogged Honey brainless last night, she'd be over there like a whippet to find out more about him. Honey knew for a fact that Hal wouldn't take kindly to anyone knocking on his door, morning, noon or nighttime. He'd be rude and abrasive, and for reasons she couldn't fathom, she didn't want her friends to take against him.

She saw Tash out of the house a couple of minutes later with a pensive glance towards Hal's door, thankful when Tash left in a blur of kisses, red hair and promises that piano man number two would be different.

'You, you, and you,' Christopher strode into the charity shop early the next week and pointed his bony index finger at Honey, Lucille and Mimi in turn. They all stared in silence at their tall, wispy-haired boss in his ill-fitting suit.

'I take it this is your doing?' he barked, and slapped the local newspaper down next to the till. Glancing down at it, Honey saw a photo of the home beneath a headline that screamed out about residents facing homelessness.

'Pack in this bloody claptrap about saving this place. Any more of it and you're out the door right now, not in six months' time. One more journalist or angry relative calls me or stops me in the street, or badgers me about it in the sodding doctor's surgery like this morning and that's it. You're out. No ifs, no buts, no maybes. Out. O.U.T. Am I making myself perfectly clear?'

His eyes swivelled between the three women, who all tried to look sufficiently contrite. Over the years they'd all been on the receiving end of one or more of Christopher's tantrums, and they all knew him well enough not to be unduly intimidated by him. Besides, at the end of the day he was on the same payroll as they were, or as Honey, in any case. The home was ultimately owned by a private company who cared very little about its residents and very much about its bottom line. Lucille and Mimi volunteered their time for free, so Christopher couldn't fire them even if he wanted to.

'I'm not sure you can do that, Christopher dear,' Mimi said with an absent smile as she folded a pile of curtains.

Lucille reached into her pocket and extracted a packet of menthol sweets. 'Have one of these, Christopher, your throat sounds sore. Have you been shouting?'

Honey glanced momentarily down at the glass counter top to hide her smile, then coughed and looked up. Christopher's comb-over had flipped the wrong way in his agitation and now hung at an odd angle from one side of his head, and his already small eyes had narrowed into slits.

'Are these women just senile, or are they taking the piss, Miss Jones? Because if you cannot control your staff then I'll find someone to run this place who can,' he hissed loudly at Honey.

'I'm sorry that you're feeling hassled, Christopher, but I'm pretty sure we're allowed to express our concerns however we choose in our own time. Aren't you worried? It's your job on the line too.'

'You really ought to be grateful to Honey for speaking out,' Mimi rebuked him mildly whilst wafting her hand around by the side of her head and making exaggerated eyes towards Christopher's errant hairstyle. He took her obvious hint, swiping his hair back into place and losing his dignity.

'No more funny business. I'm warning you, ladies.'

'It sounds more like you're threatening them to me, Christopher old bean,' a voice said from behind him. Billy Bobbysocks strolled into the shop, resplendent in a red Teddyboy suit. 'Heard shouting. Came to see what all the commotion was about.'

Christopher puffed out his chest. 'And you're just as bad,' he said, staring boggle eyed at Billy. 'I suggest you stop encouraging this ridiculous charade and start looking for somewhere else to live. Understand?' He two stepped around Billy towards the door, who gamely put up his dukes.

'Let's settle this like men,' he said mildly, hopping from toe to toe. Christopher shot them all a long, hard, disparaging look and then stalked out, holding his comb-over down with one hand as he went.

Lucille laid her cough sweets down on the counter with a worried sigh. 'He was really quite annoyed, wasn't he?'

'And a good thing too!' Mimi shot back. 'It means we must be doing something right. No doubt he'll have a new job with the company if he manages to sweep this under the carpet.'

Honey had to agree. It was pretty obvious that for whatever reason, Christopher didn't share their worries about job security.

'If he's getting calls from reporters and relatives, then I guess Old Don's son must have put the word out,' she said. The news hadn't been intended for residents or relatives until much further down the line, but Old Don's son, the unimaginatively named Donny Jr, had called into the shop a few days back and listened with growing fury as Honey outlined the oncoming demise of the home. By the looks of the newspaper on the counter in front of them, he'd just kicked the campaign well and truly into the public arena. Honey flipped it flat and smoothed it out. Billy whistled.

'No wonder he's mad,' Honey said absently, reading the part where Christopher was named and shamed for trying to keep the news under wraps.

'We need to maximise this,' Mimi said.

Lucille nodded. 'But how?'

'Would now possibly be a good time for you gals to lash yourselves to the railings by your bras?' Billy said, the ever-present roguish twinkle in his eye brighter than ever.

Mimi elbowed him affectionately in the ribs. 'Behave yourself, William.'

'Ooh, I like it when you call me William,' he said, wiggling his eyebrows. 'Will you do it again later?'

'You're an old fool,' Mimi smiled at him, and Honey folded the paper back in half.

'Let's wait and see what happens now that the news is out. There's going to be a hell of a lot of worried people out there. Maybe we should try to organise a meeting or something?'

'I happen to know the manager of The Cock, if you need a venue,' Billy said. 'Or rather, I knew his mother, many moons ago . . .' He winked at Honey and then looked apologetically at Mimi. 'She didn't hold a candle to you my love, and she's been dead a good twenty years.'

'We could put up some posters in there inviting people to gather to talk about it in a couple of weeks,' Honey mused, trying not to dwell on her disastrous date with

Deano in The Cock Inn, because that led on to thoughts of her after-date with Hal, who'd refused to open his door ever since. She'd knocked, and she'd shouted, and he'd grunted something unintelligible back at her each time to prove he was alive and get rid of her. She'd left whisky for him a couple of nights back and yelled at him not to break his neck on it, and the fact that it had disappeared in the morning told her that he'd taken it in without incident.

'You're welcome,' she'd shouted as she'd locked her front door to go out to work, sarcasm souring her voice. The truth was that she'd started to enjoy picking out things for him as she shopped, discovering his likes and dislikes by trial and ill-humoured error. She'd certainly never buy him tinned fruit again; he'd practically hurled it back at her. 'Fresh fruit or none at all,' he'd muttered. For a hermit, he certainly had strong gastronomic opinions. Not that it mattered either way, because she'd probably never buy him fruit again, tinned or fresh, given that he seemed to have decided that their friendship had ended with the world's most epic goodnight kiss.

Next to her, Lucille unpacked a box of donations that had just been dropped off by a well-heeled woman in a sports car.

'These things don't look as if they've ever been used,' she said, laying various kitchen items and small electrical goods out on the counter. 'Some people have more money than sense, this box still has its seal on.'

Honey looked at the box in Lucille's hands. An electric razor. Divine intervention, maybe? Perhaps she would knock on Hal's door one more time after all.

CHAPTER NINE

'Are you one hundred per cent certain that he's a normal, non-heartbroken guy, Nell? Because after Deano, I'm pretty much ready to jack this whole ridiculous idea in.'

Honey looked at Nell steadily who gazed unflinchingly back at her over the rim of her cappuccino cup.

'And where exactly is that attitude going to get you, Honeysuckle?' She arched her eyebrows. 'I'll tell you where it'll get you. Nowhere, apart from lonely. So Deano wasn't the one. We were never likely to get it right straight away, were we?'

'Weren't we?' Honey said. 'Because I kind of thought we'd have one go at this and bam, I'd be marrying Michael Bublé. That's how you guys sold it to me.'

'So sue us,' Tash laughed and shrugged her shoulders. 'What's this Robin like then, Nell?'

Nell placed her coffee cup down in its saucer. 'Well, he's quite good looking actually,' she said, nodding slowly in a way that made Honey instantly suspicious.

'You don't sound very sure,' she said.

'No, he is . . . in a kind of old-fashioned way,' Nell seemed to choose her words with care. 'I mean, granted, he's no Bublé, but he has, umm . . . good hair, and he laughs a lot. You need a man who can make you laugh, Honey.' Nell nodded a little too vigorously for Honey's liking.

'So, when am I supposed to be meeting him?'

Nell studied her fingernails. 'The thing is, Hon, he's not much of a pub person, so I kind of said you'd cook for him.' The end of Nell's sentence came out twice as quickly as the beginning, as if Nell hoped it might go unnoticed if she said it really quickly.

'Nell!' Tash said. 'You know that's a bad idea.'

Relieved to have her friend's support, Honey nodded. 'No way. I can't have a stranger into my house, Nell! It's blind date rule number one, meet in a well-lit, neutral place.'

'I wasn't thinking about that,' Tash said, frowning at Nell. 'You know she can't cook; she'll probably poison him before he can get anywhere close to showing her his finger skills.'

'Well, I suggested his house first, but he said his mother would be home.'

'He still lives with his mother?' Honey said, glancing at her watch to see if it was too early for a real drink. Nope, still eleven thirty in the morning. Every few weeks the three women met for Saturday brunch in their favourite café, but this week Honey was enjoying it a lot less than usual thanks to the current subject matter. Every aspect of her life seemed to be more stressful than usual at the moment; her job was under threat, her friends were pimping her out to strange men based on a ridiculous premise, and her home had been invaded by her abusive and reclusive neighbour. Was it any wonder she was considering asking for a double shot of rum in her coffee?

'He's coming over to yours on Friday night,' Nell said, ignoring Honey's question and refusing to look sorry. 'Just make spaghetti or something. He's nice, Honey. I've met him quite a few times now, and he's really good with the kids so he must be a decent guy.'

Tash broke up a huge cookie and stuck a wedge on each of their saucers. 'You've nothing to lose, Honey-bee.'

'Just a whole Friday evening and potentially my life, if he turns out to be an axe murderer.'

'Axe murderers don't usually live with their mothers,' Nell said.

'Norman Bates?' Honey said, after a moment's thought.

Tash made stabbing motions in the air over the table. 'Just don't let him follow you into the bathroom.'

Honey shook her head. 'Tell him it's off, Nell. I mean it.'

'I can't,' Nell said. 'I'm off work on Monday so I won't see him.'

'Long weekend, Nellie?' Tash said. 'Lucky you.'

'It was Simon's idea, actually,' Nell said. 'We don't really get much day time together; we're both always knackered with work and then with Ava at the weekends. It's sort of an us day. Ava's going to Simon's parents as usual.'

Honey and Tash nodded slowly.

'A *you* day,' Honey mused.

'And did he suggest that before or after he saw your new underwear?' Tash laughed. Nell huffed, pink cheeked, and then laughed too.

'After.'

She sipped her drink demurely, clearly bursting to say more. 'Oh my God! Girls, he was . . .' Nell paused and searched for the right words. 'Well, let's just say he was impressed.'

'Good on you, Nell,' Honey smiled.

'Good on Simon, more like!' Tash said. 'So what's the plan for Monday?'

Nell's eyes sparkled. 'That's just it. I don't even know! He just told me to book the day off but still take Ava to his parents as normal. He was so . . . so masterful!' Her voice practically quivered, making Honey wonder how the usually mild-mannered Simon had morphed himself into Heathcliff behind closed doors over recent weeks.

'And has he presented you with any new sex toys over breakfast this week?' Tash asked.

Nell swallowed and shook her head. 'No. But girls, I have to tell you, that vibrator . . .' She lowered her voice and glanced from side to side to make sure no one over-heard the local primary teacher discussing sex aids, and then leaned in towards Honey. 'You should have bought one when we were in that store, Honey,' she murmured. 'I don't actually think you'd have any choice but to orgasm. Seriously.' Her big round eyes glittered.

'She's right, Honeysuckle,' Tash grinned. 'All those electrical impulses concentrated on one little spot.'

Nell did the shivery, quivery thing again and glanced at her watch, probably itching to get home to sexed-up Simon.

'Fine. I'll buy a vibrator if we can ditch the piano man thing.' Honey glanced from Nell to Tash, who frowned at each other. 'Deal?'

Her friends shook their heads.

89

'No deal,' Tash said. 'This is a job for a man, not a machine.'

'Are you sure you don't want to call the banker and check?' Honey joked half-heartedly, knowing that they weren't going to let her wriggle off the piano man hook. She was just going to have to hit the ready meal aisle so as not to poison this Robin guy on Friday, and hope like hell that he wasn't an axe murderer, because it was highly unlikely Hal would bother coming to her aid if she screamed.

Glancing at her watch again, Honey pushed herself off the couch and headed for the counter. It was three minutes after midday, and she needed a glass of wine.

A couple of hours and a couple of glasses later, Honey turned the key and let herself back into the square, cool lobby. What was Nell thinking? She didn't know this man very well at all, yet she'd invited him into Honey's home.

'I need whisky,' Hal shouted through the door without preamble, more like a testy ninety-year-old than a sexy thirty-something. 'And cigarettes.'

'You don't smoke, rock star,' she called, debating whether she was glad he was speaking to her again or not, given his tone.

'I'm going to start,' he yelled.

Honey flicked her eyes towards the ceiling. 'No, you're not.'

'Did my mother die and leave you in charge? Have you adopted me, Mary Poppins?'

'You know what, Hal? Piss off. I've had a nice morning, I can do without you spoiling it.'

Honey stood still in the silence, waiting on his reply. Had he taken her at her word and pissed off?

'I take it today's date was better than the last one then,' he said, more quietly, more honestly, more Hal.

'It wasn't a date,' she said. 'I've been with Tash and Nell – you know, my friends. I have got another date on Friday, though.'

'You're not giving our Deano another chance, are you? Because a man who doesn't walk you home won't get any better second time around, you know.'

'What do you think I am, an idiot? Of course it's not Deano. It's someone called Robin, if you must know.'

'Nobby name.'

Honey laughed under her breath, despite herself. 'Maybe. He'll probably still be fabulous though.'

'Probably? You've never met him, have you?' Hal said. 'Don't tell me. He's another fucking pianist, isn't he?'

'He's another fucking pianist,' Honey said agreeably, enjoying the fact that she could wind him up. 'And he's coming here, so you better not disrupt things by yelling for whisky like someone's grandad, you hear me?'

'You're having some random bloke you don't know from Adam in your flat? Are you completely stupid?'

'And I'm cooking for him too,' Honey said. 'Dinner.' Hal's answering bark of laughter annoyed her to hell. 'What's so funny?'

'Nothing,' he muttered, making no attempt to hide his clear amusement.

'I can cook,' she said, even though it was a blatant lie.

'No you can't . . . But I can,' he said, and the change in his voice pulled Honey up short. He wasn't kidding around

91

anymore, that was for sure, although she couldn't put her finger on where the conversation had turned serious.

'I might make him spaghetti hoops à la toast,' she said.

'You could. Or I could teach you how to make bolognese properly,' Hal said softly. 'If you like.'

Honey swallowed. 'I'd like . . .' she said, eventually, 'I'd like that a lot.'

'Go get a pen and paper, Strawberry Girl. You're going shopping.'

CHAPTER TEN

An hour later, Honey found herself wandering around the supermarket armed with a long list, at the bottom of which she'd grudgingly written, *whisky*. If Hal was going to teach her to make bolognese from scratch he was going to need a drink by the end of it. She was only glad he was allowing her off making the pasta by hand too, a reluctant concession to the fact that she didn't own a pasta machine. Eyeing the box of ready-made bolognese in the fridge, she resolutely approached the butcher's counter to buy minced beef and pancetta.

Just heading for that counter at all was a bit of a first; meat generally came pre-packed into Honey's shopping basket, most often already prepared or cooked. And carrots? Who put carrots into bolognese? Not the man from Dolmio, surely. She'd never spotted carrots in her bolognese, but then she'd never eaten bolognese that wasn't produced in a mass-market kitchen by people in white hairnets. Throwing carrots into her basket, she added celery and bay leaves, smiling benignly at another woman as if this was just her regular weekend shop.

Wine was next on the list. Thank God, something she understood. Hal had insisted she was to buy something decent, which frankly seemed a waste on cooking, but all the same she added a mid-price rioja, and after a moment's hesitation she went back and added a second bottle. If she didn't drink it beforehand, she'd need more wine to recreate the bolognese for Robin on Friday anyway, so it wasn't an extravagance.

Queuing at the checkout, Honey basked in a small glow of pride as she eyed her items. A wedge of parmesan, a bunch of bay leaves, fresh pasta. She felt practically cosmopolitan, which made a refreshing change from the mild embarrassment she experienced with her usual ruck of ready meals and tins. Maybe she should do this cooking lark more often. She dismissed the thought as fleetingly as it had surfaced; baby steps. She needed to make this bolognese first without burning the house down or being killed by her irritable neighbour if she failed to follow instructions.

'Do you have an apron you can wear?' Hal perched on a stool at her breakfast bar.

'I don't need an apron to warm soup up,' Honey said. 'But I've washed my hands, if that's any consolation.'

'Is your hair tied back?'

'What is this, a military operation?' she huffed. 'Yes. It's in two plaits.'

Hal raised one eyebrow over the top of his sunnies. 'Like a milk maid?'

The off-hand, suggestive tone of his throwaway comment warmed her cheeks.

He'd been in her flat for a few minutes, and he was turning over the ingredients she'd bought in his hands. He brought the garlic close to his face and inhaled deeply.

'Will it do?' she asked, made nervous by his overwhelming presence in her small sanctuary. He looked like an exotic bird who'd landed in a common-or-garden budgie's cage, out of place and temporary.

He nodded curtly. 'Frying pan. Olive oil. Chop the onions.'

She bit her lip and grabbed the frying pan out from the drawer beneath the oven.

'I'm no good at chopping things,' she murmured, halving the onion and hacking it with inexperienced fingers into thick slices. Hal reached across and felt her handiwork then shook his head and scowled.

'I said chop them, Honeysuckle. These are the size of fucking house bricks. Smaller.'

'Have you been taking lessons from Gordon Ramsay?'

He didn't laugh. 'Smaller.' He listened to her efforts for a few seconds. 'Relax with the knife. Find your rhythm, and keep your fingers behind the blade and out of the way.'

Honey breathed out with relief when he accepted her second attempt with a curled lip, and reached for the garlic when instructed.

'Break off three cloves and smash them with the blade of a knife,' Hal said, and Honey turned the bulb over in her hands and stared at it. 'How do I get to the cloves? It's sealed up.'

Hal's mouth opened and then closed, and he rubbed the palms of his hands slowly on his jeans. 'You're kidding, right? You just . . .' he said, and then shook his head. 'Give it to me.'

Honey handed him the bulb of garlic and watched as he turned it in his fingers then broke it open easily, feeling the cloves and snapping a few off for her. He offered them to her flat on his palm as if he were feeding a donkey, and she certainly felt like one as she took them from him.

'Do I need to peel them?'

He sighed. 'Just smash them with the flat of a large knife. Press down on them until they split.'

Honey reached for her carving knife and tentatively did as he'd suggested, amazed when it actually worked.

'Well, what do you know,' she laughed, extracting the raw garlic from the skin. 'I did it! Do I chop it like the onions now?'

Hal nodded, checking her work with his fingertips when she pushed the chopping board towards him after chopping.

'Warm the olive oil and add the bacon, then after a minute or so add the onions and garlic too.' He listened as she sparked the gas beneath the pan. 'Not that high. Burnt garlic is bitter and will spoil the dish.'

Honey adjusted the flame and tossed in the pancetta.

'Watch it carefully. We both know you can get in trouble with bacon,' he muttered, and she rolled her eyes and shook the pan as she'd seen chefs do on the TV.

'Once, Hal. I've only ever burned bacon once in my life, and it just so happened that you were there at the time. I'll have you know I usually make a killer bacon sandwich.'

'I'll bear that in mind if you ever make me breakfast,' he said, and images of him waking up in her bed assaulted her brain and threatened to make her burn bacon for a second time.

'Now add the onions and garlic to the pan.'

She scraped the onions and garlic into the pan, excited by the gentle sizzle as they hit the oil.

'Oh my God, Hal, it smells like an Italian restaurant already in here, doesn't it?' She grinned with delight and sniffed the air.

He shook his head, but didn't disillusion her. 'How are they looking?' he asked after a few minutes. 'Don't let them brown or overcook.'

'How will I know when they're ready?'

'Use your bloody eyes,' Hal muttered. 'And taste them.'

'What are they supposed to taste like, beside onion and garlic?'

'Fucking hell, Honey, this is painful. Here, let me taste them.'

She glanced from the pan to the man on the other side of her breakfast bar, and then tentatively forked up some onions.

'Open your mouth,' she said, holding the fork out across the bar.

'You don't need to spoon feed me,' he muttered. 'I can feed myself.'

'I know that. I just thought it'd be easier from across this side of the bar, that's all. I didn't mean to be patronising,' she said, aware that it probably seemed like it from his perspective. He shrugged, and then surprisingly, he opened his mouth and let her slide the fork in. Watching his mouth, Honey felt the stir of sexual awakenings in her gut that was always close by when he was around. She slid the fork slowly from between his lips and waited for the verdict.

'They're ready,' he murmured.

So am I, she thought. 'Ready for what?' she said, flustered.

'Turn up the heat and add the beef.'

Oh, the heat was already well and truly turned up. Honey was breaking into a sweat that had nothing to do with the onions and everything to do with the man opposite her. She was actually glad he couldn't see the effect he was having on her right at that moment; she was like a starry-eyed teenager meeting the man who usually lived in posters on her bedroom wall. It defied all common sense – Hal was thoroughly objectionable and rude, but she couldn't seem to control the way she reacted to him. He had her so nervous that she worried she'd slice off her shaking fingers as she chopped the carrots and celery, and when he asked to test the food for a second time she swallowed hard and had to look away as his lips closed around the fork.

'Hot,' he breathed, and she could only agree. He was, and she was because of him. Why the hell had she promised that she'd never mention that kiss again? Did he know what he did to her? If he could see her she'd have nowhere to hide, but was it obvious to him anyway?

Stirring in the meat, Honey watched it brown as instructed, taking the couple of minutes to pull herself together.

'Now we need a couple of glasses of wine.'

Jeez, if she had a drink she'd probably jump his bones. 'Hal, I don't think that's a very good idea right now.'

'In the bolognese, Honey. Pour the wine into the bolognese and bring it up to boiling.'

Honey passed a hand over her hot face. 'I knew that,' she muttered, ignoring the half laugh from across the breakfast bar as she upended a glass of wine into the pan, refilling it as the meat sizzled violently in the alcohol. She threw the second glass of wine in after the first and screwed the lid resolutely back on the bottle.

'Now pour out two more glasses of wine,' Hal said.

Honey didn't want to get caught out twice. 'Won't that be overpowering?'

'They're not for the dinner. One's for me because it's killing me teaching you to cook, and the other is for you to calm you the fuck down.'

'I don't need to calm down,' Honey lied.

'The hell you don't. You're giving me a headache with all your nervousness, and trust me, you won't like me when I have a headache.'

'I don't like you very much as it is,' she said, clinging to the safe ground offered by throwing mild insults.

'Just pour the damn wine, will you?'

Honey deliberated between the lure of a glass of wine or staying sober, because although she did in fact need to calm the fuck down, she feared it might loosen her tongue and her hands in a way that would send him back into hiding again for weeks on end. In the end, her nerves won out and she unscrewed the wine again and poured them both a drink.

'There,' she said with bad grace, shoving the glass towards him until it bumped his knuckles. He picked up the glass and tasted the wine, and his lips twisted into an almost favourable expression.

'Not bad, Honeysuckle. Not bad at all.'

She raised her own glass, sipped, and found herself glad to have paid more than she usually would for wine. It was delicious, and dangerously smooth as it slid down her throat.

'Better?' Hal asked, almost as if he were watching her, which of course he couldn't have been. It was just that he seemed to know what was going on under her skin, to hear the quickened beat of her heart, the loud dash of her blood around her veins, the bloom of heat over the skin on her throat.

'Mmm,' she said noncommittally, unsure if she felt better or worse for the wine. 'So, what do I do next?'

Hal instructed her through the remaining couple of steps, his fingers lingering on the base of his wine glass as if he thought she might try to take it from him. As it was, she wasn't thinking any such thoughts. She was more pre-occupied with not burning the bolognese because she was admiring his strong, sexy hands.

'And now you turn it down to a simmer, and we wait.'

'Really? How long for? What'll we do in the meantime?'

He shrugged. 'Well, I'm not so great at cards these days, and hide and seek might take a while.' He drank the last of the wine from his glass. 'So I guess you should refill my glass and we'll do that other thing you're so good at.'

Was he talking about their kiss? Honey couldn't help but preen at the fact he'd said she was good at it, but they probably needed to clear the air about it.

'Look, I'm sorry I kissed you the other night.' In truth, it was hard to be all that sorry about something so knee-tremblingly good, but she didn't want it to make their fragile friendship awkward. 'It was completely my fault. I promise not to do it again. I won't even mention it, if you like.'

Hal smirked. 'Talking, Honey. I was referring to talking. You've been banging on my door for days asking to talk to me, so here I am. Now talk.'

Panic set in as she finished off the last of the wine between their two glasses.

'I was just trying to be neighbourly. Friendly. I thought we'd become friends.'

'Did you? Do you kiss all of your friends like that?'

'We just agreed never to talk about that again.'

'Did we? Only I think you said it and I didn't answer. Not that I want to talk about it, because you were spot on when you said it wasn't going to happen again.'

'For the record, seeing as you didn't say we were never going to talk about it, no, I don't kiss all of my friends like that, Hal. I've never kissed anyone else like that in my life. Or rather, no one else has ever kissed me like that before in my life.'

Hal put his glass against his lips and let it linger there, and then set it down slowly. 'Well, maybe this Robin guy will. You better go easy on the garlic on Friday, just in case.'

'Noted. Thank you,' she said, stirring the bolognese for something to do. 'I doubt it though. He still lives with his mother and the best thing Nell could think of to say about him was that he had good hair.'

Honey ran her eyes over Hal's rumpled dark hair, which was probably longer than he usually wore it and all the sexier for it. It constantly looked as if he'd been pushing his hands through it, and it made Honey want to push hers through it too. She picked up her wine glass to give her fingers something else to do.

'Will your special knickers get another outing on Friday?'

101

Was he flirting? It was difficult to tell with Hal, because sarcasm was his modus operandi.

'I might wear my Saturday pants, just to confuse him,' she shot back, and then realised that she'd basically just said she was planning to show Robin her knickers, which she categorically wasn't.

'Lucky Robin,' Hal murmured, raising his glass to his lips. 'My bolognese and your Saturday pants. The man's in for a treat.'

Honey's hands were still begging to reach out and touch him, so she turned back to the stove and stirred the sauce. It looked amazing, easily the best thing she'd ever made, which admittedly wasn't difficult given her limited repertoire.

'Robin won't see my pants, just so we're clear.'

Hal laughed. 'How do you expect him to make you orgasm if you insist on keeping your pants on?'

'Piss off, Hal. This whole stupid idea is destined to fail, because for one I don't have sex with strangers, and for two, as everyone and his uncle seems to know, I don't orgasm.'

'Well, it's not because you're frigid. I can tell you that much and I only kissed you briefly. In fact, you wanted sex with me and I'm practically a stranger.' He shrugged. 'Don't discount Robin too soon, that's all I'm saying.'

You kissed me too briefly, she thought, taking a mouthful of wine and remembering how his kiss felt.

'I never said I was frigid, and you're not a stranger, Hal,' she said softly.

'No? What am I then?'

He was definitely flirting, and it frightened her. She'd lost

102

him for days after the last time they'd strayed over this line, so why on earth Honey said the thing she said next was anyone's guess.

'You're my neighbour. And my friend. And the only man who's ever touched me and made me think that I might be able to orgasm after all.'

For a few moments the air between them sizzled hotter than the pan on the stove.

Honey lost her nerve and broke the silence first.

'How long should I let this cook for?'

Hal's breath left his body in a strangled hiss and he coughed a little to clear his throat before he spoke.

'Low and slow is the rule with food like this. Leave it to do its magic for a good couple of hours. It's even better if you can cook it the day before you eat it.'

The way he'd muttered 'low and slow' caused Honey's stomach to perform low and slow somersaults.

'So how come you're such an expert on bolognese?' she asked, aiming to lighten the conversation. His brooding silence implied that she may have got it wrong. Eventually, he shrugged.

'I'm not an expert. Not anymore.'

She swallowed, sensing him open and then close, clam-like. 'But you used to be?'

'I used to be lots of things. Now I'm just your miserable neighbour who taught you to make bolognese so you don't burn the house down on Friday.'

He'd opened up the line of conversation about his previous life, and then neatly shut it down. A win, and then a lose. Honey noticed and didn't push him, but all the same she hoped the day would come when he let her in closer.

103

'Will you ever let me live the bacon incident down?'

'Probably not.' He slid from the stool and stood up. 'I should go. You'll be alright on your own with that now.'

'Stay and eat it with me?'

He shook his head and drained the last of the wine from his glass. 'It needs hours. If I stay, we both know you won't be able to avoid talking about that kiss again.'

Honey laughed softly, relieved he'd made light of it. 'Stop bringing it up then. I can't even remember it.'

He smiled, one of his rare, real, gorgeous smiles that melted her knees and made it hard to stay upright.

'Good to know,' he said. 'Me neither.'

'Then we're cool,' she said, watching him leave and wishing he'd stay. He turned back as he opened his own door.

'Remember the rules, Honeysuckle. Low and slow.'

Honey stared at his all-too-familiar closed door after he'd closed it and shook her head. Dinner for one it was then.

Later that evening, Hal heard a tap at his door and stiffened. It could only be Honey, and he couldn't handle any more of her today. It wasn't that he didn't enjoy her company; the opposite, in fact. Little by little he was allowing himself to rely on her, and that wasn't fair. The more time he spent with her, the more he looked forward to the next time, and that was only ever going to lead to problems for both of them. Maybe she saw him as a challenge, or, being uncharitable, maybe she saw him as a novelty, but she certainly didn't see the man he really was. She didn't see the darkness in him, the anger, the abyss he teetered on the very edge of much of the time. He was using her in a way that was wholly unacceptable, she just hadn't realised it yet. She didn't see that he was using her as a guy rope to stop him from falling over the edge altogether.

Honey was screwing him up with her funny-girl lines, and her good intentions, and her kisses that made him forget about the bad stuff. She'd practically begged him to be the man who helped her find her orgasm, and in the heat of the moment he'd wanted to be that man too, not Deano the unchivalrous one, nor Robin who still lived with his mother, or anyone else, for that matter. Him. He'd wanted nothing other than to take her to bed, to learn her curves with his hands and his mouth, to build her up until he felt her body shudder and break underneath him. He could do that for her. He'd kissed her only once, but it had been enough for him to know that he could make that girl come, and come, and come.

But then what? He didn't want a relationship, so he'd hurt her, and how could he live here after that? The harsh truth was that he had nowhere else to go, and nothing to offer.

He'd come here to learn how to stand on his own two feet, and he was increasingly learning how to lean on Honey's shoulder, and it had to stop. And so he sat on the edge of his sofa and listened to her call out his name, lightly at first and then tinged with panic when he didn't reply. He couldn't go out there. She'd brought him dinner, she said. Too much bolognese for one, she said.

'You've got a fucking freezer,' he called out, to let her know he was still alive. 'Use it for something other than vodka for a change.'

He could feel her confusion, and her ensuing silence told him that his harsh words had probably hurt her, which only pissed him off more. He didn't have the energy to think of someone else's feelings; yet another reason not to let her any deeper under his skin.

'I'll just leave it out here then,' she said quietly, and he heard her door close a few seconds later. A wash of frustration flooded through his veins, at Honey for not giving up, and at himself for being glad that she hadn't.

CHAPTER ELEVEN

Honey shrugged out of her jacket and flung it over the back of the only chair in the tiny staffroom at the shop. Lucille and Mimi had been waiting for her when she'd arrived to open up and had followed her into the staffroom, each wearing matching chiffon scarves around their necks and frowns etched onto their brows.

'What's wrong, ladies?' Honey said, pushing the kettle under the tap and filling it up. 'Nothing a Tuesday morning cuppa can't fix, I'm sure.' She snapped the lid down and switched the jug on, reaching for the cups as she looked over at Mimi and Lucille again. The evident worry etched on both of their faces pulled her up short.

'Hey, what is it?'

Lucille placed her black patent handbag down on the table and pushed the gilt clasp open. She withdrew an official-looking brown envelope and smoothed it out on the table top beside her bag.

'It's this,' she said. 'It came in this morning's post.'

Mimi picked it up and held it out towards Honey. 'Right out of the blue,' she said, looking uncharacteristically rattled.

Honey took the envelope and scanned it, noting the way it was formally addressed to Lucille and Miriam Dreyfus, rather than their respective married names. It seemed oddly vulnerable to see their childhood titles printed alongside each other on the paper, just as they'd have been on their class registration sheet many, many years previously.

'Can I?' she asked, glancing at the sisters, who nodded emphatically.

Honey eased the letter from the envelope and opened the single sheet of headed paper from The Adoption Support Agency. Glancing quickly up at Mimi and Lucille, she flicked her eyes back down and started to read.

'Wow,' she said quietly as she read its content. 'Wow.' Folding the piece of paper and replacing it carefully in its envelope, she handed the letter back to Lucille. 'I'm guessing from your reactions that neither of you knew anything about this?'

The two women shook their heads.

'Not a thing,' Lucille murmured.

'Not a sausage,' Mimi said, her eyes misty. 'As far as we knew, our mother only ever had us. How could there have been another baby that we never even knew about? It's ridiculous.'

'An older brother,' Lucille added, her blue eyes wistful. 'I always wanted a brother to look after me.'

'You have me,' Mimi pointed out. 'I think it must be a scam, although goodness knows why anyone would go to the bother because we haven't got two brass farthings between us. We can't possibly have a brother. It's always been just the two of us.'

Honey heard the clear anxiety behind Mimi's bluster, her fear of losing her place in the world, both as Lucille's only sibling and as her best friend.

'It might be best to take a little time to think it over. There's no need to rush into anything,' Honey soothed, trying to walk the line between the sisters' clearly differing reactions about the news.

'Ernest,' Mimi muttered. 'Our mother would never have called a child Ernest.'

'I like it,' Lucille smiled. 'Ernie Dreyfus. He sounds like someone important, a doctor, or a teacher.'

'Phhfft,' Mimi scoffed. 'I don't care what he was. I've managed eighty-three years without a brother, why would I want one now?'

Honey made the tea as she listened to Mimi and Lucille bat the conversation back and forth between them. They were digesting the news in real time, each of them in their own unique way.

Lucille, ever the romantic, secure in her place as the baby of the family. Mimi the firecracker, feeling threatened and ready to battle for her position as the eldest sibling. Honey knew them both well enough to know that given time, their opinions would meet somewhere in the middle, hopefully in a place that allowed them to explore the extraordinary news of a possible brother, and the equally extraordinary news that he'd got in touch at the ripe old age of eighty-nine and if they'd like to, he'd dearly love to meet his sisters. The letter didn't go into any further detail about Ernest, just a request for Lucille and Mimi to reply via the agency to let him know if they'd be prepared to make contact. Honey had faith in Mimi that time would allow her to see the wonder of the situation, as well as the pitfalls. She had a brother, a brand-new family member who'd been waiting in the wings her whole life, had she only known. If nothing else, Mimi was helplessly nosey; the tip of an iceberg had nosed its way into her life and she'd need to know more, despite herself. Honey watched her pick up her cup of tea and bustle away to make a start on the newest donation bags, talking to herself as she went. Wrapping an arm around Lucille's stiff shoulders, Honey gave her a little squeeze.

'She'll come around. Give her time,' Honey said, rubbing Lucille's forest green velvet-clad arm.

'I do hope so, Honey dear, we're none of us getting any younger. Carpe diem, as they say.'

'Very true.' The hot tea warmed Honey's throat as she considered the simple Latin phrase. She might not have a long-lost brother, but there was still much in her life that she needed to seize. Perhaps she could start by trying to be less churlish about Nell and Tash's attempts to fix her up, enter into the spirit of the piano man mission a little more. Maybe, just maybe, they'd send someone her way who could kiss like Hal. It was, after all, a physical reaction. It would be a blessed relief to feel that level of attraction for someone who wouldn't give Dr Jekyll a run for his money in the split-personality stakes. He'd seemed fine when he'd been in her flat, and then back to business as usual again when she'd tried to take him dinner as a thank you for teaching her how to cook it.

But then what did Honey know about him, really? She

hadn't asked him any questions about his life before he'd moved into the house, because he closed down any conversation that veered even close to personal territory. She'd sat outside his door and poured her heart out. He knew her dress size, her best friends' names, her shampoo preferences, and her romantic history. He even knew more about her underwear choices than most people, yet her knowledge of him was minimal to say the least. Maybe her friendship with Hal, if it could be termed a friendship, was something else she needed to seize, or at least take more control of. It was completely on his terms at the moment, which wasn't really a friendship at all, when she came to think of it. Honey drained her teacup and resolved not to be so needy where Hal was concerned from here on in. If he wanted her friendship, he could come and get it.

Lucille and Mimi circled each other like boxers in the ring for most of the morning, until something happened at lunchtime that forced them to lay down their arms and join together against their common enemy.

Christopher.

He bounded into the shop, scanned the empty place for customers and then flicked the 'open' sign over to 'closed' and dropped the bolt.

'Hey, we don't close for lunch,' Honey said, crossing to turn the sign back and finding Christopher blocking her path. Outside, she saw Nell jog up the path, and then lean forward to squint between the various posters on the door to check if there was anyone inside when she found it locked.

'You do today. Staff meeting.' Christopher looked at his

watch for dramatic effect, straightening it on his skinny wrist. 'Thirteen hundred hours in the dining room. Paid staff only, remember,' he added, curling his lip at Mimi and Lucille. 'You two take an afternoon nap or something.'

Honey watched him spin around and leave, imagining herself bouncing the sellotape in her hand off the back of his head as she crossed to let Nell in.

'Take a nap,' Mimi muttered, with murder in her eyes. 'I'll give him take a nap . . . Honey, dear. Waylay him at his precious meeting for as long as you can,' she said, heading for the lingerie bin at the back of the shop. 'Lucille, fetch your handbag. We've got work to do.'

Nell deposited a black bag on the floor beside the counter and gave Honey a quick peck on the cheek as she gestured towards the bin liner.

'A few bits Ava has outgrown, and I've had a wardrobe clear out.' She twirled a curl of her dark hair around her fingers, and it struck Honey how unusual it was to see her with it down. Glancing down quickly, she could see a couple of Nell's demure ivory work blouses lying on top of the bundle of clothes.

'Change of image?' she joked, and then raised surprised eyebrows when Nell nodded.

'Something like that. I just feel like I need more colour in my life, you know?' She arched her black shirt-clad back to stretch it out. 'Why was the door locked?'

Honey's shoulders slumped. 'Christopher came to call a staff meeting, which can only possibly mean one thing. Bad news.'

Mimi and Lucille appeared from the staffroom. 'We're not invited,' Lucille sniffed. 'Paid staff only. Hello Nell, dear.'

'Pah. As if we'd want to go anyway.' Mimi scowled ominously. 'We've got bigger fish to fry this afternoon. You should probably call Old Don's son, Honey, see if he can get a journalist down here.'

'Mimi . . . are you sure about this? I don't know what you're planning and I'm worried.'

Mimi patted Honey's hand on the counter. 'Better that you don't know, then you can't be incriminated,' she said darkly. 'I don't suppose anyone has donated any handcuffs lately, have they?'

Honey rolled her eyes, and then Nell silently opened her handbag and withdrew a pink fluffy pair, dangling them in the air by one cuff, her cheeks a good match with the fur.

'My goodness, handcuffs have come a long way since my day,' Lucille said. 'The police only ever carried silver ones, nothing pretty like those. Although, I'm not sure I agree with them making things too comfortable for criminals.' She frowned with disapproval at Nell's fluffy cuffs, and Honey glanced at the floor to hide her smile, as Nell looked horrified with herself.

'Are these some of those sex aids, dear?' Mimi asked, squinting to get a closer look at them. Catching Nell's mortified look, Mimi lifted her shoulders. 'What? You think I'm too old to know about these things? I'll have you know I read that *Fifty Shades* on our coach holiday around the Peak District last year, didn't I, Lucille?'

Lucille nodded. 'I prefer a good murder, myself,' she said.

'You might get one this afternoon,' Mimi said dramatically, taking the handcuffs from Nell and dropping them into Lucille's handbag.

'You better carry these. If Billy sees me with them Lord

only knows what might go through that head of his.' Mimi smiled sweetly and linked arms with Lucille. 'Come, sister. There's much to be done and little time to do it in.'

'I see what you mean about adding a little colour to your wardrobe now, Nellie,' Honey murmured as they watched the two old ladies leave, and Nell laughed and covered her face with her hands.

'What was I thinking of? I just heard Mimi ask for handcuffs and flicked into helpful teacher mode.'

'I'm actually afraid to ask why you have them in your handbag,' Honey said, wincing in anticipation of Nell telling her something so lurid it would make it impossible to ever look at Simon in the same light again.

'I didn't know what else to do with them. The cleaning lady comes on Tuesdays! What if she found our new things? She might polish them or something, and think of the skin irritation you could get from that. Or worse, she might resign.'

'So . . . you have other things in your bag beside the handcuffs?'

Wide eyed, Nell opened her bag and gestured for Honey to look inside. Beside Nell's phone and sunglasses lay a vibrator, a long feather and a string of pearls.

'I don't think they're meant to go around my neck, are they?' Nell squeaked. 'Simon left them for me this morning! Honey, I don't even know what to do with them. Help me!'

'Uh-uh. You're asking the wrong person. You need Tash.' Honey laughed at the askance expression on her friend's face. The last few weeks must have been a real period of revelation for Nell, and in all that she'd still given enough thought to the piano man mission to arrange Friday's date with Robin. She really was the best kind of friend, and probably a good person to talk to about Hal, if Honey ever felt it was time to share. Now was definitely not the time though, not with Christopher waiting over in the home, itching to deliver more bad news.

CHAPTER TWELVE

Sitting down to listen to Christopher an hour or so later, Honey found herself distracted by worrying thoughts of Mimi and Lucille. What were they up to? Or rather; what was Mimi orchestrating and Lucille being accomplice to? Whatever it was, she was certain of two things: Billy would involve himself as much as he could, and Christopher was likely to go ballistic. Beyond that she was in the dark, aside from the fact that Nell's pink handcuffs were likely to feature too. She'd managed to grab a quick word with Old Don's son, and he was heading down in his lunch hour with a photographer riding shotgun. Pressing her fingertips against her temples, Honey prayed that whatever they did wasn't drastic enough to get her fired – at least not before they saved the home, anyway.

At the front of the room Christopher stood and clapped his hands for everyone's attention, and a hush fell over the disparate gathering. Three care workers representing the care staff as a whole; two cleaners; Patrick the huge Glaswegian chef and his fresh out of school trainee; Cheryl and her mother from the office, and Honey. The fact that the gathering was so disparate did nothing to diminish Christopher's apparent sense of self-importance as he tapped an experimental finger on the huge green felt microphone he'd just plugged in. It looked like something from a 1980s TV outside broadcasting. They'd all watched him set it up in the centre of the room, discover the lead wouldn't reach the plug, and end up standing at the far end of the room as if he'd been sent to stand in the naughty corner.

'One-two, one-two,' he said like a cheesy wedding DJ, and the screech of feedback had the whole room clapping their hands over their ears as one. Christopher said something that really shouldn't be uttered into a microphone, turned it up to full volume and kicked the stand.

'Unless you want the whole town to hear what you're gonnae say, I'd turn that thing off, Sonny Jim,' Patrick said, clearly enjoying the chance to add to Christopher's discomfort.

Christopher shot him daggers, yanked the plug out of the wall and dragged the microphone stand into the centre again.

'Right then, to business,' he said, both hands on the stand as if he were about to break out into karaoke.

Patrick raised his hand. 'You probably don't need to speak into the microphone, seeing as it's unplugged.'

Christopher stepped in front of the mike stand, muttering, 'I knew that,' under his breath then cleared his throat, looking slowly around at each of them.

'If we're *quite* ready, I'll make a start,' he said, as if the delays had been everyone else's fault rather than his own.

'As you're all aware, the home is scheduled to close in a few months' time,' he looked pointedly at Honey, 'the shop too. Well, the powers that be at head office have updated me personally this morning,' his chest puffed out, 'that they're looking at bringing that date forward by five weeks owing to the fact that I've already secured places for more than fifty per cent of the younger residents, and, taking natural wastage into account, they feel that they can reasonably expect to rehome the remaining residents within the shorter timeframe. Are you all still with me so far?'

Honey stared at him. Five less weeks to work with.

'Are you saying that we're going to lose five weeks' pay?' one of the cleaners piped up.

Honey shared their worries, but something else in Christopher's speech had outraged her even more. She found herself raising her hand, and all eyes turned towards her.

'"Natural wastage"?' she repeated his phrase, getting to her feet. 'Natural wastage? Are you saying that you're counting on some of our older residents dying before the time comes for them to be "rehomed", as you put it?'

Christopher had the good sense to look contrite. 'Well, I wouldn't put it exactly like that, Ms Jones, but owing to the advancing years of many of our residents, it's not unreasonable to think . . .' his voice trailed off as a commotion kicked off outside the open window. He cocked his head like a police dog and narrowed his eyes.

'What is that racket?' he muttered, backing into the microphone stand and sending it flying, then climbing over it to get to the window.

'Oooh no,' he said, wagging his finger. 'No, no, no. Not happening. No. Excuse me, ladies and gentlemen.' He said all of this through an almost-maniacally unpleasant smile as he took off towards the door at a Basil Fawlty half run, and everyone else in the room bolted to the windows to see what was going on out front.

Honey clapped her hand over her mouth, holding in her quiet 'Oh my God!' as her gaze moved along the line of residents who'd fastened themselves to the home's railings using anything they could find. Mimi stood at one end, handcuffed to the bars with Nell's pink fluffy cuffs, with Billy Bobbysocks on the other end of the line, lashed to the railings by various bras Honey recognised as stock from the lingerie bin in the charity shop. At least eight other residents were strung out along the footpath in between Mimi and Bill, including Lucille, who'd chosen women's support tights for her restraints, and Old Don, who'd fastened his wheelchair to the railings with his prized collection of men's neckties and sat eating a cheese and onion sandwich out of tinfoil with a blanket over his knees.

There was nothing for it. She needed to go outside, this was likely to get nasty. Turning quickly, Honey made for the door, followed hotly by Patrick and the rest of the staff from the meeting.

Christopher emerged onto the pavement as Old Don's son from the newspaper pulled up with his photographer buddy in tow.

'No press!' he shouted, waving his arms frantically at the car.

'There's nothing to see here, gentlemen. Kindly move along.' Christopher adopted the tone of a community police support officer and tried to push the photographer's door closed even though the guy already had one leg out of the car.

'Out of my way, lanky,' the photographer grinned, pushing the door wide and sending Christopher barrelling backwards onto his backside, much to the amusement of the quickly assembling crowd. He snapped off a quick shot before holding out a hand to help the other man up.

'No hard feelings,' he said jovially as Christopher ignored the proffered hand, brushed himself down and glared at him.

Honey stood beside Mimi, who was nearest to her, and leaned close.

'You okay?' she said, because after all, Mimi was in her eighties and currently handcuffed to the railings.

'Never better!' Mimi hooted, clearly in her element. She, along with all of the other protesters, wore long white t-shirts on which they'd written bright red slogans: 'Save Our Home!' or 'Help! Homeless and Ninety!' Old Don, still serenely eating his lunch, had his medals pinned proudly to his t-shirt.

'When did you make all these?' Honey gestured at their shirts, and the painted placards placed between the residents along the railings.

'Oh, we've known this day was coming for a while, Honey. My generation lived through the war. We know a thing or two about preparing for the worst.'

At the far end of the line, Billy Bobbysocks had teamed his t-shirt with electric blue drainpipes and a bum-bag, and he'd rolled the sleeves of his shirt up until it resembled a vest, veteran rock star-style. His silver grey quiff stood prouder than ever as he led the group in a rousing rendition of 'We Shall Not Be Moved'.

120

Christopher pranced along the pavement, every now and then trying his luck by attempting to unleash one of the residents from the railings, only to be met with a swift kick from a wooden leg or a feigned cry of 'you're hurting me!' from one of the ladies before he'd so much as laid a finger on them.

Glowering, he puffed his chest out and tried a different approach. Beside the railings stood a large, low stone block bearing a plaque engraved with the name of the home, and he stepped up onto it to give himself an air of authority. For a few seconds it had the desired effect, and a hush fell over the now not-insubstantial gathering.

'Ladies and gentlemen,' Christopher called, his back turned rudely towards the chained residents, holding his comb over in place in the breeze. 'I'm sorry for the disruption to all of your days, I realise how inconvenient this is for everyone,' he said, gesturing towards the queue of traffic that had developed on the road. 'The combined age of this group of people is over eight hundred. It's a terrible shame, but I'm afraid they don't know what they're doing.'

A cacophony of boos and hisses followed his words, and Honey felt her blood start to boil at his dismissive tone.

'Ms Jones,' Christopher's eyes picked her out in the crowd. 'Kindly help me to unfasten these poor people at once. They're confused, and lunch is on the table inside for them.'

'Not while I'm oot here, laddy!' shouted Patrick, his tomato-stained chef's apron belted around his girth. The photographer snapped shots of the scene as Christopher carried on.

'We're not confused,' Billy shouted. 'We're angry! This

place is our home, and no one seems to care that we're being thrown out!'

Christopher's grin turned into a rictus as the crowd brayed in agreement, and he waved his arms as if he were directing a plane in to land.

'Every care is being taken to approach this matter sensitively, Mr Hebden, as you well know,' he said, addressing Billy loudly. 'But these things happen every day, I'm afraid it's how the modern world works. Now, if I'm not mistaken, it's time for your medication, so if you'd kindly come inside we can put all of this nonsense behind us.'

'No fear!' Mimi called, rattling her fluffy handcuffs. 'I'm not going anywhere!'

Christopher laughed rudely and shrugged. 'Hand over the keys to those cuffs, Miriam.'

'She would, but she's a little tied up at the moment, old chap,' Billy shouted, making the crowd laugh and Christopher even more furious. 'And anyway, she doesn't have the key.' He grinned cheekily, thoroughly enjoying himself until Christopher walked down the line towards him.

'I take it you have the key, Mr Hebden?' Christopher's eyes swept down the older man's outfit and came to rest on the bum-bag slung around Billy's waist. Honey had followed her boss along the pavement, and when he reached out to unzip the bum-bag she stepped between the two men and found Patrick at her side, obviously equally incensed by the way his boss was treating the residents.

'Dinnae even think about it, dunderheid,' Patrick muttered, his thick Scottish accent coming out much more strongly than usual. 'Touch any of these folk and I'll smash yer lights oot!'

122

In the hot exchange of words that followed, Billy leaned forward and whispered in Honey's ear.

'Take the key.'

Fumbling behind her back, she unzipped the bum-bag and felt around until her fingers closed around the small key, and then zipped the bag back up as someone started to sing.

Quietly at first, a sweet, clear voice with only the slightest of nervous shakes, the instantly recognisable opening lines of 'Amazing Grace' rang out. A hush fell, and a lump rose in Honey's throat as she turned and saw who the singer was.

Lucille. Laying her hand over her fast-beating heart, Honey listened as Lucille's voice gathered strength, a beautiful, fragile songbird to still the shouting. Pin drop silence had fallen by the time Lucille began the second verse, and then a baritone voice joined her in the hymn. Old Don. Tears rolled down Honey's cheeks as she listened to the note-perfect duo, and a quick glance at the crowd through watery lashes confirmed that she was far from the only one moved by the impromptu performance.

Mimi's eyes shone with pure pride, and the crowd broke into huge, appreciative applause as Lucille and Don reached the end of the song.

Christopher, thoroughly rattled and aware that he'd all but lost the battle, cupped his hands around his mouth like a loudhailer.

'Enough! Everyone inside. Now!' He looked around, wild eyed, until he found Honey. 'Ms Jones. Help me unfasten these people this instant. They're cold, delirious and they all need a nap.'

Honey stared at him. How could this man be in charge of a home for the elderly, when he had no respect for them? Backing away, she shook her head slowly.

'No,' she said, walking back along the line. 'I won't help you, Christopher.' She reached Lucille and gave her shoulder an encouraging little squeeze as she passed, whispering, 'Well done.'

Honey carried on along the line until she was close enough to Mimi to kiss her papery cheek and whisper to her that she had the key to the handcuffs in her jeans pocket. Then, shaking inside, she stepped up onto the stone that Christopher had recently vacated.

'I won't help you dismiss the concerns of the residents of this home, or reduce the efforts of those brave, wonderful people to nothing. Do you think they're out here just to wind you up? What do you see when you look at them, Christopher? A bunch of old people who you can dismiss and boss around like school kids?' Honey glared at him.

'Billy doesn't have the keys to Mimi's handcuffs. I do.' She dug in her pocket and produced the tiny key, holding it up so it glinted in the sunshine.

Christopher saw red and swiped for it, and without thinking, Honey shoved it in the only place she could think of where Christopher couldn't get it – her mouth. His eyes bulged as she swallowed it with a painful gulp. The crowd broke into cheers, and solidarity with the residents burned hot in Honey's chest.

'What do you know about all of these people, really? Take Don, here.' She smiled encouragingly towards Don in his wheelchair, and he raised a slow, shaky hand at the crowd. 'I'm sure Don won't mind me telling you that he's the home's oldest resident. He's lived in this place for almost twenty years. Twenty years. And what do you know of him, besides the fact that his wheelchair sometimes takes the paint off the walls in the hallway?' Honey had heard Christopher complain on more than one occasion about the cost of redecoration because of Don's chair.

'Look at the medals pinned to Don's shirt. He was a pilot in the war, a flight lieutenant, a courageous soldier who fought for his king and country.' Don bowed his head at the gentle ripple of applause, his hand over his medals. 'Every single one of these people has a story. Look at Mimi and Lucille,' Honey said. 'You dismiss them as two crazy old ladies, but you couldn't be more wrong. They're brilliant, vivacious women who deserve your respect and your kindness. They were both Land Girls, keeping their family farm going to provide food for their neighbours during the war, and even now they give up their time every day to help me run the charity shop.' Honey looked from Lucille's tearful smile to Mimi's fierce nod, and was reminded of Mimi's earlier words about her generation.

'You were quite right when you said that these people have amassed over eight hundred years on this earth between them. But that's something to be celebrated, not mocked, Christopher. Eight hundred years of experience, and of sacrifice, and of hard work. Eight hundred years of love, and of sadness, and of loss. Eight hundred beautiful years of brilliance, and I won't let you belittle what they're doing here today.' Honey looked along the line of residents tied to the railings haphazardly, knowing she sounded like a soapbox politician at an election rally, but forged on regardless.

'Yes, they might look odd. Yes, their picture will make an amusing front page for the local newspaper. But their reason for being out here tied to the railings isn't funny at all. They're out here because they're scared. This place isn't just a business, it's their home, their safe haven, and they don't want to leave it. And why should they have to? Why is it right that they should have to be scared at their ages? It's not fair and it's not right, and our town needs to stand with them and do something about it.'

Breathless, Honey finally stopped speaking, and the street erupted into cheers and clapping, and Nell stepped forward and held her hand out to help Honey down from the stone, her makeshift soapbox. She pulled her into a tight hug.

'My God, Honey, I'm so proud of you,' she whispered fiercely. 'You were magnificent. I thought your boss was going to have an actual heart attack when you swallowed that key. For your own sake I'm never going to tell you where that's been.'

Honey found she was shaking a little, a delayed reaction to having inadvertently made herself the Svengali of Hope for every resident caught up in the battle.

'Three cheers for Honeysuckle, our very own Boudicca!' Billy shouted, and the photographer's flashbulbs almost blinded her when Nell turned her gently to face the expectant crowd, murmuring 'smile' in her ear as she stepped away.

Honey smiled tremulously, shaking inside, trying not to think ahead to the consequences of her actions. Or to wonder what Nell and Simon had done with the sex-cuff key before she'd swallowed it. She might get a tetanus shot, just in case.

'Er, Honey dear?' Mimi called out. 'I think someone better call the fire brigade. I can't get these cuffs off and my hands are going numb!'

The fire crew turned up in record time, and as one advanced towards Mimi with the bolt cutters, another questioned Honey on the nature of the issue.

'So . . . you chained an elderly woman to the railings with your kinky sex cuffs and then ate the key?'

'They're not my kinky sex cuffs,' Honey tried to explain for a second time.

'That's what they all say, love,' he said with a cheery wink. 'Although to be fair, these things usually happen in the bedroom, rather than in the street with little old ladies.' He shrugged. 'I'm a broad-minded sort of fella.'

On that, Billy ambled up.

'Alright, chaps?' he said, slinging an arm around Honey's shoulders.

Honey smiled gratefully. 'This is Billy,' she said. 'He was the one who chained Mimi to the railings.'

The fireman looked Billy up and down, and then slid his gaze back to Honey. 'And then you ate the key,' he said, nodding slowly. 'Bit of a ménage à trois, as they say.' He looked incredibly pleased with his own sophistication.

'Petit pois, mon amigo,' Billy replied knowledgeably, and Honey turned her eyes to the skies.

'Any chance you might go and crap that key out, love?' the firefighter poised over Mimi with the bolt cutters shouted. 'Last chance before I go in!'

Honey shook her head, mortified by the fact that a couple of journalists still lingered around, laughing openly and scribbling in their notebooks. How had she managed to go from heroine to member of a weird sex trio in the matter of an hour?

'I'm going to go and check if Mimi's okay now,' she said, smoothing her hair.

As she walked away, she distinctly heard the fireman mention the words sugar daddy, and Billy say yes please, two sugars.

Honey sat on the floor outside Hal's door that evening, her head tipped back against the wall, her jean-clad legs stretched out in front of her. He'd ignored her knock of course, aside from the obligatory curse to confirm he was alive. She hadn't really expected more, but she'd hoped all the same, because she found that of all the people she knew, he was the only one she wanted to tell about the bizarre afternoon she'd just lived through. She'd been sitting there for almost an hour already, telling him the story, even though he wasn't interested and most probably wasn't listening.

'And then the fire brigade had to be called out to cut Mimi's cuffs off because I'd swallowed the key and they were stronger than they looked. I mean, you'd imagine they'd be pretty flimsy given that they're designed for the bedroom, but no, not those ones. God knows where Simon got them from, they were bloody industrial! And of course Nell had scarpered by that point and Mimi gave the firemen the impression that the cuffs were mine, which, given that I'd eaten the key, wasn't that big a stretch of the imagination really, was it?'

Honey shook her head, remembering the barely concealed laughter on the faces of the firemen.

'I'll most probably get the sack. I'd have walked out this

afternoon if it wasn't for the fact that I'd just given my very own war speech; I can hardly desert the troops now, can I? They think I'm some kind of brave heroine who's going to lead them to victory. Except I'm not brave, Hal, and I'm no one's heroine. I'm ordinary, quite often stupid, and I'm scared stiff I'm not going to be up to the job.'

On the other side of the door, Hal thought how very, very wrong she was. She was the least ordinary person he'd ever known. Funny, yes, and fearless, yes, but ordinary, never. She just hadn't realised those things yet.

He wasn't going to answer her tonight, that much was obvious.

'I better go in,' she said after a while. 'I'm tired Hal, and this one-way conversation thing is wearing me out tonight. Just for the record, I could have done with a friend right now, and I hoped it'd be you. But then I don't suppose we're friends, are we really?'

Nothing.

Resigned, Honey went home to curl up in bed and wait for sleep to come and rescue her.

CHAPTER THIRTEEN

Friday dawned cool and grey, and found Honey knocking off work early to go home and cook bolognese for her hot date with Robin. She'd gone into work full of trepidation that morning, only to find that Christopher was out of the building for a meeting at head office and wasn't expected back all day. Honey tried not to wonder if he'd been called in as a result of Tuesday's shenanigans. There would undoubtedly be fallout from their actions, but it seemed that thankfully it was to be staved off for the weekend at least.

Mimi, Lucille and Billy had been waiting for her at the door when she'd arrived at work, presenting her with a fruitcake baked by Patrick and a rousing rendition of 'For She's a Jolly Good Fellow'. Much as Honey loved cake and appreciated the support, she left work filled with worry about next week. Lucille followed her to the door.

'Put it all out of your head for now and have a lovely

weekend, dear,' she said, holding on to Honey's forearm with a twinkle in her eye. 'Carpe diem.'

Honey smiled. It was fast becoming Lucille's catchphrase.

'Thank you, Lucille. I needed reminding of that today,' she planted a kiss on the older woman's cheek. 'Wish me luck with Robin.'

'Well, if he doesn't think you're wonderful he won't be worth your efforts,' Lucille said, and Honey hugged her, especially glad of her loyal support after Hal's apparent abdication from their friendship.

Making bolognese on her own turned out to be far more stressful than making it with Hal there for guidance. Honey couldn't quite remember the order things were supposed to go in, and although the end result looked pretty much as it should, it had gone seriously off-piste in the flavour department. Robin certainly wasn't going to be bowled over by her cooking skills, that much was for sure. Just before five o'clock she nipped to the off-licence for more wine. She'd tipped an extra glass into the bolognese in the hope of adding flavour and ended up with something alcoholic enough to take the roof off an unsuspecting diner's mouth. The addition of yoghurt to calm it down hadn't helped much, either. She did a double take when she opened the front door, because Hal was standing in the lobby.

'Waiting for someone?' she said casually, still hurt by his latest withdrawal.

'You,' he said. 'I smelled your cooking and thought I'd better ask if you needed any help. I don't want you killing your date and blaming me.'

Hmm. Honey toyed with refusing his help out of pique,

but the bolognese really wasn't good and he was her only hope of rescuing it.

'Go on then, you can come in for ten minutes,' she grumped, letting him know he was still in her bad books. 'I've ballsed it up somehow and I can't work out what to do.'

Hal followed her into her flat, sniffing the air. 'It doesn't smell too bad,' he offered, and Honey knew enough to realise that was as much of an olive branch as he was likely to offer.

'Yeah, well. Wait until you taste it.' She took the lid from the saucepan, spooned a little into a dish, and handed it to Hal. She watched him bring the bowl close to inhale the smell, and then dip the spoon in and test it with a grimace.

'You haven't put any salt in,' he said. 'No wonder it's weird.'

'Salt. Of course,' Honey said, feeling stupid for missing the most basic of things.

'Give it a good season and cook it through for another hour or so to really soften the meat and cook off the alcohol. Have you added extra wine?'

Honey flicked the gas on beneath the pan and added salt.

'Yup. It didn't help.'

'No shit.'

'Nope.'

Silence reigned. As churlish as it was, she didn't feel like making it easy for him.

'So, the big date with Robin's still on then,' he said, placing the bowl with the failed bolognese carefully on the work surface.

'Can't wait,' Honey clipped.

'I'll go then, leave you to beautify.'

'You do that. And there's no need to wait up for me tonight, okay?' she said, and then wished she hadn't because he was actually trying for once.

'Just don't burn the bacon in the morning if he stays over,' Hal said, already moving towards the door. 'Knock on my door if you need a condom.'

Honey pulled a face at his back. 'I'm sure Robin will carry his own protection, should he need it. Which he won't.'

Hal laughed, and Honey wished he'd turn so she could see his smile.

'The man still lives with his mother,' he said. 'He won't carry condoms.'

'Well, it doesn't matter anyway, because I'm a modern woman. I've got my own supply in the bathroom cupboard,' Honey said, annoyed again, and she followed him down the hall and banged her door shut behind him.

There was a tap on her door a couple of hours later, and Honey knew straight away that it wasn't Hal because it was quiet and polite, both traits her neighbour didn't possess.

Well, that was hurdle one jumped – Robin had actually turned up. Honey had swung between mild excitement in case he was wonderful and hoping he didn't bother to come at all, and she checked her reflection quickly in the hallway mirror as she went to let him in. She'd made an effort; her blonde waves hung loose around her careful no-make-up-look made-up face, and she was wearing her favourite vintage tea dress and high heels. The dress cinched her waist and gave her a cleavage, and the heels gave her confidence and height in case he was another tall guy. Taking a deep breath and opening the door, she immediately wished she'd opted for barefoot, because Robin only came up to her shoulder.

Aside from being vertically challenged, Nell had been quite right about his hair being a feature. There was just so much of it, and it seemed to grow in all directions in Leo Sayer-style curls.

He thrust a bunch of flowers at her and grinned.

'You must be Honeysuckle. Fabulous name, darling!'

Honey accepted the flowers, noticing that they were actually gorgeous, awarding him extra points because they included honeysuckle, which wasn't an easy thing to pull off in a bouquet. She smiled and swung the door wide for him to come in, hurriedly kicking off her shoes and flicking them into her bedroom as she followed him along the hallway. That was better. They were pretty much the same height now; all wasn't lost, although that hair was going to take some getting used to.

'And you must be Robin,' she said, waving for him to sit down on the sofa as she dug out a vase for the flowers. 'Nell tells me you teach music.'

He nodded, and his hair seemed to move independently of his head.

'Love it,' he said. 'Music is in my bones.' He flung his arms wide and burst into the opening lines of Abba's 'Thank you for the Music', complete with jazz hands. A huge belly laugh erupted from him as he finished, and Honey found herself relaxing and started to laugh with him. Robin was a funny guy. Maybe this was going to be a good evening after all.

'I hope you're not vegetarian, I made bolognese,' she said, and he rubbed his round tummy beneath the straining wool of his pullover.

'It's my absolute favourite,' he declared. 'Besides chicken madras. And lasagne. And my mother's lime cheesecake.' He wagged his finger at her like a guest on Jerry Springer. 'Don't you judge me,' he drawled in a dead-on Deep South accent, and then that sunshine laughter erupted from him again.

'Well?' she said a few minutes later, having watched him theatrically twirl his fork into the heaped plate of spaghetti she'd placed in front of him and then close his eyes while he savoured his first mouthful.

His eyes pinged wide open again in shock. 'Should I just give up and join Alcoholics Anonymous now, my darling?' He put his cutlery down and clutched at his throat, laughing, and then flapped his hands for her to sit back down when she reached for the water jug.

'It's fine, it's fine. I like a woman who's serious about her drink.'

He wiped at his eyes, and Honey was unsure if he was damp eyed from laughing or because of the food. Testing it gingerly herself, she suspected the latter. How could it have turned out so perfectly when Hal had been around and so badly without him? Even the addition of salt hadn't managed to rescue it.

'I'm sorry, Robin. I'm not sure what went wrong,' she said, poking half-heartedly at her dinner.

'I think you're supposed to add meat to the wine,' he said dryly, gamely scooping up another mouthful. 'It's really not that bad once you get going.' He waved his fork towards her plate. 'Eat up. We'll be drunk as lords in no time and I'll be able to have my wicked way with you.'

Honey giggled and did as he'd suggested, sensing from the twinkle in his merry eyes that Robin's wicked way was more likely to involve belting out Kylie hits on karaoke than kinky sex.

Nell must have known that Robin was never going to be Honey's type in the romantic sense, yet still the evening turned out to be one of the best she could remember in quite some time. As she cleared away their dessert plates, Honey quizzed him more on his piano skills.

'By rights I shouldn't really be able to play the piano with these sausage fingers, but I can. I get it from my mother. She's as round as a watermelon and yet she plays the piano like a light-fingered woodland nymph. It's the same with dancing – we're both as light as feathers on our toes.' He lifted his foot and circled it in Honey's direction, revealing rainbow-striped socks. 'You haven't seen anyone line dance until you've seen *me* line dance.'

'You'll have to teach me one day,' Honey laughed.

Robin looked serious for the first time that evening.

'Cards on the table, Honeysuckle. You're a wonderful girl but you're just not my type at all, my love. I prefer my dates to be over six foot with an Adam's apple, but if it's any consolation you do cook a striking bolognese.'

Honey stared at him, round eyed. 'Well . . . in the interests of complete honesty, you're not my type either, Robin. I prefer my evil twisted neighbour who habitually ignores me and then occasionally flirts with me to keep me dangling on a string.'

136

Robin's bushy eyebrows moved up into his equally bushy hair.

'Tell me everything, darling, he sounds divine!'

And so she did, and Robin topped up her glass every time she reached the bottom of it and then offered to nip across the hall and punch Hal on the nose. 'If I can reach it,' he added, making Honey laugh for the hundredth time that evening.

'Now. Enough maudlin, Jolene. Shall we line dance?'

He jumped up out of his chair and dragged the coffee table to the side of the room.

'I don't think I have the right music,' Honey giggled, three sheets to the wind from the way he'd constantly refilled her glass.

'Don't worry about that. I'll sing,' Robin said, gesturing impatiently for her to stand alongside him on the rug. 'You here.'

And so they line danced, and they laughed until Honey collapsed on the sofa with mildly hysterical tears rolling down her cheeks.

'I give up. I'll never be Dolly Parton,' she said, her arm flung dramatically across her brow.

'Probably for the best. I don't think I've ever met anyone worse at it, and I teach a class of ex-offenders at the community centre on a Thursday night.'

Honey laid a hand over her heart. 'Leave. You've wounded me.'

Robin checked his watch and then leaned down and kissed her hand with a flourish.

'Actually, I should bid you goodnight. It's almost midnight; I might turn into a pumpkin if I stay beyond the witching hour. Or my mother might put the deadbolt on. One of those things will definitely happen.'

'I like pumpkins,' Honey said, as Robin pulled her to her feet by both hands.

'Fabulous in a pie,' he nodded, shrugging into his jacket as they made their unsteady way along the hallway.

'Or soup on bonfire night,' she muttered, leaning on the wall for support as he opened the door and blew her a theatrical volley of kisses.

'I won't kiss you on the mouth, darling. It would ruin you for other men.'

Honey nodded and blew him kisses with both hands in return.

Robin glanced cheekily at Hal's door. 'Shall I knock and offer to teach him to line dance?'

Honey shook her head. 'I don't think he's a dancing kind of guy. At least not these days.'

'There isn't a person in this world who doesn't like to shake their tush to a bit of Dolly, given the right circumstances,' Robin insisted. 'Get him dancing, Honeysuckle, and you'll find your way behind that wall of his. I guarantee it.' He tapped the side of his nose. 'Trust your uncle Robin.'

'That's just creepy,' she laughed, then clapped softly as he pirouetted across the hall tiles and let himself out of the front door.

She looked at Hal's door for a long minute after Robin had left. There was no way she'd ever get him dancing, but maybe Robin had been onto something anyway. There was very little in the way of lightheartedness or laughter in Hal's life, and he had the most beautiful smile on the rare occasions he let her see it. Maybe that was a way in with him. Something to think about, anyway.

Tomorrow morning she'd call Nell up and thank her. She might not have found Honey her perfect man, but she'd certainly given her a night to remember.

CHAPTER FOURTEEN

If Honey had hoped that Hal would emerge from his lair to find out about her date the next morning, she was disappointed. She'd texted both Nell and Tash and arranged to meet them for brunch, but his door had remained firmly closed when she'd left the house. It wasn't as if she'd been quiet about it either; she'd slammed her own door once, and then again a minute or two later in case he hadn't heard it the first time. Then she'd loitered for a thoroughly unnecessary amount of time in the hallway, and she may have dropped her keys on the floor loudly a couple of times too. In the end she'd grown furious with herself and him and slammed out of the house, only to nip back in again after going a few steps along the pavement, just in case that final slam had been the one that brought him to his door. It hadn't, and Honey stomped out again, even angrier than she'd been already.

By the time she reached their favourite café she'd walked her temper off and she waved at Nell and Tash as she spotted them through the window. They were sitting on low-slung sofas around their favourite table, and a wash of familiarity and contentment washed over Honey as she dropped down beside Tash, who twisted around to face her with a mug of coffee cradled in her hands and eyes sparkling for gossip.

'Well? I take it the mysterious Robin turned up then, seeing as we've been summoned?'

Honey nodded and glanced towards Nell, who looked back at her nervously.

'Yup. He arrived on the dot.'

'And . . .?' Tash said, drawing the word out.

'And he was . . . funny?' Honey said, taking her time to choose the best word to summarise Robin without doing him a disservice.

Tash's green eyes clouded. 'Funny ha-ha or funny peculiar?'

'Umm, funny ha-ha? He was actually really good company, I don't think I've laughed so much in years. Present company excepted, of course,' she said, and saw Nell's shoulders relax a little.

'I'm getting the feeling that there was no romance involved,' Tash frowned as she put her empty mug down on the low mahogany table.

'None at all,' Honey supplied merrily. 'Nell, how well do you know Robin?'

Her friend looked a little shifty and glad to see the waiter advancing on them. 'Well, not massively, obviously. In fact, not at all, really, but I've heard him play the piano and he's practically Mozart.'

'So what did he look like?' Tash asked, after they'd placed their orders.

Honey already felt a sense of loyalty to her new friend. 'He was quite sweet,' she said, and then, 'in a short, round, hairy Leo Sayer kind of way.'

Tash shot daggers at Nell. 'Jesus, Nell, what were you trying to do? Sabotage things?'

'He's nice,' Nell protested. 'And he was the only pianist I knew.'

Honey nodded. 'He was really great, Tash; you'd have loved him. Not nice in a sexy way, but then I wasn't his cup of tea either. He told me he's looking for a chubby brunette who's into line dancing.'

Nell started to laugh. 'I'm sorry, Honey. I promise to try harder next time.'

'No more.' Honey smiled, but shook her head firmly. 'That's why I wanted to meet up today. Please girls, you've tried and I'm honestly grateful, but this just isn't working out. Deano was hung up on his ex, and Robin . . . well, he was lovely, but this whole piano man idea is proper bonkers when you stop to think about it, isn't it?'

'How about we widen it to other musicians? I saw a sexy cellist at the theatre the other night, the span of his fingers was something else,' Tash said, splaying her fingers wide to demonstrate.

'The theatre?' Nell sounded more surprised by Tash's social engagements than the cellist's hands.

Tash nodded. 'I know! And it wasn't even a pantomime! Yusef is into all this highbrow stuff, I think he's turned on by the idea of educating me.' Her merry eyes danced. 'I'm not complaining. He had his hand down my shirt through most of the second half and he let me drive his Porsche home.'

142

'Not that highbrow then,' Nell said dryly.

'He's filthy rich and filthy dirty, just the way I like 'em.' Tash's grin was pure filth too as she winked at the blushing teenage waiter who'd just placed their food down. He spilt a little of Nell's soup over the edge of the bowl in panic and then tripped on the strap of Honey's bag in his haste to get away.

As usual, brunch was delicious, soul food they'd built their friendship over for many years. Honey valued these two women like sisters, and listening to them share confidences and laugh softly as they ate, she knew it was time to tell them about Hal.

'Honey, I know we haven't come up with the best of candidates yet, but let's not give up,' Nell said, her mouth set in a serious line. 'If nothing else, you're having fun, and that's better than staying home alone, right?'

'I love you both for trying,' Honey said, covering Nell's hand and giving it a squeeze, 'but the thing is, I'm snowed under with all of this drama happening at work, and I've kind of got myself ever-so-slightly involved with my neighbour, and Mimi and Lucille need my help with some personal stuff that's come up . . .' she trailed off as Nell placed her spoon abruptly down and Tash held up her hand as if to stop traffic.

'Hold it right there, lady. Back up.'

Honey had sandwiched the relevant part of her speech in the middle, not because she didn't want to tell them, but more because she didn't really know what to tell them. On the one hand, there wasn't really very much to tell. It wasn't as if she and Hal were romantically involved on any level that could be deemed as normal; one kiss was hardly enough to call off the search. But then on the other hand, it wasn't about the kiss at all, and that was where she could really use some advice.

'Your neighbour?' Nell said. 'Not the angry one with blood all over his hands?'

Tash looked from Nell to Honey. 'He sounds delightful. What have I missed here?'

Honey sighed heavily, unsure where to start. 'Yeah, that one,' she said, glancing at Nell, and then studiously lining up the bangles on her wrist as she decided how to put it.

'Have you shagged him?' Tash burst out, staring at Honey. 'Oh my God, he made you orgasm, didn't he?'

The beetroot-faced waiter, who'd just plucked up the courage to clear their plates, put them straight back down and walked away.

'No! No. Tash, keep your voice down will you?' Honey hissed, trying not to look at the suddenly silent couple at the next table. 'Of course I haven't shagged him. He's . . . he's complicated.'

'The last time we talked about him you said he was vile,' Nell said, looking unconvinced. 'What changed?'

'I got to know him,' Honey said simply. 'A bit, anyway.'

'Have you been on a date?' Nell said. Honey half laughed at the idea of a date with Hal. 'God no. Not unless you count endless hours spent sitting outside his closed door being ignored or swore at.'

She didn't miss the concerned look that passed between her friends, and she couldn't blame them for their reticence. She wasn't painting the best of pictures. She tried again.

'The thing is, Hal's not like most men. He's going through a hard time, and he's angry, and he's blind, and he kisses

144

me like there's no air, and he doesn't leave the house, and he drinks too much whisky.'

It was a toss up which of her friends looked more shocked.

'He's blind?' Nell said softly.

'You kissed him?' Tash said, leaning forward.

'Yes, and yes. I don't know what happened to him, but I get the impression that his blindness is quite recent. He doesn't like to talk about it. To be honest, most of the time he doesn't like to talk about much at all.'

'You're not selling him, Honey,' Nell said.

'I know. It's hard to explain,' Honey said. 'There's just something about him that gets me. He's a mass of contradictions. He's a terrible grouch, but then he's funny and endearing. He dresses like a rock star and acts like a recluse. He ignores me for days on end and then every now and then he is so, so incredible that he knocks the breath out of me.'

Tash ordered a bottle of wine. 'Aside from the fact that he's a hot kisser, he sounds like bloody hard work to me.'

Honey nodded. 'I can see that. And he is, but I don't think he means to be. But here's the thing.'

Tash and Nell both sat statue-still as they waited to hear what 'the thing' was.

And so Honey let the thought out, the one that had lingered around in her subconscious like a squatter, refusing to leave until she gave it the attention it deserved.

'I think he's The One.' Honey's words came out barely above a whisper.

'The One . . . as in the one who can make you orgasm?' Tash said.

'Or the one . . . as in The One?' Nell said, her big brown eyes round and watchful.

Honey dropped her head in her hands, trying to make sense of her feelings along with her friends.

'I don't know,' she said, and Nell and Tash moved around the table to squish on the sofa either side of her. She slumped back between them and took the glass of wine Tash offered. 'I honestly don't know, and it scares me stupid. Both, maybe?'

When she let herself into the house later that afternoon, Honey took the hall at a run in case Hal opened his door. She couldn't face him yet, not after spending the last few hours dissecting her burgeoning feelings for him with Nell and Tash. They'd both wanted to come back and meet him, which she knew he'd hate and had vetoed straight away. Nell wanted to vet him for suitability, and Tash wanted to get a look at the man Honey had billed as the sexiest kisser alive. Another time, she'd said, meaning *never*, if Hal had anything to do with it.

After much deliberation, they'd arrived at the shaky conclusion that Honey had a stonking great schoolgirl crush on her neighbour. Nell had ruled out the possibility of love, based on the fact that Honey had only kissed him once and eighty per cent of the relationship seemed to be one sided.

They'd also decided that Honey should explore the possibility of further physical contact with Hal in order to reassess her reaction to him. He'd kissed her when she'd just been rejected by Deano; she'd been at her most vulnerable, which would have rendered her susceptible. 'In other words,' Tash had said, 'you need to snog his face off again and see if he gets your juices flowing a second time.'

So there it was. Piano man mission aborted, and operation snog-Hal's-face-off underway. She'd just go to bed for a few hours, and then she'd think about it again.

CHAPTER FIFTEEN

Sleep, sobriety and coffee threw fresh light on things. It was a hideous plan.

She could hardly march over there and demand to be kissed, and Honey wasn't prepared to try to inveigle him into it. If Hal ever kissed her again she wanted it to be because he wanted to, not because she'd artificially seduced him in order to conduct a very unscientific experiment.

Honey thought of him as she went through the motions of eating leftover bolognese for dinner – he'd been right about it being better the day after, thankfully. She could of course try taking some over to him again, but he'd probably ignore her or insult her. She swung between being spitting mad at him for being so pig-headed and feeling compassion towards him because if she didn't call on him no one else would, which ultimately led her back to being pissed off at him because he was such a royal pain in the ass that he'd most likely driven away anyone who cared about him. Hal hadn't just landed here from the moon. He was a man; a man who must have friends, family, a past, yet none of it seemed to have followed him here. How could that be? Did they even know where he was? Christ, he could have a wife and children for all she knew.

Honey thought about him some more, decided sobriety was overrated, and poured herself a glass of red. The man lived here under the same roof with her, for God's sake. Surely she was entitled to know more about him than just his first name.

Was he asleep over there? Or was he awake, drinking whisky straight from the bottle? Would he be mad at her for not knocking today, for denying him the chance to yell at her to piss off? Or would he be lonesome? The thought of Hal being lonely over there because she'd neglected him had her glancing at the boxed-up razor that had been sitting on her living room shelf for days.

It was as good a reason as any. She wouldn't sleep unless she at least tapped his door. Did that make her an interfering neighbour? Was Honey the wannabe girl guide he accused her of being? Perhaps, a little. But the bigger part of her couldn't resist the chance to see him. Maybe he'd answer. Maybe he wouldn't. Either way she found herself suddenly between their doors, the floor tiles cool beneath her bare feet.

'Hal.' She spoke quietly without knocking, sounding like a teenager at her forbidden boyfriend's bedroom window. 'Hal, are you awake?'

It was only a little after nine so she was almost certain he must be. When he didn't answer, she tapped lightly on his door.

'Hal, please. Talk to me.'

The lengthening silence made her sigh and lean her

forehead against his door. There was no sound from inside his flat. Talking to him had become rather like writing a diary, cathartic but solitary.

'Please, Hal. Open the door. Or at least let me know you're alive in there. Throw something at the door or something.'

He didn't, but Honey didn't panic. This had happened regularly enough now for her to know he was most likely listening and choosing to ignore her, which pissed her off beyond measure. She glanced down at the razor box in her hand.

'I have something for you, though I don't know why I'm bothering seeing as you can't be arsed to answer me. I'm getting pretty sick of this, for the record.' She banged her forehead lightly in the silence. 'Is this it, Hal? You're going to keep giving me the silent treatment until I give up and go away forever? Is that what you do to everyone in your life? To your family, your friends? Treat them like crap until they stop bothering anymore? Because I'm there too now. Just so you know, I'm right on the edge of never knocking on your door again.'

Honey knew that she was probably overstepping the mark, but then wasn't that the whole point to this conversation? To push his boundaries, to force him out of this interminable, painful silence? She wanted her nightly companion back. She wanted her five minutes of Hal-ness, that precious time that had all too easily become the highlight of her day. How had he even done that? He certainly hadn't charmed her into wanting to spend time with him; he was borderline offensive most of the time. He called her Mother Teresa and mocked every aspect of her life, and then he kissed her until she saw stars and wanted to rip his clothes off. So yes. Maybe she did want to offend him a little. To piss him off the same way he pissed her off, to rile him out of his goddamn complacency and back into the real world, a world where people took risks and sometimes hurt each other and sometimes kissed each other until they felt better again.

At some point during these thoughts she heard him moving along the hall, and her heartbeat inched up several notches.

'Open the door, Hal. I know you're there.'

'Don't ever mention my family again, you hear me?' He bellowed at her full force, making her step back from the door in shock. 'You know fuck all about me, or my family, or my friends. You hear me, woman?'

'Oh, I hear you, Hal,' she shouted back, feeling her temper snap. 'Is it even Hal? Or have you lied about who you are? Not that I've any right to ask, of course. I'm just the idiot who likes you enough to bring you food and whisky and take your shit when no one else does. Well. Excuse. Bloody. Me.' The wine had loosened her tongue just enough to reach the point of absolute honesty, and it felt treacherously good to let the words out. Liberating, in fact. She considered storming back to her own flat, but because she knew with one hundred per cent certainty that he wouldn't follow her she stayed where she was.

His door opened. Not the way she'd grown accustomed to; inch-by-inch, just enough to hear her. This time it was thrown wide on its hinges, and Hal stood there in the doorway, seeming to tower over her tonight in her bare feet.

'What do you want from me? A potted fucking history?' he blazed, his body stiff with anger. 'What exactly is it you'd like to know, eh? My name? My name is Benedict Hallam, and yes, I have a family. A mother, a father, a sister. And yes, I have friends. Or else I thought I did, until the fuckers decided a friend who couldn't see anymore didn't quite fit in with their party image. I had a life, Honeysuckle, and it was a fucking good one. I was *someone*. Someone with a girfriend, with my own fancy fucking restaurant and my own fancy fucking customers, okay?' His chest heaved. 'And now I'm no one, just some sad bloke who can't see and relies on the charity of his do-gooder neighbour for scraps from her table and schoolboy fumbles. Fucking pathetic, in other words.'

Honey stared at him, trying to process everything he'd said around the hurt of his dismissal of their kiss as a schoolboy fumble.

'I don't see pathetic when I look at you,' she said quietly. 'I just see someone in trouble.'

He laughed harshly. 'And you just can't resist the urge to jump right in and save me, can you? But who are you really doing it for, Honey? Me, or so you can feel good about yourself when you close your eyes at night?'

'I don't feel sorry for you, if that's what you're getting at,' she said, wanting to shake him. 'I mean, of course I'm sorry that you feel so . . . so shit, and that something awful happened to make you lose your sight, but don't for one minute think that I knock on your door and bring you things because I feel sorry for you.'

'Then why, Honeysuckle? Why don't you just leave me the hell alone?'

'Because for some unfathomable reason even I can't identify, I happen to bloody like you! You make me laugh when you're not being downright rude to me, you're randomly sweet when I don't expect it, and your smile does weird

152

stuff to my brain, probably because it's like one of those endangered animals that you have to wait forever to see at the zoo and then you stare really hard at because you know you might not see it again for a really long time. Or ever. Okay? I just like being with you.'

Okay, maybe that wine had loosened her tongue a little too much. She felt as winded as he looked.

'Don't treat me like your pet fucking project, Honeysuckle. I'm not some endangered goddamn panda that you get to come over and visit with bamboo sticks to tempt me out of my hut.'

She glanced down at the razor in her hands. Not bamboo sticks, but was he right? Was she here with an offering to tempt him out? And if she was, what was so sodding wrong about that anyway? She didn't see anyone else queuing up here for no other reason than to brighten his day.

'You know what, Hal? You're absolutely right. About everything. All of it. I don't know what I was thinking bothering to come over here and bring you a gift you so blatantly don't bloody want!' She thrust the razor into his hands hard enough to catch him in the guts with the corners of the box.

'Here. Stick your bamboo where the sun doesn't shine.'

She turned on her heel before he had a chance to respond, stomping across the hallway and slamming her door.

'Honey? Open the door.'

She was still standing with her back against her front door when Hal's voice vibrated through it a couple of minutes later.

'Thank you for the bamboo.'

153

His gentle tone caught her off guard, too close to her ear. She swallowed hard.

'It's a razor,' she mumbled, opening the door.

'So I gathered,' he said, turning the opened box over in his hands. 'You better come over and help me work out how to use it then.'

He said it oh-so-softly, then he held his hand out. Honey stared at his hand for a second, her breath lodged almost painfully in her throat. It was such a simple, powerful gesture, impossible to ignore or resist. She knew that she would get herself into all kinds of trouble really fast if she went into his flat, yet she placed her hand in his anyway and let him lead her across the hallway.

She'd never been inside the flat before, but it was a mirror image of her own place across the hall, or as hers had been when she'd moved in. Pale walls, simple, uncluttered spaces designed for the rental market. Over time she'd made her place her own; bright, primary-coloured coat hooks, a pretty blind that had come into the shop, a string of fairy lights woven into her bedstead. Small touches that made a big difference. Hal's place lacked any of those things, but then he hadn't been here long and it was pretty obvious that soft furnishings were meaningless in his life right now. His earlier speech had told her many new things about him that she needed to mull over, but not right now. Right now he was giving her that ten per cent of fabulous, and she didn't want to waste a second of it.

'In the lounge?' she said.

'It's more conventional to do it in the bathroom,' he said. 'Assuming we're still talking about shaving?'

Honey appreciated his attempt to make light of this unexpected turn of events and followed him along the hallway to the bathroom. He pulled the cord and illuminated the room with a wash of bright light, and then lowered the lid on the loo and sat on the closed seat.

'So have you ever shaved anyone before?' he asked.

'You want me to do it?' she said, surprised. She'd sort of figured on unpacking the razor and passing it to him to do it himself.

'I'd think twice if it were a cut-throat, but I'm assuming it's an electric safety razor. I'm fairly certain you can't kill me.'

Honey picked open the seal on the box and slid the razor out into her hands.

'Is there a trimmer?' he asked. 'You'll need to take off the length with that before using the razor.' He skimmed his hand over his jaw. 'It's too long to go at with a razor right away.'

Honey located the trimmer using the instruction leaflet and slotted it together, then plugged the cord into the socket beside the bathroom mirror. The tiny room felt as if the walls were closing in, pressing her closer to Hal. He turned his head to one side, exposing his neck, and then sighed and dropped his head.

'Hold on, Honey. There's something I need to do.'

After a couple of still seconds he lifted his face and reached for his dark glasses. Honey froze, realising what he was going to do a second before he slid them slowly off, folding them and placing them carefully beside the sink. Honey drew in a quiet breath and looked at him, really looked at him. He sat as tense as a man in the dock waiting for judgment. This was the first time he'd allowed her to see him without the protection of his shades, aside from the few seconds when he'd fallen in the hallway when they'd first met.

Hands down, Hal had the world's most beautiful eyes. Warm brown flecked with golden amber shards, fringed all the way around with long dark lashes. Eyes to melt in, and it hurt her heart to know that such incredible eyes could no longer see.

'Thank you,' she breathed, thinking, *thank you for trusting me.*

He turned his head in profile again. 'You could hardly do it with them stuck on my face. Start at one side and work your way around.'

Honey buzzed the trimmer into life in her hand, getting a feel for it before putting it anywhere near his face.

'Are you sure about this, Hal?' she said, suddenly apprehensive as she moved the razor towards him and then away again.

'Relax, Honey. It doesn't really matter if you balls it up. My social calendar is embarrassingly empty,' he said. 'Just do it.'

Honey braced her shoulders. She could do this. Stepping around into the tight space between Hal's denim-clad legs and the bathroom counter and holding his chin lightly with one hand, she touched the trimmer against the dark fuzz at the side of his neck.

'Like this?' she said, uncertain and hyper-aware of the heat of his body close to hers.

'Like that,' he murmured as she stroked it up the length of his neck towards his jaw. 'Try to keep your hand steady. You're shaking.'

Honey watched as the trimmer sliced away the length from his beard in slow methodical strokes, revealing dark stubble in its place. Dark, sexy stubble. 'Nice and easy,' he whispered when she tried to go too fast, and then he closed his eyes. His words. Oh his quiet, sexy words.

The urge to kiss him was overwhelming. Stifling. She wanted to hear him murmur those same words when he was naked and hard in her hand. Was he turned on, too? His eyes were still closed as she pressed her fingertips to his jaw and tilted his head the other way.

'No one's ever done this for me before,' he said, his words gravel in his throat. 'I like it.' His arm rested along the counter behind her, and her backside grazed his splayed palm when she squeezed around him.

'I like it too,' she said simply, no longer sure if she meant she liked shaving his beard or she liked the feel of his hand on her backside. 'It's hard to reach the other side of your head from here, the cord isn't long enough. Do you think you can twist around?' She cast a critical eye over the small space.

'I could. Or would it be easier if you . . .' He reached out and put his hands on her waist to move her to stand in front of him, then pulled her closer so she had to straddle his knees. 'Maybe you could sit here?'

Honey held the trimmer away from them for fear of doing him damage, because her whole body felt like it was shaking with awareness of his. Hal's hands were still on her waist, and he applied gentle pressure, just enough to encourage her down until her backside hit his knees.

'Better?' he said, low and teasing.

'Yes,' she breathed.

157

'Finish the job then,' he said, and turned his head for her to carry on where she'd left off. Breathing carefully, she touched the trimmer against his Adam's apple as he swallowed and wanted to follow every sweep of the razor with her mouth.

Hal's hands still rested on her waist, warm through the thin cotton of her dress, and his thumbs started to stroke back and forth, as slow and easy as he'd told her to be with the razor.

'How's it looking?' he asked as she swept it close to his ear and wanted to lick the hot skin there.

'Really good, rock star. Really good.' If only he knew. She turned the razor off and laid it down. 'You're probably done.'

He didn't move his hands – in fact if anything, he held her down a little more firmly onto his lap.

'Good. Now you need to run your hands over it to check it's level.'

Honey swallowed hard, breathed shallowly, and lifted her hands up until she cradled his face between her palms. She couldn't help herself; she closed her eyes and luxuriated in him as she learned his features with her fingers. The proud slant of his cheekbones, the contours of his jaw, all of the time aware of his fingers massaging her waist.

'I think I did a pretty good job for a beginner,' she said, opening her eyes again to watch his lips part on a low sigh. He sighed again, more audibly this time, and his hands slid from her waist to cup her backside, pulling her forward until there was no space between them.

'And I think that's probably the best shave I've ever had,' he said, and then he slid his hands into her hair and kissed her; the hot, open-mouthed kiss that she'd been fantasising about for weeks.

'Hal,' she breathed his name into the heat of his mouth and let her arms slide around his neck. She wasn't kissing him because Tash and Nell had suggested it; at that moment they never even entered her head. They couldn't, because there was no room in her head for anyone but Hal as she threaded her fingers into the thick, dark silk of his hair, their bodies pressed together, banging heart against banging heart.

Hal was lost. He knew he had to call a halt, but the words wouldn't come because Honey felt so damn good in his arms. He'd imagined how she'd feel a hundred times over, and she felt a million times better. Softer. Warmer. And responsive, so fucking responsive.

Over the last few weeks he'd told himself *no* over and over again when it came to Honey. No, I won't answer when she knocks tonight. No, I won't eat dinner with her. No, I won't kiss her. He'd denied himself constantly, and then she'd pushed his buttons tonight and he'd opened the door and lost the battle. She smelled of strawberries and she sounded like he'd hurt her, and yet still she found it in herself to tell him how much she liked him, and she'd bought him a goddamn gift.

No became yes all too easily when she was around, and he held her close and let his resolve melt like ice cubes in an inferno.

'I want you,' he heard himself gasp. 'I want you so fucking much.'

'I'm yours,' she whispered, dragging his t-shirt over his

head. Honey was the first woman he'd touched since the accident, the first woman to touch him, and he only wished like hell that he could see the beauty of the girl on his lap. He knew she was beautiful, because his hands and his heart told him so. Yours, she'd said. She wasn't, and she never could be, but right now he desperately wanted her to be.

Honey learned something from Hal that no other man had ever taught her; the art of taking it slow. The men she'd been involved with in her past had always rushed through the kissing part to get her clothes off. Not Hal. He took his time over kissing her, slow and searching, cradling her face between his hands as his lips moved over hers. Reverential, beyond intimate, the way every woman should be kissed and few were. His body was hot and hard against hers from shoulder to hip, moulded, perfectly fitted together, but at that moment his mouth was the centre of her world. Naked from the waist up, he more than lived up to her rock star nickname. He was incredible. Lean. Hard. Beautiful. Tattoos ran riot over his arms, dark marks of his misspent youth and impulsive nature. There was an edge to him, a seam of danger that ran through him. Don't get too close unless you're prepared to risk it all. If Honey had to sum him up in one word, she'd call him lethal.

'Remember to breathe, baby,' he murmured, tipping her head back in his hands to slide his open mouth down her neck, kissing the dip between her collarbones. His fingers were unpicking the small buttons down the front of her dress. Remembering to breathe was harder than it ought to be when he eased her dress down to her waist and then slid his hands up her ribcage. She heard him groan as he dipped his head and moved his mouth over the slopes of her breasts, his hands warm over the lace of her bra, stroking her nipples into peaks with the pads of his thumbs.

So this is what it's supposed to feel like, she thought, as Hal reached behind her and unclipped her bra. There was something in the way he held her, in the way he cupped her and lowered his dark lashes when he kissed her that somehow brought a lump to her throat. She stroked her hands over his hair when he mouthed her nipples, watching the slow slide of his tongue and the almost holy expression on his face. She'd never seen him look that way before, and it was deeply moving, insanely erotic.

'Please, Hal,' she said, stroking his shoulders until he raised his head again and kissed her, this time hard and hungry. If she'd thought his kiss special up to then, this kiss sent her reeling. He clamped her against him until the skin of his abdomen welded to hers, one hand tangled in her hair, the other on her neck, her breasts, sliding up her thighs beneath her dress.

'Let it be you,' she whispered, 'I want it to be you.' Rocking on him, she wanted everything he had to give her and found herself closer than she'd ever been before – to orgasm or love, she wasn't quite sure.

Her words tumbled into his mouth as his fingers grazed the lace edge of her knickers. 'Let it be you,' she'd said, 'I want it to be you.' In his whole life Hal had never wanted a woman more. He was so hard it was painful, and he could almost feel her heat through the lace of her underwear. It seemed that size thirteen was his definition of perfect,

161

and the heady power of being wanted, of feeling like a man again was a hard drug to kick.

'Honey,' he whispered, slowing down their kiss because he never wanted it to end. 'Stop me.'

'No way,' she smiled against his lips, her fingers working the top button of his jeans. He could tell that she didn't think he was serious, and he could hardly blame her. He'd stripped her and he'd kissed her like a man on death row. She was shaking in his arms, and there was nothing on earth he wanted more than to slide his fingers inside her underwear and give her what she needed.

'Honey,' he said, moving his hand out of her dress and easing his head back. 'I can't do this.'

He felt her stiffen and knew she'd registered that he was serious this time, and for the first time in his life he was glad he couldn't see, because he didn't have to witness the hurt that had to be written all over her face.

'You can, please . . .' She clung to him, her mouth on his ear as he rocked her in his arms. 'Let me in, Hal. I want you so much . . .' she whispered, stroking his back. Her breasts were pressed flat against his body, and his hands ached to hold them again. It would be so, so easy to let her in, but she wouldn't like what she found if he did.

He dipped his head and buried his face in her neck, drinking in her scent and then pushing her gently back in his lap.

'This can't happen, Honey. I'm sorry, it just can't.'

Frustration crackled from her like electricity. 'It can. It already is. You want me, Hal, I can feel it in you here,' she touched his mouth, 'and here,' she lowered her fingers to his chest, 'and here,' she dropped her hand down again and he caught it before she could reach his crotch. It pained him to know that the only way to make this any easier on her was to lie.

'Right now, maybe. But I won't want you afterwards, and then where will we be? It's just ten minutes of madness, Honey, because I'm lonely and you're desperate.' He felt her sharp intake of breath and knew his words had wounded her. 'Put your dress back on and go home. You'll thank me in the morning.'

He heard her cry, felt her stumble as she backed away from him and hated himself.

'You're wrong,' she said, low and unsteadily. 'I won't thank you in the morning, because I'm done with you.'

He hauled himself up in the tiny bathroom and followed her along his hallway. 'I'm done with your anger, and your fury, and your . . . your throwing me the occasional bone . . .' she heaved a breath in, upset.

'You know what, Hal? If you were a woman, they'd call you a prick tease. You're a horrible, hateful man who gets a kick out of blowing hot and cold just to keep me dangling.'

She sounded surprised by her own word choice and as unhinged as he felt. He stood still in his hallway, feeling wretched as she stamped out of his flat and slammed the door behind her.

CHAPTER SIXTEEN

Operation snog-Hal's-face-off is over. I hate him.

Honey slammed her way around the shop with her mobile in her hand, stabbing her fingers at the screen as she group-texted Nell and Tash. She'd woken up as angry as when she'd gone to sleep, angrier, if possible. The morning had dawned as grey as her mood, and she'd seriously considered kicking his door as she'd left the house bundled up in her boots and raincoat. What was this to him? A game, something he did to entertain himself? What kind of man did that make him? He might be sexy as sin but she was mad as hell with him. He'd given her a bad case of sexual frustration, and it infuriated her to death that he seemed to be the only cure for her ailment.

Her phone pinged in her hand, and Tash's name popped up.

Project Piano-Man is back on then?

Honey huffed and texted her straight back. No. No piano

men, and no revolting hot neighbours. No men full stop.
I'm done.

After a few moments, her phone pinged again.

So you're saying we need to look for a lady pianist
instead . . .?

Honey laughed under her breath, despite her bad mood.
Trust Tash to have a smart answer for everything.

'Honey dear, can you help me with this? It's heavy.'
Glancing up, Honey shoved her phone into her pocket and
took off across the shop towards the doors.

'Lucille, what are you doing?' She took the heavy box
from Lucille's arms. 'You should have called me to pick this
up, it weighs a ton.' Honey staggered to the counter with
the taped-up brown box in her arms. 'Where's it come from,
anyway? There weren't any deliveries outside when I arrived
ten minutes ago.'

'You must have missed it, it was right there,' Lucille said,
putting the glasses on from the golden chain around her
neck and peering at it. The neatly sealed box didn't offer
up clues in the way of labels or addressees.

Honey shrugged. 'Must be a donation. The door was
open though, they could have brought it in.' She reached
for the envelope opener in the drawer beneath the counter,
and just as she was about to slit it open, Lucille put a hand
on her arm.

'What if it's alive?' Lucille said. 'A mother donated her
teenage son's pet snake to a charity shop once, I read it in
the newspaper.'

'No air holes,' Honey said, surveying the box. Lucille
looked at it sniffily.

'Just be careful, that's all I'm saying.'

Honey slid the blade beneath the tape and ripped it open, unfolding the flaps of the box for them both to peer inside. After a few seconds Honey started to laugh. Lucille reached inside and pulled out one of the many pairs of handcuffs, all fluffy and in every shade of the rainbow. The accompanying unsigned note simply said that they were a gift for the residents to use in further protests and wished them every success with their campaign to save the home.

'How bizarre,' Honey murmured. 'There must be thirty pairs in here.'

Mimi and Billy wandered in at that moment and gazed into the box alongside Lucille.

'Ooh I say, darling!' Billy said, rubbing his hands together with glee. 'That's a rather racy way to start the morning. I'll take four please,' he waggled his eyebrows at Honey. 'No eating the keys this time please, Honeysuckle. We don't want Mimi being left in a compromising position.'

'They're not for sale,' Honey said. 'They just arrived from a mystery donor to support the campaign.'

'Very timely,' Mimi said. 'We decided amongst us in the home last night that one of us should be chained to the railings at all times. Or until it goes dark, in any case.'

'Every day?' Honey said, surprised. It was a big ask of people with a median age of eighty-six.

Mimi, Lucille and Billy nodded staunchly.

'Sort of like a prisoner's hunger strike, if you will,' Billy said. 'Except Patrick's going to supply us with a packed lunch.'

'So nothing like a hunger strike at all, really then,' Honey laughed. 'I think it's a great idea. The press could really latch on to something like that.'

166

'It was my idea,' Mimi preened. 'So I'll go first. Honey, call Old Don's son at the paper and get them down here.'

Billy picked up a neon green pair of handcuffs and dangled them in the air. 'Can I do the honours, my love?'

Mimi nodded. 'Not with those though. I'll have some red ones to match my cardigan, thank you very much, Billy Hebden.' She spun on her low heel, winked at Honey, and then marched outside to be chained up.

Lucille shook her head as she watched her sister leave, her arms folded over her chest.

'She's always been the same. Had to be first at everything,' she said quietly. 'First at the dinner table when we were children. First to leave home.' She paused, frowning. 'First to be born.'

Honey noticed the chagrin behind Lucille's words, more noticeable on Lucille because she was usually content to fall in line behind her more fiery sister.

'But she wasn't, was she?' Lucille mused, almost to herself. 'Mimi wasn't the first-born. Ernie was.'

So that was what this was about. Honey nodded slowly. 'Have you decided what to do about the letter?'

Lucille sighed. 'Mimi has decided that there's no point in us meeting him.'

'And you?' Honey said, taking care to stay neutral.

'He's my brother, Honey.' Lucille's rouged lips bunched tightly together, sending pucker marks zinging all around her face. 'I'm going to meet him next week, and Mimi can't stop me because she doesn't know about it.'

Honey's mouth dropped into a silent 'o', sensing trouble brewing on the horizon. Mimi and Lucille barely disagreed about anything, mostly because Mimi made the decisions and Lucille kept the peace. It was highly unusual for them to have such differing opinions on something so important, and a sense of anxiety settled over Honey at her own unwitting duplicity now that she knew of Lucille's plan.

'I really think it might be best if you told Mimi,' she said softly. 'I'm sure she'll come around to the idea.'

'Oh no she won't,' Lucille said. 'She's as stubborn as an ox, and besides . . .' she wrapped her arms around her middle, hugging her secret to herself, 'I want this just for me for a while.'

Honey looked at Lucille's wistful and unusually defiant blue eyes. As tactics went, she couldn't help but feel it was a dangerous way to proceed.

'Why don't I go and make us a cuppa,' she said, leaving Lucille with her secret and her faraway smile, a deepening feeling of unease in the pit of her stomach.

The tap on Honey's door later that evening didn't come as a complete surprise. Never one to wait unduly for gossip, Tash deposited a bottle of red on the kitchen counter and shimmied out of her jacket, eyeing Honey speculatively.

'Come on then,' she said. 'Out with it.'

Honey shrugged as she carried two wine glasses to the coffee table and sagged down into the corner of the sofa. 'There isn't much to tell. I threw myself at him and he blew me off.'

'There has to be more to the story than that.' Tash poured the wine and handed a glass to Honey, then curled herself into the other end of the sofa, bookends. 'Did you just knock on his door and demand to be kissed?'

'No, of course I didn't,' Honey said with exaggerated

168

patience. 'I . . . well, I wasn't even going over there at all, because it was an incredibly stupid plan that was never going to work.' She sipped her wine, glad of its deep, black-curranty comfort. 'And then I realised I hadn't given him the electric razor I'd bought for him from work, so I popped over anyway. Not to kiss him. Just to deliver it.'

'You bought him a razor? You know that's random, right?'

'He needed one,' Honey said. 'He was veering danger-ously close to Grizzly Adams territory.'

Tash waved a hand for her to move the story on from the shaver. 'So then what happened?'

Honey huffed. 'I knocked on his door and lost my temper when he ignored me, then he opened his door and lost his temper too. Yelled at me that his name was Benedict Hallam and he used to have a life before he met me.'

Tash frowned, and then her eyes opened wide and round.

'Shit! Hon. Benedict Hallam is your nutso neighbour?'

'Do you know him?' Honey said. His name had seemed familiar to her when he'd said it, but she'd spent the time since concentrating too hard on loving him or hating him to dwell on why.

'You do too,' Tash said, sliding her glass onto the table. 'Benedict Hallam, the hotshot celebrity chef?' Tash frowned, obviously thinking. 'He had a posh restaurant in London . . . and oh God, that's it! He had an accident . . . he was an adrenalin junkie . . . a snowboarding injury I think?'

Honey nodded slowly. It all sounded vaguely familiar, but she was less of a fan of the celeb magazines than Tash.

'Is he over there right now?' Tash said, instantly animated. 'Can I go and meet him?'

'No way, Tash! You're not talking to him, and he wouldn't answer the door anyway. He'd hurl abuse. He's the most ignorant man you've ever met. I'm not even kidding.'

'From what I remember of him from the papers he's sex on a stick,' Tash said.

Honey took a bigger gulp of her wine than she'd planned. 'He's alright, I suppose.'

Tash shot her a meaningful look. 'He's sex on a stick and you know it.'

'Fine. Whatever. He's sex on a stick,' Honey grumbled, knowing there was little point in arguing the point because Tash was right. 'But he's miserable as sin, and he led me on and then threw me out.'

Tash refilled their glasses, frowning again. 'So going back to your story. You shouted, he shouted, and then what?'

'And then he flipped into sexy mode and asked me to shave his beard off for him.'

'Fuuuck,' Tash sighed. 'I love him.'

'And then he pulled me onto his lap, unbuttoned my dress and kissed the life out of me.'

Tash licked her lips, her eyes sparkling. 'I know you're going to say this is bad of me but I read in a magazine that blind men are better in bed. More thoughtful and skilled with their hands because they're not rendered stupid by the sight of a naked woman. In the absence of a pianist, he might just be the perfect candidate to help you get over your little problem.' Tash's mischief-filled eyes shot to Honey's crotch.

'That's just the thing, Tash. There's something about him that I just can't put my finger on, he only has to touch me and I turn into a jelly-kneed idiot. He's rude to me, like proper obnoxious, and then he kisses me and I melt.'

170

Tash nodded slowly. 'So he stripped you, kissed you, and then what?'

'And then he let me practically beg him to do me before he decided he'd had enough and told me to get dressed and go home.'

Tash grimaced. 'Classic clit-tease.'

Honey glanced up doubtfully.

'Male equivalent of a prick tease,' Tash supplied, reaching for her glass off the table.

Honey half laughed, wishing she'd known the phrase the other night.

'He didn't give you any explanation for breaking it off?'

Honey shook her head. 'Just that I'd thank him in the morning. Which I absolutely sodding didn't, by the way.'

'Harsh, babe,' Tash said in sympathy, and then blew out heavily. 'Total horndog though. Christ.'

'You're supposed to be on my side, remember?'

'I am. I am.' Tash swirled the wine around in her glass. 'It was a shitty thing to do to you. My advice?'

Honey nodded. All advice gratefully accepted, even Tash's.

'You either have to go over there and demand he finish what he started, or stop mooning over him and move on.'

'I'm not mooning.'

'When you told Nell and me about him, you were definitely mooning.'

'I've never mooned in my life.'

Tash shot her a *whatever* look. 'I recommend the first option, just so you know. You have a hot celeb chef holed up next door. Make use of him. Get him to cook you dinner and then do some more of that magic knee-melting thing he does to you.'

'Umm . . . he rejected me last night, remember?'

'Oh, Honey.' It was Tash's turn to adopt the exaggerated patience. 'You're a woman. He's a man. You're both lonely. He was probably just having an off day or something. Try again.'

'My head says no. He drives me crazy. Honestly Tash, I don't even like him half the time.' Honey sliced her flat hand across her throat. 'From here up, I think stop mooning. But then from here down . . .' she skimmed her eyes towards the ceiling and then knocked back the contents of her wine glass, 'I want him in a way I've never wanted anyone else.'

CHAPTER SEVENTEEN

A few days of abstinence from Hal did little to make Honey's heart grow fonder. She hadn't knocked on his door, and he hadn't shouted obscenities at her as she came and went through their shared lobby. If there was one thing she was sure of it was that she wouldn't be the one to back down this time. She knew he'd never offer her an explanation for his behaviour but he owed her an apology at the very least. If he didn't give it, then he could consider their friendship over.

It wasn't usual for Honey to be so bloody-minded, but Hal seemed to bring out both the very best and the very worst in her; he made her lighthearted and sexy and even culinarily capable, and he made her stubborn and furious and frustrated. It was a lot of extra emotion to handle, and Honey was almost glad of the time out afforded to her by his most recent bout of silence. Besides, the campaign to save the home was gathering pace daily, especially since the residents had begun their daily vigil at the railings.

Honey leaned back on her stool at the till and glanced out of the window of the shop. It was Billy's day today, and unlike Elsie yesterday who'd sat sedately humming to herself and smiling benignly at passers-by and the reporter from the paper, Billy was approaching his stint in the manner of a union leader whipping up a rally. He'd managed to find a pair of prisoner-style orange overalls, which clashed violently with the lime cuffs he'd used to chain himself to the railings by one wrist. In his other hand he brandished a loudhailer, and for most of the morning he'd been entertaining passers-by and the growing clutch of reporters who'd come from further afield as word of the story spread.

From her vantage point, Honey saw Patrick appear in his chef's apron, ambling down the path with a tray laden with lunch for today's activist. Soup, from what she could make out, and a plate of sandwiches. Billy laid down his loudhailer and sat down in readiness. A moment later, Christopher flew down the path behind the chef and bobbed in front of him, a human barrier between Billy and his lunch.

'No. No feeding residents off the premises please, Patrick. I'm afraid it breaches our health and safety regulations.' He waved his hand away towards the tray, his other hand holding his hair down as he leaned in and hissed for the chef's ears only. 'And you're only encouraging them.'

'I'm old.' Billy had picked up his loudhailer again, his voice suddenly thin and wavering. 'And I'm hungry. Please let me eat my lunch, sir.' He all but doffed his cap at Christopher.

174

Honey stepped out of the shop to keep an eye on proceedings.

'No can do I'm afraid, Mr Hebden. What if you were to choke on food prepared inside the home whilst you're out here? You could get the place closed down. You're more than welcome to come inside and eat in the dining room with the other residents though.' Christopher turned and smiled at the photographers.

'The place is being closed down anyway, you numpty,' Billy boomed into the loudhailer, and Patrick started to laugh.

'He's got a fair point there, Chris. Out of the way so I can put this down, eh?'

Everyone knew that Christopher hated his name being shortened. Even Honey winced.

'I absolutely refuse to permit eating on this pavement,' Christopher said, reaching out and placing a warning hand against the edge of the tray. 'Observe the law.'

'"Observe the law"? Observe my bloody front door! It's being slammed in my face!' Billy wailed. 'I'm being made homeless, I'm old and I want my soup!'

Honey wondered if Billy had ever been on the stage – he was a natural.

'It's coming, Billy,' Patrick thundered, tussling to get around Christopher who refused to take his hand off the tray. 'Let go,' the chef muttered, and Christopher shook his head quickly.

Honey watched as they seemed to tug the tray back and forth between them, each man entrenched in winning the battle.

Billy peered hopefully between them. 'Is it tomato?' he boomed, still holding the loudhailer.

Christopher clenched his teeth and yanked hard at the tray, sending the food flying, the soup landing all down the front of Billy's overalls. It was hard to say if it was deliberate or not, but either way Billy made the most of the situation, turning to the press, virtually in tears.

'It's burning,' he moaned into the loudhailer, loud and pitiful, even though it had at best been lukewarm and he could barely feel it through the boiler suit and his clothing beneath it.

Honey ran across the pavement to help but found her way blocked by Patrick, who puffed himself up to Popeye proportions and swung a left hook at Christopher's chin, sending him sprawling.

'You just assaulted an OAP!' the chef thundered, puce in the face.

'And you just assaulted your boss!' Christopher yelled back, sliding around the pavement on his backside in the sandwiches.

'Up yours! I resign, ya great streak of piss!' Patrick shouted, louder than Billy even without the aid of a loud-hailer. He unfastened his striped apron and dragged it over his head then threw it at Christopher's head before storming back into the building.

The press pack scribbled furiously and flashed their cameras, hardly able to believe their luck. This was turning into the story that just kept on giving. Honey stepped around Christopher to help Billy step out of the soup-covered overalls, revealing the slogan-painted t-shirt beneath it. 'You say old, I say experienced. Fancy dinner?'

'How do I look, darling?' he winked.

Honey grinned at how much Billy was obviously enjoying himself. 'Never better, Billy.'

He turned to smile winsomely for the cameras, and Honey stepped back into the shadows, hoping it was all going to be enough. Billy might seem clownish to the passers-by, but behind all of his showmanship was an elderly man who was genuinely frightened for his future, and that wasn't funny at all.

'We're all starving, Honey. Skinny Steve is trying his best, bless him, but he's wet behind the ears and burnt all the toast this morning. Old Don almost broke his false teeth trying to eat it.'

Honey grimaced in sympathy at Mimi and pushed a pack of shortbread towards her. Patrick's dramatic exit from the home had seen his seventeen-year-old apprentice, Skinny Steve, elevated to head chef overnight. Wet behind the ears and eight stone on a fat day, he was never going to be up to the job of caring for the delicate diets of a bunch of fussy elderly residents. It was Christopher's job to sort out a replacement, but as he'd been last seen sitting on the pavement in a pile of sandwiches the day before, it clearly wasn't on his priority list.

'What will we do at dinnertime? It's alright for me and Mimi, we're as strong as oxes,' Lucille said, her face pinched as she sipped the sweet tea Honey had made for her. 'But some of the others are really frail, Honey. If they go without food, well . . . it just doesn't bear thinking about.'

It was a problem alright, and despite her assertion Lucille

and Mimi were nowhere near as strong as oxes, despite their sprightliness.

'Okay. Look.' Honey smiled at the sisters with more confidence than she felt inside, noticing that they'd already eaten half the packet of biscuits between them. 'You ladies hold the fort here and I'll nip across and make sure Skinny Steve's on top of lunch.'

CHAPTER EIGHTEEN

Skinny Steve wasn't on top of lunch. He was in a complete flap, his usually pale face pink and sweaty.

'I can't do this,' he'd said, staring at her wild eyed as soon as she'd walked into the kitchen. 'There's hardly any butter, and the bread's still frozen!' He looked up at the clock. 'Lunch is due out in two hours. What am I going to do?'

He really was asking the wrong person, but Honey could see he was on the edge of a panic attack so held up her palms in a calming way.

'Steve. Calm down. Take some nice, deep breaths. I'm here to help.'

His skinny shoulders sagged with relief as Honey almost felt him hand over the baton of responsibility to her. His face brightened considerably as he slipped gratefully back into his apprentice role and awaited instruction. Which would have been absolutely fine, if Honey had any clue how to run the kitchen.

'So, err . . . is there a weekly plan or something we can follow?'

Steve nodded. 'Yes. It's . . .' He glanced at the huge aluminium fridge door and the smile slipped from his face. 'It's here, but this is last week's. Patrick usually changes it today.'

'Okay. Let's have a look. We can always follow it for this week too if needs be.'

Skinny Steve shook his head. 'They'll know,' he whispered, nodding towards the door to the residents' dining room as if they were a bunch of zombies from *Night of the Living Dead*.

'Skinny Steve,' Honey said, using his full title in the stern way a mother uses a child's full name when they're reprimanding them. 'At this point it'll be a miracle if there's any lunch on the tables at all. Work with me here.'

He swallowed hard and squared his bony shoulders. 'Okay.'

Honey reached for an apron off the pegs on the wall and slid it over her head. A search through the cupboards revealed several catering-sized tins of chicken soup, and there was a mountain of cheese. Chicken soup and cheese and tomato sandwiches. That wasn't so bad, surely?

'Come on. Let's get this bread defrosted in the microwave. We've got sandwiches to make.'

Honey helped Steve clear the plates from the dining room after lunch, a small glow of pride warming her belly at the fact that between them they'd managed to supply food for the hordes without incident. It may not have been gourmet, but the plates and bowls were mostly empty and the residents were mostly full, so that had to be considered a good result.

She placed the last plates down in the kitchen and dropped her backside onto a stool.

'That wasn't too bad, was it?'

Steve looked up from loading the dishwasher and said something that horrified her.

'What will we give them for dinner?'

The small glow of success popped like a pin-pricked bubble. 'I have no idea. What does the plan say?'

'Roast pork.'

Honey huffed. 'Not a chance. What else can we do?'

She opened the huge fridge and stood contemplating its contents. Ham. Lots of ham. Vegetables. Cheese. Boxes of mince beef. Steve came and stood beside her.

'I bet chef was planning cottage pie. He's defrosted mince beef.'

'Do you know how to make it?' Honey turned to him with hopeful eyes.

Skinny Steve pulled a look of intense concentration that really wasn't very attractive at all. 'There's definitely mash in it,' he said eventually. Honey sighed. She knew that much already. Opening the vegetable drawers, she saw onions. And garlic.

Onions, garlic, and minced beef. Maybe . . . just maybe . . .

'Have you ever made bolognese, Steve?' she asked.

He paused, then nodded. 'There's definitely minced beef in it.'

Honey wiped her clammy palms on her apron and reached for the beef, hoping like hell that she could remember what she was doing. She'd spotted tins of tomatoes and bags of pasta earlier in the store cupboards. With the right wind behind her, there was an outside chance that she might just be able to pull this off.

It was after eight in the evening by the time Honey pushed open the door at home and let herself into the lamplit lobby. She was exhausted, but still buzzing with elation that the residents had, on the whole, declared her spaghetti bolognese a roaring success. It might not have included pancetta and other fancy ingredients, but the basic taste had been there and this time she'd skipped the red wine and made sure to season it properly. The results had made for a more than passable dinner, enjoyable even, if the fact that Billy had eaten two and a half platefuls was anything to go by. Dessert had been even less designer; strawberry magic whip from the corner shop, but even that had seemed to charm the residents with its nod towards wartime austerity treats.

She glanced longingly towards Hal's door. He'd as good as fed those residents today.

'Hal?' she said, her voice small in the cool lobby. 'Hal?'

He didn't reply, as ever, but she told him none the less. She told him of the fracas on the pavement yesterday, and of Patrick's shock resignation from the kitchen. She told him of Skinny Steve's burnt toast breakfast, and how she'd felt obliged to step into the breach. Even in the silence, Honey could practically hear Hal thinking that it was yet further evidence that her girl guide complex was alive and kicking. She told him of her forage through the cupboards for lunch, and then she told of her bolognese success, almost laughing with relief when she added on the bit about the magic whip.

'God knows what I'll do tomorrow though. Skinny Steve

182

is taking care of breakfast while I open up, but he's relying on me going over there again by ten o'clock. I don't think they'll be as pleased with bolognese two days on the run, will they? I definitely saw chicken breasts. What the hell can I make with a huge bag of chicken breasts, Hal?'

He didn't answer. Honey had known he wouldn't. She wasn't even sure whether she'd told him about her day to impress him or annoy him. After a few minutes she trudged across the hallway to her own flat and microwaved herself a ready meal for one before she fell into bed, all in.

'Bake them.'

Honey stopped dead in the lobby the next morning, halted by the sound of Hal's voice through his door.

'Hal?'

'The chicken breasts. Lay them on trays over some tinned tomatoes and garlic, add herbs if you have any. Remember to season them. Cover with foil and cook low and slow during the afternoon. Did you get all that?'

Honey could feel her heart beating too fast.

'Lay the chicken over tinned tomatoes. Add garlic and seasoning. Cover and cook,' she repeated slowly.

'Serve with boiled rice and vegetables,' he said.

Honey walked towards his door and laid a hand on the cool wood. She turned her ear and concentrated; could just about hear him breathing.

'Thank you,' she said softly.

'Just don't kill any of them,' he said. 'It'll badly fuck with your Mother Teresa complex if one of them chokes on a chicken bone.'

CHAPTER NINETEEN

Hal listened to her leave and slid down to sit on the floor in his hallway. He'd been relieved to hear her key in the lock last night, even though he'd never acknowledge that he'd noticed she was late home from work. And then she'd stopped by his door and told him about her day, another sequence of unlikely events that made him hold his head in his hands and wonder how she, and those around her, made it through each day alive. One day the heroine on the front of the local paper. The next day dating random men because they happened to play the piano. And then somehow cooking dinner for thirty OAPs even though she could barely cook for herself. Honey seemed to get up each morning and approach life like a beautiful, haphazard firework; the distinct possibility of disaster balanced against the high probability of brightening someone's day. She'd brightened his day yesterday just by being in it, and he'd returned the favour by providing an idiot-proof way to cook the chicken. It seemed like a deal weighted heavily his way.

'Skinny Steve forgot to re-cover the chicken again after he'd checked it so it all went a bit dry, but on the whole, it wasn't too bad.'

'I'd have fired Skinny Steve on the spot,' Hal said that evening, listening once more to Honey regale him about her day. She'd come in around eight, late again, and this time when she'd come to his door he hadn't ignored her. She sounded tired, and his curiosity had got the better of him. She was cooking, and he was a chef, after all.

'You're joking. Steve's all that stands between me and starvation for the residents. He knows more than he thinks he does when he just relaxes and trusts his instincts,' Honey said. 'He needs a proper teacher, that's all. He could probably become a good chef in the right kitchen.'

Hal suspected it was encouragement and support from Honey that had given Skinny Steve a boost; he'd seen it time after time in professional kitchens. Chefs made by praise and chefs broken by criticism.

'You should trust your own instincts too, Honey,' he said. 'They're good.'

She didn't reply, no smart comeback. In fact, he couldn't be sure, but it sounded as if she might be trying to hide the fact that she was crying. He couldn't stop himself. He reached out and closed his fingers around the latch of his door, on the very edge of opening it.

'Are you crying?' he said, for want of something more tactful.

She definitely was. 'It's your fault. You said something nice to me and I'm bloody knackered and Skinny Steve almost ruined dinner.'

Hal processed the three bits of information, and then sighed and swung the door open. 'Would you like a cup of tea?'

He heard her snivel. 'Yes.'

She followed him down the hall into his kitchen.

'Should I make it?' she asked, her voice small and laced with uncertainty.

'Knob off. I can make tea. Go and sit down, I'll bring it through.'

Hal made Honey a sandwich while he waited on the kettle, taking it all through and placing it on the coffee table when it was ready.

'You didn't have to . . .' she said. At least it sounded as though she'd finished crying now.

'Just eat,' he said roughly, not especially proud of the chicken and brie salad sandwich he'd made her but glad to be able to offer something.

'You make good sandwiches,' she said after a while. 'And nice tea.'

'Feeling better now?' he asked, even though her voice already told him the answer.

'A bit. Thank you.'

'Want some whisky?'

'Best not,' she laughed, and then she stopped laughing. 'Know what I really would like, Hal?'

Danger. He could almost smell it; the hairs on the back of his neck stood up.

'Honey . . .'

186

Her hand moved to his knee, warm and firm, her fingers grazing the skin where the soft denim had split open.

'I shouldn't have asked you to come in,' he said quietly.

'And I shouldn't have come to your door when you piss me off so much, but I did, so I guess we're even. I can't stay away from you, Hal.'

'Try harder,' he frowned, distracted by the slow stroke of her thumb over his kneecap.

She took a while to speak again. 'I've been thinking about something. I have a proposition for you,' she said, her voice brave and breathless.

He swallowed hard. 'What kind of proposition?'

He heard her swallow even harder. Gather herself. 'One night, Hal. No strings. No dates. One night, show me how good sex feels for everyone else.'

Fuck, fuck, fuck. How could you make your mouth say one thing when your brain really wanted to say something else? Hal couldn't, so he said nothing at all.

'I know you don't want a relationship, and that's okay because I don't either. In fact I think we'd be bloody terrible together. I'm not asking you for romance, just sex. God knows why, but when you touch me, I feel more. More than I've ever felt with other men.' He felt her shrug, as if it was a mystery to her. 'My body likes yours, Hal.' The break in her voice cracked his resolve, reached into the nooks and crannies of him. She'd moved nearer on the sofa, and he couldn't move away because he wanted to move towards her instead. Instinct took the driving seat when she touched his jaw; he turned his mouth and kissed the softness of her palm. What kind of a man could refuse an offer like that? One no-strings-attached night with a beautiful, pliant woman? Especially a woman whose arms had slid around his neck, her lips a breath from his. He didn't stand a chance.

'Honey, we talked about this,' he murmured, trying even as her lips brushed tentatively against his.

'*You* talked about it,' she sighed, stroking his hair as she opened her mouth a little.

'It's a bad idea,' he said, even as his tongue touched hers, barely there and slow.

He heard her low sigh, felt her body lean into his.

'You said,' she whispered, as he moved his arms around her and held her to him. She fit him all too well, her curves melding into his chest. 'But this feels too good to be a bad idea.' Her breathing quickened in his mouth as she sank her teeth into his top lip, licking along it. 'Just kissing you is better than sex with anyone else.'

'Honey,' he breathed, not sure if he was going to say something to stop her or just needed to say her name.

'Name the night, Hal, and I'm yours. Tomorrow. Tonight. Right now. Show me. Please?' She spoke around his kisses, her lips soft and open for him, her tongue sliding over his between her words. Oh, he wanted so much to say yes, to press her backwards on the sofa and slide her out of her clothes. He could practically feel her naked beneath him, and she was right. He could make her body need his so badly that she'd shiver with it, that she'd have no choice but to come for him. She'd be transcend-fucking-ent, and it'd feel amazing, to be the man who gave her what no other man had ever given her. It was heady; intoxicating.

'We can't keep doing this, Honey,' he managed, holding

her face in his hands. 'Because however much I want to say yes, and you have no fucking idea how much I want to say yes, the truth is that you're lying to yourself. It wouldn't be one night.'

'It would,' she pressed. 'Hal, one night. No lies, no promises, no relationship. We don't even like each other.'

Her words said one thing, and her tone of voice something else.

'You're not that kind of girl, Honey.'

'I could be. With you.'

'Liar.'

She thumped his leg out of frustration, then grabbed his hand and slammed it flat over her heart. 'Can you feel my heart banging? You must be able to, because I feel as if I'm going to have a bloody heart attack here. I haven't just plucked this out of the air you know. I've been thinking about this ever since the other night.' She gulped and carried on. 'Hal, if you don't do this one thing for me, I'll go out there and find someone else who will and it'll all be your fault. I'm not even joking. My entire life is up in the air at the moment, and more than half of that is on you. You've woken my body up, and it won't go back to sleep again until someone sings it a goddamn lullaby!' Her voice rose in both volume and octave as she made her impassioned speech, the queen of her own debating society. 'I want that person to be you, more than anything I want it to be you, but I swear to God, Hal, if not you then it'll be someone else, and soon.'

She stopped speaking, finally, and Hal found his hands had moved to grip her shaking shoulders.

'Don't do this,' he said. 'You don't mean it.' Even as he

said it he thought that actually, she sounded as if she meant every word.

'Oh, I do,' she said hotly. 'I've had a bloody epiphany these last few weeks. Pianists. Campaigns. And you, Hal, you shouting and swearing and kissing me like no one else ever has. Is it so bad that I want you?'

Hal was rarely speechless, but this was one of those times. She was actually serious. Strawberry Girl, his beautiful, crazy neighbour wanted him – or to be precise, she wanted him to teach her how to orgasm.

'You know how crazy this sounds, right?' he said, scrubbing his hand over his stubble after a few moments of contemplation.

'Yes,' she said. He could hear how much depended on what he said next, so he chose his words with care.

'Let me think about it, okay? Just promise me you won't go out there dragging strangers in off the street when you leave here.'

She sniffed. 'You're not making this easy on me.'

He was tempted. Of course he was. He missed sex, the intimacy of a warm body against his, the mindless release. She'd woken his body from its slumber too, but unlike Honey it made him want to run a mile away rather than tumble into bed. If he gave her what she wanted, he'd be giving himself a fast pass to a place he didn't want to go. A place he'd closed the door on, a door he'd had to brace his back against and fling the bolts across to keep it in place. Opening it was a monumental mistake, but saying no to Honey felt like a mistake too. He was caught between a rock and a hard place, or in this case a door and a soft, seductive, strawberry-scented place. He'd come here counting on the hope of making peace with himself, of saving his sanity, of forgetting, of learning to be the man he needed to be. He just hadn't counted on Honey.

Standing up, he held out his hand and pulled her to her feet. Leading her to his front door, he walked her across the lobby to her own threshold.

'There. I walked you home. No strange men tonight, okay?'

Her hand still warmed his; she didn't let go. He felt her body rub against his as she rose on her tip-toes, and tasted the subtle longing in the brush of her mouth against his.

'You told me that every date should end with a goodnight kiss.'

'That wasn't a date.'

'You made me dinner.'

'You see? Back there you said no dates. No complications. I told you you couldn't do it.'

'I can so. I'm a woman of the world,' she said, and he felt her small smile against his lips. Hal had known many worldly women in his life, and Honey wasn't one of them. He'd even loved one of those worldly women, and she was one of the many reasons he'd needed to slam that door so tight. Could he open the door just enough to let Honey in as a temporary guest without being crushed by the stuff that would try to force its way out of there? The weight of rejection, the heartache, the crush of having it pushed down his throat that he was no longer man enough to be a husband or a father? He was broken. Broken eyes, broken heart.

He pressed his lips against her forehead. 'Go to bed, Honey.'

She nodded, a tiny movement. 'You promise you'll think about what I've said?'

He mirrored her actions, the same small nod. 'Bed.'

It was only as he closed his door that he put his hand down and discovered his dark glasses lying on the hall table. They were his armour, yet he hadn't given one single thought to them all evening.

CHAPTER TWENTY

'Do you think you could come with me?' Lucille whispered the next morning, twisting her string of bright blue glass beads around her fingers and looking beseechingly at Honey. Glancing towards Mimi, who was chatting to a customer across the shop floor, Honey struggled for an answer that didn't compromise her neutral position between the two sisters. It was bad enough that she knew of Lucille's clandestine meeting with her brother at all, let alone tagging along as well.

'Lucille, don't you think it would be better if you told Mimi? If you wait until afterwards it's going to be ten times harder to tell her. She might even want to come with you.'

'She wouldn't. She won't even talk about him with me. I've tried, Honeysuckle, but it's up to her. She can't stop me from meeting him.' Lucille fired a nervous glance towards her sister, who was now engrossed in teaching a nervous-looking student how to tie a Windsor knot for an upcoming job interview.

'I know that. I just think you're setting yourself up for an argument by keeping secrets.'

'I'll tell her as soon as I've been,' Lucille promised. 'I just want to meet my brother. How can that be wrong?'

It wasn't wrong, and Honey could completely understand why Lucille felt she needed to do this, with or without her sister's approval. The letter from the adoption agency had opened the lid on a can of worms that couldn't just be closed again without action, and in some ways it reminded Honey of the proposition she'd put to Hal last night. Lucille was asking for help because she needed answers, and in her own way that was what Honey needed too. It was all becoming quite exhausting. Maybe if she helped Lucille, and Hal helped her, they could all move on and get back to business as usual.

'You absolutely promise you'll tell Mimi as soon as we get back?'

Lucille beamed. 'I promise. Thank you, Honey, you're a poppet.'

Glancing across at Mimi, Honey didn't feel like a poppet. She felt compromised, and she tried not to wonder if she'd made Hal feel the same way last night.

Later that afternoon Honey glanced around the busy shopping street, trying to pick Nell out in the crowd. She'd received a strange text earlier, an SOS of sorts. Emergency. Meet me by that sex store on the High Street at 4pm. Tell you later. Nell. xx

Honey had to double-check the sender; she wouldn't have batted an eyelid if it had been from Tash, but from Nell it seemed entirely out of character.

194

'There you are.' Nell appeared at her side, neat and efficient in her teacher's attire. 'Thanks a million, Honey, I didn't fancy going in on my own, I might see someone I know. This way I can say I'm with you.'

Honey rolled her eyes. 'Thanks a lot. I have a reputation too you know.'

'Not with the school gate mafia you don't. Trust me, one whiff of scandal and I'll be in the head's office.' Honey glanced at the St Trinian's-clad model in the sex shop window behind Nell and tried not to laugh.

'What are we here for anyway?'

'It's my turn,' Nell said, leaning in.

'Your turn to what?'

'To buy something new,' Nell tilted her head towards the store. 'From in here. For our . . . collection.'

'Ohh. I see.' Honey wasn't certain she wanted in on helping Nell choose their next sex toy, but . . . 'Come on then. Let's go in. Do you think we're going to need to go behind the curtain?'

Nell's eyes flickered around as they went inside, already viewing the shelves with a more practised eye than the last time she'd been in there. 'Possibly.'

They trailed amongst the lingerie, pale lace to hot pink nylon, something for every taste. Honey paused by a pale peach wisp of a bra with matching silk knickers, beautiful and sexy without being too much. Would Hal like her in that? It was all too easy to imagine his pleasure as his fingers discovered the slender velvet bra straps, the silk-encased bones, the cobwebbed soft lace. Her fingers had found her size even as she ran through the scenario in her head, and she carried the set in her hands as she followed Nell behind the curtain into the strictly adult zone.

'Any idea what you're looking for?' Honey said, and Nell shook her head, perplexed.

'None.'

Honey's eyes slid over the packed shelves. 'You should probably have asked Tash to meet you rather than me. She'd have known what to suggest in a heartbeat.'

Nell laughed. 'I guess. But then she'd also have made me buy something that probably isn't even legal.'

Honey browsed the shelves and picked up a black silk blindfold thoughtfully, her mind already miles away from Nell's bedroom conundrum. Running the silk through her fingers, she could almost feel Hal's fingers tying the strip of silk behind her head, putting them temporarily closer to a level playing field. She looked down as Nell plucked it from her fingers with a grin.

'You're a lifesaver, Honey. Perfect.'

Honey watched Nell walk towards the tills, and after a moment's hesitation she hurriedly grabbed a second blindfold and followed her friend.

Hal hadn't answered his door when Honey tapped it after work that evening, but as she was heading to bed just after eleven there was movement in the hallway and then a knock on her door.

'Don't open it,' Hal said. 'Just listen.'

Honey stood perfectly still behind her closed door, her hand flat against it.

'I've thought about what you asked me,' he said, the rumble of his voice low and rich and sure.

196

'And . . .' Honey said, biting her top lip and crossing the fingers of her other hand behind her back without realising. 'What did you decide?'

He paused. 'Did you mean it when you said you'll go out and find someone else to do it if I won't?'

'It wasn't intended as a bribe, Hal,' Honey sighed, laying her forehead on the wood.

'No dates. No relationship. One night, and then we never mention this again.'

Honey's hand covered her mouth in shock as she reached for the catch on the door.

'I told you not to open the fucking door,' Hal warned, stilling her fingers. She wanted to see him very much at that moment, but she sensed that it was more important to him that she didn't.

'Okay,' she said, dropping her hand away from the catch. 'Hal . . . when?'

He was quiet again. And then, 'I'll come over again on Friday.'

She swallowed hard. Friday was three nights away. 'Friday it is then,' she said, so quiet that almost no sound came out.

'It's not a date,' he reminded her.

'Roger that,' Honey said, rendered stupid by nerves.

An amused silence, then: 'Try not to throw yourself at passing strangers between now and Friday.'

Honey could hear traces of dry humour in his voice. ''Kay.'

He went to move away, and she called out: 'Hal . . . shall I buy nibbles?'

He was silent for far longer than she knew what to do with.

'No nibbles, Honeysuckle. No funny stuff. Buy whisky if you feel the need to shop. This is how this thing will go down. I come over here. We do it. I go home again. Are you crystal clear on how this is going to go?'

'Crystal,' she said, wondering what the hell had possessed her to suggest nibbles. She'd never used the word nibbles in her life.

'I'm going now,' he said. 'Do me a favour. Don't say another word.'

Honey screwed her eyes shut and nodded.

He really needed to go home, and she really needed to shut up.

CHAPTER TWENTY-ONE

'This is it, I think?' Honey looked up at the large, well-kept terraced house with steps leading up to the shiny green door. The kind of house that estate agents might describe as a *gentleman's residence*, with neat tubs of flowers in the vestibule.

'It looks nice, doesn't it?' Lucille said, holding on to Honey's arm as she looked up at the gleaming windows of the house. 'Should we go and knock?'

Honey squeezed Lucille's hand and smiled. 'Well we didn't come all this way just to admire Ernie's hanging baskets, did we?'

'They are very nice though,' Lucille said. 'I wonder if he did them himself? I'm hopeless with plants, but Mimi is wonderful. She looks after all those flowers in the window boxes at home, you know. Green fingered, as they say.'

Honey recognised Lucille's words for what they were; an early attempt to draw parallels between her beloved sister and her brand new brother, to find common ground between them to help her to win over Mimi when they spoke later. It had been Honey's only condition, and she was in no doubt that Lucille would honour it.

'Come on,' Honey said, steering Lucille gently along the pavement. 'He's probably ten times more nervous, you know. You have Mimi, and all of your memories of your parents. He's on his own in all of this.'

Lucille nodded and braced her shoulders. 'Let's go and say hello to my brother.'

They didn't have to wait long for the door to open. A few seconds after Lucille rang the bell, a dark-haired, efficient woman opened the shiny green door.

'You must be Lucille,' she said, putting Honey and Lucille at ease with a smile. 'I'm Carol, Ernie's assistant. Please, come inside.'

The interior of the house was just as well kept as the exterior, bright and fresh; well-polished floor tiles, gleaming woodwork, the scent of polish, and fresh flowers on the coffee table in the sunny lounge Carol ushered them into.

'Ernie will be through in a minute or two. Can I get you some tea while you wait? Coffee?'

Lucille nodded and Honey shook her head, and Carol smiled widely. 'Ernie's been a bit like that today, too. Can't make his mind up on anything.' She leaned towards Lucille. 'I don't think he slept a wink last night, his covers had hardly moved when I made his bed up this morning.'

'Told you,' Honey whispered, when they were alone. 'He's as nervous as you are.'

'Is my lipstick crooked?'

Honey could just about feel Lucille's slight frame shaking

on the sofa beside her. She'd asked about the condition of her lipstick twice that morning already.

'Your lipstick looks perfect, your hair looks fabulous, and that dress is wonderful on you. Lucille, will you please just relax?'

They both looked up at the quiet hum of a motor in the hallway, and a couple of seconds later a wheelchair appeared in the wide doorway. Ernie. Honey hadn't really anticipated what he might look like, but it wasn't just green fingers that Ernie shared with his eldest sister. The shock of seeing someone so like Mimi in male form took her breath. She heard Lucille gasp beside her, and passed her a tissue to stem the tears already on the older woman's cheeks.

'Mimi should be here,' Lucille murmured, getting to her feet because Ernie couldn't. He pressed a button and moved his chair forward to the middle of the room, and Honey watched with a lump in her throat as Lucille bent and embraced her brother for the first time in their lives.

'So many years,' Ernest said, his voice strong even if his body wasn't. 'I've wanted to meet you my whole life, Lucille.'

'I never knew,' Lucille whispered, her shaky voice full of emotion. She pulled back, scrutinising his face. 'You're the image of our sister, Mimi.' Lucille glanced across at Honey. 'Isn't he, Honey?'

Ernie looked towards the sofa, and Honey smiled and nodded. 'You are. It's uncanny.'

'Sorry Ernie, where are my manners!' Lucille said. 'This is Honeysuckle.'

'Your . . . granddaughter?' Ernie said, looking hopeful.

'No. As good as, mind,' Lucille said, and the lump in Honey's throat threatened to spill over into full-blown tears.

She'd come along today as a support for Lucille. She hadn't anticipated finding it so emotional herself. Hauling herself to her feet, she touched Lucille lightly on the shoulder.

'Why don't I leave you guys to it for a while? I'll go and grab a cuppa and come back later.'

Lucille nodded, still holding on to Ernie's hand. 'I think I'd like that. We've a lot to catch up on, haven't we Ernie?'

Honey let herself out of the front door and found Carol sitting in the sunshine on the front steps. She looked up at the sound of the door opening.

'I thought I'd leave them to it for a while,' Honey said, nodding back towards the doorway.

'Lots to talk about, I expect,' Carol said, lighting up a cigarette and then holding the box up towards Honey, who shook her head.

'Thanks, though. Mind if I sit for five?'

Carol tucked the cigarette box into the pocket of her navy tabard and waved her arm. 'Take a pew.'

Honey dropped down onto the steps and the other woman switched her cigarette into the hand furthest from Honey.

'Sorry. Bad habit. Menthol though, not that they're much better. Ernie's been nagging me to give them up for years.'

'You've worked here for a while then?'

Carol nodded. 'I've been with Ernie for over twenty years. He's more like family to me than my own lot.'

Honey traced her finger along a crack in the step, feeling rather like they were sizing each other up as much as Lucille and Ernie were inside, representatives and supporters from the blue and the red corner. She well understood the concept of friends feeling more like family; Lucille and Mimi had been surrogate aunts for several years.

'It's a shame his other sister couldn't make it today,' Carol said mildly.

Honey tried to find neutral words. 'It was a shock for both of them, Ernie's letter. Mimi will come around. She's . . .' Honey paused thoughtfully. 'She's strong willed, that's all. I think she's troubled by the whole idea of her mother having had a child before she was born, coming out of the blue like that.'

Carol bent and put the cigarette out in an ashtray concealed behind a low wall. This was clearly her favoured smoking spot.

'I can see that. Ernie's known about his sisters for the last forty years. I guess he's had longer to adjust.'

Honey frowned, perplexed. 'Can I ask why he never got in touch before now?'

Carol turned her head to look at Honey. 'Oh he did. He wrote to his mother. To their mother,' she corrected herself.

'Really? But . . .'

'She wrote back by return post and told him not to contact her again. That she'd put everything to rest years ago and she couldn't bear to rake it all back up again.'

'Wow. That's just so sad,' Honey said, floored. She knew that Lucille and Mimi would be equally as shocked. They sat in the sunshine for a moment, each digesting the information that was new to them.

'Has Ernie always been disabled?' Honey asked, trying to slot the pieces of Ernie's story into Lucille and Mimi's.

Carol shook her head. 'Injured in the war. He was about twenty-three I think, been in a chair ever since.'

'And he never married, or had any kids?' Honey asked, wary of sounding as if she were prying but fascinated to hear Ernie's story.

'No one. He barely leaves the house. It's a crying shame. He's lived here all of his life, his ivory tower against the outside world ever since the war. He came home, closed the door, and that was pretty much that.' Honey shook her head. Ernie seemed such a kind, gentle soul, it wasn't fair or right that he'd cloistered himself away. She found herself holding back tears all of a sudden. The parallels between Ernie and Hal were there in plain sight. All those years Ernie had spent alone couldn't be rewound, but she was damned if she was going to allow Hal to resign himself to the same reclusive fate.

'His adoptive parents were nice enough from what I can gather, but he doesn't have any other family left to speak of,' Carol said. 'I'm the only person he sees, besides his physio nurse who comes in most afternoons.' A dark cloud passed over her features. 'His health isn't what it used to be.'

Poor Ernie, he seemed to have been dealt a bad hand of cards all round. Honey found herself feeling very glad that he'd been brave enough to write to Lucille and Mimi, and wishing that Mimi had been able to find it in herself to come and see him. Hopefully she'd be in a different mind about it after Lucille spoke to her about today.

'So why get in touch again?' she asked. 'Why now, after all these years?'

Carol looked at the floor with a heavy sigh. 'Like I said. His health isn't great, and he's not going to get any better. He's a lonely man.' The shadow that crossed Carol's face told Honey that there was more to be said on the subject. It was clear that Carol was immensely fond of Ernie in the same way she herself was of Lucille and Mimi; she couldn't bear the thought of either of them being unwell. So she didn't pry, and her quiet reflection gave Carol time to speak at her own pace.

'He's put all of his affairs in order over the last month or so. He thinks I haven't noticed, but of course I have. If I'm honest, I didn't think it was a good idea for him to write to his sisters. The last thing he needed was another disappointment.'

Honey had already wished that Mimi had been there several times that day, and she wished it again now.

'Ernie has never said a bad word about his mother. Do you know anything about her?'

Honey cast her mind back through scattered conversations with Mimi and Lucille over the week since Ernie's letter had arrived and stirred up long-undisturbed memories. 'She was a singer, from what I can gather. They haven't exactly said anything untoward about her, but I get the impression she was hungry for fame and didn't make it.'

'Charming,' Carol huffed softly. 'Too ambitious to want her first-born.'

'I honestly don't know many more details, except she would have been young and unmarried. I suppose a baby out of wedlock would have been a scandal back then, and would have definitely killed her chances as a singer.' Honey smiled sadly. 'They didn't have things like *The X Factor* back in those days.'

Carol grimaced. 'Probably a good thing.'

The two women sat companionably in the sunshine,

probably both wondering how things were going inside the house.

'I'll try my best to get Mimi to come soon,' Honey said.

Carol nodded, her eyes cast to the ground. 'Do me a favour. Make it as soon as you can?'

Nodding, Honey glanced away. She would. For both the men she now knew in self-made seclusion, she would.

CHAPTER TWENTY-TWO

Friday morning rolled in grey and cool, but Honey woke up early and in a hot sweat.

It was today. Or tonight. Friday. No-date night with Hal. In an attempt to play it down in her head, she hadn't told a soul. Not Tash, nor Nell, nor Lucille and Mimi, a choice she regretted as she threw up her breakfast five minutes after eating it. Her nerves were off the scale. Tash would have been the perfect person to help her dial it back down with her jokey good humour, but Honey knew that she'd be somewhere thirty thousand feet up at that moment and in no position to offer comfort. Nell . . . Nell was probably being politely boffed over her muesli, so no joy there either, and it wasn't a conversation she should have with Lucille and Mimi. That left no one. No one except the one person who was aware of the arrangement. Hal. But what was she supposed to do? Knock on his door, and then what? Ask him if he was still on for casual sex later? She pulled a 'you idiot' face at her reflection as she tied her hair back in the hall mirror, shook herself into her mac, and left the flat.

Across the lobby Hal heard Honey's door open and close, and listened for her footsteps. He was able to discern whether she was heading over to his or towards the front door, and today she paused just outside her own door. Was she deciding which way to go? Had she bottled it? Should he? He had grave misgivings about the whole situation. His body was undeniably turned on by the fact that Honey wanted him, and his head was certain that it was a mistake of monu-fucking-mental proportions. His hand touched the cool lock on his door, ready to open it and cancel. He stood still, bated breath. If she walked his way, he'd open it, call it off because that was no doubt why she'd be coming over. If she went out of the front door, he'd . . . and then the front door banged, and she left for work, robbing him of the luxury of choice. She hadn't cancelled, and neither had he.

Hal greeted the pleasurable emotion that surged around his body like an old friend. Adrenalin in his veins. The feeling he'd lived for before the accident, the one where you're right on the edge of doing something incredibly stupid and have to screw up insane amounts of courage to throw yourself off the ledge.

Except sometimes you didn't have the safe landing you'd banked on. Sometimes it really was incredibly stupid. Sometimes it could wreck your life. Hal's problem was that he honestly didn't know which way this one was going to play out.

He heard her come in as he'd heard her go out hours

before, from the front door to her own flat without devia-
tion towards his door.

He could do this. There was a way to give her what she
wanted without taking what he did. She probably wouldn't
like it, but this was his gig, his terms.

He reached for the whisky bottle.

Honey had spent her day in a swan-like state; serene on the
surface, frantic on the inside where no one else could see.
Her heartbeat was erratic, pounding too fast every time she
thought about the night ahead. Her brain wouldn't function
when it came to shop-related matters, and she was hugely
relieved by the arrival of an agency chef to help Skinny Steve
because her brain wanted to think about Hal and their non-
date all day. What should she wear? Where would they do
it? She'd changed her sheets before work that morning to fill
the time between throwing up her breakfast and leaving the
house. Maybe the sofa would be a better idea; they might
be able to slide naturally from conversation into sex. 'How
was your day, dear? Fine. Fancy a shag?'

In the end she'd decided that it would be best to just
stop trying to plan it and let Hal take the lead. She was
after all, the pupil, and he the teacher. By the time there
was a knock on her front door just before eight o'clock
that evening, she was mildly hysterical and badly in need
of a fortifying drink.

'Shit,' Honey whispered, struck silent and statue still by
the sound of the knock. 'Shit!' Her heart seemed to bang
around behind her ribs almost as loudly as Hal had banged
on the door. He was here. He hadn't forgotten, or backed
out. He was outside her door and she needed to let him in.

'Coming!' she called out skittishly, and then cleared her throat and put her hand over her mouth to hold in the horrible urge to gaily add, 'or else I hope I will be,' as she opened the door.

'Honeysuckle,' he said, and just the sound of her full name on his lips was enough for her to want to gasp, *do me*. Hal looked the same but subtly different, an ever-so-slightly less grungy version of himself. It was probably the fact that he was wearing a shirt rather than a t-shirt with his jeans, a shirt that followed close against his body and was as inky dark as the hair he'd made an attempt to tame.

'Shall I come in, or would you like to do it in the lobby?' he asked, and Honey belatedly realised she had yet to invite him in.

'Sorry . . . sorry. Come through.'

In the lounge, Hal took a seat on the sofa, and Honey prevaricated between the other end of the sofa and the chair. The chair won.

'Unless you expect me to make you orgasm from three feet away using just the power of thought, you're going to need to come closer.'

Honey laughed nervously. 'Ha. Yes. Would you, umm, would you like a drink first?'

'I already had one, but you go ahead. You sound as if you need it.'

'Do I?' she said, knowing full well that she did. 'I'm fine, really. Totally fine. Cool as a cucumber.' She moved from the chair to balance on the other end of the sofa. 'See? I'm right here, being cool and calm.'

After a minute's awkward silence she jumped up again and shot across to the kitchen. 'I might just get that drink.'

In the kitchen, she banged her forehead three times against the fridge door, called herself an obscene name, and returned with two big glasses of red.

'I bought wine,' she said, putting the glasses down on the table. 'Shiraz. Australian.'

'There aren't nibbles too, are there?' Hal said, low and dry as a bone.

'No nibbles.' She sat down alongside him, not quite touching and wishing she'd put the TV on before he came over because it was so quiet and it looked rude to put it on now, as if he were boring her.

He took a sip of his wine, and she took a gulp of hers.

'So. How was your day?' she asked, feeling ridiculous.

He put his glass down slowly. 'Really?' he said, incredulous. 'You want to do this that way? Shall we talk about the weather next?'

'It's just conversation, Hal,' she shot back.

'I haven't come here to talk. Let's go to the bedroom.'

Whoa. 'Easy, caveman. You'll be flinging me over your shoulder next,' she said, and when he said nothing, she stood up and muttered, 'I'll bring the wine through.'

Hal made his way to the edge of the bed and sat down on the edge like someone in a bed showroom. Honey watched him, unnerved by his big, dark, brooding presence in her light, Scandinavian-style bedroom.

Placing the glasses down on the bedside table, she eyed Hal nervously.

'What are you wearing?' Hal asked.

Honey's eyes opened wide in surprise. He'd gone from caveman to sex line operator in a flash. How to respond?

'Oh, erm . . . well, my dress is black with a zipper all

the way down the back, easy access,' she all but purred, and screwed her eyes tight with embarrassment. 'And . . . my underwear is new. I chose it for you. It feels . . .'

'Just take everything off and lie on the bed on your back.'

Honey picked up her wine glass and threw the entire contents down her throat, then sat down on the other side of the bed. The last man to say anything like that to her had been her doctor.

'Hal. I'm going to lie down here with all of my clothes on, and I'd like it if you lay beside me. You're going too fast for me, okay?'

It was something she hadn't anticipated that she'd need to say. Previous encounters with Hal had been sexy and slow and had melted her bones, but this just wasn't working yet.

She lay back on her pillows, and he did the same alongside her.

'Happy now?' he said, his face angled towards the ceiling.

'Not especially,' she muttered. 'Is this what it feels like when you've been married for years, do you think?'

'It really would help if you got rid of your clothes,' Hal said.

When she'd dressed that evening, she'd subconsciously opted for things that were tactile, things she hoped Hal would enjoy peeling off her later.

'I umm . . . I brought a blindfold. I wondered if you'd like me to wear it?' Honey heard her own upward inflection, like an Aussie waitress asking if he'd like an extra shot in his espresso.

'Not especially. Strip off.'

We'll, he'd missed the point of that entirely.

'Do you think you could possibly kiss me first?'

Hal paused. 'I wasn't planning on kissing.'

'What?'

'This isn't a date, remember?'

'Yeah, and I'm not a prostitute either,' she said. 'Just bloody kiss me. I am one hundred per cent certain I won't orgasm without being kissed first.'

Hal sighed, then rolled towards her until his body half covered hers and pressed her down into the mattress. Lowering his head, he kissed her too lightly, lingering for just a couple of agonisingly good seconds.

'There. Now are you going to strip, or does this dress ruck up enough to get your knickers off?'

'For God's sake, Hal!' Honey huffed. 'This isn't what I expected from you!'

'No? What did you expect, Honey?'

'I don't know,' she said, flustered. 'A bit of romance, maybe? I know it's not an actual date, but can't you pretend it is?'

'You want me to lie to you?'

'Yes Hal. I want you to lie to me,' she said, surprising herself. 'Tell me you've been thinking about this all day. Take my dress off and tell me how sexy I feel to you. Tell me I turn you on. You don't have to mean it, and we won't mention it again once we're outside of this bedroom, but right here and right now, lie to me.'

Hal dropped his head and kissed her again, this time hot and open mouthed. Sliding the heat and weight of his body over hers, he held her face in his hands and took the kiss as deep as it could go, and Honey wrapped her arms around his back and dragged his shirt up to get at the warmth of his skin.

'You know you turn me on, Honeysuckle,' he breathed, his mouth hot against her ear as she arched into him. His fingers found her zipper and slid it all the way down, and he shifted just enough to slide her dress away from her body.

'And you feel like a goddamn fucking goddess,' he said, kissing her again, slower, tracing his fingertips from the dip between her collarbones to her navel.

Was he lying? It didn't feel like it in the heat of the moment. His body told her that he was telling the truth, hard against her softness.

'Hal,' she said, her fingers picking at the buttons on his shirt. He stilled, and then covered her hand with his own.

'Not me,' he whispered. 'Just you.'

Honey opened her eyes. 'What?'

'We're not going to have sex tonight, Honey,' he said quietly, massaging her hip. 'This is all about you.'

'But, I want you to have tonight too,' she said, realising that she meant it. Tonight had been as much about pleasuring Hal as it had been about being pleasured herself. It had to be a two-way street.

He shook his head, trailing his lips over her jaw. 'Shh. Relax.'

'I can't,' she said, pent up with longing to take his shirt off.

Smoothing his hand down the length of her body, Hal let his fingers come to rest over the silk of her knickers, and then slid under the material to cup her.

'Yes, you can,' he said, his hand warm and still and heavy. 'It's just you and me. Open your legs.'

'I don't think I can do this,' Honey said, feeling her body

214

tense even as his fingers started a slow massage. Hal smooched the sensitive skin beneath her ear.

'Let me touch you the way you want to be touched, Honey,' he whispered, covering her mouth with his as his fingers began to move. To explore. To stroke. 'Let me do this for you, baby,' he said, opening her slickness with his fingers, taking her small gasps into his mouth, breathing encouragements and endearments back into hers.

For a second Honey stopped thinking about sex, or about pleasing him, because the things he was doing to her took away every last thought and replaced them with sensation. This was good. So very, very good, and it made her want all he could give her.

'Change your mind, Hal,' she murmured. 'Take your clothes off and stay with me tonight. I can feel how much you want to.'

He stopped what he was doing.

'Do you want me to do this for you or not?' he said, changing down the gears from raw Hal to in-control Hal again.

'I don't think I can do it unless you're naked,' she said. 'And don't tell me you don't want to because, er, hello?' she skimmed her hand over his swollen crotch.

'You asked for this,' he said. 'You asked me to come here and make you orgasm. We were well on the way for a minute back there, and then this. What is it with you? You get something, you always want more. *Lie to me, Hal. Tell me you're turned on, Hal.*'

'Were you lying?' she asked, hoping he hadn't been.

He drew in an exasperated breath and extracted his hand from her knickers. 'A man tells you you're beautiful when he has his hand down your pants. Go with it. He probably means it.'

'So you were lying, or you weren't? Which is it?' It suddenly felt important to know, because if he'd been faking it he was world class.

'Honey. Can you just stop this? I'll say this one more time, because we seem to have a communication failure. Take off your underwear and spread your legs, and I'll crawl between them and give you what you want. I'll lie to you. I'll make it so good for you that you won't remember your own name, let alone mine. But you need to be really clear on this. We are not going to fuck. Not tonight, not tomorrow, not ever.'

And with that, any hope of saving the situation left the building. Honey reached for her dressing gown on the bottom of the bed and pulled it tightly around her body.

'Was it something I said?' Hal muttered, reaching for his wine and knocking it back.

'Just go, Hal. I don't know why I thought it would be any different with you than with other men.' She stood up. 'My mistake.'

He threw his hands up in the air. 'Have it your own way.'

'I will. With someone else.'

'Good luck with that,' he said, sauntering down her hallway and opening the front door.

'I won't kiss you goodnight,' he said.

'I wouldn't let you,' she shot back.

'Goodnight, Honeysuckle,' he said, as he opened his own door. 'Sweet dreams, baby.'

CHAPTER TWENTY-THREE

Honey didn't have sweet dreams. Instead, she finished the wine and tossed and turned all night in a temper, while across the hallway Hal drank himself into a whisky-induced stupor on the sofa.

Headaches, lazy mornings and bad moods were the order of the weekend on both sides of the lobby, and Honey wasn't impressed to find herself out of milk for a much-needed coffee.

'I'm going to the shops,' she yelled as she closed her door, her cross-body bag slung over her denim jacket, and her hair dragged back. 'And I don't care if you need anything, because I'm not your bloody servant!'

'Try not to bring any random men home with you,' he shouted back.

'I will if I bloody well want to,' she shouted back. 'I'm sure they'd all be a damn sight more considerate than you are in bed.'

'We haven't been to bed, and we're not going to,' he said.

'You're not wrong there, buster,' she yelled, opening the door. 'You had your chance to spend the night with me and you blew it, big time.'

It wasn't the best time to find herself eyeball to eyeball with the postman. He lifted his eyebrows at her appraisingly, handed her the morning's mail and walked away down the pavement sounding suspiciously as if he was laughing under his breath. Honey glanced through the letters; bills, pizza menus and junk mail. She threw them all on the table in the hall, including the brown envelope addressed in stark black handwriting to Mr Benedict Hallam. Up to then he hadn't received so much as one piece of mail, leading Honey to conclude that he'd redirected everything on purpose.

She cursed him loudly a few times for good measure and then slammed out of the house hard enough to rattle the windows.

Monday morning, and there had been no further communication, across the lobby or otherwise, between Honey and Hal. Neither of them had enjoyed their weekends much. Honey just didn't get the man at all. Why had he agreed to sleep with her and then treated her the way he did on Friday night? Was it just too good an opportunity to yank her chain? Even after two days removed from the situation it was hard to see it as much else.

For his part, Hal brooded in silence, mad at himself for the way he'd made such a monumental botch of the situation. He'd been so concentrated on not letting it cross the line into romance that he'd turned it into borderline assault. Was this it for him now? A lifetime of misread situations and mistakes? He knew exactly where he'd gone wrong – he should never have agreed to it in the first place.

'Would you come outside and cuff me, dear?' Mimi asked Honey an hour or so later. It was her turn to be chained to the railings that day, and she was all decked out in her slogan t-shirt and hot pink leggings in readiness. She'd tied a pink polka dot headscarf in a jaunty bow on top of her dark curls, and looked for all the world like the star of an OAP production of *Grease*. Honey grinned at the thought. She'd pay good money to go and watch that on the stage. Mimi would definitely be Frenchy to Lucille's Sandy, and Billy's snake hips would make him a shoe-in for one of the T-Birds.

Honey shot a look towards Lucille, stacking glasses over on the far side of the shop. Had she mentioned her visit to Ernie yet, she wondered? The cordial atmosphere suggested not.

'Of course. You ready now?' she said, picking up Mimi's fluffy red cuffs from the counter.

Mimi nodded. 'Although I'm starving. That chef the agency sent over is awful. He gave us biscuits for breakfast this morning,' she grumbled. 'We oldies need our All-Bran or there's hell to pay.'

Honey grimaced. 'How did he do over the weekend?'

'Terrible. I can't even talk about it,' Mimi shuddered. 'Even your cooking was better than his.'

Honey swung between being insulted and proud. She went with proud; there was little point in being insulted by the truth. She followed Mimi out, calling back to Lucille that she'd be five minutes.

Lucille looked up sharply. 'Honey, dear,' she called out as Mimi left the shop. Honey turned back, and Lucille zipped her lips together with her thumb and forefinger then shrugged apologetically.

Honey shook her head. 'This can't go on, Lucille,' she hissed, as Lucille walked towards her and shooed her out the door.

Outside, Honey found not only Mimi but Billy too, along with two women in their forties who she didn't recognise.

'Honey, fetch some more of those frivolous little hand-cuffs, my darling,' Billy called, slinging his arms around the shoulders of the two identical-looking women. 'We've got company today. Michelle and Lisa here have come to help the cause.'

The women nodded in unison, and Honey found herself distracted by their uncanny likeness to both each other, and to Susan Boyle. 'My auntie Titania lives here,' one of them said. 'She's my auntie too,' the other said, rather redundantly adding 'we're sisters,' for clarification. 'Twins,' the other said, and they both nodded solemnly. Honey slipped back into the shop for more cuffs and then dutifully chained all four of the protesters to the railings.

Billy had opted for red skinny jeans and a t-shirt that declared 'Old boys do it better!' and when the twins removed their Pac-a-Macs they revealed matching white t-shirts hand-painted with 'We Love You Auntie Tit!' across the front. It was unfortunate – or fortunate, depending on how you wanted to look at it – that both women were extremely well endowed, because their ample cleavages had eaten several words from the slogan, leaving them proudly announcing

'We Love Tit!' across their busts. They smiled serenely, and Billy nodded and threw a theatrical wink towards the press, who'd gathered as on most days in the hope of action.

'Quite right too, ladies. Don't we all!'

Light bulbs flashed, and Honey knew that thanks to the sisters' t-shirts, the campaign would once again be flashed across the front of the papers. It had made the local TV news for the first time last week too, which had sent Billy into a Brylcreemed spin of excitement. Surely it must be having some effect up at head office by now? They might say that no press is bad press, but surely being made to look heartless was bad PR for a company who made their money on retirement homes?

'I think it's amazing what they're all doing here,' a passer-by said, pausing next to her on the footpath while the press took their shots. Honey smiled at the woman with the buggy laden down with two young children and shopping.

'Thank you. It means so much to everyone to stay here,' Honey said. She was fast becoming accustomed to her role as public spokesperson. 'I just can't imagine what would happen to them all if the home closes.'

'If I didn't have these pair with me I'd have joined in.' The woman grinned and gestured to the kids, and then smiled and went on her way. Honey stood and looked down the length of the railings, her mind whirring with ideas. How many people could they fit along there, she wondered? The railings wrapped around the street corner and carried on, so actually, quite a few. Thirty? Forty? More? As she turned to head back to the shop she met an anxious-looking Skinny Steve coming in the other direction laden down with warm tea for the protesters.

'You're doing a great job, Steve,' she said, patting his shoulder as she walked by.

'Don't go!' he whispered loudly to her retreating back, and she stopped and turned slowly, unnerved by the desperate edge to his already thin voice.

'You okay?' she asked, carefully.

He shook his head, wide eyed. 'The agency chef is going crazy in there, Honey. He won't listen to a word I say.'

Honey frowned. 'I heard there might be a few problems.'

Steve huffed and picked nervously at a spot on his chin. 'Problems? Even I know better than to give this lot a prawn vindaloo.' Steve spoke urgently, as if it were a relief to get it off his chest. 'The staff have been going crazy because everyone wants the loo all the time. Old Don shat on Elsie's slippers this morning because they couldn't get him there quick enough.' He shook his head and pulled a face that indicated he'd probably witnessed the incident. 'It's bad, Honey. Really bad.' He shook his head.

'He's in there right now making a chilli hot enough to take the skin off the roof of your mouth. I know, because he made me try it.' Steve swallowed painfully. 'I don't think he likes old people very much. In fact . . .' He looked at Honey fearfully, as if she were a police officer taking his statement. 'I think he might be trying to kill them all with spicy food.'

Honey almost laughed, but held it in because actually, it wasn't at all funny. It was highly unlikely that the agency had sent them a chef who harboured homicidal tendencies towards the elderly, but this was clearly a problem that was too big for Skinny Steve's skinny shoulders. There was little to no point in suggesting he take the matter up with

Christopher; in fact there was every chance Christopher had handpicked the worst chef he could find himself.

'I'll nip over there and have a word with him when I get a chance, Steve,' she said, smiling encouragingly. 'In the meantime, just try to steer lunch in the right direction, okay?'

Steve nodded, a vigorous duck of his head that almost spilt the tea on his tray.

Thirty thousand feet above ground level, Tash was also serving tea, and as the plane hit a pocket of turbulence it sloshed from the pot onto the lap of the passenger closest to her.

'I'm terribly sorry, sir,' she said, putting the pot down quickly and grabbing a cloth. Dabbing at the guy's paperwork, she noticed it was sheet music rather than the usual reports or graphs passengers studied in transatlantic business class.

He put out a hand and stopped her, and when she looked him in the eyes she found him smiling. 'Hey, it's fine,' he said, his accent placing him as American. 'It wasn't very good anyway. You've just saved me a job.'

'You write music?' Tash asked, always ready to take the time to chat to passengers, especially ones with sexy blue eyes and an easy smile.

'I try, anyhow,' he nodded ruefully. 'I'm a pianist.'

CHAPTER TWENTY-FOUR

Honey left it until after lunch to go over and look in on the new chef. Pushing the kitchen door open tentatively, she could hear shouting and clattering from within. Inside, the new chef had his back towards the door and held a frying pan held aloft, waving it around in the air as he yelled at Skinny Steve. Honey was sure he didn't intend for it to look threatening, but nonetheless it did rather look as if she'd walked in thirty seconds before Skinny Steve took one for the team.

'Whoa there,' she said lightly, clearing her throat, and then 'Er, hello?' a little louder when the chef failed to even register her presence. He spun around, frying pan still in the air.

'What?' he spat in heavily accented English, his dark moustache bristling with contempt. Judging from his appearance, Honey hazarded a guess at Spanish, or possibly Mexican. He wasn't a tall man. An unkind person would have even called him short, but what he lacked in height he made up for in volume. 'What do you want, woman!' he shouted, and Honey watched the pan carefully in case it came down on her head as she approached him slowly.

'Do you think you could, umm, put that pan down?' she tried, summoning scant hostage negotiation skills gleaned from the movies.

The chef looked slowly up the length of his arm and stared at the pan as if he was as surprised as anyone to see it there.

'You means this pan?'

Honey nodded and smiled the small, quivering smile of the mildly terrified.

Chef's eyes moved from the pan to Honey, and then across to Steve, which was the point when he started to growl.

'Ooohkay,' Honey said, and catching Skinny Steve's eye she flicked her head towards the back door that led to the garden. He didn't need telling twice. Like the worst hero in the world, he made a dash for freedom and left Honey to dodge around the chef and slam the door to stop him from chasing Steve.

'Whaddya do that for!' he shouted, and slammed the pan down hard on the counter. Honey jumped, but stayed splayed over the door like a police cut-out.

'You were frightening him,' she said.

'What is he? A man or a mouse?' The chef's chin wobbled. 'He tell me all morning, *don't do this, don't do that. They won't like this, they won't like that.*' He picked up a whole chilli from the work surface. '*And they definitely won'ta like these!*'

He bit the chilli in half and ate it without turning a hair.

'My mama in Mexico has these for breakfast and she is one hundred and three.' He shoved the rest of the chilli in and swallowed. 'These people,' he waved vaguely towards the dining room in disgust. 'Bland. I just try to spice up their lives, and that boy . . .' he looked murderously through the window for Steve. 'He won't let me. Who is in charge here? Him, or me? My chilli con carne won three red peppers in the Chihuahua Chilli Awards 2010. Three peppers!' He picked up three more chillies, and quite alarmingly shoved them all in his mouth at once. Honey stared, transfixed, as he stood with his hands on his hips and chewed them all up with difficulty.

'Would you like a glass of water?' she whispered, as tears ran down his cheeks.

He spat out a chilli seed. 'I not cry because of the chillies. The chillies are delicious. I cry because my soul is crushed. Crushed by these people who look as if they are made of paper and will only eat bland, bland food.' He'd gone from angry to maudlin in a blink, impressive for someone stone cold sober. 'I cry because I miss my mama. These people remind me I should go home and kiss her wrinkly cheeks again.' He mopped his tears with the corner of his apron, which he then took off and slung on the stool. 'I will go now,' he declared. 'This minute. I will go and see my mama.'

'But . . .'

He held up both his hands to stop her speaking. 'My mama. I will go now.'

'In Chihuahua?' Honey said doubtfully, and he glared at her with a curt nod.

'But what about dinner?'

'I made chilli.' He waved towards the bubbling vat on the stove. 'Skin and bones knows what to do with it.'

Honey could only presume he was referring to Skinny Steve, and furthermore she guessed that the only thing that chilli was going to be useful for was stripping paint. She watched helplessly as the diminutive chef slung a bag across his back and flounced out of the kitchen, flounced back and grabbed his bunch of chillies, and then flounced back out again, this time for good.

'We can't serve it like this,' Honey said, having braved a tiny taste of the chilli on the end of a teaspoon. Prickles of sweat had broken out on her brow and she'd reached instantly for water. 'Do you have any idea how to calm it down?'

Steve shook his head, his brows knitted together into a unibrow. After a full minute's thought, he finally spoke.

'No.'

Honey took a calming breath and tried to summon her inner Nigella. 'Water, maybe?'

Steve shook his head. 'Don't think so. It'd turn into soup.'

He was most probably right, but he'd also given Honey another idea. 'Soup? Do we have any tomato soup? That might work.'

Steve considered her suggestion, and then turned to rummage in the wall cupboards. Lining up four huge tins of soup on the counter, he turned back to Honey.

'It's worth a shot,' he said. 'Shall I put them all in?'

Honey nodded. Even her complete absence of cooking knowledge didn't stop her from knowing that the chilli needed as much dilution as they could throw at it. She nodded encouragement at Skinny Steve as he tipped each can in and stirred the pot.

'Now test it,' she said.

'Why me?'

'Because you're the chef,' Honey exclaimed.

'I don't like chilli,' Steve muttered, looking doubtful.

Honey sighed and picked up a spoon. 'Move out the way.'

The consistency had certainly changed; it was way too gloopy and vivid red, horribly like road kill you'd avert your eyes from on a country lane. She wouldn't want it for her own dinner, and she felt sorry for the residents come mealtime tonight. Dipping the spoon in, she gingerly put a little into her mouth.

Laying the spoon down slowly, she shook her head.

'It really hasn't helped much,' she croaked, reaching once more for the tap.

'What are we going to do?' Skinny Steve whispered, looking stricken. 'It's almost two. If I don't have something on the table at half five they're going to lynch us.'

Honey briefly considered mentioning that she wasn't, in point of fact, kitchen staff, and running for the hills, but she'd seen Skinny Steve sprint just now and had no doubt he'd tackle her and bring her down before she made it as far as the door. Besides, he was desperate, and she wasn't hard-hearted enough to desert him in his hour of need. Which kind of left them both with a monumental problem. They had to serve dinner for around thirty people in just over three hours and didn't have a clue between them how to do it.

'Do you think the agency could send a replacement in time?' Steve asked.

Honey really doubted it. She crossed the room and swung the fridge door open, feeling a sinking sense of déjà vu about the whole situation. The last time she'd done this she'd managed to pull off a coup, but that wasn't likely to happen twice in one lifetime. The chiller offered up very little in the way of inspiration, definitely nothing that looked like it might save their bacon. Although there was actual bacon . . .

'Do they eat bacon and sausages?' she asked.

Steve screwed up his nose. 'Some of them. Bacon gets stuck in their false teeth. Or they don't have any teeth.' He shrugged apologetically.

'And sausages?'

He looked more hopeful. 'Yeah. We could do sausages.'

'With . . .' Honey tried to coax him into creating a dish. He was the more experienced cook of them both, he did this every day.

'. . . Mash!' Skinny Steve practically shouted, lighting up like a just-plugged-in Christmas tree. 'Bangers and mash!'

Honey grinned, relieved at yet another disaster averted. 'Now you're talking. Get some potatoes, there's peeling to be done. You do peel potatoes for mash, right?'

You know that warm glow of pride you get when you do something really well and everyone tells you you're a marvel? It wasn't quite that good, but by Honey and Steve's standards the sausage and mash feast followed by their trademark magic whip pudding was a roaring triumph. It was only as they were gathering in the dishes afterwards that Steve checked the kitchen calendar and went a sickly shade of green.

'Oh no,' he muttered, making Honey look up from stacking the plates.

'What is it?'

'It's Old Don's birthday tomorrow. There's a party at three o'clock.'

'A party?' Honey repeated, her tired brain hurting with the effort of more frantic thinking. 'As in a party that needs party food? Like sandwiches, and sausage rolls and things?'

'And a birthday cake,' Steve mouthed, the look of a hunted deer back in his eyes.

'Can you bake?' Honey asked, already knowing the answer before he shook his head. She was no Mary Berry either, despite having watched every series of *The Great British Bake Off*. She freely admitted to having taken more notice of Paul Hollywood's baby blues than the technicalities of baking, an oversight she now bitterly regretted.

'Shit.' She dropped onto the nearest stool. 'We're sunk.'

Steve looked like a defeated featherweight boxer, all slumped shoulders and downturned, dejected lips.

'I've had enough of all this,' he mumbled. 'I'm sorry, Honey. I know this is bad of me, but I quit. I can't do this.'

'What? No!' Honey stood up and grabbed the lapels of the tracksuit top he'd just dragged up his arms. 'Steve, you can't do that to me! Or to them.' She jerked her head towards the dining room. 'Please, we'll sort something out. I'll buy a cake from the supermarket. We'll get another chef in soon, I promise.'

'Honey, we need one here first thing in the morning, and

it's not gonna happen.' He shrugged. 'They pay me minimum wage for this. It's too much shit for too little pay.'

Honey's mind raced, and then she made a rash and desperate offer. 'What if I promise you that there will be a chef here tomorrow? Someone to take over and teach you again, like Patrick did?'

Fragile hope lit his teenage grey eyes, making Honey feel like the Child Catcher trying to lure him to stay with lollipops.

'You promise?' he said.

She nodded, closing her eyes briefly and hoping like hell that she'd be able to come good.

'I promise. Just be here on time in the morning, okay?'

Skinny Steve shot her a small smile and left her alone in the kitchen looking longingly at the cooking sherry.

Hal heard Honey come in later that afternoon and listened to her footsteps as she stopped outside his door.

'Hal,' she called out. The fact that she called out at all surprised him, and her non-confrontational tone of voice surprised him even more. He'd seriously started to doubt that she'd ever decide that she wasn't furious with him any longer.

'Hal!'

She called his name again. It was hard to judge her mood; she sounded stressed, kind of worked up.

'What is it?' he said, trying for middle of the road, conversational.

'I need to talk to you,' she said.

There was something in the words she didn't say that told him more than the words she did. He sensed her weariness, and that she didn't really want to be at his door about to say whatever it was she was going to.

'I'm listening,' he said.

It sounded as if she was pacing outside his door.

'I need your help,' she said.

He really hoped that it wasn't the same favour she'd asked for the week before.

'Honey, I don't think we should go there again,' he said, trying to be gentle.

'Get over yourself,' she huffed. 'This is about work.'

'Work?' he said, genuinely perplexed. 'Your work?'

She was moving again, and then he heard her come to rest outside his door and slide down the wall. She really did sound all in.

'Yeah,' she sighed. 'You know I told you about Patrick, the chef who hit the boss and then resigned? Well his replacement turned out to be incapable of cooking anything that didn't include at least eight million chillies; the residents were in danger of internal combustion. Anyway, I tried to talk to him about it and he threw a wobbler and stropped off back to Mexico on an afternoon flight.'

'Wow. He really didn't like you,' Hal said, impressed.

'I didn't like him much either. Anyway, that left me and Skinny Steve scrabbling to make dinner, which actually wasn't so bad.' She paused for breath. 'Sausage and mash, seeing as you asked.'

'I didn't ask.'

'I'm pretending you did, I like to kid myself that you're a nice person. Anyway, it wasn't terrible, but oh my God, Hal, I can't keep this up! You know how bad I am in the kitchen and Steve has the imagination of a goldfish on a bad day. I think I'll have a sodding heart attack if I have to do this for much longer, poor Lucille and Mimi are having to hold the fort at the shop and it's too much to ask of them at their age. And then, to top it all, it's Old Don's birthday tomorrow and we have to throw him a bloody party. His family is coming and everything. I need a cake! How do I make a cake?' She sounded terrified. 'And what else can we feed them? Steve's threatening to walk out and I don't blame him, and I kind of promised him that I'd make sure there was a proper chef there in the morning to supervise him, and Hal, the only chef I know in the world is you.'

She gasped in a strangled breath, and he sank to the floor on the other side of the door with his head in his hands. He'd sensed where the conversation was leading and he already knew he couldn't do it. It was unfair of her to ask it of him.

'I can't, Honey. I just can't.'

'Hal, please,' she rushed in again, words tumbling out of her mouth too fast. 'I know it's short notice and you don't much like leaving the house, but I'll get you there and back safely, you'd literally have to just sit in the kitchen and tell Steve what to do. I know I said that he's got no imagination but he's really good at following instructions, honestly, he is.'

The pang of desperation in her voice sliced through him. He had to make a choice between his own fears and hers, and however big hers were, his won.

'I can tell you what you need to do, Honey,' he said, trying to compromise. 'I can give you lists, and instructions. I can do all of that. Go grab paper and a pen now if you like. I'll wait.'

'You don't understand,' she said quickly. 'I don't need

lists, Hal, I need you. If I walk in there without a chef tomorrow none of those old people are going to get breakfast. Nor lunch, or dinner! And Old Don won't get a party and he's a sodding war veteran!'

Her voice grew high pitched and thick with frustrated tears. 'Even the protesters won't get fed!'

He wanted to help her more than he could even put into words. She made it sound so easy, as if he'd be churlish to refuse. It probably seemed easy to her; she didn't view the world the way he'd been forced to since the accident. She couldn't possibly, and he didn't have the words to make her understand, so instead he used ones that were tactless and deliberately unkind to make sure she knew that he absolutely meant it.

'It's not my fucking problem, Honeysuckle. I'm not your go-to man to fix all your problems. Last week, sexual frustration. This week, you want my professional skills. What's it going to be next week? Just don't come to me if you ever need a spider catching, because I'm not the man you fucking need.'

He expected vitriol, and he got silence, and then she said just one quiet word, which turned out to be much, much worse.

'Coward.'

Moments, and then minutes, and then he heard her haul herself up off the floor. He felt her dejection, and he heard her door close, and he loathed himself more than ever. Of all the things he'd never been, it was a coward.

Not my fucking problem, he'd said.

I'm not the man you fucking need, he'd said.

Honey lay in bed that night and cried big fat tears. Tears because she was tired. Tears because there was so much responsibility on her shoulders that she didn't know how much longer she could stay standing upright. And tears because of all the things that had upset her lately, Hal's words tonight had hurt her most of all.

CHAPTER TWENTY-FIVE

Honey's phone buzzed, waking her up too early the next morning, which was a bummer given that she'd barely slept. Squinting at the phone, she read Tash's message.

Piano man number 3 identified. You cannot say no. He is to die for and you're meeting him for lunch on Saturday at the pub.

Honey groaned and closed her eyes again. Tash was just going to have to cancel the date, because the piano man project was dead in the water. If Honey never had another date again, it'd still be too soon to re-address the subject of romance.

She really didn't want to get out of bed, because it signalled the start of another long day of trying to juggle more balls than a Covent Garden street performer and she'd never been the best at catch. Concentrating on her breathing in the fetal position worked for a couple of minutes; it soothed her body, if not her mind. Her mind refused to be soothed. Too many thoughts about whether salmon sandwiches posed a choking hazard to octogenarians and whether the Smartie-covered caterpillar cake she'd noticed in the supermarket last week would cut the mustard. Not that one would be anywhere near big enough; she'd need at least six or more. Was there a collective name for a group of caterpillars? A hive of caterpillars? A clutch of caterpillars? All these thoughts and more chased each other wildly around inside Honey's skull until she crawled, caterpillar-like, out of bed and under the shower.

'I'm not a coward.'

Hal's stark words reached Honey as she closed the door to her flat a little later. She paused.

'I'm sorry if my choice of words offended you,' she said, even though she kind of was and kind of wasn't. On the one hand she could see that by allowing himself to hide away Hal was taking the easy option, but then on the other hand, he was probably the bravest man she'd ever met.

She heard the mechanism of his lock move, and a second later his door swung slowly open. Hal stood there, looking exactly the same as ever, except for one thing. He was wearing a coat.

'Hal, oh my God!' Honey moved swiftly to his door and instinctively reached up and kissed his cheek.

'How do you know I'm not just going for a morning stroll?' he said, making light of the decision he'd wrestled with all night.

'I doubt you've ever strolled in your life,' Honey said, and then faltered. 'So how do we do this?'

'Do what?' he said.

'Do you have a cane?'

Hal made a sound that sounded horribly huffish. 'No, I do not.'

'Don't you need one?'

'So they say.'

Honey could only agree with them, whoever *they* were. She scanned the hallway for potential pitfalls and her eyes alighted on the umbrella stand, and more specifically her Orla Kiely full-length brolly, a gift from Nell for Christmas the year before. Making a grab for it, she pushed it into Hal's hands.

'Use this?'

He ran his hands along it, feeling the curve of the handle. 'Is it raining?'

Honey knew that he knew perfectly well that it wasn't raining. 'I was only trying to help.'

'By giving me an umbrella that is too short and no doubt hideously garish in order to draw attention to the fact I can't see a fucking thing?'

Honey rammed the brolly back into the stand. 'It's very tasteful, actually. Nell gave it to me and she doesn't have a tasteless bone in her body.'

'If you really want to help, just stand next to me once we're outside. Hold my arm casually as if we actually like each other and tell me if there are steps or kerbs. Can you do that?'

'I'm not an idiot, Hal,' she said, but lightly, because she really didn't want him to change his mind.

'You do idiotic things quite often,' he said, pulling his door closed. Honey didn't miss the way his chest rose and fell heavily beneath his navy woollen pea coat.

'I've never seen you in a coat before,' she said, to keep the conversation going. 'It's quite, er, sexy fisherman.'

238

'"Sexy fisherman"?' Hal sounded incredulous.

Honey opened the front door. 'Two steps down to the pavement, quite shallow,' she said, stepping down ahead of Hal. 'Yes, you know. Captain Birdseye and all that.' She held his elbow lightly and scanned the quiet, early morning street. 'We're walking left down towards the bus stop, there's no one else around.'

'Just don't ask me to run for the bus,' he said. 'Captain fucking Birdseye?'

Honey realised what she'd said wrong, too late as usual. 'Crap. Sorry.'

'I'm more offended by the fact that he was a fat man in his sixties than by his name.'

Honey heard the thread of humour and the louder thread of tension in Hal's voice. She sensed that the best thing she could do for him right now was keep up the inane chatter. If there was one thing Honey was good at, it was inane chat. A half smile touched her lips as they stood together at the bus stop wrapped up in warm coats, making catering plans for Old Don's birthday party. He was coming to help her. He was really coming.

'Skinny Steve, meet Hal. He's a chef.'

Honey had installed Hal on a stool in the kitchen, and practically floated two inches off the floor with pride when Steve arrived for work half an hour later.

Skinny Steve almost genuflected.

'You did it,' he whispered. 'I didn't think you would, but you did.'

For a brief moment Honey understood how it felt to be Santa Claus. 'I promised, didn't I?'

Steve nodded and stuck his hand out towards Hal.

Honey shook her head emphatically and Steve lowered his unshaken hand again uncertainly.

'Hi Steve,' Hal said. 'Honey tells me you're the sous chef around here.'

Steve frowned. 'Why'd you tell him I can cook soup?' he shot at Honey out the side of his mouth.

Honey coughed. 'Would you excuse us for just one second please, Hal?' she said, and yanked Steve into the dining room.

'Skinny Steve,' she said, and sucked in a deep breath. 'That man in there is one of the country's top chefs. He had an accident and he can't see anymore, but he's here to help, so don't blow it, okay?'

'You still shouldn't have said I can cook soup, Honey,' Steve frowned. 'What if he tells me to do it today?'

'He didn't say soup,' she hissed. 'He said *sous*. It's French, Steve, for . . . for super chef,' she lied. 'Yes. I told him you're a super chef and he's really looking forward to teaching you, so get your act together and just do as he tells you, okay?'

She pushed him back into the kitchen with both hands and offered up a silent prayer.

Alarm bells went off in Honey's head when she glanced up from pricing a stack of shirts to see Nell and Tash advancing towards her across the shop floor. One or the other of them during the working day was a welcome sight, but both of them together usually meant trouble.

'Hey you guys,' she smiled. 'Lunch break ambush?'

'I'd prefer to think of it as a friendly pep talk,' Nell said,

240

as smoothly as only a teacher used to fractious parents knew how to be.

Tash pulled her phone out of her huge handbag and pushed her sunglasses up on top of her head. Clicking through it quickly, she twisted the screen towards Honey, who looked at it and then glanced away again quickly.

'Ew. Is that Yusef?'

'Nope.' Tash shook her head and grinned. 'It's your lunch date for Saturday. I told you he was hot.'

'So hot he needed to take off all his clothes?'

'What?' Tash frowned and whipped the phone back, then grinned, thoroughly unabashed.

'Ha! Sorry, Hon. No, that's Yusef. What a horse, eh?'

She clicked through a couple of shots and turned the phone around again.

'Christian.'

Honey looked down again into a profile shot of an admittedly good-looking guy, this time thankfully fully dressed.

'Couldn't get a better shot without him noticing,' Tash said. 'See what I mean now? He's even better in the flesh. All blue eyes and yes ma'am, no ma'am. Honestly, it was like talking to Elvis without the rhinestones.'

'Tash, it isn't that I'm not grateful, but I just have so much going on right now, you know?'

Nell glanced at Tash with I told-you-so eyes. 'It's only lunch,' she said. 'One little lunch. Everyone needs to eat, Honeysuckle.'

'Not with random men who sound like Elvis, they don't,' Honey said.

Tash's green eyes flashed with determination. 'What

241

would you be doing otherwise? Mooning after your Emo neighbour?'

'No,' Honey scowled, not willing to elaborate on how badly wrong things had turned out with Hal on that front. 'Meeting you two in the café, probably.'

'I'm busy on Saturday,' Nell said quickly. 'Me too,' Tash smirked, and they both looked at her expectantly.

She was saved from having to say anything more by the wail of a siren outside.

CHAPTER TWENTY-SIX

All three women spilled out onto the grass outside the shop, along with a rag-tag line of shoppers trailing behind them. Billy brought up the rear wearing a frilly pinny, having sportingly offered to fix a leaking tap in the staffroom.

'Oh my God! What's happened?' Honey set off at a sprint at the sight of the ambulance with its flashing blue lights pulled up beside today's protesters, Lucille and Mimi, along with at least six people Honey didn't recognise. A strange thing had started to happen since Titania's twin nieces and their provocative t-shirts had been splashed across the local news; people from all over town were coming to help, three, four or five different strangers every day to boost the protest numbers. It was turning into a story that people were following with interest, and the press were more than happy to oblige.

'Give us some room please,' the paramedic called out, shouldering his way across the pavement to where Mimi sat on a stool someone had fetched for her from inside the home. Still chained to the railings by one wrist, she huffed and puffed about being the centre of attention for all the wrong reasons.

'All this fuss over nothing. It's just a sprained ankle,' she grumbled.

Honey was torn between relief that it wasn't something more major and concern for Mimi, because even a sprain could be nasty and Mimi was no spring chicken.

Honey rubbed Mimi's shoulder affectionately. 'Let them take a look at it, hopefully it's fine. What happened?'

Mimi glowered and pursed her lips. 'Did you know Lucille had been to see Ernie?'

'Oh,' Honey said. 'Well, yes. It wasn't my place to say anything, Mimi, I'm sorry. She's told you, then.'

'Just now. She waits until I'm chained to the fence and then blurts it out, just like that.'

'Right . . . and how did that end up with your ankle being sprained?'

Mimi sighed and looked into the distance. 'I might have lunged for her arm. I'd have reached her too, if it wasn't for this.' She rattled the fluffy handcuff viciously.

'Where's Lucille now?' Honey scanned the pavement as the paramedic rotated Mimi's ankle, making her wince and slap his shoulder.

'Hiding from me, if she's got any sense,' Mimi muttered darkly. 'We'd agreed not to see him. Why did she do it, Honey?'

Still rubbing Mimi's shoulder, Honey sighed and tried to choose her words carefully. 'It wasn't something she did lightly, Mimi. I don't think she could help herself.'

Mimi shook her head. 'She's got me. She doesn't need him.'

Honey wanted to hug and shake Mimi all at the same time. 'There really isn't any need to make her choose, Mimi. You know Lucille loves you, and nothing will ever change that. Not husbands, or friends,' Honey glanced at Billy, who'd thrown off his frilly apron and had hunkered down on Mimi's other side, 'nor brothers. But he's so like you, Mimi. It took my breath away.'

A tear rolled down Mimi's cheek, and the paramedic looked up, concerned.

'Is that painful?' he asked, pressing carefully in case he made her cry more. Mimi shook her head and dashed away the tear.

'Okay, I think you've slightly sprained it,' the paramedic said, placing Mimi's ankle to the floor. 'Try to go easy on it over the next couple of days, and remember to elevate it when you're resting. Use an ice pack if it's painful, and your usual preferred painkiller if it's playing up, okay?' He looked at Mimi with kind eyes. 'I think it'd be for the best if you unchained yourself and took a couple of days off.'

Honey expected Mimi to refuse, but the older woman just nodded instead and fished a key out of the pocket of her cardigan, looking thoroughly dejected.

'Let me help you,' Honey said, unnerved by Mimi's capitulation. Passing the shop keys to Billy she unfastened Mimi's cuffs gently, massaging her wrist as she helped her to stand. Over the years, Honey had never needed to acknowledge the age difference in her friendship with Lucille and Mimi. Not so today. Mimi leaned heavily on her arm as they made their way slowly back up the path towards the home, oblivious to the cameras flashing behind them, or to Christopher appearing on the pavement to deliver an oily speech about cancelling the protest on health and safety grounds.

'Well that's that, then,' Mimi said, resigned, so quietly Honey barely heard her. 'I'll go to my room please, Honey. I'm tired, and I need to lie down.'

Honey clicked Mimi's door closed and headed instinctively for the kitchen. Her life suddenly felt as if it was bursting all of its dams; Tash and Nell trying to railroad her into yet more dating disasters, Mimi and Lucille at each other's throats, the campaign to save the home in peril, and now Hal in the kitchen with Skinny Steve. Passing through the dining room, she came to a sudden halt and stared around her. It looked different, and it smelled delicious, as if she'd walked into a restaurant from the street.

The clock on the wall told her it was a little after two, and the array of food laid out told her that there was going to be a party soon. She could have cried with relief at the sight of tables pushed together under the window to form a buffet bar, neat white cloths covering the joins. The dining room door swung open from the kitchen and Lucille appeared, laden down with a covered platter of cheese and onion rolls.

'Old Don's favourite,' she smiled weakly as she made room for them on the table. 'How's Mimi?'

'She's not too bad. The paramedic said it's a mild sprain. I've just left her resting in her room.'

Lucille shook her head. 'I should never have told her like that when she was chained up. I just thought it might be easier.'

'Maybe you should go and have a chat now everything's

quietened down. It looks as if everything's under control here.'

Lucille smiled, properly this time. 'That man in there is marvellous,' she sighed like a teenager, her hand fluttering near the neck of her spring green floral dress. 'So charismatic.'

Another victim of the Benedict Hallam peculiar school of charm. 'Go and see Mimi.'

As Lucille left through one door, Skinny Steve appeared from the kitchen with a large, ornate cake, and a heavy one too if the way his slight frame swaying with effort was anything to go by.

His face broke into a wide grin when he spotted her standing in the middle of the room. Depositing the cake quickly on the side table laid out in preparation for it, he opened his mouth and let out a silent yell and waved his hands around in excitement. If this were charades, Honey would have guessed at 'Man overcome with excitement at meeting Bono'. And then she realised. It was 'Man overcome with excitement at meeting Benedict Hallam'. Victim number two. Hal's hit rate was impressive.

Steve jerked his thumb towards the kitchen.

'He's proper famous,' he mouthed. 'And he's taught me how to make sausage rolls.'

Steve pointed at the evidence, a plate of golden gorgeousness on the table.

'Looks like that isn't all he's taught you,' Honey said, her gaze travelling over the plates of sandwiches and niceties on the table.

'Where did the cake come from?'

Steve shrugged. 'I don't know,' he stage-whispered, as

shiny eyed as a five-year-old who'd just got his first bike for Christmas. 'Hal made some calls and a van arrived with it ten minutes later. He's, like, amazing.' His expression turned suddenly serious. 'But listen, Honey. You can't tell anyone he's here, okay? He's undercover.' Steve's brow furrowed. 'Do you think he might be making one of those programmes for the TV where the boss pretends to be somebody else?'

Loving Steve's enthusiasm but doubting his sanity, Honey smiled. 'I don't think so, no, but his secret's safe with me. Is he through there?'

Steve nodded furtively, and then ambled out of the dining room in the direction of the loo, leaving Honey looking at the door leading to the kitchen.

'It's beyond weird seeing you here,' she said from the doorway, looking at Hal perched at the work surface, eating a bowl of soup.

'It's beyond weird being here,' he said, seemingly unsurprised to hear her voice. 'There's soup in the pan if you haven't had lunch.'

Honey ladled out a bowl of the creamy soup, sniffing the steam.

'It's just leek and potato. Steve made it.'

'Skinny Steve made this?'

'Went down a storm at lunchtime.'

'I'm not surprised. I don't think they've eaten soup that didn't come out of a tin in the last five years.'

Honey grabbed a spoon and sat down along from Hal at the counter.

'You met Lucille, then,' she said, blowing on her spoon before eating it. 'Jesus, this is gorgeous!'

248

She didn't miss the pride that slid over Hal's features before he shut it down. 'It's just soup.'

'Yeah, and Brad Pitt is just a man. Not all men are born equal.'

Hal mulled on that. 'Just eat it.'

Honey was more than happy to do as she was told, and took the chance to properly observe Hal outside of his comfort zone for the first time since she'd met him. He hadn't strayed far from the stool, but all the same he looked more at home than he had when she'd left him this morning.

'Yeah, I met Lucille,' Hal said. 'Classy lady. She speaks highly of you.'

'She speaks highly of everyone,' Honey smiled, warmed by Hal's admiration of Lucille. 'Thank you for sorting out Old Don's party too. Where did you get that cake?'

Hal shrugged. 'I know people.'

It was no doubt one hell of an understatement, but she knew enough not to expect further elaboration.

'There's enough food and soup for everyone to have dinner tonight,' he said. 'And we've worked out the menu for the next few days.' He stopped and pushed his bowl away. 'Steve asked if I'll come back tomorrow.'

Honey's spoon stilled halfway to her mouth. 'And will you?'

Hal ran a hand over his stubble. 'I'll think about it.'

Gathering both of their bowls and sliding them into the dishwasher, she turned to leave.

'I better get back. Billy's holding the fort, he'll probably be giving the stock away in exchange for kisses.'

Hal rewarded her with a half smile, one of those that did odd things to her synapses.

'Sounds like a fair deal to me,' he said softly. 'Don't forget me at home time, Honeysuckle.'

'I'll try not to,' she said, swinging out of the kitchen. Forget him. As if.

Billy was waiting for her when she got back to the shop and, contrary to her concerns, he'd made a magnificent job of holding the fort.

'We need to talk about the campaign, Honey,' he said as he placed a china cup and saucer of tea down in front of her ten minutes later. 'I'm afraid Mimi and Lucille's fisticuffs has rather put us in a tricky spot.'

Honey couldn't help but smile at Billy's choice of phrase, but she knew he was right. Christopher must be rubbing his hands together over at the home; they'd played right into his hands by fighting amongst themselves.

'Who called the ambulance?' she said.

Billy glanced out of the window. 'The finger has to point towards the establishment,' he said, anarchic, looking down his nose towards the home.

Honey didn't doubt it. 'What did he say in his speech?'

'He mentioned the words *regrettable* and *senile* a few times, and then I threw my shoe at him.'

'Did you really?'

'I most certainly did, darling.' Billy waved his red suede, thick crepe-soled shoe in the air. 'I think he has a suggestion of a black eye.'

Honey sipped her tea thoughtfully.

'Billy, do you think you could watch the shop for a little longer this afternoon? There's someone I need to catch up with.'

'Is it that rather dashing chef in the kitchen, young lady?' Billy wiggled his eyebrows at her suggestively. 'Very enigmatic, with those dark glasses.'

'He's blind, Billy.'

It was a rare thing for Billy to look surprised, and even rarer for him to be serious. Nevertheless, he pulled off both emotions simultaneously at Honey's revelation.

'Well I never, I missed that. My brother was blinded as a boy,' he said, his gaze distant. 'Can't have been more than fourteen. Nasty business.'

'Is he still alive?' Honey spoke without thinking. Billy had never mentioned a brother.

'Died about ten years back. If you think I'm trouble, you should have met our Len. Or Leonard, as my mother would have preferred.' Billy's face broke into a wide grin. 'Leonard and William. Billy and Len. He was always getting me into bother.' Billy's eyes sparkled with nostalgic wickedness. 'Quite the ladies' man, he was, too.'

'Unlike you,' Honey laughed. 'But no, I'm not off to see the chef.' She glanced up at the clock. Three o'clock. 'I'll be back in half an hour so you can go over to Old Don's party.'

'Good girl,' he said, rubbing his hands together. 'You know me, never one to miss a good knees-up.'

CHAPTER TWENTY-SEVEN

It was well after seven by the time Honey and Hal sat beside each other on the bus home.

'I haven't caught a bus since I was sixteen,' he'd said when they'd boarded the bus that morning, and he looked no less outlandish and uncomfortable on the return journey.

'Of course you haven't.'

She completely believed him. People on the bus mostly blended in. Not Hal. Even aiming hard for anonymity he seemed to stand out, or maybe she was just hyper-aware of him. She was just glad it was after the rush hour and the bus was relatively quiet.

'Can you drive?' he asked.

'Technically, yes,' she said, 'although I haven't really driven much since I passed my test.'

Hal turned his face towards the window while he considered her words. Before the accident, driving had been one of his pleasures. Cars. Motorbikes. The faster the better.

Honey's easy-come, easy-go attitude to being able to slide behind the wheel any time she liked filled him with hot fury out of nowhere.

'You'd really rather ride the fucking bus? You prefer to be rubbed up against by rancid teenagers and avoid making eye contact with the local nutter than be in a car, be in control of everything yourself?'

The need to feel the power of an engine under his hands again took his breath away, along with his ability to be tactful. He tried to shut it down, to tune it out, but it wouldn't let go. He could feel it throbbing inside him like an angry animal's heartbeat. He missed it so, so much; it was visceral. Who he was, who he'd been right down to his bones. Benedict Hallam. Adrenalin junkie. It was one of the reasons he'd shut his life down to four walls since the accident, because being out here just rammed home all the things he'd never do again. The addictive smell of the petrol fumes, the throaty rumble of an exhaust. He couldn't be that man anymore, and the plain truth was he didn't know how to be anyone else. He'd been left with all of the bad stuff and none of the good, and he wasn't sure there was enough of him left to build a new man from. Worse still, he didn't even know if he wanted to try.

'You did great today,' Honey said, breaking into his bleak train of thought.

'I sat on a stool and told someone what to do. I'd hardly call it earth shattering.'

Honey laughed softly. 'You really have no idea. Hal, without you there today Steve would have walked. Thirty-odd residents would have gone hungry, and a war

253

veteran wouldn't have celebrated his birthday. You can think of it as just sitting on the stool if you like, but the way I see it you saved the day.'

'Move over Nicolas-fucking-Cage,' Hal muttered.

'Do you have to swear in every single sentence?' she snapped. 'There are other words, you know.'

'I'd say I'll read the dictionary, but I'm goddamn fucking blind,' he shot back, and folded his arms over his chest in fury.

Honey watched the cars trundle past the darkening windows. 'I like Nicolas Cage.'

'Yeah well, real life isn't like the movies, Honey. The hero doesn't always get to save the day. He doesn't always get to keep his eyesight, or his driving licence, or his livelihood, or his fiancée.'

She was silent for the rest of the bus ride home, and on the walk to the house too, besides providing enough basic information to save him from falling down the kerb. He hated the way she'd withdrawn her company long before they went their separate ways in the lobby.

'It's pretty mean to give a blind man the silent treatment.'

Honey snorted down her nose. 'You have the nerve to call me on giving the silent treatment? You're the bloody king of it.'

'That's quite some fall, from Nicolas Cage to the king of silent treatments,' he said, trying to coax her back into civility again.

'I'm going inside,' she said, tonelessly. 'Thanks for your help today.'

She sounded like a teacher thanking a PTA parent. Polite, and professionally distant. It grated on him. He slotted his key into the latch as he heard her door close, and then took it out again.

'What did I do?' he shouted, walking back to her door. 'One minute I'm a hero, the next you're in a temper. What is this?'

She opened her door. 'You never mentioned your fiancée.'

Her voice was calm and heavy with the questions she didn't ask.

'So?'

'So you should have.'

'Am I missing something here? I used to have a fiancée. Now I don't. And that's a problem for you, because?'

'Why did you split up?'

'Fuck, Honey, what is this, the Spanish Inquisition?'

'It's a simple question.'

He ran his hands over his hair. 'Fine.' Squaring his shoulders and closing his arms over his chest, he spoke again. 'Fine. We were getting married. Next summer, if you must have all the details.'

'And now you're not?'

'She didn't want to marry a blind man.'

Hal heard Honey's swift intake of breath and felt guilty for painting Imogen on a par with Cruella De Vil. The truth had been far more gradual and not at all one-sided. The accident had been the catalyst, the inciting incident, definitely, but the aftermath had been the reason they'd separated. Hal had been a man left without many choices, and Imogen had become a woman who'd had to make the toughest one.

He didn't blame her. Oh, he had. He'd railed against her, just as he'd railed against everyone else in his life. His friends, his family . . . all of them. They couldn't possibly understand what he was going through, and it reached the point where their well-meant kindnesses felt patronising, Imogen's most of all. She'd tried to accommodate the changes that forced their way through their life together, the broom that swept away the flash, materialistic lifestyle and left the brass tacks of a broken man behind. It wasn't her fault; she'd fallen for one person, one life, and overnight she'd been presented with someone completely different. It was debatable whether she'd left him or he'd left her in the end; it had become bitterly apparent that they weren't going to make it.

'Hal . . . I'm sorry,' Honey said. 'I shouldn't have pried.'

'So why did you? What does it matter?'

She was near enough for him to hear her shallow breathing and smell the familiar scent of her shampoo.

'Honestly? I don't even know.' She sighed heavily. 'Maybe it doesn't matter at all, Hal. It's just that sometimes I feel as if we know each other, and then I realise that we don't really know each other at all.'

The forlorn note in her voice resonated with him.

'Can I come in for coffee?'

She was too close not to touch. He stroked his fingers against the smoothness of her hair.

She didn't reply to his question, just leaned her head against his hand a little.

'It's getting late,' she said finally; softly. 'I don't think coffee's a good idea.'

He knew he could push the point; that she'd probably change her mind if he asked her to, and in that moment, he wanted Honey to change her mind pretty badly. He didn't want to think about driving fast cars anymore or how he should have been marrying Imogen next summer. He wanted to block it all out by pushing Honey down onto her mattress and losing himself in her curves. Her breathing wasn't steady, and he could feel the warmth of her body a footstep away from him. Swallowing hard, he dipped his head, and he felt her slide her face sideways into his hand, moving away from his kiss just a fraction too slowly, letting his lips touch hers for the briefest hint before they settled on her cheek.

'Goodnight Hal,' she murmured close to his ear, letting him linger for a second before easing back. Accepting her decision with a sigh, he brushed his thumb longingly along the softness of her mouth and then turned away.

Honey cradled a mug of coffee in her hands, the heat from the steam warming her face in the dark lounge. Curled into the end of the sofa, she sat in the quiet room and tried to make some sense of the jumbled day.

She'd woken troubled, and Hal had turned her troubles into triumphs. Then the campaign to save the home had almost been derailed by Mimi and Lucille's public disagreement. She'd taken steps to repair the damage over the course of the afternoon; she could only hope it was going to be enough.

And then there was Tash and Nell trying to push her towards some guy who sounded like Elvis, which was too random to even worry about amongst the bigger stuff she was trying to process. Like the fact Hal should have been getting married. He'd loved someone enough to ask them to marry him, and quite recently too. Was he still in love with her, whoever she was? Was that why he'd shut himself away? Was that why he pushed her away? But then, he hadn't pushed her away this evening, had he?

If she'd have allowed him in, it wouldn't have been for coffee. They'd have made for the bedroom, not the kitchen, and it would have no doubt been all of the things she'd hoped for the last time she'd invited him over her threshold. Turning him down tonight had been her heart's decision, not her head's. Her heart had said don't. Don't let him in. He's too dark, too hard. He's broken, and he'll break you too.

Somehow, he'd cured her of her girl guide complex, her need to step in and make everything better.

Somehow he'd gone from being the man she thought she needed to the one man she couldn't let close.

CHAPTER TWENTY-EIGHT

With the new day came new resolutions. She'd concentrate her efforts on the things that were within her control, and on the things that were the most pressing. Principally that meant getting the campaign back on track, and secondly it meant telling Tash and Nell in no uncertain terms that there would be no date with Elvis, nor anybody else. She'd allowed herself to get so whipped up by this ridiculous search for the elusive piano man that she'd tried to strong-arm Hal into sleeping with her – now that she knew about his own romantic woes she felt pretty shoddy about that. She'd tossed, she'd turned, and finally she'd wrestled him into the right box overnight. Hal was her neighbour, and hopefully he was her friend. Yes, there was a physical spark between them, but one that was best left to dwindle and fizzle out, all things considered.

Knocking on his door ready for work half an hour later, she was resolute.

'Morning, Hal,' she said, chipper when he opened his door, already wearing his sexy fisherman garb.

'Honeysuckle,' he said, cordially.

'Ready to go?' she asked gaily, although he clearly was. Hal followed her down the steps onto the pavement. 'Why are you being weird? Is it because of last night?' he said, cutting straight to the chase. 'Because for what it's worth, you were totally right. The last place I'd have wanted to wake up this morning was in your bed.'

Honey stopped walking abruptly. 'Well, that's charming.'

'I'm not a charming man, Honey. I'm an honest one. It was the right decision for both of us. Thank you for making it.'

The bus approached from the other end of the road and they took their places on the early morning commute, precluding any further discussion on the matter.

Mimi hobbled into the shop at around half past ten, supported by Billy and trailed by a lacklustre Lucille. A fragile truce had been settled on between the sisters over an unexpectedly excellent breakfast of Eggs Benedict and homemade blueberry muffins.

'Mimi has acknowledged that she can, at times, be somewhat bossy,' Billy said, in clear earshot of his beloved.

'And Lucille has accepted that it might have been better not to tell porky pies,' he added, earning himself a baleful look from the lady herself.

'Good,' Honey said. 'Because there's something I need to talk to you all about.'

Having ascertained that the shop was empty of customers, they all gathered around the counter.

'I've been thinking about the protests,' Honey said.

Lucille's shoulders slumped. 'I can't believe it's my fault that we've had to stop. I feel terrible.'

Mimi looked as if she might be about to agree, so Honey forged onwards. 'That's just what I wanted to talk to you about. Are you all free next Sunday?'

Billy's eyes twinkled with mischief. 'Tell us more, Honeysuckle. Tell us more.'

Hal couldn't believe how much he loved being back in a kitchen again. He was an all-or-nothing sort of man, and he'd slammed the shutters down on cooking anything beyond toast since the accident.

As a chef he'd been avant garde, a kitchen alchemist; faced with the possibility of being average, he'd chosen instead to be nothing at all. His knives had been wrapped and stored away, and even the almost-physical ache in his fingers to cook had finally started to subside. But still, at night he dreamed of food. He'd become adept at closing down his thoughts during the day, but when he slept his brain ran amok.

Complicated dishes, beautiful creations, symphonies of ingredients that would make the toughest critic weep. He dreamed of people he used to know interspersed in his here and now, of Honey dining in his restaurant, of Imogen laughing at how the mighty had fallen to running the kitchen of an OAP home. He battled against sleep because he didn't want to wake up in the middle of the night with damp cheeks and a racing heart, and because he'd have to handle those hideous in-between moments just after waking before he remembered that the nightmare was real. Brand new pain every time.

261

It really was sheer hard work being Benedict Hallam. The gap between his two lives was too big a leap for any sane man to take. It would take a man with balls of steel to jump that chasm.

Thursday ran into Friday, and finally the weekend arrived with a burst of pale sunshine. Honey woke just after dawn on Saturday morning full of nervous energy, and then forced herself back to sleep and slept in late. Most of the week before had been spent laying down surreptitious plans for Sunday. Every customer in the shop had left with a few hastily prepared flyers in with their purchases asking for their support, and Old Don's son had called in a favour from a buddy at the local radio station to ensure that the word would be spread quickly come Sunday morning. They'd been careful to keep things as covert as possible to shield the plan from Christopher's ears, and so far their luck had held.

Honey lay back on her pillows. Should she see if Hal fancied breakfast? The last few days had surely taught them how to be around each other like normal human beings, right? They ought to be able to manage bacon and eggs unsupervised without fighting or throwing themselves at each other. She could prove once and for all that she could cook bacon, or maybe he could teach her to make the American pancakes that the residents at the home had become addicted to over the last few days.

'Like little clouds,' Lucille had sighed.

'Or pillows,' Mimi had nodded.

Pillowy pancakes sounded good. Honey pulled herself up, and then reached for her phone when it buzzed and flopped back to check her messages.

Brunch? from Nell.

Café at eleven? from Tash.

Honey considered her options. A slow, chatty wake up with Nell and Tash over buckets of cappuccino and food she didn't have to cook herself, or risk being knocked back by Dr Jekyll over the way? Only one of those options offered anything close to certainty or safety, or even a guarantee of food.

She sent a text to both girls. See you there in an hour.

An hour somehow became an hour and fifteen, and Honey pushed the café door open expecting to find Tash and Nell already halfway down their first cups of coffee and berating her for her lateness. Weird then, that neither of them were in evidence at all. Tash wasn't especially known for her punctuality, but Nell hated running late for anything. She was the only person Honey knew who set her phone alarm to wake her up ten minutes before her alarm clock, just in case. She also knew what Simon had started to use those extra ten minutes for these days, thanks to a tipsy conversation when Nell had revealed far too much about their suddenly sexed-up love life. Ordering her usual coffee as she passed the counter, Honey dropped down onto a well-squished sofa and threw her bag on the floor beside her.

After leafing through the paper for five minutes with one eye on the door, Honey reached down and rummaged in the bottom of her bag for her phone.

'Ma'am, are you Honeysuckle?'

Keeping her eyes cast downwards for a couple of seconds, Honey stopped rummaging and realised she'd been had.

She knew without looking up that Elvis had just entered the building.

Turning her face up and her smile on, she slid her phone onto the low coffee table and pulled herself to her feet.

'I am,' she said, half holding out her hand awkwardly and trying to remember his name, because she was pretty sure it wasn't actually Elvis.

He grinned infectiously as he took her hand in his big warm one and dipped his head to kiss her cheek. Honey smelled fresh cologne and washing powder, and found herself impressed by his cleanliness and his big easy confident kid smile.

'Christian,' he murmured. 'Shall we?' He nodded towards a table for two by the window. 'I'm starving.'

He pulled out her chair and transferred her coffee to the new table, and while he talked eggs with the waitress, Honey fired off a quick text to Tash and Nell.

You're both dead to me.

The waitress looked enquiringly towards Honey with her pad in her hand.

'I'll have the same,' she said with a bright smile, even though she'd tuned out and had no idea what Christian had ordered.

He raised his eyebrows. 'I like a girl with a healthy appetite.'

Honey shrugged, unconcerned. She'd eaten at the café dozens of times, there wasn't anything on the menu she didn't like.

'So Tash tells me you play the piano,' Honey opened the conversation with an invitation to talk about himself, as advised by all the best guides to a successful first date.

264

He nodded, and pushed his fingers through his chestnut brown hair when it fell in his eyes. Cute, in a Clark Kent kind of way.

'My whole family's musical. My mother is a brilliant cellist, she went all around the world when she was younger. That's how she met my dad,' he said, as Honey listened to his deep, rich voice and wondered if he sang.

'Is he a musician too?'

Christian laughed. 'Actually no, he isn't. He's a surgeon. He fixed Mom's arm when she broke it and feared she'd never play again. She likes to say she was so grateful that she married him.'

Honey relaxed as she listened to him tell her about the rest of his family. They sounded a scarily bright bunch; his brother, the violinist, his elder sister, the talented flautist.

'You've got your own band right there,' she smiled, impressed.

'I know. Move over the Von Trapps, right?'

They paused as the waitress appeared with a pot of tea and placed it down on the table with a couple of fresh cups.

'English breakfast tea,' she said. 'I'll be right back with the food.'

'Tea?' Honey said, raising her eyebrows. 'Not a cup of Joe?'

Christian grinned boyishly at her hammy attempt at an Americanism.

'I thought you might like tea better,' he said, almost bashful.

Honey looked at him for a beat before she spoke, feeling an undeniable tingle of pleasure at the thoughtful gesture.

'Thank you,' she said, simply. 'I do.'

His blue eyes held hers for a second, and then the moment was gone as the waitress reappeared and placed two huge platters down in front of them.

'Corned beef hash, and eggs over easy,' she paused and smiled at Christian, who winked right back at her attempt to Americanise the perfectly standard-looking fried eggs. 'With a side of pancakes, crispy bacon,' she paused to clear away their empty coffee cups and touched the small jug on the side of Christian's plate. 'And maple syrup. Not golden.'

Wow. The man sure ate like an American. The waitress shot Honey a look that blatantly said, *I'll have him if you don't want him,* and then left them to contemplate the huge amount of food she'd somehow squeezed onto the tiny table.

'This looks good,' he said, tucking in with gusto.

Unless he was expecting his huge and super-talented family to join them for brunch, it also looked like far too much.

'Tash tells me you're something of a media star at the moment,' he said, pouring her tea before his own. Another gold star for his impeccable manners, his cellist mama had taught him well.

'I wouldn't exactly put it like that,' she laughed, and found herself telling him about how the campaign had spiralled over the last few weeks. He laughed in all the right places, and concern darkened his expression at the idea of the residents being forced out of the home they loved.

'You make light of it, but in my book what you're doing is pretty amazing,' he said, pushing the jug of maple syrup towards her. 'Have it with your bacon and pancakes. Trust me.'

There was something about Christian that told Honey she *could* do that. She could trust him. There was an innate goodness to him, a wholesomeness. Maybe it was just that he'd been lucky enough to live a gilded life that hadn't given him the rough edges of some men she could mention.

Honey turned her attention back to the pancakes with a small smile. She'd watched enough episodes of *Friends* to know they were going to be good and happily took his advice on the syrup. It was sound advice, even if the pancakes cooked especially for Christian weren't exactly as fluffy in the centre as they might have been. Not as pillowy or cloud-like as a certain bad-tempered chef's.

'I think they just needed a little more baking powder,' he said, adding, 'I'm a pretty keen cook,' to clarify his credentials.

'Me too,' she lied, although in her defence her first attempt at bolognese had been a thing of wonder.

'Cool,' he grinned, making her feel bad for embroidering the truth so heavily.

He picked up his tea and sipped it, watching her over the brim. 'I could cook something for you one of these evenings, if you'd like?'

He made it sound so easy. Everything about Christian, in fact, seemed easy. Easy eggs. Easy company. Easy on the eye. Easy to date.

'I'd really like that,' she said, and he touched his cup against hers and grinned.

Honey stayed on for another cup of coffee after Christian left, knowing she should text Tash and Nell and let them

267

off the hook for setting her up for American pancakes with the wrong man. She tapped her fingers on the wooden table top to the beat of the song playing on the radio in the background, its lyrics absurdly appropriate. 'If you can't be with the one you love, love the one you're with.' Or in Hal's case, if you can't be with the crazy bad-tempered one who swears at you and drives you to the edge of sanity, be with the self-assured one who makes things easy and managed an entire conversation without swearing once.

She picked up her phone and tapped out a message to Tash and Nell.

Elvis has left the building.

Hal called out to her when she let herself into the house a while later. She'd meandered her way through the shops on the high street after she'd left the café, picking up bits and pieces for the big event tomorrow. A couple of flasks. Poster paint. Family bags of boiled sweets for a sugar boost. Picking up the post, she put the heavy brown envelope addressed to Hal down on top of the one that had arrived a while back.

'Hey, you. Want to get rat-arsed with me?'

Alarmingly, he sounded as if he'd already had a couple of large ones. Honey looked at her watch. It was almost three in the afternoon, much too early for him to be getting plastered.

'You okay?' she asked, standing uncertainly outside his door.

'Top of the world,' he said. 'It's my fucking birthday.'

Honey winced at his bleak tone and harsh words. The contrast between Hal and Christian was stark.

'You should have said about your birthday,' she said.

'Why? Would you have baked me a cake?'

'I think we both know that'd be a bad idea,' she said, feeling bad for having been out on a fun day without realising Hal had been drinking whisky alone on his birthday.

'You're a truly shit cook,' he said.

Honey hated the slur in his voice. 'Open the door?'

She listened to him fumble with his keys, cursing under his breath. When he opened his door, he looked as crap as he sounded. Crumpled clothes. Messy hair. A glass of scotch in his hand.

'Happy birthday,' she said, even though the words rang hollow around the hallway.

He raised his glass and then downed the contents. 'To another shitty year.'

'Hal,' she said. 'Go to bed. Sleep it off.'

He shook his head and half laughed. 'I'm only just getting started. Come to my party?'

'Don't do this,' she said. 'Please.'

'I didn't have you down as a lightweight, Honeysuckle,' he said, shrugging. 'I might even have nibbles. We both know how fond you are of nibbles.'

The idea of Hal laying out nibbles to lure her into sharing his birthday with him brought a lump to her throat.

'Look,' she said, taking the glass from his hand. 'Go and get your head down. Sober up, then come over to mine later. I'll cook you a birthday dinner.'

Taking advantage of the fact that she'd surprised him into silence, she stretched up and planted the quickest of kisses on his cheek, wrinkling her nose at the smell of him.

'And take a shower. You stink like someone on a park bench.'

He leaned against the wall, suddenly melancholy. 'You have no idea how close I am to that.'

'Stop feeling sorry for yourself, birthday boy,' she said.

'You've slipped back into girl guide mode again,' he grumbled. 'I don't want dinner with a girl guide on my birthday. Can you bust out the sexually demanding one with Friday knickers on?'

'It's Saturday.'

Hal nodded and pointed an unsteady finger. 'I knew that.'

Honey looked at him for a long time. 'Go inside. I'll see you later.'

CHAPTER TWENTY-NINE

Honey went straight back out to the shops when Hal closed his door, and by the time he knocked hers a little after eight, she was ready. Dinner made? Check. Flat tidied and scented with a candle left over from Christmas? Check. Her best dress on and her hair fresh and swingy? Check. Envelope from that morning's mail, hopefully a birthday card she could read to Hal?

She'd never have guessed when she got up that morning that it was going to be a two dates kind of day. Not that this *was* a date, exactly, but birthdays were special, a kind of magical hinterland where the usual rules went out of the window and endless goodwill reigned. Sort of like Narnia appearing in the back of your wardrobe, as long as you obeyed the rules and only ever visited once a year.

She faltered as she reached for the catch on the door, almost not wanting to open it in case he'd ignored her suggestions and carried on with his party for one. He might be reeling out there, drunk as a skunk and still smelling like one.

'I know you're in there, I can smell burning,' he called out, thankfully not slurring anymore.

She smiled and opened the door. 'Liar. I've got everything totally under control in here.'

A different man stood in front of her from earlier in the day. A scrubbed-up, freshly scented one in a shirt and tie, and most significantly, a man who'd chosen to come over without the shield of his dark glasses.

He followed her down the hallway into the kitchen, sniffing as he went.

'Garlic with a hint of pine disinfectant. Unusual, even by your standards,' he said, and she hurriedly blew out the Christmas candle and steered him towards the dining table.

He examined her efforts as she worked behind the kitchen counter. She glanced at him as he turned her best cutlery over in his hands and rubbed the edge of the oilcloth between his fingers. No doubt it wouldn't pass his restaurant standards, but at least he didn't know it was covered in a kitsch Christmas print. It had been the only thing she could find that remotely resembled a tablecloth, a gift from Lucille several years ago.

Honey checked the tray of small crispy potatoes and roasted vegetables and then closed the oven.

'If you were cooking fillet steak, how long would you cook it for?' she asked, eyeing the lumps of raw meat on her chopping board as if they were her own kidneys.

'Not very long. Depends how thick they are and who I'm cooking them for,' he said, pushing his chair back and making his way over to the breakfast bar. 'Let me feel them.'

Hal tested the meat's thickness between his thumb and forefingers, and Honey tried not to admire his hands.

'Do I grill them?' she asked.

'Jesus, no.' He looked aghast. 'Get the frying pan. And some butter.'

'Am I about to have my second cooking lesson?'

'I can't let you ruin good steak,' he said. 'Now melt some butter until it foams.'

She did as he'd instructed.

'That sounds about right,' he said after a minute. 'Season the steaks well and then lay them in the sizzling butter.'

Honey grinned at the satisfying sizzle as she placed one of the steaks in the pan.

'Both together?' she said.

He nodded, and then fell silent.

After a minute or more, she pushed a fork into one to check the underside.

'Leave it,' Hal said; an order, not a suggestion. Honey eased the fork out of the meat with raised eyebrows and stepped away from the pan.

A minute or so later, he finally spoke again. 'Now baste them in the butter and turn them over.'

Honey followed his advice to the letter and then stepped away.

'Don't touch them until I tell you they're ready.'

'You haven't asked me how I like my steak.'

'It's fillet. You're having it the only way it should ever be cooked.'

'Rude,' she murmured, and saw him smirk into the glass of buck's fizz she'd just pushed his way.

'Eurgh. What the fuck is this?' he said, frowning.

'Buck's fizz. It's for your birthday.'

'Am I fourteen again?'

'No, but seeing as you were half cut a few hours ago I thought we'd go in easy,' she chided.

Hal placed the glass down. 'Take them out, they'll be ready.'

Honey frowned. She'd have left the steaks in for far longer.

'Already? They've only just gone in . . .'

He sighed pointedly. 'Do I try to tell you how to sell dead people's clothes and cast-offs?'

Honey huffed. 'Pre-loved and upcycled, actually.'

'Take the steaks out. Now.'

He waited enough time for Honey to obey his instructions. 'We can't eat them straight away, they need to stand for five.'

Honey stared at them. 'But they're ready. You just said so yourself. They'll go cold.'

Hal rubbed a hand over his mouth as if holding in a string of swear words. 'You can do everything else while you wait. Warm the plates. Pour some actual wine. Put some music on. Sing "Happy Birthday". Do anything you like, just don't touch those goddamn steaks.'

Honey stuck her tongue out at him, and immediately regretted it because it seemed mean.

'It's rude to stick your tongue out at a blind person,' he said.

She didn't even ask him how he knew.

'So how old are you today?' she asked, turning the oven down and sliding a couple of plates in with the potatoes and roasted vegetables. She loosened the plastic lid on a tub of ready-made chilled red wine sauce and stuck it in the microwave, waiting for him to reply.

'Thirty-four,' he said. 'Thirty-four years old and going nowhere fast.'

Honey opened the bottle of cabernet sauvignon that the supermarket advice tab had reliably informed was great with steak.

'Don't say that,' she said, pouring the wine into the glasses she'd set on the table and reaching across to flick the radio on in the background. 'Come and sit down. It's almost ready.'

Hal listened to Honey moving around the kitchen. The clank of plates, the rush of heat from the oven when she opened it, the scent of food. It was intoxicating, all of it, even more so than the decent glass of red she'd finally given him.

He could practically feel the pride radiating off her in waves when she placed his meal in front of him.

'Voilà,' she said. 'Fillet steak, little potato things, roasted vegetables, and a red wine juice.'

'Jus?' he said.

'Don't question the chef,' she warned, sliding into the chair opposite him.

'Are there any lit candles on this table?' he asked.

'Yes, because I'm stupid and want to set your head on fire,' she said. 'Of course there aren't any candles.'

He didn't reply, mostly because he'd actually been thinking that her first homemade steak dinner deserved the romance of a candle.

'Oh my bloody God,' Honey suddenly said. 'This steak.

Hal, it's perfect,' she sighed, with something that sounded like rapture. 'I didn't think it was going to be anywhere close to cooked, but you were totally right.'

'Don't question the chef,' he quipped lightly, and found that he could only agree when he tasted his own steak. It wasn't a masterpiece, but given his diet over recent months it was pretty damn close to perfect. They ate with the sound of the radio in the kitchen, low music to accompany the chink of cutlery against china and their idle chat about the well-oiled plans for the covert event she'd planned at the home the next day.

'Will you come?' she asked. 'They say an army marches on its stomach, and Skinny Steve is no born leader.'

'I like him,' Hal said, jumping to Steve's defence. His young apprentice for the week might not be a culinary genius, but he was a hard worker and good at following instructions. 'He'll make a decent chef one day.'

'Yeah, but not by tomorrow,' she wheedled. 'Say you'll come?'

'Fine,' he relented. 'I'll come. But I'm staying in the kitchen, okay?'

'Deal,' she said, and he knew he'd pleased her from the smile behind her voice. Considering the volatile nature of their relationship, Honey was actually a pretty easy person to please. He'd been accustomed to a life surrounded by high-maintenance people before the accident; demanding customers, his party hard friends, and of course, Imogen. Had he himself been high maintenance too? Probably. If a penchant for expensive clothes, good food and fast cars made someone high maintenance, then maybe so.

Honey stood and cleared the plates.

'I didn't buy dessert,' she said. 'I don't know why, but you don't strike me as a dessert man.'

He didn't argue. He'd always choose a cheeseboard over a cheesecake. 'I'll take some Stilton?' he said, teasing her.

'You're welcome to a Dairylea triangle,' she laughed lightly.

'I'll pass,' he said, pushing his chair back. 'Shall we go through to the lounge?'

He followed Honey and settled on the sofa, accepting his refilled glass with thanks.

'I have something for you,' Honey said, hovering close enough for him to smell the light scent of her perfume and sounding uncharacteristically shy. 'For your birthday.'

He put his glass down carefully on the coffee table in front of him. 'You brought me a present?'

In years gone by, he'd given and received many extravagant gifts. This year his only wish had been for his birthday to slide in and out again unmarked, so quite why he'd had a skinful and blurted it out to Honey was beyond him. The fact that she'd gone to all of this trouble and rustled up a late notice gift had actually touched Hal greatly. Although, knowing Honey, he should probably approach any gift she'd chosen with a certain degree of trepidation.

She perched beside him on the sofa and placed a package into his hands.

'It's not much,' she said. 'I didn't know whether to wrap it or not,' she said. 'It's in a box so I left it.'

He felt around the contours of the box and picked open the lid, feeling inside until his fingers closed around something cool and metal.

'It's a hip flask,' she said. 'I thought it might help you drink less whisky if it comes in a smaller bottle.'

'There's that girl guide again,' he said, but without malice. 'Thank you, Honey, for all of this. You didn't have to.'

'I wanted to,' she said quickly. 'It's your birthday. No one should drink alone on their birthday.'

Hal placed the flask back into its box. 'I haven't always drunk this much,' he said. 'I used to be too busy.'

Taking the box from his hands, she laid it on the table. 'I don't think badly of you for it, Hal.'

He shook his head. 'You should. I don't like the man I've become, Honey. I don't like the life I have now.' He tried to choose his words to make her understand. 'I'm not talking about the material stuff. I mean sure, I miss the trappings, but it's not that. It's in here.' He tapped his fingertips on his chest like a builder testing the soundness of a wall. 'My heart needs to race. It didn't matter what it was, as long as I was pushing myself over my limits. Faster cars. Bigger bikes. Higher slopes. I was always restless for the next big thrill.' He rolled his shoulders and scrubbed his hand over his stubble. 'I don't know who I am anymore without all that.' He shrugged. 'I feel like a dead man walking. Nothing makes my heart race.'

'Maybe, in time . . .' she said, tentatively. 'There's loads of things you could still do, when you're ready, I mean. Tandem skydiving, even. Stuff like that.'

'Yeah,' he said. 'It's just I like to be the one in charge, not the passenger.'

Honey sipped her wine. 'I bet you were a scary boss to work for.'

'You wouldn't have liked me.'

Would she have liked him? Aside from doctors, Honey was the first person he'd let anywhere near close enough to become a friend since the accident. She hadn't known the man he was before. She only knew this pale, watered-down version of him.

'Probably not,' she said, candidly. 'You frightened the living daylights out of me when I first met you.'

'I don't believe you. You're Honeysuckle Jones, freedom fighter, bona fide Wonder Woman.'

She laughed gently. 'Tash dressed up as Wonder Woman on New Year's Eve last year. She had a terrible wardrobe malfunction in The Cock; Superman had to save her virtue with his cape.'

One of the things Hal had come to value most about Honey was the fact that she didn't take life too seriously – never more so than in that moment. He loosened his shirt collar and tie as he sat back against the sofa, his arm along the back of it when she scooted back beside him.

'Is your life always on the edge of ridiculous?' he said, leaning his head back on the cushions.

She was silent for a moment. 'Not always. Quite a lot more so since you moved in though.'

'No way,' he said. 'It's not my fault you've become a female version of Robin Hood with a band of merry pensioners, or that your crazy friends have some bizarre insistence that you can only date pianists.'

'They did it again today,' she said.

'Did what?'

'Tash and Nell set me up on a blind date,' she said. 'I was supposed to meet them at the café and they sent a pianist to meet me instead.'

279

'Oh.' The idea that she'd been on a date and then returned home to his drunken *poor me* rant pissed him off. 'Was he better than the last two?'

Honey sighed. 'I guess he was, yeah.'

She didn't elaborate, and her hesitancy to share details frustrated him. He wanted to hear her laugh and tell him it had been another dating disaster, but she didn't. Frustration had him reaching for his wine. He wanted to see her face, to be able to see the things her face wouldn't be able to hide rather than pick through her words for clues. And he wanted to see her face because when he dreamed of her she was always indistinct, more of a feeling than an image. A good feeling.

'Two dates in one day. It's my personal best,' she said, making light and sounding anxious as her head rested on his arm.

Hal's need to be top dog at everything kicked in hard. Honey was beside him on the sofa, bumping against him from hip to knee.

'Did he kiss you goodbye?' he said.

'It was lunchtime and I was stuffed full of American pancakes. He gave me a peck on the cheek and his number.'

Even that sounded too promising for Hal's liking. He found that he didn't want Honey to use that number. He knew well enough that he was being unreasonable, but it was his birthday and she was, well . . . right now, she was *his* date, and it wasn't lunchtime, and they weren't stuffed. They'd skipped dessert. He could hear her breathing, feel her waiting for him to take his turn to speak.

'I don't have a number to give you,' he said, winding

silky strands of her hair around his fingers. 'And I don't kiss on the cheek.'

He heard her intake of breath when he wrapped his fingers around the back of her neck and drew her head to his.

He hadn't intended on kissing her tonight, in fact he'd planned not to as he'd tipped his face up into the beating rain of his shower earlier. He needed involvement like he needed a hole in the head; but he wasn't too big to admit that he was lonely. What he really needed was a friend. He just wished his body had got the memo from his brain, because in that moment he didn't want Honey to be his friend. He just plain wanted her.

If she'd have resisted for even a second, it would have been enough. But she didn't. She was pliant and warm, and she turned into his kiss rather than away and opened her mouth under his.

When he'd kissed her before, it had been urgent, frantic. This time it was neither of those things, deliberately so. She moved closer into the circle of his arms, and he stroked his thumb along the curve of her jaw. He took his time, because she was a luxury and his life was so starved of luxury that he needed to drink her in. He could feel the tremble in her lips when she sighed against his.

'I'm glad you don't kiss on the cheek,' she whispered. He felt her reach over and click the lamp out, and then all of a sudden it wasn't so easy to go slow because her hands were inside his shirt and his blood was roaring in his veins. He'd been wrong earlier. There was still one thing that could make his heart race. This, here and now. He pushed her down onto the sofa, or maybe she pulled him down, he couldn't tell and it didn't matter. Either way he found himself lying on top of her, feeling himself yield into her softness, wanting her so badly that his whole body ached with it.

She pulled his tie loose and unpicked the buttons of his shirt. He pushed it off when she eased it back off his shoulders, kissing the skin she revealed.

'Why did you turn out the light?' he said, trailing his lips over her face with his hand buried in her hair.

'To make it even,' she said. They both knew it would never be anywhere close to even.

'Crazy girl. Did it work?' he asked, opening the buttons on her dress and kissing the curves of her breasts.

'Not really. I can still see you,' she whispered. 'You're beautiful, Hal.'

No one had ever called him beautiful. He paid the compliments. So Hal let himself get lost completely in the wonderland of being here with her, in the soft warmth of her compliments and in her efforts to make him feel good, because he mostly felt so goddamn awful. It moved him that she'd turned out the light. It moved him because she wanted this experience to be as good for him as it was for her. He remembered back to their previous terrible attempt at sex, to her telling him that she'd brought a blindfold. He'd scorned it at the time, deriding her in his head for not having a clue how he felt, but right now, he got it. She'd never understand the reality of how this was for him, but the fact that she even wanted to try turned out to be a huge fucking turn on.

'Pass me my tie?' he said, and took it from her fingers when she'd reached it from the floor.

'Are you sure you want it to be even?' he murmured, running it between his fingers to find the centre.

Her nails dug into his back, and he heard her low gasp as she lifted her head to help him. Her breath tickled the skin beneath his ear, and her hips rocked up to meet his.

'Blindfold me, Hal.'

CHAPTER THIRTY

It had been shadowy in the lounge, and Hal's tie took it back to complete darkness. He'd secured it well, no slivers of light to guide her way.

'Okay?' he whispered, and she stroked her hands over him, learning his body; the lean compacted muscles of his shoulders, the smooth length of his back. She saw his inked biceps in her head as her fingers curled around them, and felt the strength in his hands when he held her face between them.

'Better than okay,' she said, finding his mouth in the darkness, feeling more for seeing less.

'I bought this bra for you,' she said. He ran the slender velvet straps between his fingers and then traced over the lace cups, making her nipples stiffen.

'I like you in it,' he said, kissing her as his fingers slid beneath her to the catch. He opened it easily, the assured touch of a man who knew exactly what he was doing. Honey lifted her shoulders to help him slide it from her

284

body, loving the way he wrapped her against him. He had a vulnerability, a capacity for tenderness she hadn't anticipated from him; he usually hid it well. He didn't hide it from her now. She heard her own low moan when his hand moved between them to her bared breasts, his tongue an erotic slide over her lips as his thumb circled her nipple.

'Pink,' he murmured, not really a question. 'Like turkish delight, or rose streaks across the morning sky.'

'Yes,' she said, helping him paint her picture in his head. Her heart aching for him that he'd never see either of those things again, and for herself that he'd never see her at all.

And then he moved slightly, dipping his head to take her nipple inside the warmth of his mouth, and she pushed her fingers into his hair, overwhelmed. He wasn't the first man to touch her, but in that moment it felt brand new and more powerful than she'd ever realised it could be.

At that point other men might have stepped the gear up. If anything, Hal knocked it down, sighing low in his throat as his hips moved languidly against hers.

'It's been a while,' he said.

'Forever,' she said, because she'd never known this before. 'What do you see in your head right now, Hal?'

He laughed softly against her mouth, easing his weight slightly away from her. She'd have happily stayed right there forever, cradled between the back of the sofa and Hal's body.

'I don't need to see you to know how beautiful you are, Honey.' He stroked a single fingertip from the dip between her collarbone to the edge of her silk knickers, and the raw, honest edge to his words intensified the feeling tenfold.

'My hands tell me.' He covered her breasts with his

hands; warm, firm, massaging. Honey arched into his touch when he squeezed her nipples and then lowered his head to lick each one in turn.

'My mouth tells me,' he whispered, sliding his lips back up her neck and pressing her against the sofa with his weight. Honey could feel her breath becoming shallow in her chest as Hal's hand moved slowly down between her legs.

'Your body tells me,' he murmured, sliding his hand inside the silk. She held her breath, as if she were walking along the very edge of a cliff path, and he held still and kissed her slowly until she had a secure footing again.

He stilled her fingers when she reached for the button on his jeans. 'Not here. Not now. And not because I don't want to, or because we never will, but because this is yours. It's all for you.'

He was the best man she'd ever known by a country mile.

'Okay?' he asked her for a second time that evening, and she couldn't find the words to tell him how much more than okay she was. He shifted slightly to remove her knickers, and then came back again, lying on his side and gathering her against the length of him.

Being naked and held by Hal in the darkness turned out to be the sexiest thing that had ever happened to Honey in her life.

He was a sensory feast; the low sounds of pleasure in his throat, the smooth heat of his skin, the sensual weight of his body moving against hers. His hands travelled over her, sweeping her spine, cupping her backside as he rocked into her, kissing her open mouthed and breathless. When he opened her knees with his own and moved his hand between her legs, Honey could only cling on to the slick breadth of his shoulders and gasp his name into his mouth.

In those moments, it never occurred to her to wonder if he might be the first man to make her come, or if it was time to fake it to please the man she was with. Hal had her mind totally relaxed and her body as tightly wound as a spring, completely in the moment, and there was only one way it was ever going to go.

He smoothed her damp hair from her forehead, kissing her jaw, her ear, her mouth. His words, his hands, his body, his mouth. Honey let them all move over her, let him pull her under, push her further than she'd ever been. Her blood raced in her veins, pounded in her head, and there was nothing but him, and here, and the intense, spiralling tension he'd created between her legs. Even when she could feel her tears dampen the blindfold it didn't stop, like a tightening screw, every thrust of Hal's denim-clad hips against his hand ratcheting her closer, and closer, and closer, and then he opened her knees wider and moaned deep in his throat, the sexiest sound she'd ever heard, and she couldn't hold on anymore. She took a running jump right off the edge of that cliff path holding tightly on to Hal for safe harbour, free falling, and utterly, utterly dazzled.

'Easy as that, Honey,' he whispered, barely there kisses as her breathing came in almost painful gasps.

Benedict Hallam had set the bar high. It was the kind of climax that could give a girl unrealistic expectations for the rest of her born days.

'Oh my God,' she said, still trembling as she pushed his tie from her eyes a couple of minutes later. 'Oh my bloody God.'

287

'Fucking hell,' he probably said; she couldn't be certain. He wrapped her close in his arms, holding her to his bare chest, stroking her hair while her breathing steadied.

'I never knew,' she whispered.

'And now you do.'

'Even if it never happens to me again, I'll always know.'

'It'll happen to you again, Honey. Trust me, it'll happen again.'

'I'm going to do something for you now that I've never done for you before,' Honey said a little later, still curled against the warmth of Hal's chest.

He traced lazy fingertip circles on the back of her shoulder.

'Does it involve my cock and your mouth?'

Honey laughed and shook her head.

'Nope. I'm going to make you a cup of tea.'

'You sure know how to look after a man,' he said, and Honey could feel his smile against her hair.

'Never let it be said that I don't have good manners. You gave me an orgasm, I'll give you tea. How'd you like it?'

'Is on your knees out of the question?'

'Sugar?' she asked sweetly, extracting herself from his arms.

'Two,' he grumbled, pulling himself up to sit, his denim-clad legs thrown out in front of him. He was a sparely built man, long and lithe, the kind of guy who could eat Ben & Jerry's out of ice cream and still fit the same jeans he'd worn at twenty-one.

Knotting her robe around her waist, she busied herself making tea, her mind back on the sofa with Hal. He'd made

288

it so easy, just brushed aside her hang-ups with his easy touch and his gentle mouth. Ordinarily he was just about the toughest man she'd ever known, and paradoxically, he'd turned out to be the most considerate lover. He'd held himself back tonight and made it all about her, despite the fact that it was his own birthday. That was the thing with Hal. He rarely played by conventional rules, and it made him addictive company. Maybe that was why she'd sought him out as a confidant so many times, sitting on the floor outside his door and pouring out her heart even though he barely acknowledged her presence.

Honey crossed the kitchen to grab the milk from the fridge, and her eyes fell on the envelope that had arrived a few days ago for Hal. Addressed to Mr Benedict Hallam in bold black pen, it definitely looked like personal mail rather than the bills that made up her own usual morning haul of letters. Surely it was a birthday card? The green glow of the oven clock informed Honey that there was still an hour or so left of Hal's birthday. She stuck the envelope on a tray with the cups and a packet of chocolate digestives and headed back through to the lounge.

'A letter came for you,' Honey said, and she felt the temperature in the room plummet from afterglow warm to snowstorm cold. Good job Hal had slid his jeans back on while she made the tea or he'd die of frostbite.

'A letter?' he said, completely failing to pull off the casual tone he'd aimed for because of his ramrod-straight shoulders. 'What kind of letter?'

'Well, it's a brown envelope with your name and address written on the front in bold, black writing,' Honey said, turning it over in her hands. 'if I had to guess I'd say it's a man's handwriting, and by the feel of it it's probably a birthday card?'

'Miss Marple's granddaughter is back in the building,' Hal muttered.

Honey ignored his barbed comment.

'Should I open it?' she asked.

Hal didn't reply right away. His heavy sigh was the only sound in the quiet room, and he rolled his shoulders and cricked his neck to the side like a boxer limbering up for a fight.

'It'll be from my brother,' he said, grinding the heels of his palms against his jaw. 'He's the only one who has this address.'

Was that so bad? Honey wondered silently. A birthday card from his brother? From Hal's reaction, the answer was most probably yes.

'Just open it,' Hal said, so quietly that Honey felt the need to double check.

'You're sure you want me to?'

He didn't reply. Honey looked at him, feeling his simmering anxiety and hoping that the letter turned out to be nothing after all. Dragging her gaze away from him and back to the envelope, Honey slid her finger under an open edge and ripped it carefully.

As predicted, it was a birthday card, heavy and cream, and again as predicted, the front said 'brother' in embossed gunmetal letters. It definitely wasn't the kind of card Honey would have found in the corner shop; it screamed money and understated elegance.

'Well?' Hal ground out, still facing the floor.

'Well,' Honey began, 'it's, umm, it's a birthday card saying "brother", so you guessed right there.'

'Inside?'

She hadn't opened it yet, and in truth, she was frightened to. Hal had arrived in her life as if he'd been dropped from outer space. No family or friends intruded into the bubble, and it had allowed Honey to get to know him in isolation as a man, rather than as a son, a friend, or as someone's brother. The arrival of the card served to highlight that she didn't really know him well at all, and that there were people out there who did. With unsure fingers, she cleared her throat and opened the card.

It wasn't just a birthday card. There was a second, smaller envelope nestled inside the card, and written across it in cerise ink was just his name. Hal. The writing was different to that on the previous envelope, very distinctly feminine. Honey's heart sank. This wasn't just a birthday card after all, or a minor intrusion. It was a letter; it was two worlds colliding. Hal's old life and his new life about to intersect.

'What does it say?' he asked, his anxiety coming through as impatience.

Honey forced her eyes to read the writing in the card. 'It says: *"Hello brother, couldn't let your birthday pass without contact. I miss you. We all do, Imogen especially, if the amount of times she's called me is anything to go on. She's been after your address constantly, that's why I asked her to write a letter, so I could send it to you. I don't know what she wants, but she wasn't giving up. Get in touch when you can, I hope that taking some time out*

291

has helped you in a way that we obviously couldn't.

Happy Birthday, big brother.

Damien x".'

Honey and Hal sat in silence for a few seconds after she stopped reading. The unopened letter burned in her hand. Part of her ached to know what lay inside, and another part of her wanted to run a thousand miles. This was not her business, and Hal was not her boyfriend. Was he still Imogen's boyfriend, officially? It was another question that she didn't have an answer for, and now was definitely not the right time to ask it.

'Fucking Damien.'

Hal spoke at last, and the despair in his voice made Honey's heart ache for him.

'He sounds nice,' Honey ventured, wondering how such a plain adjective could be applied to any relative of Hal's. It certainly wasn't a word that ever came to mind about the man himself.

Hal laughed harshly.

'What the fuck am I supposed to do with her letter?'

Honey knew exactly what Hal meant. They were in the most awkward of positions. Half an hour back they were having sex, and now she needed to read him a letter from his ex-girlfriend. Was it a love letter? A Dear John letter, maybe?

Either way, it was going to be the most personal of letters, and she was the last person on earth who should read it to him. But then she was also the only person on earth who could, so they found themselves on uncharted territory.

'I'll read it to you.' The words left Honey's mouth before

292

she'd had time to consider the implications. Purposely so, because if she let herself think about it, she wouldn't have the courage to read it.

'No fucking way,' Hal said. 'No fucking way.'

'Who else is going to read it to you?'

'No one. No one is going to read it, because I am not remotely fucking interested in anything she has to say.'

The fact that the letter had raised such anger in him told Honey otherwise. He was interested alright, and so was she, in a perverse, nigglingly self-destructive kind of way. She was emotionally invested, and she found that she needed to know how invested Imogen was too.

'Hal, let me do this. It might be important. It must be, for your brother to go to the trouble of sending it.'

'He's doing it to get Imogen off his back. He said so himself. Nothing more, nothing less.'

'Please, Hal. Let's just get it over with, okay?'

He sighed heavily, and Honey accepted his lack of complaint as agreement. Reluctant and begrudging, but agreement nonetheless.

The small white envelope looked innocent enough, yet Honey still opened it as if it might contain a nail bomb. One that was definitely going to cause damage to the two people closest to the impact.

The paper crinkled in her fingers as she opened it out. More swooping cerise writing, pretty and feminine, probably a reflection of the woman who had written it. All of a sudden, she regretted pushing him to let her read it. Once inside her head, these words would stay with her forever.

'You really don't have to do this,' he said, practically a whisper.

'I know that,' Honey said. 'It's okay. Just give me a moment.'

She sucked in a deep breath. She would do this.

'"*Dearest Hal,*"' she read, trying to keep her voice level and free of emotion, because these were not her emotions to feel.

'"*I hate that it has come to this. I need to see you . . . God, I don't even know how or if you will get to hear this, just hoping you have a friend or a neighbour around to oblige. A cleaner even - I know how much you hate doing that stuff yourself!*"'

Honey paused for a second, already hating the familiar tone. She wasn't his cleaner; she wasn't even sure if she was his friend. Was 'neighbour with benefits' an actual term?

'"*I miss you so much. Come home, baby? Come back, your life is here, not wherever it is you've holed yourself up now. Your friends, your family, we all need to know that you are okay, Hal. It isn't fair to cut us all off like this. How are you spending your days? I know I handled things badly, but I've had time to think about it and I would do better this time around. Give me another chance, we can still make a life here. We could open a new restaurant together, hire a chef in to do most of the cooking. You'd still oversee the menu and have complete creative control . . . it would be okay Hal, I promise, I'd make sure it was for you. It doesn't have to be the end, we can still have that dream life we* wanted. You, me, a restaurant, celebrity clients . . . remember?

We had some amazing times, didn't we? I can't think about our time in Venice without crying, Hal, it was the best weekend of my life. I've still got that awful street cartoon drawing of us on my bedroom wall, remember how we laughed about the fact that it looks more like Charles and Camilla than us?"'

Honey paused, winded by the details, the intimacy, and Hal dropped his head in his hands, hiding his expression from her.

'"I'm not saying things will be the same, obviously, but it will be better than just giving up on everything, won't it? Jesus, I know the accident was hard on you and I want to be there beside you again as your girlfriend . . . your wife, even.

Do you want to know a secret? I didn't cancel the wedding, Hal. I couldn't bring myself to do it. It's all still there for you if you want it. Come back. Come home to me please? Back where you belong, in the limelight. You worked too hard to let this go just because of the accident. Or to let me go.

I'm still here waiting for you, still loving you, despite everything that's happened.

Imogen x"'

Honey put her hand over her mouth as she read the last words, almost as if she wished she could push them all back in again and not even tell him that he'd received any mail that morning.

'"Despite everything",' Hal muttered darkly, repeating Imogen's sign-off. 'She means *I still love you despite the fact that you can't see anymore*. She always fucking blamed me, right from the moment I opened my eyes in the hospital.'

Honey was well and truly out of her depth. She couldn't offer any real advice because she'd never even met the woman, but from the letter Imogen sounded like a petulant teenager who'd cobbled together a desperate plan to hold on to the fantasy lifestyle she'd mapped out for herself on Hal's coattails.

'Tea?' she said inadequately, reaching for his cup.

Hal shook his head and huffed. 'I need a proper drink.'

He'd long since drunk her out of her leftover Christmas spirit supplies. 'There's some wine left?'

'Just fold the letter up and put it away,' Hal said, ignoring her offer of wine and visibly pulling himself together. 'Where's my shirt? I should go.'

'Hal, please. You don't have to leave so quickly,' Honey said, picking up his shirt from the floor and handing it to him.

'I think we both know that I do,' he said sourly, shrugging his shirt over his shoulders and pushing his arms roughly into the sleeves.

'It's okay. Honestly, it is,' Honey said, feeling everything but okay.

'Don't be fucking stupid,' he said, sounding bone weary. 'Of course it isn't. Okay is the last thing this is. It's fucked up and you know it. I shouldn't be here.'

Honey cast around for the right thing to say. He was right. It was fucked up and crazy, but what did he mean by he

296

shouldn't be here? Was he already regretting tonight? Was he still in love with his ex-girlfriend? It was a huge, tangled mess, the kind of mess that Honey had no clue how to clean up. She watched him prepare to leave, feeling his emotional detachment and wishing she could turn the clock back.

'I'm sorry,' she said softly.

'What do you have to be sorry for?'

She shrugged, agonised. 'I don't know.'

'Then don't be sorry,' Hal said, monotone and low. 'For what it is worth, I'm the one who's sorry. Sorry that I've dragged you into my shit.'

'Don't say you're sorry either,' she said urgently, laying her hand on his bicep and massaging because she needed to touch him, to offer him some sort of physical comfort in the absence of a hug. Hal was not a man given to hugging. She was grateful that he didn't shrug her hand off. He let her touch him briefly, and then he laid his hand over hers to still the movement.

'I'm monumentally fucking sorry that you've been dragged so far into my shit that you'll never get clean again. Trust me Honey, no one spends time around me and comes out of it wearing rose-tinted glasses anymore.'

For a few seconds he bumped his fingers over her knuckles, like a mountain rescue worker warming up someone they'd found wandering on a remote moor.

'Look,' he sighed. 'The fact is that you're a nice girl, and I'm not a very nice man. I emotionally manipulated you into asking me over here tonight, played the only card I had, the poor lonely drunk on his birthday. I'm not proud of it, and if I do it again, slam the door in my stupid, sorry face, okay?'

'What if I want you to?' Honey couldn't hide the thick sound of tears in her throat. 'What if I like you best of all in those moments when, for whatever reason, you let me in?'

He was fully dressed now and in the jumpy, agitated state of a cheating husband keen to flee the bed of his lover. It left her at a loss, not knowing how to feel or react. Too many emotions knocked around in her chest, fighting for sovereignty. She was angry; with him for leaving, with herself for being needy enough to want him to stay, with Imogen for writing the letter and laying out a bridge for Hal to cross or not cross. She was wistful; already missing the skyrocket feeling of being in his arms. And she was hurting; for herself, yes, but she was also hurting for him. Hal cut a lonesome figure as he stood.

'I don't know what to say to you.' He shrugged apologetically.

And with that, anger won out, because it offered her the most protection from his awkward discomfort.

'How about you say what you're really thinking, Hal? Or shall I save you the bother? You're grateful and all that for dinner and a birthday fumble on the sofa, but now you've had a better offer so you'll be on your way.'

Her outburst earned her nothing but his silence. He seemed about to say something, and then he said nothing at all and walked out of her flat, closing the door softly behind him.

Hal lay flat on his back, welcoming the numbness afforded to him by the whisky he'd drunk straight from the bottle as soon as he'd crossed his own threshold. He'd always known that life would catch up with him sooner or later, but he hadn't counted on it crashing back in and flattening Honey as well as himself. Bloody Imogen. She'd been his everything, and her letter had caused him all kinds of pain. How could she do this now? How could she come back and lay out their future in a few simple words. *Hire a chef*. Did she even know him at all? Didn't she understand how excruciating it would be for him to own a restaurant and not run his own kitchen? She'd clearly assumed him incapable of taking it on himself, and maybe he was, but was that her decision to make? He didn't want to trade on his past reputation for the sake of hanging on to a lifestyle that no longer had any meaning to him. Life in general had precious little meaning, but these last few days he'd allowed a few chinks of light into the darkness. He'd found moments of hope teaching Skinny Steve in the kitchens at the home, he'd found moments of laughter listening to Honey regale her haphazard life through his door, and tonight on Honey's sofa he'd felt like a whole man again for the first time in a long time. And then, the letter. Listening to the woman he'd just had sex with read a letter from the woman he'd planned to marry had screwed him up on just about every level. He hated himself for letting Honey read it to him. It had been selfish and unkind, yet he'd allowed it to happen because he'd been desperate to hear it. His needs over hers. An orgasm in exchange for a clerical favour. It hadn't been a fair deal.

CHAPTER THIRTY-ONE

The following morning came with indecent haste, and Honey had never felt more ill-prepared to lead her troops into battle. It was with tired eyes and a sore heart that she opened her door at a little after half past seven in the morning. It came as a shock to find Hal leaning against the wall outside her door. She'd assumed she wouldn't see him again for days.

'What are you doing lurking around in the hallway?'

'I told you I'd be there today to help feed the protesters. That hasn't changed.'

It was just about the only thing that hadn't.

'We can manage without you,' Honey said, even though they patently, clearly could not.

'Don't be stupid. You'll have mutiny on your hands if you leave Skinny Steve in charge of the kitchen,' he said, then dropped his voice. 'There's no need for us to be awkward around each other. We're adults, not school kids.'

So that was how he was going to play it. Achingly cool,

terribly sophisticated, it happens every day kind of thing. Well she'd never be able to do that.

But he was painfully correct about one thing; her army could not be expected to march on an empty stomach, and Skinny Steve was no sergeant major. She desperately didn't want to spend today around Hal, but so many people had invested too much time and effort, not to mention hope, into this day, and she had to put their needs before her own.

'Fine,' she said reluctantly. 'Let's just get on with it then, shall we?'

Outside it was one of those early autumn days to relish; the leaves turning, yet still enough warmth and the promise of washed-out lemon sunshine. Linking arms with Hal out of necessity, Honey tried not to feel any of the emotions he'd stirred in her last night, or BL, as she now referred to it in her head. Before Letter. They were now to adjust their relationship to AL status, or After Letter. Or neighbours without benefits, to put it another way. It was going to be a long, long day.

At the shop she found the troops already in the trenches. As it was closed on a Sunday, there were no customers, but the shop was heaving nonetheless. The majority of the residents had gathered inside, wearing oversized t-shirts over their woolly cardigans and jumpers with slogans painted on them, no doubt Billy's handiwork. Today they would not be one or two residents chained to the railings. It was to be all hands to the pump, a human chain of as many people as they could muster, residents, their families, friends, customers . . . anyone who cared enough to give their time was welcome. They'd put the word out as

301

surreptitiously as possible, and Old Don's son had tipped off the press to expect something newsworthy. Honey could only hope now that their plan came together. They were banking on the fact that Christopher didn't usually work the weekend shift. Without his eagle eye on the scene, they were hoping to make one last-ditch attempt to save the home.

'Honeysuckle, our modern day Joan of Arc,' Billy raised his hand and hailed her from the counter behind the till where he was busy handing out fluffy handcuffs from the large box he'd brought through from the staffroom. Mimi and Lucille flanked him, each with polka dot scarves knotted on their heads.

'Nice headscarves, ladies,' she grinned.

Mimi patted her dark curls. 'Once a Land Girl, always a Land Girl.'

'It feels a bit like those days in here today, doesn't it?' Lucille smiled fondly, her red lipstick the perfect match for her scarlet scarf.

'Let's just hope to God that we win this war, too,' Billy murmured with unusual gravitas. He was all bluff and dander, so much so that it was easy to forget that beneath it all was a man approaching ninety and frightened of losing his home.

Honey cast her eyes around the shop, soothed by the low hum of chatter and the chink of teacups as the residents readied themselves for their scheduled ten o'clock start. They'd planned the protest carefully to begin after breakfast and the medication run, the inauspicious time when residents usually retired to their own rooms or to the communal lounge or gardens.

'We will, Billy. We will.'

She patted his wrinkled, weather-worn hand, and he gripped her fingers tightly for a second and nodded, his resolute eyes over-bright.

'Let go of her, you silly old goat,' Mimi said mildly. Billy grinned and did as he was told, snapping back into his modus operandi as if nothing had happened. Honey turned her face towards the window while she swallowed the sudden lump in her throat. They didn't make men like Billy anymore, or for that matter, women like Mimi and Lucille. Fashioned out of sterner stuff by necessity, accustomed to hardship and fighting for what they believed in. In every way but physically, they were actually far better equipped for today than she was.

At a couple of minutes before ten, Billy and Mimi made their way out to the railings as if it were business as usual. Five minutes later, Lucille joined them, a trio of chained OAPs. Honey glanced at them through the window and Billy threw her a wink. He was enjoying this. In fact, everyone seemed to be in high spirits, and camaraderie ruled as they united together in their common cause. Safety in numbers, Lucille had said when they'd talked over the plans for the day, and it had become the unofficial name for the protest. Watching the residents walk out every few minutes to join the line, Honey's pulse beat a little faster. Operation Safety in Numbers was go.

By eleven o'clock, they were all there, standing if they were able, seated if they weren't. Thirty-three of them in all, each fastened by fluffy sex cuffs to the railings, or in Old Don's wheelchair's case, his vintage tie collection again.

Honey locked the shop doors and went outside to join them. Much as she wanted to join them on the railings,

303

they needed her for other things. She was their designated spokesperson, and just as importantly given their ages, she was the welfare officer. It was up to Honey to make sure they were all okay, grab seating for those who were flagging, put blankets around shoulders, and make sure they were all well fed.

'Hey, Honey!' She turned at the sound of her name and found herself flanked by Tash ready for action in her gym gear, and Nell in jeans, Hunter wellies and a buttoned-up Barbour. The girl even had a whistle around her neck.

'You came,' Honey grinned, gladder than she could have imagined to see them. The weight of making sure today went well sat heavy on her shoulders, but having her two best friends beside her lightened it.

'As if we'd be anywhere else,' Nell said, looping her arm around Honey's shoulders. 'What can we do?'

'We need to make sure everyone's warm, comfortable and fed,' Honey said, going through the basic list that had been running through her mind constantly since she'd woken. The whole thing would be for nothing if they gave Christopher any ammunition to use on them again. Honey had had to look away to hide her smile earlier when she'd overheard Billy giving Lucille and Mimi a strict talking-to about not brawling in the street again, but the fact was that they couldn't afford to come across as anything other than the fabulous band of elders that they were.

'There's a box of blankets by the gate,' Honey said, pointing towards the large box that she and Mimi had put together in the charity shop yesterday. Blankets were one of the things they received lots of, and they'd certainly be put to good use today.

'And there are chairs stacked just over there by the shop door.' She gestured at them. 'Basically, we need to make sure everyone is okay at all times, you know?'

Tash nodded. 'Easy-peasy, Honeysuckle.'

Nell's professional eye skimmed the line. 'Thirty-three. Eleven each,' she said briskly. 'Honey, you take from Billy onwards to eleven. I'll take the central chunk. Tash, you look after the last eleven. Right?'

She turned expectant eyes towards Honey and Tash, who could only nod, wide eyed. It was not for nothing that Nell had spent the last five years marshalling schoolyards of rowdy children.

'Will you blow your whistle if you see any of them playing up?' Tash asked innocently.

Nell smirked at Tash's sarcasm. 'I'm more likely to blow it at you than them. Chop chop.' She craned her neck as the doors to the home opened and Skinny Steve appeared with a large tray of plastic cups, a thermos of tea, and a mountain of muffins.

'Is Skinny Steve on his own in the kitchen today?' Nell frowned, having heard all about the recent kitchen woes from Honey.

Honey inspected her fingernails rather than look her friends in the eye.

'He has help.'

'If chilli-chef has returned from Spain, my eleven aren't going near those muffins,' Tash said, holding up her perfectly manicured hands. 'These babies are so not made for wiping OAP bottoms.'

'You're safe. It's not chilli-chef.'

Tash nicked one of the lemon and poppy seed muffins

from the tray as Steve passed. 'Christ, they're still warm! Have you actually made these, Steve? Because if you did, you're coming home with me, mister.'

Skinny Steve turned an unattractive shade of purple and his hands shook enough to make the plates on the tray rattle.

'Umm, it wasn't just me,' he said, struck by an up-to-that-point-in-his-life-unheard-of stammer. 'Hal did most of the work.'

'Hal?' Nell muttered as Steve moved away down the line.

'Hal as in your dirty sexy neighbour who has officially been declared bad for your health?' Tash said, breaking off a chunk of muffin with her fingers.

'He's a good cook,' Honey said evenly.

Tash nodded, her mouth full. 'Heavenly.' She swallowed, narrowing her eyes at Honey. 'As long as that's all he's doing for you. I've bust a gut finding you the perfect pianist.' She grinned. 'He's good, isn't he?'

With difficulty, Honey pulled Christian into focus in her mind. So much had happened in the intervening hours that it seemed days since she'd sat in the café with him.

'He's really nice,' she said, noncommittally.

'"Nice"?' Nell said, picking up on Honey's tone. 'Nice doesn't sound very impressive.'

'No, nice is . . . good,' Honey said, really wanting to change the subject, because all she could hear in her mind was Hal telling her that she was a nice girl and he wasn't a very nice man. Actually, he hadn't been wrong. Nice might be appropriate for Christian, but it wasn't a word for men like Hal.

306

'Looks like the cavalry are starting to arrive,' Nell commented, and looking along the line Honey saw Titania's middle-aged nieces had joined the end of the line, their splendid bosoms once more graffitied in honour of their aunt.

'That plays hell with your numbers,' Tash said. 'How many people am I in charge of now?'

A frown creased Nell's brow, and Honey stepped into the breach. 'Just keep a close eye on the residents as planned, and a general eye on everybody else, okay?' She nicked a muffin from the tray as Skinny Steve walked back down the line, drawing him aside for a second.

'How's it going in the kitchen?'

'Pukka,' Steve beamed, clearly channelling his inner Jamie Oliver. 'Hal's, like, all over it. These muffins? Twenty minutes from scratch. He's, like, a genius.' The upward inflection at the end of his sentence reminded Honey how young he was, and his words pressed home the fact that he held Hal in godlike esteem. Someone had to. She smiled encouragingly, despite the fact that her opinion of Hal was far less clear cut. She kind of agreed, and kind of violently disagreed. It wasn't an easy position to be in, and it made being anywhere near him almost impossible. They'd barely spoken on the journey in that morning. Honey would have sat at the other end of the bus from him to avoid any more awkwardness if she could have gotten away with it without seeming childish. For a while last night she'd trusted him to take care of her, and then this morning she could only trust him to take care of other people. But he was here, and looking down the line at the residents happily eating the muffins, she knew she ought to be grateful. Skinny Steve was grateful enough for both of them.

'Hal said he'll help me get a job in a professional kitchen if I want,' he said, his eyes shining.

Honey frowned, annoyed with Hal for widening Steve's horizons beyond the home, even though she knew it was selfish of her. 'Don't even mention leaving right now,' she smiled. 'We need you here.'

'I'll stay while he does,' Steve said, obviously still in hero-worship mode. 'I can't believe I've got him to myself.'

Yeah, don't count on keeping him, Honey thought darkly. He's only yours until he gets a better offer. She held her silence diplomatically as Steve meandered away back up the path towards the home, towards the kitchen, towards his idol.

'Looks like you better tell Steve to up the numbers for lunch,' Nell said, and Honey followed her gaze to the end of the line, to a group of seven teenagers in hoodies who'd been walking past and decided to join the protest.

She watched as one of them turned, lowered his hood, slid his phone into his pocket, and shook the hand of the nearest resident.

'My granddad used to live here,' he said. 'He'd have hated to see it closed.'

They fell into easy conversation, and Honey made her way towards Lucille and Mimi at the other end of the line.

'It's all going rather well so far, isn't it?' Billy said, his roguish blue eyes full of mischief.

Honey nodded. 'Seems to be.'

She glanced down at Mimi sitting on a chair beside him, her strapped-up ankle visible beneath the hem of her dress.

'How are you holding up, Mimi?' she asked.

'I'd be better without this damned chair,' Mimi scowled, too proud to admit that she needed any support.

'Actually Mimi, I think the chair adds to the visual impact of the protest.' Honey rubbed Mimi's shoulder. 'You're obviously injured, but you haven't let it stop you from coming out today. It shows everyone how much this means to you.'

Mimi sniffed, but her mollified expression told Honey that her words had helped soothe pride-ruffled feathers.

'Protester number fifty just chained themselves up!' Tash called from the other end of the railings, and a cheer of appreciation rippled along the line, along with the clank and rattle of cuffs against metal.

'You better make that sixty,' a familiar voice called out, and there, line dancing towards her, was Robin, his hair doing a dance all of its own choosing as he boot-scooted along the pavement. Behind him trailed what could only be described as a rugby scrum of questionable-looking characters, all of them twice the size of the oddest pied piper in history.

'Robin,' Honey laughed, thrilled to see him. 'How did you know?'

'A little bird might have told me,' he winked, and then winced at the shrill sound of a whistle.

'A little bird with a big whistle, by any chance?' Honey looked over to where Nell was good naturedly marshalling newcomers into place.

Robin nodded. 'And these marvellous boys are my students,' he said, emphasising the word 'students' in a conspiratorial, *you get my drift* kind of way. 'Strictly speaking I'm supposed to conduct these sessions in the

309

community hall to comply with their tags, but today my dance company is on tour, baby!' His voice dipped in the middle of his sentence to spare the parole gang from embarrassment, and then rose at the end to almost operatic levels. He clicked his Cuban heels for good measure, and then pirouetted away towards Nell and her whistle. Honey smiled at each of Robin's charges as they filed past her, most probably just relieved to not be spending the day listening to country music and doing the grapevine.

Hope flared hot in Honey's chest. This was happening. It was really happening, even better than she'd dared to hope.

Skinny Steve reappeared with more tea and biscuits to rally the troops, walking along the line and chatting amiably. Honey watched him, struck by the change in him since Hal had arrived. There was a confidence to him, a baby swagger learned from his new master. It suited him well.

'Get off me!'

A braying, male, distinctly alarmed voice reached her from down the line, and frowning, she hurried down to find Tash snapping purple fluffy cuffs around Christopher's wrist and chaining him up next to the line dancing ex-cons.

His eyes lasered in on Honey as she approached.

'Honeysuckle Jones! Unfasten me this instant or you're fired!'

A boo went up in the crowd, and Robin's line dancers all glowered in a way that made it clear they'd really love to break their parole conditions.

Tash grinned and dangled the little keys between her thumb and forefinger in front of her face.

'She can't. I've got the keys.' She gave them a little shake for effect, and then let them go right over the drain in the road. They teetered for a second on one of the metal ridges, and she nudged them lightly with her toe until they slipped over and tumbled into the water beneath with a faint splosh. The crowd were behind her every step of the way, laughing as she put her hands to her expertly made-up cheeks in fake shock. 'Oops. Sorry.'

Honey took advantage of the fracas to slink back down to Lucille and Mimi at the far end.

'Christopher just arrived,' she said, with a worried grimace.

'That's all we need,' Lucille said, her blue eyes clouding with apprehension. 'Where is he?'

'Tash just chained him to the railings down the other end.'

Billy hooted. 'I love that young lady.'

'I love you too, Billy Boy,' Tash laughed, appearing beside Honey. 'This is fun! I sort of recognised him when he hopped out of a taxi and had him in cuffs before he could even pay the driver.'

'What if he calls his bosses?' Honey dithered. If head office got wind of things they'd no doubt come down hard to shut the protest down before it grew any bigger. And going on the way things had gone so far, it was going to grow quite quickly.

'Call them on what?' Tash grinned. 'This?' She fished a mobile out of her pocket and shrugged casually. 'It kind of fell out of his suit pocket when I was chaining him up.' Honey knew Tash well enough to know that 'fell out of his pocket' was a loose interpretation of the truth. The girl was a brilliant liability. 'Don't look so worried,' she said,

311

squeezing Honey's shoulders. 'I'll keep it safe for him. He's bloody lucky I didn't drop it down the drain along with the handcuff keys.'

Honey often wished she were as bold as Tash, or as efficient as Nell. They'd each brought their own unique skills today, and between them they seemed to be pulling things off.

'You really should go and let the kitchen know how quickly the numbers are growing,' Mimi said, her beady eyes on Honey.

'I can do it,' Tash volunteered, and Honey almost shoved her towards the home out of relief at not needing to see Hal.

Billy had other ideas though, grabbing Tash's arm with his free hand as she moved past him.

'My darling, I think I've got a frozen shoulder. Do you think you could give it the quickest of massages? You look like you've got the perfect hands for it.'

Tash flexed her fingers. 'Go on then. These hands have had a lot of practice.'

Mimi, usually territorial over Billy, just smiled serenely. 'The kitchen, Honeysuckle.'

Coerced, Honey sighed and picked her way along the path towards the home. Towards the kitchen. Towards Hal.

Inside, the Sunday staff had gathered, bewildered. Without anyone to care for they were rudderless, and they turned to Honey as she walked through the doors.

'What are we supposed to do?' Nikki asked, one of the carers who Honey knew vaguely.

'Well, it's up to you guys. You can stay in here, or you

can go out there and make your voices heard. Your jobs are on the line here, as well as the residents' home. You have a dog in this fight too.'

She left them there, straightening her shoulders as she heard their murmurs of assent, when the door swung shut behind her. Maybe Tash was rubbing off on her after all. Outside the kitchen door a moment or two later, she regulated her breathing and hoped like hell that she could keep the kick ass attitude in place, at least for the next five minutes. Thank God Skinny Steve was in there too. 'Safety in numbers' had never felt a more appropriate phrase for the day.

CHAPTER THIRTY-TWO

Staying at the flat hadn't been an option for Hal that morning. He'd promised Honey and Steve that he'd be there, but his reasons for being at the home were more selfish than that. He didn't want to be alone with his thoughts today; he made bad company and even worse decisions. His brain was under siege, held hostage by the past. How had things gone so wrong? He'd woken yesterday with a plan to let his birthday slide past unmarked, and it had somehow ended up being the most significant birthday of his life.

He could blame the whisky. He could blame Honey. He could blame his brother. He could blame Imogen. He could blame all of those things and all of those people, but he didn't. Hal blamed himself for yet another spectacular fuck up, and he was reaching the point where he couldn't stand to make many more. That was the real reason he was here today. This seemed to be the one and only thing he was capable of doing right. Imogen's letter had opened doors that he'd long since slammed shut, and only the simple beauty of cooking could offer him respite from deciding which doors to open and which ones to close.

'I'll make a start on taking the soup out,' Steve said, heading out of the back door. 'I'll be back in ten.'

Hal nodded, and then turned as the door from the dining room opened. He knew who it was before she spoke. Strawberries, the slightly irregular sound of her breathing, the crackle of attraction, the complicated emotions.

'Where's Steve?' she said, in lieu of a greeting.

'Honeysuckle,' he said cordially. 'He's just gone down to take soup for the protesters. Did you need him?'

As he said it, he wished he'd chosen different words. He didn't want her to say she needed anyone else.

'It was just about the numbers.' She stumbled slightly on her words. 'There's already more than seventy people down there, more arriving all the time. We're going to need, umm, a lot of soup.'

Hal wasn't concerned by the numbers. He'd designed food today to specifically cater for a crowd. What concerned him more was the widening chasm between himself and Honey, and he didn't know how to bridge it.

'Honey, about last night . . .'

'Soup! Lots of it please!' she squeaked.

'It doesn't have to be like this.'

'I think we should work on well over a hundred,' she shot back, still hovering over by the door, ready to bolt. 'More, even.'

'We can make enough soup for the whole damn town if they all show up, Honey. It isn't a problem, okay?'

He heard her swallow. 'Good. Well, that's good news about the soup,' she said, trailing off. 'I'll get back then.'

315

'Honey. Just hang on a minute, please?' he said, even though he had no idea what he was going to do or say to make things better.

She didn't ignore him and leave. That had to be something, right?

'Come here.'

He needed her closer. She moved quietly, nearer, not touching him.

'I need to say some things, Honey, and I don't know how to say them without hurting you,' he said, reaching out for her, aiming for her shoulder, finding the soft skin on the side of her neck, his thumb on the warm pulse between her collarbones. She'd tied her hair back.

'Hal, do we really need to do this?' she said.

'Yes. Yes, we do,' he said. 'I don't want you to think I had a better offer than you. That isn't what that letter was. It's a different offer, but I don't want to ever hear you call anyone better than you again, okay?' A loose strand of her hair brushed his fingers and he stroked it back behind her ear, and then he just stroked her hair because he couldn't stop himself.

'What do you want, Hal?' she said, and he heard the question she was really asking. *Who* do you want, Hal?

'I don't know,' he said, because honesty seemed the only way to get through this. 'I don't fucking know. I just know that I can't think straight until we're okay again. I shouldn't have leaned on you yesterday, but I can't say I'm sorry for what happened because it was the most fucking alive I've felt since the accident. Being with you, it just feels . . .' Hal stopped, sighed. 'It just feels simple, Honey. It comes naturally.'

Beneath his fingers, her pulse trembled.

'Listening to you read that letter from Imogen was like scraping nails down my own eyeballs,' he said, hating even the memory. 'What kind of fucked-up prick does that to a woman?'

She sighed. 'It doesn't matter. You needed to hear it from someone.'

'Did I? I don't even know, but even if I did, then not from you. Anyone but you.'

'What difference does it really make who you heard it from, Hal? Maybe I was exactly the right person you needed to hear it from, and maybe that was exactly the right time for you to hear it. We're kind of done, aren't we? You gave me my orgasm, and now you get your life back. We both win.'

Except winners didn't cry when they delivered their speech, and Honey's voice shimmered with tears. And winners didn't feel like they'd been punched in the heart.

'We both know you don't mean that,' he said, knowing he should take his hand away from her face and cupping her cheek anyway.

'I don't think it even matters whether I mean it or not, because the fact is that you're going to decide to go home in the end. You know it, and I know it. There are wedding invitations out there being printed with your name on them, and a restaurant waiting to have your name over it. Your life's out there, waiting for you to step back into it.'

She was right. It would never be the same, but he could try to pick up the pieces and put them back together again into a similar but slightly altered picture. How had he gone from being certain that his future held no romance

317

to being someone's lover and practically another woman's fiancée?

'I don't know if I want that life again,' he said.

'Well, only you can decide, Hal.' She sounded tired. Unravelled.

'What do you think I should do?' he asked, even though he knew he had no right to.

He felt her shrug and breathe out shakily.

'Whatever you can't not do, I guess.'

It was a typically Honey kind of answer.

'I need to get back outside,' she said eventually, and he felt her hot tears run between his fingers on her cheek.

'Whatever happens next, I honestly didn't mean to hurt you,' he said, breathing in her scent, resisting the crazy, desperate urge to kiss her better.

She laughed softly, shook her head. 'Let's just call it collateral damage.'

He made his way to the back door after Honey had left the kitchen, and stood there on the step for a few minutes to feel the warmth of the sun on his crawling skin. How much more collateral fucking damage was his accident going to cause before it was done with him and everyone around him?

Skinny Steve bounded back into the kitchen a few minutes later to refill his thermos with more soup.

'This is going down a bomb out there,' he said gleefully. 'We're going to need to make more.'

'Yeah. Honey was in here just now and said as much.'

'Honey was here?' Disappointment rang clear through Steve's voice, and the penny dropped. Steve had a crush on

Honey. He was certain that Honey had no clue. She was totally guileless when it came to understanding the effect she had.

Steve was quiet as he assembled the vegetables for the soup on the bench for Hal to start work on. As they chopped onions side by side, he paused.

'Did you ever see pictures of Marilyn Monroe, Hal? You know, before your accident, like?'

Hal nodded, aware from Steve's voice that he was being taken into his confidence.

'Sure I did.'

'And you know that woman who played Bridget Jones? Renee something?'

'I think I know the one, yeah. Why?'

Steve paused. 'Because that's what Honey's like. Curvy like Marilyn, and always getting into trouble, like that Bridget Jones chick. She's blonde as well, but kind of kick ass.'

'So like Uma Thurman in *Kill Bill* too?'

'Man, I'd like to see Honey in that yellow tracksuit,' Steve murmured, and then coughed and seemed to gather himself. 'Yeah, like that.'

Funnily enough, all of the women Skinny Steve had listed resonated with the image of Honey he'd built in his head. She certainly had Marilyn's curves, he knew because he'd held them in his hands. He knew her dips and her hollows, they'd burned themselves onto his brain so clearly that he'd be able to mould her body from clay. And a penchant for getting herself into trouble? Bridget Jones was strictly amateur compared to Honey. She'd been trouble from the first time he'd met her in their hallway, which seemed like a lifetime ago now, and it followed her around like toilet paper stuck to the heel of her shoe. She was a trouble magnet.

And kick ass? Hell, yeah. She didn't think so herself, but that girl could rule the world if she wanted to. It'd teeter on the edge of disaster the whole time, but she'd somehow keep it balanced and make every one of her subjects adore her without even trying. Personally Hal could live without the yellow tracksuit, but as summaries went, Skinny Steve had pretty much hit the nail on the head.

'Pass the carrots, Steve.'

CHAPTER THIRTY-THREE

'Jesus, Honey, there's more than two hundred people here. We're going to need a police marshal at this rate,' Tash said. 'We ran out of handcuffs ages ago, people are using anything they've got. I've just chained four men up by the belts from their trousers. The women next to them were cheering, they thought they were going to get a performance of *The Full Monty*!'

Honey shook her head, overwhelmed with pretty much everything about the day. The protesters lined the street along the railings, snaked around the corner, and then doubled back on themselves along the other side of the railings. They were almost back at the beginning again, a complete loop of residents, friends, family, and locals who'd heard about the protest and come to show their support. Banners waved, t-shirts were emblazoned, and the gathered press pack had expanded in numbers almost as quickly as the protest.

'Are the residents all okay?' Honey asked as Nell came to join them on the pavement.

'Absolutely. They've all got a chair and a blanket each now, and we made sure they all had lunch. We had help, too. They've all had their medication,' she said, nodding towards Nikki, the care home worker, who was kneeling beside Old Don laughing at something he'd said. Looking around, Honey noticed other staff from inside too, some chained up, others milling amongst the residents. There was something about the whole event that had her permanently on the edge of tears, which was handy really, given that she felt like an emotional wreck. She was determined to keep her mind focused one hundred per cent on being out here doing her best, and not on the man inside providing sustenance for everyone. Making a success of this campaign had become crucial, because it was a battle she had at least some control over. Hal was his own man and needed to make his own decisions, but in her heart Honey already knew which way he was going to jump. He just needed to get there in his own time.

'Honey my darling, over here!' Billy called out, waving her over to the railings. Throwing his free arm around her shoulders, he turned her to face the flashes of what felt like dozens of cameras.

'Smile for the cameras, darling,' he said in her ear, and she bared her teeth in a rough approximation that probably looked more like a snarl than a smile but was the best she was capable of right now. Her tearstained cheeks would just add drama. Who knew heartbreak could be so helpful? She stilled, feeling a million miles away from the flashing bulbs. Was she heartbroken? To be heartbroken you needed to be in love, and she didn't love Hal, not precisely. Did she? Just because she wanted to be with him whenever she wasn't, and dreamed of him, and craved his touch, and loved the rare sound of his laughter, and held his happiness as more important than her own, and couldn't stand the thought of him walking out of her life, it didn't mean she loved him, did it? She'd felt all of those things for . . . thinking about it, she'd felt those things for no one else, ever.

'Could you unfasten my cuffs for a few minutes, dear heart?' Billy said close to her ear. 'There's a loudhailer in my room; I think we're going to need it.'

Honey nodded, opening his cuffs with shaky fingers, turned mute and stupid by her private epiphany. She didn't want to love Hal. He was the most difficult, recalcitrant of men, and he didn't love her back. How damn inconvenient to love someone who was marrying someone else next summer.

Billy detoured to the kitchen, loudhailer in his hand, and found Skinny Steve and Hal building sandwich mountains.

'I'll take the first lot out,' Steve said, walking cautiously and peering over the top of one of the huge platters. 'Billy, have you met Hal? He's our new chef, and he's brilliant. Hal, this is Billy.'

And with that, Steve stepped out of the back door and left them to it.

'Billy,' Hal said, aware of the older man's presence before Steve had made formal introductions. 'Honey's told me a lot about you.'

'She hasn't told me an awful lot about you, old bean, aside from the fact that you can't see,' Billy said. 'Rotten luck, by the sounds of it.'

Hal swallowed, taken aback by Billy's frankness. 'That's one way to put it,' he said, dryly.

323

'Happened to my brother,' Billy went on.

'It did?'

'Not much more than a kid at the time. It didn't stop him of course, still grew up to be the bane of my mother's life. More trouble afterwards, if anything,' Billy grinned at the memories. 'Sink or swim. He was a swimmer.'

Hal sat down hard on the stool at the bench, wondering if he was a swimmer. He didn't feel like one most days. He felt like a child in armbands frightened to loose hold of the side. He was surprised to feel Billy's hand on his shoulder.

'You'll get there, son. Early days yet.'

Outside, a police cruiser had indeed turned up, alerted to the size of protest by the almost non-stop coverage on the local radio.

'Who's in charge here?' the officer asked Tash, who'd just appeared from the shop with the staff radio in her hands and set it up on the ground so they could all listen to the coverage.

Tash led him over to Honey, who'd flopped into Billy's empty chair beside Mimi and Lucille to catch her breath.

'Are you in charge of this event?' the officer asked, pulling a pad from his pocket and looking over it at Honey. She stood up and wiped her hands down her jeans and then held one out in an attempt at professionalism. Her tearstained face and messed-up hair did little to back her up, but thankfully she didn't realise that she looked every inch a woman who'd found and lost the love of her life in the space of five minutes.

She nodded. 'I am.'

'And I assume you have the necessary permits, and you applied to the council to have this road closed?'

Honey opened her mouth and closed it again. There were no permits, or closed road applications. They'd hoped the event would attract a crowd of course, but by crowd she'd envisaged forty or fifty, rather than hundreds. It was peaceful, but it was undeniably huge, and traffic had ground to a halt when drivers stopped to see what was going on and left their cars to join the protest. Horns honked, and Nell had eventually made a sign and put it up at the end of the road to politely advise people to come and join the protest or go round a different way.

'Are you an officer of the law?' a voice bellowed from down the pavement, and they all peered down to see Christopher hanging as far out from the railings as he could manage and waving his free arm to attract attention. 'I'm the manager of this home and I demand . . .'

His demands, however, went unheard, drowned out in a flash by the sound of Robin clapping his hands and yelling 'Five, six, seven, eight!' in a theatrical singsong voice and swinging an invisible lasso above his head before performing a tight grapevine along the pavement. Beside him, all nine of his parole boys fell perfectly into step, completely obliterating Christopher from view aside from the occasional flash of his hand wildly poking out. The crowd went wild for them, joining in the boot-scooting chorus and doing their best to pick up the steps until a good half of the gathering were line dancing in the street, and the residents clapped along and cheered from their seats.

Honey clapped her hands to her face, tears coursing down her cheeks as she watched Robin's diminutive frame and huge hair bounce around, his pied piper status forever cemented, along with their friendship.

The police officer cleared his throat. 'Those permits we talked about?'

Honey opened her mouth to confess all, and at the same time Billy's voice boomed through the air as he strutted down the path with a loudhailer against his lips.

'Officer Nigel Thomson, as I live and breathe. I knew you when you were knee high to a grasshopper and your mother kept The Cock!'

Honey watched as the middle-aged police officer narrowed his eyes at Billy as he drew near, then broke into a huge smile and pushed his notebook back into his pocket, permits forgotten.

'Uncle Bill!' The officer put his hand out and pumped Billy's arm, and then pulled him into a stiff bear hug.

'I wasn't actually his uncle,' Billy mouthed at Honey over his shoulder with an arch wink. Watching Billy walk Officer Thomson back to his car a little while later, she let out a small sigh of relief at another near-disaster averted. When today was over, she needed to take a long holiday in a quiet place, preferably alone on a desert island with a fridge full of chocolate and wine.

'Umm, Honeysuckle, dear,' Lucille piped up, craning her neck towards the end of the road. 'Is that a TV van?'

Hold that thought. It looked as if that one-way ticket to paradise would have to go on hold for a while longer yet.

'Troy Masters can put his boom mike down my pants any time he wants,' Tash murmured as they stood watching the TV cameraman get himself set up while Troy Masters, a well-known face from the BBC twenty-four-hour rolling news channel, chatted easily to the crowds.

326

'You've been watching too many American TV shows, Tash,' Nell said. 'We still say trousers here, remember?'

'Oh, I know the difference perfectly well, Nellie,' Tash's laugh was pure filth.

'Never mind all that,' Honey said. 'They want to interview me on screen in half an hour, and we all know that I'm going to be rubbish!'

Nell and Tash exchanged a worried look over her head.

'Do you happen to have your make-up bag with you?' Tash said, way too casually.

Honey shook her head. It had been the last thing on her mind that morning.

'Hairspray? A comb?' Nell said, tucking Honey's wild hair behind her ear optimistically.

'Nothing. I've got nothing, and no clue what to say.'

After a moment, Nell took charge.

'Where's the key to the shop?'

Five minutes later, the contents of Tash's make-up bag were spread across the counter in the shop and Honey perched on a stool next to it. Tash walked around her, one way and then the other, casting a critical eye as she went.

'Let's just not bother,' Honey said, suddenly feeling as if she were in the middle of a department store about to be given a drastic makeover by a perma-tanned assistant who hadn't had enough training.

'Are you kidding?' Tash said, frank as always. 'You look like the bride of Dracula. Did you just wipe mascara down your cheeks for a laugh this morning?'

Nell rooted in her bag and produced a packet of baby wipes. 'I dread the day I have to stop buying these. I used them to polish the TV in a panic last week when Simon's mother turned up unannounced.'

Swiping one lightly over Honey's cheeks, she sucked in her lips. 'I see what you mean, Tash. Bloody hell, Hon, have you really cried this much today?' She rubbed harder at the streaks, making Honey screw her face up and take the wipe from Nell's fingers to do it herself. Nell picked up a gilt, long-tailed hand mirror they used to show customers how necklaces looked on them and held it up for Honey.

The face looking back at her wasn't the one she'd seen when she'd applied the ill-advised mascara that morning. It was similar, certainly; the same features, the same apple cheeks, cheeks that were now glowing like airplane landing lights thanks to Nell's ministrations. But her eyes weren't the same. These were the eyes of a woman, not a girl. Hal hadn't just made a woman of her last night on her sofa; he'd been making a woman of her from the very first moment she'd met him.

As a child, her mother had gone through a stage of taking them to church every Sunday, and scraps of an oft-repeated reading drifted back.

When I was a child, I reasoned like a child. When I became a man, I put away childish things.

Today, Honeysuckle Jones had finally put away her childish things.

She took the mirror from Nell and laid it face down on the counter, and then put her hand over Tash's to still it as she rooted through the cosmetics she'd laid out.

'Forget the make-up, Tash,' Honey said softly. 'And the wipes,' she half laughed, holding on to Nell's hand too. 'I don't care what I look like on telly. What matters is what

I say out there.' An unexpected wash of absolute calm settled over her bones. 'If I can find the right words, this is a real chance to actually save the home. That's pretty bloody amazing, isn't it?'

Nell nodded and squeezed her fingers in support, and Tash rolled her eyes.

'Troy Masters might be a grade eight pianist in his spare time. That's all I'm saying.'

Nerves rattled through Honey's body as she stood on her mark beside Troy Masters and the cameraman ran through his lighting and sound checks. Lined up beside her were Lucille and Mimi, Billy, and on the end, Old Don in his wheelchair with his war medals pinned proudly to his t-shirt.

'We'll be on air in five minutes, guys,' Troy said, smiling to put her at ease, his rich voice as familiar as an old friend's from years on the TV.

Honey nodded, and tried to swallow with difficulty. The inside of her mouth seemed to have turned to sandpaper. The cameraman had chosen to set up the interview site close to the shop with the protesters in the background, which hopefully meant that viewers would be able to hear her clearly as well as get a good idea of the ever-growing scale of the protest. Even as she watched, newcomers arrived, by now bringing their own shackling methods having been advised to do so by the radio. Neck ties had proved to be popular, as had yards and yards of silver tinsel one of the staff from the home had found in the storeroom. In reality, tinsel wasn't going to effectively restrain anyone, not even the many children who were happily playing on the grass, tied loosely to their parents' wrists. The method of restraint wasn't the point – it could have been a single strand of cotton and it would have had just the same visual impact. We all stand together, it said, every last one of us, from the ribbons fastening the pram of a six-month-old baby to Old Don tied by his vintage tie collection.

'Can someone shut that ice-cream van up?' the camera-man yelled, and the white-haired Italian ice-cream man zipped back across the grass to kill the music. He'd heard about the protest on the radio and turned up an hour or so back to hand out free ice creams to all the kids. It would have been another streaked-cheek moment for Honey, had she had any mascara left on to cry off.

'One minute and counting,' the cameraman said, and they all squared their shoulders in readiness.

Troy opened with an introduction to camera about the protest, and then turned to Honey with his mike in his hand.

'So Miss Jones, did you anticipate that the protest would be so well attended?'

Honey smiled. 'We hoped, obviously, but no, I never expected this many people to come out in support. We're grateful beyond measure, and only hope that it makes the owners of the home think again. There's more than thirty residents living in the home, and the idea of having to leave has most of them terrified.'

Troy nodded with a solemn frown on his face. 'And your own job is presumably on the line too?'

'Mine and everyone else's who works here too,' Honey said. 'The home employs more than fifty staff, it's a lot of jobs to lose. But in all honesty, this is about the residents, not the staff. We can get other jobs, but would you want to be homeless at ninety? Or would you want that for your

330

parents, or grandparents?' Honey could feel her blood starting to heat up in her veins, all of her frustrations from the day channelling themselves into that one important moment.

'This home is full of amazing people. War veterans. Women who kept the home fires burning and raised their babies in a blackout. A generation of people who've already seen more hardship than most of us will ever encounter. How can it be right to toss them out onto the street like yesterday's newspaper, or to rehome them scattered across the county like a pack of stray dogs?'

The look on Troy's face told her that she'd already given him far more than he'd counted on from her, but the words wouldn't stop falling from her mouth, and worse, hot tears were gathering in her eyes.

'These people . . .' she looked at Lucille and Mimi. 'These people stood up for us when we needed them, and today we're standing up for them.' A tear slipped down her cheek and she swiped it with the back of her hand. 'We're standing with them, and we're asking everyone out there watching this to stand with us too. Stand in your living rooms, stand with us on Twitter, or on Facebook, or in your local pub right now!'

Troy looked alarmed, and the cameraman was drawing a line across his throat with bulging eyes. Honey could understand it, but couldn't find it in herself to be bothered if she'd made a fool of herself. She stood stiffly beside the others as Troy threw back to the studio, and finally the cameraman raised his hand and switched off the light on the camera.

It was only then that Honey realised that the protesters had fallen silent to listen to what she said, and as she turned to look across at them a ripple of applause began, quietly at first, rising to a thunderous noise as Honey clamped shaking fingers over her mouth. Troy Masters shook her by the other hand, and then Billy grabbed it from him and lifted her arm aloft as if she were the victor in a boxing ring. Honey's ears rung with the noise, and she found she was half laughing and half crying. They hadn't won yet, but maybe, just maybe, they'd just moved a step closer.

In the dining room Skinny Steve had turned on the TV to watch the segment, and he sat alongside Hal at the nearest table as Honey appeared on the screen.

'She looks hot, just so you know,' Steve muttered.

'She sounds nervous,' Hal said, listening to her as she started to speak.

They sat in silence as her speech gathered pace and passion, and heard the crowds outside begin to clap when Steve turned the TV off afterwards.

Hal laughed and shook his head. Honeysuckle Jones, slayer of evil giants, Svengali of the masses. He pushed his chair back and stood up.

'I think we're going to need some extra help in the kitchen, Steve,' Hal said.

A mile or so away in The Cock Inn, the Sunday afternoon drinkers watched Honey's impassioned plea go out live on the news and to the last man, they stood up and raised their glasses.

CHAPTER THIRTY-FOUR

By three o'clock, Nell had given up trying to count the newcomers or marshal them into position. The pavement was packed, the grass was covered, and the road itself was three or four deep with people sitting on the tarmac. Strangers happily fastened themselves onto the human chain in any way they could; Honey had even seen a gaggle of little girls tying Old Don's wheelchair back to the railings with daisy chains after he'd appeared on the TV. Tash winked at her as she clicked away with her iPhone, recording the day for them all to look back on when it was over. She wasn't the only photographer there by a long way. The press were all over the protest in earnest now it had made the national news, snapping pictures and interviewing as many of the protesters as they could. Every once in a while the radio blasted out a country hit especially for Robin and the parole boys, and they'd lead the crowd in a heel-clicking line dance to keep the morale sky-high. It was unfortunate for Christopher that he was chained up right next to them and thus found himself regularly hauled to his feet and forced to half-heartedly dance, all arms and legs, rather like an outraged puppet on a string.

The kitchen played its part valiantly too, ordering in more supplies from a local supermarket who delivered within half an hour once they realised that they'd get a boatload of feel-good free publicity when their vans arrived in the street. They even threw in freebies; sweets and biscuits that lent the whole affair a 'picnic in the park' atmosphere, regardless of the fact that it wasn't the warmest of days. It was good-natured, and as the TV station ran the story regularly across the day, their numbers continued to swell.

'I think we might have to start turning people away soon,' Nell worried.

'No bloody way,' Tash said. 'We'll just go around the corner and start filling the next street when this one's chocka.'

Honey shook her head. 'I just can't believe it's turned out like this. It's huge!'

'Fucking gargantuan,' Tash nodded sagely. '*And* we met Troy Masters.'

They looked up as someone picked their way through the crowds.

'Nell!'

Nell's face broke into a big smile when she saw her husband.

'Simon, you made it. I knew you would.' Honey was surprised when Simon pulled Nell into his arms and placed a lingering kiss on her mouth until she pushed him away, laughing.

Tash made heaving motions behind them. 'Get a room, kids.'

'There's no handcuffs left, Simon,' Honey smiled warmly at him and leaned in to peck him on the cheek. He glanced at Nell, and a private look passed between them before he reached into his pocket and withdrew a pair of silver ones.

'No need. I've come prepared,' he said, and had the good grace to go slightly red-cheeked. In the whole time Honey had known Nell's husband she'd never before thought him impish, but in that moment, being led away by his wife with his handcuffs and his schoolboy embarrassment, it was the only way to describe him. Honey could only wonder at how it might feel to be with someone who understood you as innately as Simon understood Nell, someone who celebrated your strengths and encouraged you to be more than you imagined you could be.

Tash had drifted away and was caught up in conversation, so Honey wound her way between people until she made it to Mimi and Lucille. Dropping gratefully into Billy's empty seat between them, she looked from one perfectly lipsticked sister to the other.

'How do you two still look as fresh as daisies when I look as if I've run a marathon?' she grumbled, pulling out her hairband and re-tying it more securely.

'Because we've just sat here while you've done all the hard work, dear,' Lucille smiled, patting her knee.

'Some people would call that plain lazy,' Honey laughed. 'How's the ankle bearing up, Mimi?'

Mimi waved the question away airily. 'I ploughed fields when I was twenty-one and still managed to jitterbug with the GIs in the evening. My ankle is perfectly fine, thank you very much.'

'She asked Nikki for an extra painkiller earlier. I heard her,' Lucille supplied, and Mimi shot her a look. There had been the smallest of power shifts between the two sisters since the incident with Mimi's ankle; less of an imbalance in Mimi's favour and it suited Lucille well.

Honey looked over her shoulder. 'Where's Billy got to again?'

'The Scarlet Pimpernel,' Mimi grouched. 'Give him an audience, and the man has to act the goat. He's been here, there and everywhere all day.'

Honey rolled her shoulders and stretched her legs out in front of her, suddenly aware of how much her feet were aching now that she'd sat down. She could easily forgive Billy for deserting his post if it meant she got to spend five minutes recharging her batteries between the two main reasons she was doing any of this in the first place.

Gazing down the road, her eyes came to rest on a small dark-haired woman pushing a wheelchair in their direction. Catching her eye, the woman broke into a wide smile and raised her hand.

Beside her, Honey heard Lucille's soft gasp and a second later felt her fingers grip her wrist.

'I know,' Honey said, raising her hand and smiling in acknowledgment. 'I see them.'

'Who?' Mimi said, peering around them to see who they were looking at.

From a distance, it might have been Mimi in the wheel-chair, the resemblance was so strong.

Honey reached out and picked up Mimi's hand in her own. She didn't miss the fact that it was shaking slightly. Lucille's fingers tightened around Honey's wrist and they sat in silence until their visitors came to a halt in front of them.

'Well there's no denying whose brother you are, is there?' Mimi said brusquely, dashing her spare hand across the back of her eyes.

'Ernie!' Lucille cried, springing up and kissing his cheek.

'I saw you both on the news and I had to come,' he said, holding on to her hand. 'You girls are being so brave, I thought I should be too.' His gaze moved to Mimi, uncertain. 'Is that okay?'

Honey stood and moved her chair out from between Mimi and Lucille.

Mimi sighed. 'You better park yourself up here,' she nodded at the freshly vacated space. 'Honey, you better go and get Ernie a nice cup of tea.'

Billy wasn't acting the goat or entertaining the crowds. Shirtsleeves rolled back and pinny on, he was working up a storm alongside Hal and Skinny Steve, reacquainting himself with knife skills gained in the army kitchens. There was something about their new chef that intrigued him. Maybe it was the fact that he reminded him in some ways of his much-missed brother. Maybe it was that he sensed a deep melancholy in him, and innately understood it. Maybe it was purely selfish, that every now and then Billy needed to turn the showman off for a while. Or maybe he wanted to check Hal out as a potential suitor for Honey, because it was written all over the girl that she was in way over her head. Perhaps it was a jumble of all of those things that placed Billy in the kitchen, but whatever it was, Hal was grateful for both his help and his company.

A second TV company had been and gone by half past four, and the protest had managed to make most of the national news channels as well as the local ones. It was the kind of story that caught hold of everyone's imagination, and Honey's impassioned speech had set Twitter on fire with the hashtag #standwithus trending across the country. Going make-up free had been an unintentional stroke of genius; she'd become the tearstained poster girl that everyone wanted to wade in and support.

'Five hundred tealights,' Nell puffed, dropping a straining carrier bag down and rubbing her fingers where the plastic had bit into them. They were going to lose light soon and no one was showing any sign of going home, so they'd decided to break just about every health and safety rule in the book and hand out tealights.

'Candles create atmosphere,' Tash had reasoned. 'They make people feel all sentimental. Imagine how it'll look on the TV, Honey, like one of those vigils that makes everyone pick up the phone to give money they don't have.'

'Have we heard anything at all from the owners of the home?' Simon asked, standing with his arm around Nell's shoulders.

Nell shook her head. 'The only thing they're saying on the TV is that they've declined to comment.'

'Well, they're just about the only one who has,' Nell looked up from her mobile and grinned. 'Phillip Schofield's just tweeted the standwithus hashtag to over three million followers!'

'Oooh, I love Phillip!' Lucille piped up, her hand fluttering over her hair as if he might appear at any moment. 'What's a hashtag?'

'Oh my God, look,' Tash said, turning her screen around to show Honey the shot of Davina McCall in daisy chain handcuffs underneath #standwithus. 'If this doesn't make the difference, I don't know what will.'

Skinny Steve couldn't believe anyone would ever want to interview him, and he fell over his words when a reporter from one of the nationals waylaid him en route back to the kitchens with empty coffee flasks.

'You're doing a fantastic job here today, congratulations,' the pretty reporter gushed.

'Thank you,' Steve stammered. 'But it's not all down to me. I wouldn't have known where to start without Hal to tell me what to do.'

The woman smiled winningly, and Steve really liked the way her kind blue eyes twinkled.

'Hal?' she said.

Steve nodded. 'He's amazing. I can't believe I'm being taught to cook by someone as famous as him.'

The reporter tipped her head to one side. 'Do you think we could meet him too?'

Steve frowned, realising that he might have said too much.

'I don't think so. Hal doesn't want anyone to know he's here.' He bit his lip. 'You won't tell anyone, will you?'

The reporter drew lines over her heart with her shell-pink nails.

'Cross my heart.'

She reached inside her shirt and pulled a business card

out of her bra, then reached out and tucked it into Steve's apron pocket.

'In case you think of anything else to tell me,' she said, and then tripped away on her high heels.

Skinny Steve breathed a sigh of relief and headed inside for more coffee.

As dusk fell just before six o'clock, the candles turned the pavement into a flickering carpet of light and Honey returned to her sweet spot between Lucille and Mimi.

'Ernie's gone then?'

Lucille nodded with a little smile. 'He stayed for ten minutes or so, but he was worn out. He's promised to come and see us again soon though.'

Mimi's expression was inscrutable, and Honey decided not to push her on the matter.

'Still no sign of Billy?'

'He appeared a while back with a plate of sausage rolls,' Lucille said. 'Odd, really.'

'Nothing surprises me where that man's concerned,' Mimi said. 'He's a loose cannon.'

Honey laughed softly. 'He is that.'

'How's that handsome friend of yours doing in the kitchen?' Lucille asked, her blue eyes keen and wise.

Honey shrugged. 'Well everyone's eaten, so I guess he's doing fine.'

'Haven't you been inside to check on him?' Mimi asked sharply, and Honey suddenly felt as if she were caught in the centre of a 'good cop bad cop' routine.

'Not this afternoon, no. I've been busy out here, there hasn't been time.'

'There's time now,' Lucille said reasonably. 'Take five minutes.'

Honey picked at a loose thread on her sleeve. 'Maybe later.'

'I used to say things like that,' Mimi said. 'And then you get old and there isn't a later, and you wish you'd done it sooner.'

'You didn't say that about meeting Ernie,' Lucille said, her tone laced with hurt.

Mimi shot Lucille a look for going badly off script and ignored the barb.

'I'm just giving Honey the benefit of my wisdom. If there's something that needs to be said, don't let your pride stop you from saying it.'

Lucille nodded and laid her hand on Honey's arm.

'She's right, dear. We both think that you've fallen for him. You should tell him.'

Honey let her head drop back and gazed at the stars.

'It's more complicated than that.'

She didn't bother denying the truth. Mimi and Lucille knew her inside out and backwards, and besides, it was a relief to talk about it out loud.

'It's only as complicated as you make it,' Lucille said.

Honey sighed heavily. 'They aren't my complications, Lucille. They're his. He's got to make some choices, and I've got to wait and see which way the chips fall.'

'That doesn't sound fair to me,' Mimi said. 'Never give a man all the power, Honeysuckle. They don't know what to do with it and will more than likely blow their own hands off before they've even got started.'

'His ex-fiancée wants him to go back to London. She

341

sent him a letter asking him to step back to his old life.'
Honey folded her arms over her chest and kept her eyes
on the dark sky. 'They're supposed to be getting married
next year.'

Mimi and Lucille fell silent while they mulled Honey's
revelation over.

'People change,' Lucille said, eventually. 'Going back isn't
always possible.'

'Get yourself in there this minute and tell him to choose
you,' Mimi said, suddenly fierce. 'Or do you want me to
do it for you?'

Honey laughed softly and rubbed Mimi's arm. She was
pretty sure that however fierce Hal could be, Mimi could
be fiercer.

'I think this is one battle I need to fight on my own,' she
said, knowing that Mimi and Lucille were both right in
their own ways. She needed to pull up her big girl pants
and be honest with Hal about how she felt before he made
his decision, or else she might never get the chance to. It
would be better to cope with rejection and get over him
than to spend the rest of her life wondering what if.

'I'll tell him. As soon as today's over, I'll tell him.'

Skinny Steve heaped piles of warm sausage rolls onto plates
and prepared to go out on yet another food run.

'Try not to get paparazzied this time, Stevie-boy,' Billy
warned.

Hal grinned. 'Are you becoming a celebrity out there too,
Steve?'

'It's not funny,' Steve muttered. 'I almost blew your cover
earlier.'

Hal paused, hating the fear that prickled the hairs on his arms. 'Only *almost* though, right?'

'Yeah, I only said Hal, not your whole name, before I remembered.' Steve put the sausage rolls down by the door and rustled in his apron pocket for the reporter's business card. 'Alicia Caughton-Black. What kind of a name is that?' he laughed, picking up the plate again and shaking his head as he headed outside.

'Fuck.'

Hal scrubbed his hand over his mouth hard. He knew exactly what kind of a name Alicia Caughton-Black was, because he'd met Alicia Caughton-Black on several occasions. A reporter who loved to court the celebrity circuit, she'd eaten in his restaurant; he remembered her well because she'd made a fuss about being vegan every time and asked to see him personally to discuss her choice of dish. He'd known at the time that she was trying to draw gossip from him rather than food facts, but he'd paid little attention because no publicity was bad publicity for the restaurant.

Skinny Steve would have been like Bambi in her lioness paws; the kid wouldn't have stood a chance of outwitting her.

'What's the matter, son?'

Billy.

'I need to get out of here, Billy,' Hal said, aware that his voice wasn't as even as he'd like it to be.

'You mean you need a breath of fresh air? A ciggie?' Billy said, sounding doubtful.

'No. I mean I need you to call me a cab and not tell a soul.'

'You can't walk out of here now, son. We need you.'

Savage fury ripped through Hal's chest, and he kicked

the cupboard beside him. 'Why now?' he said. 'Why the fuck right now?'

'Tell me what's going on, Hal. I might be able to help you.'

Hal shook his head. 'The only thing you can do now is call me that cab, Billy. I'll tell you exactly what you and Steve need to do to keep things going tonight, but I can't stay here. I'm sorry. I just can't.'

CHAPTER THIRTY-FIVE

At that moment, Honey, Tash and Nell all sat side by side on the grass outside, their bellies full of Hal's delicious food and their ears full of the sound of singing. Lucille and Old Don had reprised their roles as choir leaders, starting things off with the opening lines of 'Morning Has Broken'. Slowly and surely, people had joined them. Residents, family and friends, singing, humming, their faces illuminated by the flicker of the candles as they swayed gently. The parole boys moved things along with a heartrending rendition of the opening verse of 'You'll Never Walk Alone'; they were no Welsh choir, but they moved the crowd to join in with them come the chorus.

It was a scene that burned itself onto Honey's heart forever, and was absolute TV gold for the news channels. Troy Masters had once more returned to the site with his cameraman, and they watched as he filed a piece to camera on the unfolding events.

'I still think you should have a crack at him, Honey,'

Tash said, her eyes on his pert backside. 'You're practically a celebrity in your own right now. You could be one of those cute TV couples who host *This Morning*.'

'Piss off,' Honey said, knocking Tash in the ribs with her elbow.

'I don't think she needs us to set her up anymore,' Nell said. 'Do you, Honey?'

Honey had known that her friends were too perceptive to miss what was going on under their noses.

'Don't say it,' Tash said suddenly. 'I know you think you love him, but it'll pass.'

Honey turned to her. 'Not so long ago you were telling me to seduce him.'

'Yeah. Seduce him. Have hot sex. I never told you to bloody love him, did I?'

'We can't help who we fall in love with, Tash,' Nell chided.

'Bollocks can't we,' Tash shot back. 'He's trouble. He's already broken her heart before he even knows she loves him.'

They lapsed into silence.

'I don't think he meant to,' Honey said, her voice small.

Tash leaned in against her one shoulder, and Nell propped her up on the other side. They sat there like that for a fair while, and Honey felt her breathing regulate and her heartbeat calm down. Whatever happened, she wasn't going to have to get through it alone.

'Nell! Get Honey over here, quick!' Simon called a few minutes later. 'Troy Masters needs her on camera right now!'

Simon wasn't given to drama, so his tone was enough to have the girls scrabbling to their feet and heading across

346

the grass to Troy. He beckoned Honey across to stand beside him, and then switched on his professional smile and spoke into the camera.

'Thank you Sarah,' he replied to the presenter back in the studio. 'Yes, you join us back here at Greyacres where we have breaking news, and I'm joined once more by Honeysuckle Jones, the protest leader.'

Honey smiled quizzically. Breaking news? She glanced towards Nell and Tash beside the cameraman, and they both shrugged, obviously none the wiser either. Troy looked down at an iPad in his hands, and then back to camera.

'This has really caught the public's attention today, nowhere more so than on Twitter,' he said. 'The hashtag #standwithus has been trending throughout the afternoon, and in the last ten minutes there's been something of a first, Sarah, a celebrity auction taking place,' he said, flashing his cosmetically correct smile again. 'It seems that there's at least three stars vying to buy the home for the residents, Honeysuckle,' he said, and held the microphone out for her to reply.

'Really?' she squeaked, rendered almost speechless by shock and glassy eyed with yet more tears. Troy, who had her number this time, held out a tissue and grinned.

'Mick Jagger was first to offer, and then Jamie Oliver threw his hat into the ring,' Troy said.

'His pukka white chef's hat,' Honey whispered in wonder, and earned herself a warning look from the cameraman.

She saw Tash lean towards Nell. 'I'm gonna fucking die laughing if the third one's Michael Bublé,' she whispered.

The cameraman's head whipped around so hard that he was lucky not to break his neck. Tash had just sworn live into the living rooms of thousands of viewers up and down the country.

Troy coughed spectacularly to cover it up as best he could and hastily threw back to Sarah in the studio, while Tash and Nell threw their arms around a shaky-kneed Honey and danced her in a wonky circle.

'Oh my bloody God,' Honey whispered, as Tash whipped her phone out and loaded Twitter.

'Look at the list of hashtags that are trending right now,' she said, running her finger down the list. #standwithus sat in pole position, closely followed by #goodonyoumick and #jamiesavestheday.

Honey stared at the screen, hardly able to believe it. They'd done it. They'd bloody well done it. Her face ached from smiling, and then that smile melted from her face like butter in a hot pan. Touching Tash's mobile screen, she looked up slowly at her friend.

'Why is #benedicthallam trending too, Tash?'

Honey ran. She ran through the crowds, desperate to get inside, dogged every step of the way by people wanting to congratulate her, shake her hand, or drag her into a hug. It was obvious that quite a few people had taken the arrival of dusk and candles as a prompt to crack open the wine, so there was a definite party vibe going on. Everyone gleefully threw off their shackles and made merry, but Honey couldn't have felt less like joining in the revelry. She threw herself gratefully through the doors of the home, relieved when they slid shut and cut out much of the noise behind her. She needed to think fast, and most of all she needed to get to Hal. She had no clue what she was going to say

348

to him; whether to warn him that he'd been discovered, tell him that the home was saved, or tell him that she loved him more than life. She needed to say all of those things, and she could feel her heart hammering as she pushed open the kitchen door and prayed he'd be in there alone.

Billy sat in the kitchen, no Hal or Skinny Steve, a bottle of whisky and two empty glasses on the counter in front of him. Honey didn't stop to wonder why Billy was in the kitchen at all. The only thing that mattered was that Hal wasn't there.

'Where is he, Billy?' she whispered.

'Come and sit down, Honey,' Billy said kindly, patting the stool next to his. She stood rooted to the spot, her hand over her heart.

'Where is he?'

Billy sighed, his eyes troubled and his trademark sparkle nowhere to be seen.

'He's gone, sweetheart.'

'Gone? How can he be gone?' Honey said. 'He goes home with me. We go home together.'

'Not this time,' Billy said, as tactfully as he could. 'He asked me to call him a cab about an hour ago.'

'A cab? You called him a cab?' Panic sent her voice shrill. 'For God's sake, Billy, he doesn't do this! He can't . . . he hasn't . . .' She stopped, because she was gasping, struggling to get her breath.

'Yes he can,' Billy said quietly. 'He's not a child, Honey. He's a man. Let him be one.'

She sagged against the doorframe. 'Did he say where he was going?'

Billy looked down and shook his head sadly.

'He had a lot on his mind,' he offered.

Honey dashed the back of her hand over her cheeks.

'I know that,' she said. 'How did he seem to you?'

Billy paused. 'Like he needed space?'

'From what?' Honey said, stricken. 'From me?'

In that moment she reminded Billy of an evacuated child, a lonely little girl suddenly bereft without the person she loved best. It fair broke his heart that her day should end like this.

It was well after midnight when the last of the protesters-turned-partygoers packed up and left, and Honey dropped down on the cool grass and wrapped her arms around her knees. People had been kind and taken all of their rubbish home with them, aside from a few lonely strands of tinsel glittering in the moonlight. Running her fingers over the grass, she found a discarded daisy chain, its flowers closed up and yellowing without the benefit of sunshine on its petals. Picking it up, she slipped it carefully in her pocket, and then accepted Tash's outstretched hand to pull her up.

'Dust yourself down, Supergirl,' Tash said, leading her away from the home by the hand. 'Come on. I'll take you home.'

CHAPTER THIRTY-SIX

Someone was banging on her head. They had to be, because it was loud and it hurt. Honey roused from her bed on the sofa, still dressed in yesterday's clothes and groggy with the need for more sleep. She'd slumped down as soon as she'd walked through the door last night, not even bothering to take off her shoes. The fact that she was now barefoot and had a pillow and a blanket told her that Tash had stuck around long enough to see her off to sleep. The world needed more Tashes, unless of course she was the person banging on the front door, because whoever that was clearly had no respect.

'Stop banging, I'm coming,' she yelled, standing up and rubbing her hands through her hair in a vague attempt to straighten herself up. Not that it mattered, because she had no intention of going anywhere today, not unless she ran out of wine or the house burned down. Maybe not tomorrow either, or even the next day. Honey had officially shut up shop, pulled the shutters down on life and declared herself gone fishing. She was exhausted, and she couldn't rely on her legs to hold her up or her brain to string a sentence together that didn't include the word Hal.

'Hal!'

Honey frowned. The hammering hadn't stopped, but now she was finally awake she realised that it wasn't her own door being assaulted, it was Hal's, and from the sound of it the assailant was female.

'I know you're in there, Hal. Damien gave me your address.'

Honey inched along the hallway, drawn like a cobra from its wicker basket by a snake charmer.

'Please, Hal. Open the door.'

Whoever was out there didn't sound as if they were going to take no for an answer. They obviously hadn't counted on Hal's belligerent, stubborn-as-a-mule attitude. She cricked open her door, hoping to sneak a look at Hal's visitor before they realised she was there.

Wow. They were good shoes. Honey started at the bottom and worked her way up, letting go of her shoe envy to take in the skinny hips in dark skinny jeans, and the slick, buttery leather jacket that clung to the woman's slender body as if it had been peeled directly from a newborn calf and moulded around her. Gleaming, honey-blonde hair hung poker straight to her shoulder blades, swishing violently as she rapped her knuckles on the door yet again.

'For God's sake, Hal,' she called out. 'I know you can hear me. Half the street probably can.'

'He won't answer it,' Honey said, surprising herself as much as Hal's visitor.

The stranger swung around, and for a couple of seconds

the two women took each other in. As glossy from the front as she'd been from the back, everything about her screamed money. She looked like a woman made to sip champagne on the deck of a footballer's yacht, utterly out of place in Honey's hallway.

The cool look in her grey eyes seemed to assess Honey, and then recognition dawned.

'Aren't you that woman from the TV yesterday?'

Honey shrugged.

'Hal won't answer his door. He never does.'

'Maybe not to you,' the woman said, folding her arms over her small-but-perfectly-formed chest. 'But he will for me. He's probably sleeping.'

'Or drunk,' Honey muttered.

The woman narrowed her eyes.

'Don't you have a key to his door?' she said, and then added, 'for emergencies or anything?' to unnecessarily reinforce the fact that she wouldn't expect Honey to have a key for any other reason.

Honey shook her head. 'Don't you?' she snapped back, sure by now that this must be Imogen. The brief flicker of uncertainty in Imogen's eyes didn't make Honey feel as contrite as it might have done on a more normal kind of day.

'I can tell him you came by if you like,' Honey said, leaning on the doorframe and mirroring Imogen's cross-armed pose.

'I'm not going anywhere.'

Honey lifted one shoulder, going for disinterested even though the woman in front of her had come to take Hal away. She flicked a glance at his door, wondering what was going on on the other side of it. If she knew Hal at all, he'd be passed out from too much whisky after fleeing the home last night. For once, she was glad to see his door stay closed.

'Then you're in for a long wait,' Honey said, and stepped back to close her door.

'Wait.'

Against her better judgment, Honey didn't close the door. She was tired and ratty, but she couldn't bring herself to be downright rude. She lifted her eyes to Imogen's and waited for her to speak again.

'I sent him a letter,' she said, the uncertainty Honey had glimpsed in her eyes now apparent in her voice too. 'Do you know if he got it?'

Honey wished she'd closed the door. She wasn't sure she had the strength for this conversation.

'He got it.' She swallowed, a painful sound in the quiet lobby.

Imogen nodded.

'How's he been?'

Annoyance flashed hot in Honey's brain. She had no right, not after months of not caring.

'Up and down. He gets lonely.'

She didn't feel any thrill of victory at Imogen's troubled expression, and she certainly hadn't counted on the girl bursting into tears.

'Shit,' Honey muttered, and pulled out some scrunched-up tissues from her dressing gown pocket and handed them over.

As Imogen patted her cheeks, Honey noted the lack of mascara streaks and silently envied her smart waterproof choice.

'He shouldn't be stuck here in this hole,' Imogen gulped, and Honey suddenly lost all sympathy again. 'Do you know who he really is? I suppose you must after yesterday.'

Honey nodded.

'I know who he is.'

Imogen shook her head. 'He was a different man before the accident,' she said. 'Smart. Sexy. The talk of the town. Wow, was he going places.' She ripped the tissue to pieces as she remembered, dropping tiny shreds like wedding confetti on the floor. Honey glanced down and tried not to let her knees crumble at the sight of the huge rock glinting on Imogen's left hand.

'You should have seen him in the kitchen, he was a wizard,' Imogen sniffed. 'He was always the coolest guy in town.'

Honey could feel her temper running through her fingers like sand through an egg-timer.

'He caught the bus with me yesterday,' she said, limbering up.

Imogen yelped as if she'd been nudged in the ribs with a poker. 'Hal caught the bus? As in the public bus?'

Honey nodded.

'And he's still a wizard in the kitchen. He's been running the kitchen in the residential home for a while now. The residents can't get enough of his shepherd's pie.'

Imogen's fingers flew to the necklace around her neck, and the tilt of her chin warned Honey that her opponent had realised that she was being needled.

'I'm sure you've all been very sweet to him,' Imogen said, smiling her princess smile. 'And we all really appreciate it, but he needs to come home now and pick up his life again.'

355

Honey didn't doubt that he would, but she wouldn't give this woman the satisfaction of the upper hand.

'He's smart. Just about the smartest man I've ever met,' she said quietly. 'And the sexiest, too. Still the coolest guy in town. Just not your town anymore.'

'You didn't know him beforehand,' Imogen said, pulling rank.

'And you don't know him now.'

They faced each other down, one immaculate, the other bedraggled with dark circles around her eyes.

'I love him. I love him for the man he is right now,' Honey said. There was little to lose, and nothing to gain, but she said it anyway and saw the fury harden Imogen's pretty features.

'He's marrying me.'

'I know.'

'He could never love someone like you,' Imogen spat, rattled by Honey's honesty.

'I know that too.'

Imogen shook her head, as if she were disgusted. She had every reason to be. The man she'd pinned all of her hopes on had fallen down a mountain and taken all of her dreams down with him, and now a ratty-haired blonde had the nerve to make her feel bad for wanting to resurrect them.

'I'll tell him you came by,' Honey said a second time, and this time Imogen stalked out of the lobby on her fabulous heels without looking back, leaving only the trail of her perfume and a bad taste in Honey's mouth.

Had Hal heard them? Honey ran a bath and immersed herself beneath the water, wishing she could stay under there forever. Just wallow forever in the warm, peaceful solitude. Life had been a waltzer ride lately, and there under the bubbles it finally stopped spinning. No campaign. No love rivals. No blind dates. And no Hal. In the absence of a desert island, her own bathtub would have to do.

As the morning slid into afternoon, Honey replied to texts from Nell and Tash to stop them from racing into the breach with wine and shoulders to lean on. Oddly enough, she didn't need any shoulders today. What she really needed was to stand on her own two feet and prove to herself, more than anyone else, that she could cut it at life as a grown up. She was proud of the way she'd handled Imogen, and she was beyond proud of the way things had turned out where the campaign was concerned.

Lots of people had tried to give her advice yesterday about Hal, and actually they'd all said the same thing in a different way. *Tell him.* Make damn sure he knows that you love him before he walks away. And they were right. Honey didn't want to be a passive voice waiting for him to cast judgment. She had a part in this play, although it probably wasn't going to be leading lady.

Squaring her shoulders, she opened her door and crossed the lobby.

'Hal,' she whispered, tapping her knuckles on his door. It didn't surprise her when he didn't respond.

'Hal,' she said again, louder this time. 'There's something I need to say to you, and this time I'm not prepared to say it to your closed door.'

Pin drop silence, and Honey felt her serenity start to slip.

'Open the door, Hal. I mean it.'

Nothing. She waited a full minute, counting in her head to keep her nerves steady.

'Jesus, Hal, you infuriate me! Open the goddamn door!'

Okay, so her serenity had left the building. After another couple of failed attempts, panic started to edge its way under her skin. Even in the early days he'd rarely ignored her so blatantly. He'd sworn, called her names, even thrown things at the door on occasion, but at least she'd known he was okay. Not knowing he was okay wasn't okay.

'Don't make me break this door down,' Honey called out loudly, expecting him to laugh at the idea. She hadn't been able to turn off a smoke alarm the first time they'd met; the chances of her breaking down his door were slim to none. Given the fact that she knew that, she ought to have known better than to take a run at it from her own doorway anyway. All she ended up with for her trouble was a jarred shoulder, a still-closed door and a growing case of full-on panic.

'Hal!' she shouted, battering on his door with her fists. Christ. He had to be hurt, she was yelling loud enough to wake the dead. She opened the door and walked out onto the pavement barefoot, pressing her face against his front windows with her heart in her mouth. His wooden blinds were half open, and squinting, she could make out the clinically tidy room. She let out her breath and leaned her back against the window for support, winded by the relief of not seeing him sprawled on the floor. Turning back to look again, she watched the empty space for a few minutes.

'Come on, Hal,' she whispered. 'Walk in with bed hair and whisky in your hand. Walk in, scowling. Just please God, walk in.'

The possibility that he'd fallen and banged his head in the bathroom or asphyxiated himself in bed tortured her. Should she call the police to break in? Would they even bother to look for a grown man who'd been seen less than twenty-four hours previously? She made her way around the back and shouldered the scarcely used side gate open with a hard shove, more frightened than she'd ever been in her life.

His bedroom blind was unhelpfully drawn and his bathroom window was opaque, but his backdoor handle turned freely in her hand.

It wasn't locked.

'Oh my God, oh my God, oh my God,' she whispered, stepping inside, as terrified as the heroine in a horror movie even though it was broad daylight and she knew better than to make the schoolgirl error of running up the stairs. Scanning the lounge and kitchen quickly, she confirmed what she already knew. They were empty. Returning to the hallway, she looked at the bedroom and bathroom doors, both of them closed.

Placing her clammy hand over the bedroom door handle, she turned it slowly, and then at the last moment threw it open and almost jumped inside in her haste to speed up the agony.

Empty.

Honey almost doubled over with relief, gasping, able to put away the horrific images she'd conjured of him lying ghost pale on the bed.

And then she remembered the bathroom.

Stepping back into the hallway, she stood still outside the final door.

'Please don't let him be in here,' she said out loud. 'Please no.'

She turned the handle and pushed the door slowly, all the time expecting resistance from his body on the floor in the small room. It swung easily, all the way back. Only when she was one hundred per cent certain that he wasn't in there did she let the air back into her lungs and the tears rain down her face.

She'd spent the last half an hour terrified that she'd find him, and now she at least knew he wasn't dead, she was even more terrified that she wouldn't.

CHAPTER THIRTY-SEVEN

A silver people carrier pulled up outside the home a couple of mornings later and a dark-haired care worker wheeled her charge into the building.

'Could I possibly speak with Lucille and Mimi please?' the man in the wheelchair asked the care worker walking through reception.

Nikki smiled. 'Of course. Who can I tell them is calling?'

The man straightened his shoulders.

'Please tell them it's their brother.'

And so it was that Mimi, Lucille and Ernie sat down together for the first time in their lives that morning and shared a pot of tea.

Mimi found herself stripped of any lingering anger or reticence by the kind, frail man who so resembled her, and when he held both of their hands in his trembling ones and his tired eyelids drifted down midway through their conversation, she held on to him until he woke again and apologised for his terrible manners.

'It's not you who needs to apologise,' she said. 'It's me. I was a silly old fool not to see you sooner.'

Mimi hated the fact that time obviously wasn't on Ernie's side. What had she been thinking of? She was thoroughly ashamed of herself.

'I couldn't believe it when I saw you both yesterday on the news,' he smiled. 'You first, Lucille, and then of course you, Mimi. I'd have known you anywhere.'

'You both look like our mother,' Lucille said.

Ernie's face turned wistful. 'I've never looked like anyone else before.'

'Two peas in a pod,' Lucille smiled, pouring them all more tea.

'I came to give you something,' Ernie said, looking around for Carol, who'd tactfully taken a seat across the other side of the conservatory with a magazine. She caught his eye and crossed to hand him a file from a bag on the back of his chair. Once she'd faded away again, he pushed the file into Lucille's hands.

'What is it?' she asked, looking down at the beige file and wishing she had her glasses with her.

'It's my savings. I want you two to have them.'

'Ernie, no,' Mimi said, agonised. 'Please, we don't want your money. Let's just all have another cup of tea, and we'll meet up again. We can do it every week, can't we, Lucille?'

She turned to her sister for back-up, and Lucille nodded.

'Of course we can.'

Ernie sighed. 'I've known I had two sisters for many, many years. Dozens of birthdays and Christmases without

362

being able to give you anything. This is for all of those years.'

'You have nothing to make up for,' Lucille rushed. 'If only we'd known about you, Ernie, things would have been so different.'

'It's no one's fault, don't upset yourself,' he said, squeezing her fingers gently. 'We're here now, and I won't take no for an answer about the money.'

'How about we say we'll talk about it another time?' Mimi tried, but he shook his head.

'I've already been to the bank this morning.'

Lucille knew that the fact that Ernie was out of the house at all was a rare thing. He must really feel strongly to have visited the bank too.

'What's going on, Ernie?'

His eyes lit with mischief that made him look more like Mimi than ever.

'I beat Mick Jagger.'

Both of his sisters frowned.

'And Jamie Oliver.'

Lucille looked down at the folder, not getting it.

Ernie nodded towards it, his expression proud.

'There's enough in there to buy this place twice over.'

Mimi and Lucille gasped.

'How on earth . . .?' Mimi managed.

Ernie looked as gleeful as a dying man can look.

'I play poker online,' he whispered his secret with wide, laughing eyes. 'Against young hotshots in Vegas, all from the comfort of my own living room.'

'No,' Lucille laughed, shocked. 'I can't believe it, how exciting!'

'Lord, don't tell Billy you can do things like that,' Mimi muttered, shaking her head in amazement.

'I want you to buy this place with my winnings,' Ernie said. 'I want to buy the roof over my sisters' heads.'

Both Lucille and Mimi were rendered temporarily speechless by emotion.

'You're the best big brother I've ever had,' Lucille said, wiping a tear from her cheek with the hankie Ernie produced.

'*We've* ever had,' Mimi corrected.

'That's settled then.' Ernie nodded, pleased. 'I never did like The Rolling Stones.'

CHAPTER THIRTY-EIGHT

It came as a shock to Honey to realise that life carried on regardless and she was still expected to take her part in it. Where was the 'stop the world, I want to get off' button when you needed it?

The shop still needed to be opened. Tash and Nell still needed to be her best friends and make a fuss, feeding her up even though food was just stuff she found hard to swallow. The sun still came up, the buses still ran, and amazingly enough, her legs still worked and words seemed to come out of her mouth in roughly the right order. How could that be, without Hal?

News of his expected return to the London restaurant scene scattered the papers, and there was talk of sightings of him in gossip columns. A vague shot that might have been any man in a beanie hat and dark glasses emerged, an immaculate Imogen clinging to his arm. Honey pored over it all, trying to piece together the stranger in the public eye with the man she'd had all to herself for a few precious weeks.

'She looks a class-A bitch,' Tash said, twisting the magazine around her way on the coffee shop table and squinting at it. 'Is it even him?'

Honey flipped it shut and shook her head. 'I'm not sure.'

'His loss.'

Honey looked listlessly out of the window at the rain. It wasn't Hal's loss. It was hers. She'd lost her peace of mind, along with her stupid, feckless heart. Romance movies and novels hadn't prepared her for the fact that the hero sometimes royally screws up the happy ending. Or maybe it was just that Hal was never her happy ending to have. Either way, she was never going to the cinema again, unless it was to watch a psycho thriller where they all died in the end and no one expected to waltz happily into the sunset.

'Did you give Christian my number? He called me yesterday,' Honey said.

Tash licked hot chocolate froth from her spoon.

'Good. Straight back on the bike, it's the only way.'

'I told him the truth.'

'Which is that you've been pissed on from a great height by an almighty cock and yes, you'd love to go on a date with him because he's handsome and kind. That's what you told him, right?'

Honey looked at Tash levelly across the table. 'You know that isn't what I said.'

'It's been a week and he hasn't been in touch, Honey. He's gone, and he's not coming back.'

She wasn't quite ready for Tash's tough love approach.

'A week. Seven days. It's not enough, Tash. I need more time.'

Tash rolled her eyes. 'God made the world in seven days. You probably haven't even made your bloody bed.'

'It's an unfair comparison,' Honey muttered.

'Yeah. You're real. And you're here, and this is your life.' Tash opened the magazine and jabbed her finger at the picture. 'And he's there, and that's his life.'

She closed the magazine, dropped it in a nearby bin, and stood up.

'Come on. Let's go get drunk.'

'I can't believe you guys are my new bosses,' Honey smiled weakly at Lucille as she placed a china cup and saucer down on the counter. 'Will you be making many big changes?'

'Well,' Lucille said, her blue eyes dancing around the shop. 'I thought we might move the books over into the other corner.'

Honey smiled and sipped her tea. 'I think I can live with that.'

They looked up as Billy strolled over to the counter, a black shirt in his hand. He held it against himself and looked at them for approval.

'Is it a bit dark for you?' Honey ventured, glancing down at Billy's mustard-yellow drainpipes.

'I thought I'd try something dark and mysterious to woo Mimi,' he said, striking a pose. 'Will it work?'

Honey did that thing with her face formerly known as smiling and hoped it fooled her friends.

'Ring it up then,' he said, squinting at the price tag. 'She's worth two quid.'

Honey folded the shirt and slid it into a carrier for Billy, who added it to another already in his hand.

367

'Buy her flowers.'

'Irises are her favourites,' Lucille said, arranging necklaces artfully on the bust stand.

'And chocolates too,' Honey added. 'Mimi loves chocolates.'

Billy grinned and pretended to make notes on his hand.

'Noted, ladies. I shall retire to my chamber to make plans.'

He bowed low with a courtly flourish of his hand and tipped his imaginary hat on the way out.

As it happened, Billy didn't retire to his chamber. Looking furtive, he sidled around the back of the home and down the path to the tree line at the bottom of the garden, and then through them to the big old shed in the corner. It had long since been his unofficial lair, and over the years he'd added various cast-out bits and bobs to make it a comfortable place to hide out. A couple of old reclining armchairs lifted from a bunch put outside because they didn't meet new fire regulations. A sideboard he'd resurrected from the dead, and a much-prized radio that had kept him company on many an afternoon. For all his gregarious nature, Billy sometimes craved a couple of hours' peace and quiet, and here in the old potting shed was where he found it.

Pushing the door open, he stepped inside and put the morning paper down on the sideboard.

'At ease, Hal. It's only me.'

Honey heaved her tired body over the threshold of the house later that evening, slamming the door against the rain and looking towards Hal's front door rather than her own. Some habits were hard to break.

'Hal?' she called out his name even though she knew perfectly well that he wasn't there. Still bundled up in her coat and scarf, Honey walked to his door and laid a hand on it.

'It's been a long, grey day out there today, Hal,' she said, world weary. Was it really any different because he wasn't on the other side of the door? She'd become well accustomed to one-sided conversations, and so well acquainted with the floor outside his flat that it was a wonder there wasn't a groove shaped like her backside worn into the Minton tiles.

Sliding down into her spot, she wrapped her arms around her knees and hugged them, shivering. She hadn't felt properly warm since the day he'd left; there was a chill in her bones that had nothing to do with the weather.

'Can you believe Ernie bought the home in the end?' she said, letting her weight sag against his door.

'I'm so glad for Lucille and Mimi. Well, for all of the residents of course, but them especially. I don't think Lucille has said a sentence that didn't include Ernie's name ever since.' The tiniest of smiles touched her lips at the thought of Mimi and Lucille as the new bosses of the home. She was pretty sure her job was safe for as long as she wanted it, although Mimi and Lucille had already floated other possibilities too.

'They asked me today if I'd think about taking over Christopher's old job,' she said, imagining what Hal would have thought had he really been sitting on the other side of the door. Something involving quite a lot of swear words, no doubt.

'I missed you today,' she whispered. 'I missed you this morning when I opened my eyes. I missed you on the bus

369

to work, and again on the way home just now. When will it stop, Hal?'

The worst thing was that she wasn't even sure she wanted it to stop, because that would mean she was moving on, and the idea of moving from him hurt like a shard of glass lodged in her heart. She closed her eyes and laid her head against the door, ignoring the tear that seeped through her lashes and slid down her cheek.

A noise, a rustling. Honey dashed her hands hurriedly over her cheeks, her heart a swooping skylark behind her ribs and then a stone falling into her boots when she realised the sounds were outside on the street rather than behind Hal's door. Voices easily recognised as Nell and Tash's floated around the hall, snippets of concerned conversation as they knocked on the door and called out her name. Honey didn't reply. She didn't have the energy.

'Hang on,' she heard Nell say. 'I think I've still got a key.'

'Why have you got a key and I haven't?'

'Maybe because she trusts me not to throw wild parties in her flat when she goes away?' Nell said, and a few seconds later she must have found the key, because they pushed the door open.

'Bloody rain,' Tash grumbled, fighting with her brolly, and then jumped back when she spotted Honey huddled by Hal's door.

'Shit, Hon, you nearly gave me a sodding heart attack!'

Nell moved across the lamplit lobby and dropped onto her haunches beside Honey, concern all over her pretty face.

'What are you doing out here, babes?' She smoothed her hand over Honey's hair.

Honey shook her head, and shrugged her shoulders, fresh tears gathering in her eyes.

'Talking to Hal,' she said.

Nell glanced up quickly at Tash, who frowned and moved around to sit beside Honey on the floor.

'He's not in there, Hon. You know that, right?'

Honey nodded. 'He hardly ever used to answer me anyway,' she said. 'It's not that different now. I just . . .' She halted mid-sentence to swallow the painful lump in her throat. 'I just feel close to him here.'

Nell slid her slender frame in on Honey's other side.

'Then we'll sit with you for a while. If that's okay?'

Tash rustled in her huge suede bag and produced a bottle of wine.

'We were kind of planning on drinking this out of glasses like normal people, but hey, the floor works for me.' She unscrewed the cap and took a drink, then passed the bottle along the row.

Honey accepted the cool bottle with a deep sigh and tipped it to her lips. Would it be wrong to drink the lot in the hope of oblivion?

'What am I going to do?' she said, and Nell rubbed her arm.

'You're going to do exactly what you always do. Get up. Go to work. Keep breathing. It's all you can do, Honey, and then one day you'll go to bed and realise you didn't think about him at all.'

'I think about him all the time,' Honey whispered, taking a second drink and then passing the bottle to Nell. 'Everything reminds me of him. He's everything I'd say I don't want in a man, and yet I love him so much that

I feel as if someone has scooped my heart out and put it back in the wrong way round,' she said, her little girl lost voice echoing around the quiet lobby. 'It hurts, right here.' She put her hand over her heart, and leaned her head on Tash's shoulder. 'In fact, it hurts everywhere. I ache so much that my bones feel too heavy to get out of the bed in the morning.'

'I'd like to smash that handsome face of his in,' Tash muttered viciously. 'He might be a hotshot celebrity, but he doesn't deserve your tears.'

'I mustn't have known him at all,' Honey said, trying to understand how the solitary man who'd lived here could be a man who courted celebrity, who'd returned to his life again.

What had this interlude been to him? A holiday from reality, and she his holiday romance? She knew better than to expect him to write. He'd disappeared from her life as quickly as he'd appeared; gone in a blink, only this time he'd taken her heart with him.

'I'm sure you did,' Nell said, passing over the wine. 'From what you've said of him, it seemed to me that he was learning who he is now right along with you.'

'You think so?' Honey said, ready to grasp at anything that painted Hal as anything other than a shallow, selfish heartbreaker. The wine had started to move in her blood, and she relaxed into her spot sandwiched between her two best friends in the world.

'It might just have been the wrong time in your lives for you two to meet,' Tash said, philosophical on her other side. 'It happens that way sometimes. You meet your soulmate on your honeymoon, or your best friend brings home the love of her life and he's actually the love of yours. The timing is off, but maybe in another place, another time, you'd have made it. It's just the shitty way love goes sometimes.'

'That doesn't actually make me feel any better,' Honey half laughed, knowing Tash was doing her best to help. And she had a point; maybe Hal was simply the right man at the wrong time. The thought of what might have been fair broke her heart all over again.

'How do you ever get over that?'

'Time,' Nell said. 'It sounds trite, but it's the only thing that's going to help. Then one day when you don't expect it you'll meet someone else, and they'll put your heart back in the right way around again. You won't always feel like this, I promise.'

They lapsed into silence, passing the wine between them.

'When did you two get so wise, anyway?' Honey said.

'I've had my share of heartbreak,' Tash said. 'Although . . .'

'What?' Both Honey and Nell turned to look down the line towards Tash.

A slow, uncharacteristically shy smile spread over her face. 'Yusef asked me to marry him last night.'

'Wow,' Honey smiled and squeezed Tash's hand, and on her other side Nell grinned and said, 'That's huge, Tash.'

Tash laughed. 'I know. And he is.'

'You've said yes?' Honey said, although it seemed almost moot given the glow radiating from her friend. Tash nodded.

'In Dubai, next summer.' She looked from Honey to Nell. 'Bridesmaids?'

'There's nothing I feel less like right now,' Honey said, smiling for Tash and crying for herself. 'But try and keep me away.'

Nell knocked back a slug of wine, pink-cheeked.

'I don't know if Simon and I will make it through customs without being arrested,' she giggled in a most un-Nell-like way. 'Are you allowed to take a suitcase full of sex toys into Dubai?'

Tash reached across Honey and high-fived Nell.

'Hats off, Nell. Simon has gone up in my estimation in recent weeks.'

'Just don't go and fall in love with your best friend's husband,' Honey murmured, repeating Tash's earlier words.

'Or someone else's fiancé,' a sarcastic voice said from the doorway, and Imogen stepped through the door that Tash and Nell had left ajar. 'Is this a private party or can anyone join in?'

All three women on the floor stared up at the Amazonian blonde in silence for a few moments. Nell was trying to place her, Tash was momentarily dazzled by the arrival of someone straight from the gossip pages, and Honey was winded by the sight of the woman who could never love Hal as she did but had won the battle anyway. Looking at her now, all long legs and glossy hair, Honey knew it had never been a fair race. A thoroughbred would always romp to victory over a pony.

'What are you doing here, Imogen?' Honey said, sliding the empty wine bottle behind her. She didn't want to give Imogen the opportunity to look down on them as if they were three drunks on a park bench. She heard Nell's soft gasp of recognition beside her, and felt Tash's fingers close firmly around hers.

'You have exactly thirty seconds, and then I'm going to knock your veneers out, lady,' Tash said.

Imogen looked momentarily wrong-footed.

'Is he here?' she said, flicking her eyes towards Hal's door.

Honey narrowed her eyes. Surely Imogen knew where he was? The combination of wine, sleepless nights and heartache made it hard to think sensibly.

Tash folded her arms across her chest. 'Have you lost him already?'

Imogen looked from one to the other, irritated, and then stepped over their legs and banged on Hal's door.

'Hal,' she called out, desperation clear in her voice. 'Hal, it's me, darling. Please, let me in.'

'He isn't in there,' Honey said flatly, staring at Imogen's spike-heeled boots. 'He hasn't been here for days.'

And then they all fell silent and turned in unison towards Hal's door, because the latch clicked, and a moment later, excruciatingly slowly, it swung open.

All three women on the floor scrabbled to their feet.

'Hal,' Honey breathed. 'You came back.' She stared at him, scared to take her eyes off him in case she looked away and he disappeared again.

'Jesus,' Honey heard Tash mutter next to her. Honey understood. He'd had the same effect on her the first time she'd seen him in this very same spot, and he'd carried on taking her breath away ever since.

'Why are you here, Imogen?' he asked.

Honey had almost forgotten Imogen had even turned up, and felt dull hurt from Hal's choice to address her first.

'I came to see you,' Imogen said, a little more confident in Hal's presence. 'Can we talk inside?'

Hal didn't step aside. Instead, he turned and picked up

a holdall from the floor and then stepped out and closed his door.

'Go home, Immie,' Hal said gently. 'You shouldn't have come here.'

Honey watched as Imogen reached out and laid a manicured hand on Hal's arm.

'I'll only go if you'll come with me.'

Hal sighed heavily and moved out of her reach. 'I'm not coming back to London.'

Imogen's eyes flicked to Honey. 'Well, you can't stay here,' she said.

'Last time I checked I could do whatever the fuck I wanted,' Hal said. 'But no. I'm not staying here either.'

Honey wondered how much a human heart could take before it stopped working. He was here. He wasn't in London with Imogen. He was leaving again. All this, and he hadn't even acknowledged she was even there yet.

'You could,' she said, finding her voice at last. 'You could stay here. If you wanted.'

'Honey,' he said, turning towards her, and every inch, every fibre of her reacted to her name from his lips.

'It's so good to see you,' she whispered, wishing everyone else would leave, terrified that he would.

'I can't stay,' he said. 'You know I can't.'

Panic fluttered in her breast. 'Yes. Yes, you can. Stay here with me.'

He breathed in deep, and then turned from Honey to Imogen.

'Immie, I owe you better than to do this here, but it seems that this is how this thing is going to play out,' he said, stepping closer to his fiancée.

'I've changed, Imogen. I've had to. You're right, we probably could go back to our old lives in London, try to pick up where we left off somehow. We could, but I don't want to.' He looked unbearably gaunt. 'I can't say this in a way that isn't hurtful, so I'll say it in the only way I know. The honest way. We had a wonderful life together, but I don't want that life anymore. I don't want London, or a celebrity lifestyle, and Imogen, I'm sorry, but I don't want to be your husband either. Or your fiancé. Or your anything.' He drew in a deep breath. 'It's over, Immie. It has been since the moment I lost my sight.'

Honey glanced down at the floor, feeling no victory from Imogen's defeat. She felt Hal's words as if they were directed at herself, and she recognised her own sense of loss in Imogen's tearful face. They both loved him in their own way, and just because the first blow had been a knockout for Imogen it didn't mean he didn't have another killer blow up his sleeve.

'I guess I'll leave you to your party then,' Imogen said, looking at Honey.

Honey looked back levelly, her chin high despite her spirits being on the floor. She watched the other woman leave, looking at the door as it closed behind her, knowing in her gut that she wouldn't be the only person leaving tonight.

She turned to Tash and Nell, holding each of their hands.

'Should we go?' Nell asked, her worried eyes searching Honey's face.

'We can stay, if you like?' Tash said.

Honey shook her head and kissed them both. 'Thank you for coming tonight. You're the best friends.'

'Fight for him,' Tash murmured as she kissed Honey's cheek.

'Make him fight for you,' Nell whispered, and with a small, sad smile, Honey ushered them out of the door.

'Here we are again,' Hal said after Honey had closed the door behind her friends. 'Just you and me in this lobby.'

Honey leaned against the door. 'We started it here. I guess it's fitting that we end it here too,' she said, because despite Nell and Tash's parting advice, she knew that it was inevitable that Hal was going to walk out of here tonight.

'Well, you have the advantage on me,' she said. 'I guess you heard everything I said earlier?'

His silence confirmed what his words didn't.

'So yeah,' she laughed shakily, a sad sound that echoed around the lobby. 'I love you, despite the fact that you're the most difficult, rude person I know. You've done nothing to earn it, yet my love is yours anyway.' She shrugged. 'Take it. Keep it. Throw it away. Do whatever you like with it, because it's not mine anymore.'

He looked anguished, not at all like a man glad to hear love declarations.

'I never intended to let things get this far,' he said. 'I tried to tell you. I tried to stop it. Don't love me, Honey. *I* don't love me. Fuck, I barely even know me, so there's no way you can.'

Oh, he wasn't getting away with that.

'You're wrong. I do know you. I probably know you better than you know yourself right now. Maybe you haven't given up on the old Hal, but I only know the new one, and he's the man I love,' she said. 'Am I not enough,

378

Hal? Is that it? Life here is boring compared to the glitzy London life? I can't compete with that. I'm not even going to try.'

Hal stepped closer and reached out, holding her by the shoulders.

'Honey, there is no competition. You win. You win hands down, okay? Life with you isn't dull. It's a fucking technicolour rainbow.'

What was he saying? She struggled to sift his words, even more so when his thumb brushed along her collarbone.

'You're not second choice. You're first. The best. The most fucking exceptional girl I've ever met in my life.'

'So why won't you stay with me?' she whispered, because despite everything he'd said, she knew he was still going to leave her.

He shook his head, and then slowly removed his dark shades and put them in the pocket of his coat.

'Because of this,' he said starkly. 'I don't want this life for you. It's my life, but I won't let it be yours too.'

Frustration burned hot in Honey's chest. 'You know what? I don't think I'd have loved the man you used to be. I love you just as you are right now. Why can't you be brave enough to love me back, Hal?'

'Because this isn't a place for exceptional rainbow girls,' he said, touching the side of his head. 'It's dark in here, Honey. I'm dark, and I'll tarnish you if you stay with me.'

'That's a crock of shit, Hal.'

He shook his head. 'Your friends are right. You'll meet someone else. Someone funny and lighthearted, someone who can love you properly, who can be the husband you deserve, give you beautiful, crazy children. I'm not that man.'

'*You* loved me properly,' she said, hot tears on her cheeks. 'No one's ever loved me as properly as you.'

He closed his eyes and rested his forehead against hers, so close she could feel his breath on her lips. His hands were still on her shoulders, his thumb still grazed the dip between her collarbones.

'I'm going away soon,' he said, slowly.

'No!' Desperation edged into her voice. 'Please Hal, don't walk away and never come back.'

'I won't leave without saying goodbye, okay?' he said, stepping away from her. 'I'm not trying to hurt you, Honey. If I stay, I'll hurt you more.'

Honey reached out and gripped the lapels of his coat.

'I'm a grown woman, Hal. I make my own choices, and I choose you.'

To a stranger looking in, they might have looked romantic, like a couple locked in a train station embrace.

'And I make mine, Honey,' he said quietly, moving to the door. 'I don't choose you.'

It would have hurt less if he'd punched her.

CHAPTER THIRTY-NINE

A few weeks living in a potting shed turned out to be the most reflective time in Hal's entire life. He'd been dubious at first when Billy had suggested it as an alternative to calling a cab on the day of the protest, but the spur of the moment choice had actually been exactly what he'd needed. Leaving only once to go home and collect his things, he'd spent his days totally off the grid, cranked back in the armchair listening to the radio, not bothering to retune it from Billy's preferred choice of Radio Four. He listened to late-night ghost stories, became well acquainted with the residents of Ambridge on *The Archers*, and found himself strangely soothed by the cadence of the shipping forecast in the early hours. It felt as if his life in the flat opposite Honey had been good training for this more extreme version of the same.

'Stilton and grapes today, old bean,' Billy said. 'And I've managed to rustle us up a dram of port to go with them.'

'That's almost sophisticated,' Hal smiled, righting his chair and sliding his dark glasses on.

He folded his blanket away as he listened to Billy unpack the food.

'I looked in on Honey just now,' Billy said.

Hal lived for and dreaded the daily report in equal measure.

'How's she doing today?'

Billy's quiet moment unnerved him.

'Poor thing looks as if she needs a good dinner. No colour in her cheeks at all.'

'But she's okay?'

Every day Hal looked for reassurance in Billy's words, and every day it wasn't quite there. *She's bearing up*, or *she's quiet*, or *she's pale*. How long would it be before Billy reported that she was laughing again, or getting herself into the kind of scrapes only Honey could get into?

'I think she'd be a damn sight better if she knew you were here,' Billy said.

'She wouldn't,' Hal said, accepting the plate that Billy put in his hands. He'd been on an eclectic diet since he'd moved into the potting shed, and had almost grown accustomed to sneaking in Billy's bathroom window for a midnight shower.

'I never married, Hal,' Billy said suddenly. 'Never settled.'

'You seem happy enough,' Hal said mildly.

Billy's throat rattled. 'I made the best of it, son, like we all do. Doesn't mean I don't regret some of the decisions I made over the years though.'

Hal heard the healthy glug of port as Billy poured it into the plastic cups.

'Can't go back and change 'em, though,' Billy reflected.

382

'And you might just spend the rest of your life wishing you could.'

'Is this your roundabout way of telling me you think I'm making the wrong decision, Billy?'

Hal lifted the port to his lips and let the comforting heat fill his mouth.

'I'm old, Hal. You get to this age, you know what matters.'

'And what's that?'

Billy huffed. 'People. Hanging on to the ones who make you happy.'

Hal slid his cup onto the table. 'You make it sound so simple.'

The creaking sound told Hal that Billy had reclined his chair.

'That's because it is simple, son. It's easy as pie. You figure out who makes you happy, and then you work your backside off to make them happy too.'

'We're too different, Billy.' Hal sighed, his heart heavy. 'Honey . . . she's kind, and soft, and she laughs more than anyone I've ever known.'

'Not anymore she doesn't,' Billy said, not pulling any punches.

'She will.'

'Have you lost your mind as well as your eyesight, lad?' Billy said brusquely. 'It's not obligatory to go through life bloody miserable, and you're not doing her some huge favour by denying yourself, and her, the chance to be happy.'

Hal wasn't offended by Billy's words. He needed to hear them. He'd been living in suspended animation ever since he'd walked out on Honey over a week earlier, knowing he should go away, yet doing nothing to make it happen. He couldn't live forever in Billy's potting shed, but he wasn't sure he could live forever without Honey either.

Billy cleared his throat. 'You've wallowed long enough, son. It's time to sink or swim.'

'What if she sinks with me, Billy?'

'She won't, Hal. She's your life jacket.'

CHAPTER FORTY

'Billy's throwing a Halloween party?' Honey said a few days later, pulling a pained face at Mimi. Anything that included the word *party* was strictly off the menu at the moment. She couldn't go to parties. Parties suggested fun and gaiety, and that was hard when you'd had your heart amputated less than three weeks ago. She was lucky to be breathing.

'It's only for an hour when the shop closes,' Mimi said. 'Humour him, or else we'll never hear the end of it.'

Lucille appeared with a cobweb lace black dress in her hands from fresh stock that she was sorting through in the back room.

'You could wear this,' she said, shaking it out.

'Please don't tell me it's fancy dress,' Honey groaned.

'Not exactly, although Billy did say he fancied dressing up as Dick Turpin,' Mimi said.

Honey looked down at her jeans and pink t-shirt. She wasn't dressed for an OAP Halloween party, but then who

385

ever was? She was supposed to be meeting Nell and Tash after work to go see a suitably gruesome slasher movie, it was a valid excuse to say no. Or else it would have been, had her mobile not pinged beside the till as she opened her mouth. Glancing at it quickly, she saw the rain check message from Tash, and then almost instantly a second one from Nell. Terrific.

'One hour and then I'm going home,' Honey grouched. 'You better pass me that dress.'

Honey locked the shop at five o'clock and found herself being frogmarched across the wet grass sandwiched between Lucille and Mimi, two unlikely witches in scarlet and black striped tights and tall hats.

'One hour,' Honey reminded them, yanking the black lace dress down to a more decent length and inadvertently revealing more cleavage. 'Where are we going?' she asked, twisting her head as they steered her down the side of the home rather than through the front doors.

'To the party,' Mimi said.

'A garden party? It's almost November,' Honey said, wishing hard that she was already on the bus home.

'It's not in the garden,' Lucille laughed, squeezing her arm and tugging her along in the darkness.

'There's nothing down here,' Honey said, and then stopped walking when a silent, shadowed figure at the end of the garden lit lanterns to guide them, or perhaps lure them, across.

'Okay. That was mildly spooky,' Honey conceded. 'What's his next trick?'

It turned out to be a treat rather than a trick. Tiny white

fairy lights flickered into life in the trees in the corner, throwing enough light to reveal the fact that there was a low-slung old shed nestled beneath the branches.

'He's throwing a party in the shed?' Honey murmured, perplexed as they drew nearer. The shadowy figure appeared on the path beside them. Billy, or highwayman Billy, given his attire and eye mask.

'Ladies,' he said, inclining his head cordially at Mimi and Lucille, who released Honey from their arm locks and inclined their witches' hats formally to Billy.

'You look divine, my darling,' he said, and even the mask didn't hide the way he looked Honey up and down. She rolled her eyes as he held out his arm, and then sighed and stepped forward to allow him to lead her into his decidedly weird shed party. She was going to need a stiff drink when she got home; the residents were showing every sign of losing their marbles.

As she stepped inside the shed, Honey automatically ducked in case of spider webs. She needn't have worried. This wasn't her grandfather's dusty shed of her childhood memories. This was . . . this was a saloon shed, or a 1930s dining car from a vintage movie. Tinkling piano music played in the background, and someone stood behind an impromptu bar fashioned from an old sideboard. Honey had to look twice to realise that the glamorous witch's red waves weren't a wig.

'Tash!' she said, letting go of Billy's arm and almost running the few steps across to the bar.

'Drink, madam?' Tash said, remaining in character, aside from a barely there wink as she pushed a glass of green-tinted fizz into Honey's hand.

'Your table's ready when you are,' someone said at her elbow, and she turned to find her zombie waitress for the evening impeccably turned out in a black dress and white frilled apron. The bolt threaded through Nell's slender neck and the blacked-out eyes were perfectly done. She'd have looked mildly terrifying, had it not been for the fact that she was beaming.

'Nell, what's going on?' Honey said, grabbing her arm.

Nell consulted her bare wrist. 'You're right on time, madam. This way please.'

She led Honey to a small dining table that had been laid for dinner with cut glass and gleaming cutlery.

Nell pulled out a chair and Honey took a seat, feeling as if she were having an out of body experience. Candles flickered all around the inside of the shed, and yet more fairy lights had been strung along the rafters.

'I'll be right back, madam,' Nell murmured, and as she heard the door close Honey realised that everyone else had left too.

Jesus, this was odd. Had she drunk herself into a Halloween stupor and imagined all of this?

The music had stopped when Nell left, and as Honey sat there, almost too scared to move, it began again. Halting, simple notes, a pretty, old-fashioned tune that Honey couldn't quite put her finger on. It was only when a bum note rang out that she realised that it wasn't recorded. It was live. Someone was behind the old piano in the corner of the shed, and by the sounds of it, someone not all that competent at playing it.

She rose, playing her part, and walked slowly across the floor until she reached the piano. She wanted to look around the edge, but then she didn't because she might not survive the disappointment.

The music stopped, her breathing stopped, and time stopped until he finally spoke.

'Billy taught me.'

Hal.

He stood up and moved around the edge of the piano, and Honey placed her hands over her heart and just looked at him, filling her eyes, her head, her heart with him. She recognised the black shirt he wore as the one Billy had bought a few days back.

He'd learned to play that song on the piano just for her. The idea of it, the image of it, brought a lump to her throat.

'Call off the search,' she said softly, trying to understand what was happening. 'Where did you go, Hal?'

He stepped closer, put a hand on her hip, and in return she laid her palm over his heart.

'I didn't go anywhere, Honey.'

'You've been here the whole time?'

It seemed impossible that he'd been so close to her and she hadn't known. He nodded.

'I'm sorry for running out on you,' he said, stroking his hand over her cheek. 'I needed to think.'

'You think too much,' she whispered, as he drew her against his body and kissed her hair. 'Did you come to any conclusions?'

He held her close, pressed together like dancers at the end of night.

'Yes,' he said, and she let her lips brush the warm skin at the open top button of his shirt. He tasted of home.

'I choose you too, if you still want me. I'm a selfish man.

Your crazy rainbow life brightens mine and I just can't walk away. I love your strawberry hair, and your weekday knickers, and your beautiful size thirteen ass that feels like heaven in my hands.' His hand slid down her back and she leaned into him, yearning. 'You make me laugh, and you make me goddamn furious. You're fucking fearless, Honey.' He paused at last and drew in a deep breath.

'I can't be happy unless you're with me,' Hal said. 'I want to try to make you happy, if you want me to.'

His hand slid into her hair as she lifted her face, and finally, finally, he lowered his head and kissed her. Honey heard his sigh and her own as she wrapped her arms around his neck and closed her eyes, connecting. He kissed her slowly, deeply, the kind of kiss that sustained soldiers going off to war. Except this wasn't a goodbye kiss. It was a hello forever kiss, long and lingering, a *thank God for you* kiss.

'I missed you so much,' she whispered against his lips. 'Will you disappear again if I tell you that I love you?'

'Only if you'll disappear with me.' He tipped her head back and kissed her neck. 'I love you too, Strawberry Girl. Every last fucking thing about you.'

Honey half laughed because his constant swearing had never sounded sexier, and then half gasped when his hand skimmed down her throat and settled lower.

'I don't think we can live forever in Billy's potting shed,' she breathed. 'Take me home, Hal.'

THE END